THE MONSTERS OF GRAMERCY PARK

THE
MONSTERS
of
GRAMERCY PARK

a novel

DANNY LEIGH

HarperCollins*PublishersLtd*

The Monsters of Gramercy Park
© 2005 by Danny Leigh. All rights reserved.

Published by HarperCollins Publishers Ltd

First Canadian edition

HarperCollins books may be purchased for educational, business,
or sales promotional use through our Special Markets Department.

HarperCollins Publishers Ltd
2 Bloor Street East, 20th Floor
Toronto, Ontario, Canada
M4W 1A8

www.harpercollins.ca

Library and Archives Canada Cataloguing in Publication

Leigh, Danny, 1972–
The monsters of Gramercy Park / Danny Leigh.

ISBN-13: 978-0-00-639555-3
ISBN-10: 0-00-639555-4

I. Title.

PR6112.E43M66 2005a   823'.92   C2005-901629-9

HC 9 8 7 6 5 4 3 2 1

Printed and bound in the United States
Typeset by Westchester Book Group
Set in Sabon

ONE

THEY ARE OUTSIDE, of course, as they always are by now. Two of them striding down the hall, practiced steps conducting them past numbered doors, dull metal. Stopping only where they have to. Their faces inert, breathing and blinking, nothing more. Flatly efficient in steel-capped shoes. Veterans in the maintenance of loathsome, frightened men.

The morning bell rings but he's conscious a second before it. Like every morning. And they are outside by now, approaching, that much another certainty. With breakfast.

His cell lies at the far end of the corridor. The guards will work through the rest until they get here. The first of the day's numb repetitions, Identikit customs, routines, samenesses.

Inside, he turns, curls on the bed and shuts his eyes again, knees hiked into his chest as the main cell light glares from the ceiling above. A thin strip, too harsh to let your eyes stray near. A second is fixed beside it, sickly, dim. That stays lit all night. Then the main light judders on and with it there's a hum, the sound of bad connections, and the light and the hum together always wake him before the bell, its electric scald redundant.

This is the pattern of things here. Sleep, then light, then noise, a moment of nothing, then the bell. After that, breakfast. Delivered from the same source as everything else.

When he first arrived, they told him breakfast was at six-fifteen. Though clocks and watches are forbidden, he has no reason for thinking the schedule has changed. Which at this time of year means it must still be dark out.

Except he doesn't think of that. Even acknowledge it as real. Better to embrace a more valuable truth: that there is only this, and here is all there ever was. The Administrative Segregation Unit of US Penitentiary Essenville, Pennsylvania. Ad-Seg ESSUSP. Isolation chiseled into art.

A snag from the blanket catches on his fingernail, and the patches of dry skin that dot his cheek are still tender. Grudgingly, his eyes draw open.

He needs to piss but the cell is glacial. So he'll wait. Do it when he has to get up anyway. Rise and fetch his breakfast.

Mindful of the pressure on his bladder, he twists, stares hard at the slot at the bottom of the door, holding still until it lifts open and a guard slides through a meal tray. As they do, they will not speak. If there is to be speech, it will come later, a demand stripped of cadence or the use of his name.

His name, he knows, is Wilson Ulysses Velez.

Somewhere in the guts of this building there's a plump manila file in which is documented the life of a Wilson Ulysses Velez. Before this. Until here. Pictures of a slight-framed man, sepia skinned, eyes bright. But all that too is better forgotten. The smart move just to lie and wait, hold still a little longer until the food.

He doesn't remember much of it anyway. That life.

The camera in the far top corner of the cell turns slowly left to right. Forever informing back to the control booth, its bank of screens, the guards.

You'd think it would be silent, wouldn't you? The camera? A mute observer, wordless snitch. The truth is different. Here, where bombs could rain inches from his door and he would doze on none the wiser, its every pivot is bedlam loud, each screw creak a cacophony.

Wilson Ulysses Velez breathes deep and clamps his thighs together. Drifts out of his body as he has so often. Sees himself as they do, from above.

The cell is exactly seven feet by ten. The size of the bathroom in an average family house. A bed cast from the same gray concrete as the walls and floor juts up in the manner of a coroner's slab. An emaciated mattress. No sheet. There is a blanket, coarse and aged, that with growing conviction he blames for the rash mottled across his chest. (He sleeps in his uniform now, the short-sleeved orange jumpsuit with the Velcro collar). The same rash he's requested cream for five times without success, that he scratches now as his eyes close until a fresh barrage from across the cell— the violent rush of water—smacks him back to consciousness.

The toilet flushes independently every three hours. With equal precision, the shower—its head caged above a narrow stall in a molded steel unit with the sink and toilet—comes on for three minutes at eleven A.M. each Sunday, Wednesday and Friday. The water, naturally, is cold.

The sink has no plug. Should he attempt to flood the cell by blocking the sink, toilet or shower, a connective valve will shut off the water. The sink also has no taps, just as the toilet has no handle. It's operated by a push button the size of a large denomination coin. Nothing removable, useful as a tool.

Between the bed and the shower, sink and toilet there's a strip of empty floor space he can stand up in if he keeps his arms at his sides.

The cell door is actually two separate doors, each bank vault thick. The internal door is fitted with the tray slot and a small porthole window made of Plexiglas. From the cell, all you can see through it is the steel of the outer door. There is no natural light.

Although he can't see it, the cell backs on to a chain-link fence and, beyond that, a bare cement enclosure into which he is allowed for thirty minutes on Mondays, Thursdays and Saturdays. The guards call it the kennel.

That's the sum of it. Concrete and metal. Pure function. And no bald accountancy of feet and inches like this was just another humdrum space could ever capture its real essence. The nada at its heart. It's as if—

How to put this?

Walk into a room, and there's an aura, an ambience. A trace of events that have gone on inside it. The psychic residue of life, lived.

There's nothing like that here. No reassuring human currents. Just a vacuum. A holding pen for the damned, somewhere between this world and what follows.

So he sees himself as they do, from above. A beetle in a shoe box, deaf and unmoving.

The food should be here by now. With his gaze still fixed on the tray slot, he reflects on possible causes of delay. A guard's shoelace working itself undone. A global apocalypse.

Breakfast, when it comes, will not only be a meal. It will also be an interaction. Here, the dual purpose is important. According to federal guidelines drawn up to protect the mental health of prisoners, even an Ad-Seg inmate must take part in six interactions daily.

At Essenville, an interaction is defined as any significant contact with another person. As such, the delivery of a meal tray and its later collection—along with any utensils used—count as two interactions. The terms of the guidelines are, therefore, satisfied by this process being repeated three times during the day. On the days he's let outside—with shackling beforehand and strip search afterward—another two interactions are added to that total. When, on Sundays and Wednesdays, a guard oversees him shaving, that's one more.

Today, however, is a Tuesday. And without the kennel or a shave or shower—requiring the provision and return of a towel—there are just the six core interactions ahead.

This is his everything.

The norms don't apply here. In his time at Essenville, he has never seen, handled or been wounded by a shank, banger or any other homemade weapon. He has been neither the victim or perpetrator of a sexual assault involving another inmate. He has not found himself obliged to fight another inmate in the prison canteen. (There is no canteen at ESSUSP.) He has never adopted an insect as a pet, become friends with a sage lifer or benevolent guard. No escape has either been planned or attempted.

None of that is what this is. This is what's left when all that's been stripped away. Just him, Wilson Velez, and this cell. Him inside it, and it in him.

The corner of the blanket slips from his legs and the air champs his skin like a mousetrap.

Which guard will it be? Who will actually stoop down and push through the tray? There was a time he'd have scrambled to the door just to find out. Kept track to mark the days. Fallen to his knees and huffed at the air for a hint of old aftershave, the linger of a recent cigarette. Lain prostrate by the slot for a glimpse of the color of the hair on their fingers. When he might have spent whole days butting his head against the concrete, a week just screaming. Bawling from the depths of his lungs, an orphan's wail of rage and grief.

But that was all so long ago. And these things pass. In time, you don't scream anymore. You just lie and wait. Hold still a little longer until the food.

Thuds and scrapes beyond his cell. Is that them now? With breakfast? It must be. It has to be. So is it? Are they here yet? Are they?

Well?

They are outside, of course, as they always are by now. Six-fifteen A.M. like they're wired to an alarm. Pitter-patter scrabbling at the bottom of the door, sounding that mawkish whine of desperation. Naturally, Tork's the ringleader. She can hear his noise inspire the others. Nes and Dolenz take his cue.

So she throws off the covers and leaves the bed, pulls on a robe, feet sweeping across the room to the door. The familiar pressure from the other side the moment she touches the handle, the frenzy as she lets it open, a melee of paws and tongues, the fleeting chaos of motion, breath, insistence. Wending a path downstairs with them beside and all around, bounding, then nuzzling or vice versa.

Such is the lot of a bullmastiff's owner. The same every morning of their staunch, rambunctious lives. Mayhem until their bellies are attended to.

Tork is eight, a canine *force majeure*. Nes is six and Dolenz three. She feels their heft against her and the carpet under her feet gives way to slate as she reaches the end of hallway. Between the dogs and the size of the house, this walk takes forever. Through the kitchen, on into the utility room, where the bowls are waiting, cavernous at the base of the freezer.

Then the feeding. Vast sacks of biscuit mixed with canned meat. A communal trough for the water. And the room fills with a brash three-part harmony of lapping and slobbering.

Lizbeth Greene takes three steps back and watches them eat. Slapstick but purposeful. She tries to recall the last time she felt that single-minded. What about.

Squirrel.

The word is written in black ink across the back of her hand, the S looped around the vein that runs to the knuckle of her middle finger. She has no idea why it's there.

People always said she had a rich imagination. Even as a child, her mind would wander, take itself strange places, seize on random thoughts, ideas. Now, all these bountiful years later, she still needs to record stray phrases, nocturnal visions, in case she might one day have use for them, waking abruptly at two A.M. or three or four to scribble a reminder on the nearest surface. And that—since her teens—has been the back of her left hand.

It's usually covered. At times of particular inspiration, the notes creep past her wrist and inch up the forearm. It's just hard when she can't recall why she's written what she's written. When the prompt comes up blank.

Lately, that's been happening every time. She'll gaze down at the words, try to summon the notion that stirred her in the night. But it mists up and disappears before she can.

Squirrel.

She steps out to the front of the house, the drizzle settling on her neck in the darkness. Picks up a newspaper, bloated with supplements.

Back in the kitchen, she makes tea, finds her reading glasses. Revels in the early morning torpor until the dogs come swarming back, contented.

And while they are, before the mad agitation for their walk, she prepares her own breakfast. Portion controlled and nutritionally precise. A single bowl of chipped wheat-bran, fruit slices, apple, pear. Natural yogurt slopped over the lot. Juice, and honey with the tea.

She sets the bowl down in front of her. Juice on the left and tea on the right. The spoon rests in the bowl at as close to forty-five degrees as possible. It has to be forty-five degrees. Anything else looks wrong.

The newspaper's front page reports on an unarmed man shot dead by an off-duty cop in Corona, Queens. Congressman Mitchell Rieber demanding the refusal of emergency health care for the families of drug dealers. Among the myriad sections she sets to rooting through, the one she needs is called the *Cultural Review*. Printed on glossy stock. Angelina Jolie on the cover. She pulls it out and opens it, thumbs through until she reaches the center pages where, across the breadth of one, her own face looms out, expressionless.

DEATH BECOMES HER, says the headline. And she pauses to stare at the photograph. Absorb its implications.

"Don't worry about them," says Lizbeth Greene, as I tiptoe around three huge and fearsome creatures she tells me are bullmastiffs. "They're very gentle. Just

So begins the accompanying profile, based around an interview she gave in the living room of this house three months ago. Now, her eyes track across the space devoted to her, just her, the text and picture together, before they return to her place.

a little boisterous." From where I'm sitting, however, they still look terrifying. Just what you might expect from Greene—a woman who, for a decade and a half now, has made murder her business. Murders, in fact: grisly and unsolved, performed in all kinds of baroque fashions and investigated by Frederick Enschell, the ever-stoical

The spoon has crept down the side of the bowl. The handle's almost in the yogurt. She puts it back as it should be, then takes a mouthful of fruit and bran. Chews hard. Glances through the next few lines. The exposition. It never changes.

Lizbeth Greene writes crime fiction. She is lauded by critics, cherished by a large and ardent fan base. Her work is read on sun-baked yachts and dankly clattering subway trains. She has written fifteen books, been translated into thirty-two languages. The adjectives with which the newspaper describes her stories—elegant, brutal—are as well worn as those it uses about her: prolific, best-selling. Frederick Enschell has been the hero of her novels since the first, *In Tooth and Claw*. A gnomic middle-aged police officer of half-Swiss extraction. Her readers' chaperone through the alleys of the underworld, the murk of human intention.

Next week her latest work goes on sale. *Black Water Elegy*. Everyone's expecting great things. This is the first major item of associated publicity. The Big Push is what her agent calls it.

So Lizbeth skims through her abridged career like she's checking a receipt in a supermarket, brisk, offhand, attentive only to factual errors (none so far, remarkably). Thinking not of the words themselves but who wrote them. A young woman pleased with her station in life, nodding as she listened or affected to.

She seems to have spent most of her time here observing the furniture. There are digressions into the hang of the curtains, the design of the fireplace. Lizbeth recalls not wanting to meet this girl in the house. Could they not just book a suite at the Four Seasons, as usual? Her agent insisted. They want to go in-depth, she said. It'll give the piece color.

I ask her if she's happy with the new book and she peers at me over the darkwood gleam of her coffee table. "I think so. As much as you can be."

She speaks quietly, almost under her breath. You find yourself leaning in to make her out.

"I think in many ways it's an evolution. Although in saying that I hope the work hasn't lost its visceral quality."

She shouldn't worry. If nothing else, Black Water Elegy is as bloody a read as she's ever produced—no small praise for a writer this famously gory. For her, after all, shootings and stabbings have always been mere drudgery, to be replaced where possible with more flamboyant MO's: bludgeonings, impalements, in one epically gruesome sequence, the surgical removal of a victim's spine. And now.

Lizbeth follows the lines back, her attention snagged on a phrase.

If nothing else

The words seeded there so casually.

More stuff about the house. You'd think this woman had never seen a floor lamp before. That or she was cloned by real estate agents. High ceilings in every room, fully modernized with many designer features, all showcasing majestic views over the signature verdant woodland of Quince Hill, central Connecticut's best kept secret.

"I think that when I'm writing," she shrugs, shifting back against the soft brown leather of her vintage couch, "what I'm really doing is exploring my fascination with consequence. That may be one of the reasons I write quickly. I create situations I'm intrigued by just so I can be first to get to the ending." She laughs, an airy giggle.

These comments, Lizbeth remembers, were made at three different stages of the conversation. She thinks the last was paraphrased. Made up even. She doesn't remember giggling either. Ever.

I almost find myself relaxing—although that soon changes once I recall the array of subjects her publicist warned me I was not to even think about raising while here. The extent of her wealth is one; the three tepid movie adaptations of her novels is another. Neither, I was told, will she welcome inquiries about whatever book she might be currently working on or may have in store for Enschell.

Then the story calls her elfin. Talks of it being hard to reconcile her *name for the prickly* with her *apparent good humor,* and then it says:

Elfin is the word I find myself thinking best suits her. In photographs, she appears petite—sitting here dwarfed by the expanse of white-walled space, speaking in that feathery voice of hers, she seems tinier still, a china doll in four-inch heels. Her image—the chic all-black outfits and the sleek brunette bob, both in evidence today—is as clearly defined as any rock star's. But it doesn't prepare you for the almost miniature scale of her hands and feet, her birdlike frame. At one point I tell her I wish I had her figure; for the first time she looks away, blushing, thanking me before resuming her otherwise unbreakable eye contact.

That at least isn't too removed from what her readers might come up with were you to ask them to picture the altogether brawnier Detective Enschell. With him too, an unexpected shyness lurks behind the steely facade. Yet their similarities go deeper. Take their professional perfectionism or unlikely fondness for reggae music—a long-standing passion of Greene's you suspect she wouldn't have shared with him lightly (not that her musical tastes have always been so exotic; in tribute to "the unrivaled ardor of my infancy," those three hulking dogs are named after members of The Monkees).

But there is, of course, a darker and more profound bond between them—a trauma endured in childhood still forever rippling through their adult lives.

I tell her it's okay if she doesn't want to talk about it. She gives me a particularly forceful stare. For the first time I sense a chill developing. "Why would I not want to talk about it?" she says. It's a reasonable question. She has, by her own admission, been talking (and writing) about it for years now.

And she pushes her glasses up onto her temples, rubs her eyes until stars whirl in front of them. Digs her spoon into the fruit and bran, keeps eating as the dogs pace the kitchen.

He could have sworn that was them. The guards. Their lumping progress and the din of the meal trolley. But it's quiet again now. Must have been nothing.

(The phantom sounds that used to torment him—the screaming baby, the pinball machine—they don't visit anymore. Haven't for a long time. Those coals have been walked.)

Among the country's glut of maximum security facilities, USP Essenville is a benchmark. The main body of the prison houses 1,086 inmates in conditions watchdogs have called "persistently inhumane." Ad-Seg is its darkest corner. A jail within a jail; quarantine for the most disruptive and dangerous inmates. Thirty identical cells inlaid down one corridor.

The guards here call Wilson Velez the star attraction.

These are the terms. You can list the terms like you can map the cell.

He exists in solitary confinement. The conditions are as absolute as federal law allows. Every two weeks he can meet with his attorney for a period not longer than an hour. Otherwise, he cannot see, speak to or correspond with anyone besides the guards and his immediate family. (He has no immediate family; none that would visit him, anyway.)

He owns—is permitted to own—nothing apart from a Bible and a pair of glasses prescribed for nearsightedness. His cell cannot be decorated with pictures or photographs.

This has been his life for the last one thousand nine hundred and twenty-seven days. Five years and pocket change.

All other Ad-Seg inmates are brought here for a specific chunk of sentences otherwise served in the main body of the facility. Most are gone in a week.

Wilson Velez is here forever.

These are the terms. Feel free to stroll around them, reach out and touch them, gape and giggle like a kid on a museum trip. But the terms can't express how each moment feels longer than all history. Can't gauge the depth of their sadism. Here in the permanent light, alone.

He gives in to the nag of his bladder, uncoils himself and leaves the mattress. Bare feet set down on the cold gray floor.

The soles slap against the concrete as he crosses the cell to piss. Before the silence returns.

You won't often find silence like this. Not beyond these thirty cells. Out there, in the world, even the softest breath of a lone desert tribesman will ultimately find another, a second tiny noise to bond with, and that in turn will echo off a third, and so on, until it's all one locked-in swirl of fuzz and chatter. Here, unless the guards are outside or the camera's in motion or he sets the flimsy metal of the shower unit ringing, the concrete and steel kill every sound. Nothing in, nothing out. The deadest end. You could sing the most beautiful song ever sung and the notes would freeze and break against the walls.

That's why the baby cried and the pinball yammered into life. Filling up the silence. And there were numbers too, endless random sequences incanted by a host of unseen voices.

In long-term solitary, aural hallucinations are only outstripped by visual ones. There was a time a day wouldn't pass without a mob crowding in here, acquaintances and strangers, long dead ancestors and characters from movies, lounging on his bed or leaning up next to it. Then the fun would really start. Oh, the sights he's seen in here.

Until all of it would drop away and the nothing—that bastard void—would be left.

The process works in stages. First you panic. Lose control in the stillness as the world is taken from you. Maybe you hyperventilate. Snatch your breath in violent little sobs. Then comes the pain. That'll settle in, hollow you out for weeks, then months, then years, until finally something cracks.

Something always cracks.

There's a scar down Wilson Velez's forehead, a fat red groove scored from his hairline to the bridge of his nose. He can't remember how it happened, but it's always going to be there. The mark of his despairing.

After that, things start shutting down. There's just the husk of a body, some memories. And the memories fade.

But then they change. They flower. Conversations, events, they bend and weave in time. Becoming fiction. Half truth.

They say that when you die you don't actually see your life in flashback the way you might expect, a calm linear review from between your mother's legs to wherever you might be as your heart gives up. Everything just plays at once. Infinite TV shows on infinite screens mounted in the windows of a skyscraper.

So this must be the death of Wilson Ulysses Velez. Because that's what he can see. Just the way God planned it.

The piss will sit now until the automated flush. A sliver under three hours. He slumps back across the cell. Falls on the bed. Scratches his rash. His balls. Coughs.

Where in the sweet and blessed name of Christ is the food? The light means food. It always has. So where are the guards with their keys and their batons?

When all you have is a routine, you cling to its upkeep. So the only thing he wants now is his two pancakes greasing up the tray beside the half ounce of gray cereal (there is no milk), the finger-thin sausage and the paper cup of watered fruit juice.

The exact menu can vary. Sometimes the juice is orange; sometimes you can't tell. Alternate days he gets waffles, not pancakes. On Mondays and Fridays there's a meat patty instead of sausage. Occasionally, once the meals have been ferried to Ad-Seg from the main facility, the trays go uncovered so long the food gets cold. Other times it was never hot to begin with.

He slides under the blanket again, pulls it over his head. Shuts his eyes and drifts back to sleep. Lets the memories take him.

To a humid afternoon in a rural village, thatched huts in a rutted line and middle-aged women chattering in Spanish, and he's younger, much younger. A boy. Heat on his back, arms frail and hairless, sweat beads dewing on his top lip and forehead, and it's just getting hotter as he barrels down a dirt track, child's stride lengthening with every step, dry leaves brittling underfoot.

Arriving at a place where there are limes. Dozens hanging low and bulbous from the spiny branches of skinny trees, their greens brilliant in the pure country light. And he stops. Rises up on tiptoes as high as he can. Fingers groping to twist off the fruit. Away from the voices now, the women. But then another noise: a whimper. And after that, a thump.

And a wetness sprays across his face. Warm and sudden, from above. He wipes his cheek and sees blood. Someone else's blood. But when he looks back up the sun blots out everything but the green of the limes. Beyond them just a blinding white. The blood still dripping. Soaking into the earth.

And he hears a rumble, closing, loud enough for him to turn and run, back through the lime trees, terrified. Until he wakes to the sound of his right hand scratching his stubble. A beard advancing down his neck. It's another two days before he can shave.

Falling back to sleep is an idiot's trick in Ad-Seg. Just means you wake up here twice.

Wilson Velez lets his eyes adjust to the cell light once more. Comes to focus on his arm. His gaze moves down, descending to his wrist. The soft inside. And there are words there, like there are everywhere on his body, but as he returns to the nothing he stares instead at the numbers beside them, marked in unfading black: 1.18.4.9.12.12.1

Just past six-twenty-five. So says the wall clock that hangs above the kitchen table. The minutes seem to pass slower this early. It's still not light outside.

She should have gotten the bran she always gets. The flakes. This new stuff tastes weird somehow: cardboardy. She saw it advertised, thought

12

she'd experiment. But this really isn't working out. Next time she'll go back to the flakes.

Lizbeth nudges the dogs away with her feet as they bustle around her, scattering them in an instant. It's a foolproof technique, honed down the years since they were puppies. She doesn't even take her eyes from the paper.

As she ponders her answer, her assistant walks in, a personable red-haired woman a few years younger than her and, unlikely as it sounds, even paler. "Tea," she announces, bringing with her a ceramic pot, milk and a jar of honey that Greene will use as a sweetener.

"I don't consider myself damaged," she says when it's just the two of us again, with a nonchalance it's hard not to take as pointed. "I'd like to think I'm more than just the product of an event that took place over thirty years ago." As a writer, or a human being? "As both."

Yet although she may dispute it, the fact is that violence and death touched her at a grievously early age—and have defined her ever since. In a tragic sense, you could even argue that she was born to write the books she does, doomed to spend her life unraveling the darkest acts of men on behalf of her readers.

First, of course, at the age of eight, there was her mother's murder. Her life until then had, she has said, been almost cartoonish in its perfection: a "little slice of heaven" in suburban Danbury. Then, in the small hours of an April morning, with her pharmaceutical executive father away on business, an intruder broke into the family home, made his way upstairs and bludgeoned the sleeping Marion Greene to death. Cowering in an attic bedroom with her older sister, Lizbeth could hear the horror unfolding below her, trapped in a nightmare until the killer fled. No arrest was ever made.

The case briefly commanded front pages. Later, its shadow would hang over much of Greene's storytelling, not least when—during what many fans consider her finest book, The Hands of Angels—*the previously tight-lipped Frederick Enschell revealed his zeal for detective work began with the grisly murder of his mother when he was a child.*

But Marion Greene's fate would not be her daughter's only contact with the most heinous of crimes. Eleven years later, now a freshman at Columbia, she was leaving a friend's apartment when a stranger pushed a gun into her ribs, knocked her unconscious and bundled her into his van. The man was Richard Cazet—the serial rapist and killer whose rampage across the New York area by then included five murders.

Cazet drove to Queens, then left the vehicle parked on waste ground for around ten minutes. In the interim, Greene came to and broke free. Still dazed, she alerted the police—only to find the van was gone. Fate, however, would intervene. The following night, Cazet argued with a clerk in a Brooklyn liquor store. When a police officer entered and threatened to arrest him, he shot himself. Greene's only injury was a concussion. It could have been very different.

And from these terrors came inspiration. From their memories, she built a career—and found her calling. The breakthrough came after In Tooth and Claw, *a modest debut with little to distinguish it from so many other routine procedurals. Her next book, however, was a phenomenon: titled* City Slicker *after its subject's nickname in the press, it was a factual account of Richard Cazet's reign of fear, lent a potent dramatic charge by its author having so nearly become his last victim. Indeed, interwoven with her portrait of Cazet were moving personal reflections on both that terrifying night and her mother's unsolved homicide.*

It was a runaway success. And when Greene returned to fiction, she quickly took her place among the nation's favorite crime writers: harder-edged than her male contemporaries but with a classically female appreciation of her characters' inner lives. Her own life—her own pain—had been her platform. I look at her, perched on the edge of the couch now, its ample cushions taut beneath her, and

She doesn't even know if she can finish this. The bran. Undecided, she picks out the fruit, a hunk of apple, then a slice of pear, holds them in her mouth as she stares around her. At everything the stories have brought. This gracious house with its perfect seclusion. The product of a life of lonely hours.

She used a typewriter back then. In the early, clear-headed days. A rackety machine that—given enough coaxing—would turn out the endless pages she kept stacked in a corner of her one-room apartment. Now she has a laptop as thin as a chess-board in a study overlooking the forest. And the phone rings from across the kitchen.

"I wanted to make sure you had the paper," a woman's voice says. "I haven't read it yet, but the pictures look great."

This is Nancy Bonchurch: Lizbeth's assistant for the last eight years. She was a fan to start with, a reader whose letters of admiration led to a correspondence and then, in time, a job. A resourceful woman. Connecticut solid. Well paid for what she does—with her weekends left free and a generous health plan—but, more than that, proud to be doing it.

"I'm looking at it now. It's fine."

"It is?"

"I guess."

"You guess?"

"No, really. It's fine."

"Okay. So I'll swing by at eleven?"

"Make it twelve. I need to get some work done."

On an average day, she writes from seven. Breaks in the late morning to meet with Nancy, have lunch. Sometimes she'll swim beforehand in the pool at the back of the house. Returns to her desk at two, works through until five.

"Do you need me to bring anything over?"

"Actually, can you pick up some bran? The usual stuff? The flakes?"

"The flakes. Sure."

After the call, she replaces the receiver. Then lifts it again. Holds it to her ear and checks the line. She's not sure why. She just waits there, listening to the dial tone.

The dogs are clawing at the foot of the door, whining to get outside. The drizzle's turning to rain now. She lets them into the garden, and they bound onto the lawn for exactly the time it takes her to sit back down. Then they hurtle inside again, snuffling and baying, being a nuisance, paws up on the kitchen table. Demanding their walk.

"C'mon puppies, cut it out. At least let me finish my breakfast."

And she raises her spoon and tries again with the bran.

Squirrel.

Still there, scrawled on the back of her hand. Undisclosed. A word without meaning.

S-q-u-i-r-r-e-l.

1.18.4.9.12.12.1

Wilson Ulysses Velez gazes down at the tattoo round his wrist. Etched in gothic script. If anyone else were with him now, they'd also see the chain of three-pointed crowns inked across his neck, rendered in gold, inset with rubies and diamonds. The rest of his tattoos are hidden, though, stashed under his jumpsuit: the mural of dates and faces that sprawls over his chest and belly; the litany of names running down both arms; the dense jumble of Incan warriors and the New York City skyline that takes up his whole back. Only his feet have the unadorned skin he was born with. Everywhere else is covered, veiled in relics and epitaphs.

1.18.4.9.12.12.1. He reaches for his glasses but even with them on, even in this ruthless light, the edges of the numbers are blurred. His sight has declined with every month he's spent here. As if with nothing to look at but this, his eyes have lost the will to function.

Five years in Ad-Seg and you change. At first he was an animal, a scream made flesh. Later, he turned silent. A penitent, his filthy soul burnt out of him. But God ignored his pleas for mercy. So now he just lies and waits. Holds still a little longer and a little longer yet.

Maybe they're giving him the loaf. That would explain it. But there's no reason. Even here where they don't need a reason, he's done nothing to deserve it.

The loaf is a punishment. In Ad-Seg, these matters need imagination. The rules, they're countless. So are the infractions. A list so long the penalties—those officially sanctioned, at least—can barely encompass them. Besides, when a person exists in a windowless space of seven by ten feet, the jailer's dilemma becomes: What next?

Next comes the loaf. The loaf is the three meals the inmate would have eaten that day pressed into a single beige slab. It provides the statutory minimum of vitamins and minerals.

Unlike regular meals, the loaf always comes at the same temperature. Cold. But he can't be on the loaf. There's no reason. But if he isn't, and they're still not here, then:

Where where where fucking where is the food and how many times is he going to have to beg for some cream for this motherfucking rash that makes him want to scratch away his whole fucking chest? It feels like it's spreading. What if it's only a symptom? Just the first hint of something incalculably worse?

In Ad-Seg ESSUSP, trained medical staff are supposed to tour the cells seven days a week. In practice, they come once. A doctor might appear in an emergency. (The cost of any treatment will be charged to an inmate's commissary account.) The rest of the time there's just the guards.

If his cell was fitted with a window he could see the rain now. Puddles forming on the kennel floor. Without one, his hip lets him know anyway. It always flares up when it rains. A gift from his time in Essenville.

He used to pace. Darting across the cell, from the end of the bed to the door and back again, as fast as he could. Four steps each way. He'd do that thirty times a minute until he collapsed. Once, on another Tuesday two years before this one, he went for sixteen hours.

Eventually his hip gave in. The cartilage worn through. Now when it rains he limps.

Outside there's noise—real noise—and he jars upright. The first door's sliding open.

Finally. At last. The guards are here. They're right outside.

But when the tray slot flips up, nothing comes through it except a voice: "Inmate, prepare for extraction."

And a pair of eyes glower through the porthole window.

In Ad-Seg, an inmate never *leaves* his cell. Whenever they step beyond the two steel doors, they are being *extracted*. Should the guards decide an inmate is not cooperating with his extraction, they will charge the cell to enforce it. There will be hollered orders, muffled protests. Screams.

Wilson Velez has been judged to be uncooperative fifty-six times during his confinement in Ad-Seg. The guards usually leave a month or so between each episode to let him recover. It will, he has always thought, be the way that all this ends: his body heaped lifeless and bloody, the result—it will be claimed—of his own belligerence.

But as he meets the eyes at the porthole he sees enough sour impatience in them to know this is not a pretext. Today, they just want him out of the cell.

It makes no sense. It doesn't have to. He gets to his feet, the throb in his hip enough to make him wince, peels apart the Velcro at the collar of his jumpsuit. Pulls it down to his waist, then his ankles. Steps out of it. Stands naked facing the door.

The rest is carried out without pause or protest.

Wilson Ulysses Velez lifts his cock and balls. Waits five seconds. Without a response from the guards he turns, bends, spreads. Waits five seconds more. Displays the soles of his feet, his armpits, the inside of his mouth. And now the tray slot squeals open. He rights himself, then he stuffs his jumpsuit through to the other side. Waits for it to be inspected.

When it's pushed back through he puts it on again. Then he passes out his shoes. Pillowy white sneakers issued by the facility. (They have no laces. Laces can be used as a noose.) Gets them back and pulls them on. Squats on the ground with his hands offered up to the slot. Feels the cuffs being fitted round his wrists. Locked.

1.18.4.9.12.12.1. And he rises.

The cell door opens, and there they are. Three of them. All dolled up in the same quasi-military garb, black boots and jackets made fat with stab-proof padding, outsize goggles covering half their faces.

The two at the front are Johnson and Abernabi. One white, one black. Their names are printed on plastic tags Velcroed to their jackets. Legally they have to be. (But tags get mislaid, like children's homework is forgotten.) He's seen them both before. The third is new. Younger. Kolin. Tubby and pale. He stands behind his colleagues.

Kolin's got the video camera. All physical interactions with the guards have to be taped. The object is to record any violent incident that might take place, for the legal protection of all parties. (But cameras malfunction, and tapes can be lost.)

Abernabi holds up the waist chain.

"Inmate, step into the doorway."

Wilson isn't meant to reply. If he did, it would be an infraction. He just shuffles forward. Sees the corridor beyond the guards. Still no windows. Lit with the same demonic strip. He flinches before Abernabi even touches him. But he can't avoid breathing him in as he locks the chain around his middle.

Two more chains hang from it. Abernabi attaches the shorter of them to Wilson's handcuffs. The other dangles between his thighs until Johnson kneels just long enough to fit the leg irons around his ankles and connect it to them. His hands are pulled in tight to his stomach, shoulders hunched, feet fifteen inches apart. Then Abernabi takes hold of his waist chain and pulls him out into the corridor. Turns him to the side. Takes up a position behind one shoulder as Johnson does the same at the other, batons ready as they each press a hand to his back.

A curt little shiver at the base of his calf evolves into a shake and in a second his whole body is convulsed. Each muscle twitching, nerves ablaze. He tries to control it. But he can't.

"What the fuck is he doing? Look at him. He's spazzing out."

Kolin is aghast behind the camera.

"He does this," Abernabi says. "Just leave him."

Every part of his body that's not cuffed in place is shuddering. His head jolts like a struck punchball. It takes an age to pass. Ebbing from the feet up.

Johnson steps in front of him, peers into his eyes.

"You think he's through?"

"As much as he needs to be."

His cell is locked behind him and the hands return to his back.

The corridor is wide enough for them to move down three abreast. With the leg irons, he can only take the shortest of steps, almost dainty in their abbreviation. Kolin follows behind and the other cells stretch out before them. A sign above announcing that should an inmate be seen here without a guard, no warning shots will be fired.

The funk of Ad-Seg breakfasts is overpowering. So the noises were real. Everyone else is eating now. The guards pushing him onward.

"I'vvvve . . . dddddddone nothhhinggggggggg . . ."

Abernabi and Johnson trade sighs.

". . . wrrrronnnggg . . . I jjjust . . . I-I-I-I jjjj—jjjjjusttt—"

"Shit. Does he always talk like that?"

Kolin is fascinated. He speeds ahead of his colleagues, nudges the camera into Wilson's face.

"So this is the star attraction. The stone gangster. A fucking vegetable. *Ag-gug-gug-gug-gug*. Shit. That's a blast, man."

"Let's just get this done, Kolin."

Johnson reaches over and bats away the camera.

"Hey, CO! What's he gonna do? Sue us for ragging on him?"

CO is what the guards call each other, and what they expect to be called. Corrections officer. They hate the word guard. Any inmate using it is guilty of an infraction.

Beyond the last cell there's the first of the gates. Then the next corridor.

Every one they proceed down has another camera aside from Kolin's. Mounted up by the ceiling, linked to the control booth. Wilson Velez glances up at them as he labors past.

Waiting on the other side of the fourth gate is Brink.

Brink's the senior guard in Ad-Seg. Day to day, all this is his. He gestures for the party to continue. Strides ahead of it. A whip of a man. Buzz-cut and steam pressed.

The five of them move on through a string of gates, down yet more corridors. Wilson still has no intimation of where he's going, what awaits him when he gets there. He just keeps taking his clockwork steps, gaze fixed on the back of Brink's head, the perfect roundness of his bald spot. The leg irons are gouging him now, the handcuffs strangling his wrists.

Brink stops dead, and they're outside a room now. Not a cell: a room.

"Wait," Brink says, and he steps inside, closes the door after him. Emerges a second later to usher in the rest of them. Mutters at Kolin as he passes:

"Shut the camera off, CO."

Inside there's a square metal table bolted to the floor and one hard-backed chair. In it sits Warden Michael Sosa. When he first trained as a guard his classmates called him Hangdog. That was the beginning of twenty-two years with the Department of Corrections. Now he stares at Wilson with eyes more bag than pupil.

"We've got something for you."

He dips his hand into the pocket of his shirt. Produces a scrap of paper.

"Your lawyer's been calling since yesterday. The talkative Mr. Ossery. He sounded pretty het up by the time I spoke with him. Anyway, I spoke with him. He thinks there's something you should know. That you *have* to know. So I've decided to pass it on."

Warden Sosa turns to Brink.

"Does he understand me?"

"It's hard to say, sir."

He turns back to Wilson.

"This is very unusual, inmate. I just hope you realize how lucky you are."

And he lays the paper on the table. For a swollen moment it sits there. Then the guards relax their grip, just enough to let him lean forward, get his face down next to the page where his failing eyes can make out the writing. As it darkens into focus he finally sees what's been left for him. The message. Three words, handwritten, evenly spaced.

GOD IS DEAD

Squirrel.

Yes, it would be easier if she kept a notebook. Lizbeth knows this. She's tried, repeatedly. Filled the first pages of a tower of them. But every time she ends up stifled. Thinks of those pages stacked on her desk, and what would happen if she died unexpectedly, in a plane crash, say, or a boating accident. Leaving them to be discovered by future literary historians, whose regard for her could only be eroded by the stumbling of her raw ideas. So she takes her chances with skin cancer and keeps using her hand. Forgetting what it was she was trying to record by the time she comes to need it.

Squirrel.

She tries one last time to recapture the thought process: nothing. No trace.

The story in the paper has moved on now, to what it calls her private life. On the third page, there's the usual references to the ways in which

the triumphs of her career aside, her private life has rarely been the proverbial cherry bowl. Her only marriage—to a former Yale professor of linguistics—was over within a year. The last time she made any comment on the subject—any mention of it here being, of course, strictly forbidden—she described herself as living in a state of "enlightened singlehood." She has no children.

    Trouble, meanwhile, found her yet again in the form of Leon Slocomb, a pool cleaner who sent her threatening letters for three years before trying to attack her at a reggae concert. The experience weighed heavily on Greene. Shaken, she retreated from public life completely. (Slocomb is currently incarcerated in Fairton, New Jersey.)

    "Would I say I was wary of people?" she ponders. "No. I'm happy in my own company. Is that a bad thing?" Going by the way her eyebrows arch, I assume the question is rhetorical. Despite her reluctance to admit it, however, her reputation continues to lie somewhere between unsociable and Howard Hughes.

That, she feels, is ridiculous. She sees her assistant every day. Speaks regularly with her agent and—if not so frequently these days—her sister, Mame. And there are friends. Several friends. She hasn't seen them in a while, not physically, not face to face, but that hardly means they don't exist. Now does it?

There are, she would admit, few unknown quantities left in her life. But she has her reasons for liking it that way. Through the slow weeding out of uncertainty, you find some kind of peace. Yet here, in print, all she appears as is

a finicky little woman deliberately removed from the world around her, hiding away in Quince Hill with her pristine furniture and rowdy dogs in a large house where, she admits, several of the upstairs rooms stand empty.

And Lizbeth understands now. This was always going to be the story. The girl must have had it planned before she even got here. Just needed to fill the space between quotation marks.

Her mouth's still full of bran. It doesn't seem to be shrinking in mass as she chews. It's like it's expanding, swelling up to fill her throat, flatten down her tongue. For a second she takes her eyes from the paper and concentrates on swallowing. Gets it down in one almighty gulp.

The dogs are going crazy as they try to escape the kitchen. Her voice cracks as she yells: "All of you! Stop! You'll go out when I've eaten! The same way you always do! What is wrong with you today?"

An awkward silence hangs over the room. Her bullmastiffs have taken up residence at her feet, their contented snoozing at odds with the frostiness of the atmosphere. I'm starting to worry she may sic them on me the next time I say something she doesn't like. Instead, I try and find out more about what it must be like spending so much time thinking about murder. Is it rough terrain, psychologically?

"It's just something you deal with. I think you have an obligation, a duty almost, to be truthful even as you're creating this fictional entertainment. To bring something real to the story. There's a gravity to murder it's unwise to ignore."

I start to ask another question, but she's on a roll. "All criminals cross a line—but the murderer crosses it in such a way I'm not sure they ever come back."

I wonder aloud how much of an insight she thinks she has into the minds of murderers? "Oh, I'm sure we've all felt that white-hot anger that leads to murder. The difference is you or I pull back from the edge." So she understands the urge to kill? The eyebrows arch once more. "How else could I write about it?" But could she act on it?

"No. Of course not. I understand osmosis—that doesn't mean I can do it."

She covers her mouth with a porcelain hand and gives a discreet cough—as if she could give any other. The silence that follows is her longest yet. Despite the wealth accrued through her career, there seems to be a heavy price attached to the material she deals in. Forever dreaming up new ways for people to do each other in, maybe anyone would get crabby.

"No," she says as the dogs begin to stir. "I get crabby when people draw absurd conclusions about me. The writing has never been a problem."

Judging by the sheer volume of books she's produced, every one since City Slicker *a commercial triumph (even if, according to industry gossip, sales may not quite be what they were), I'm sure she's telling the truth. But before*

She knows what's coming next. Realizes now where all of this was always headed. As her ears start to ring.

either of us can say anything else, her assistant reappears. She tells me I've got time for one more question. So I ask Greene how much longer she can see herself doing this? A book a year, every year? "As long as I have the ideas," she says, "then I'll pursue them. Sorry, can I ask you a question? Did you actually like my book?"

I wonder if this is the first time it's occurred to her that someone might not. She stares at me with those fearsome eyes. To my eternal discredit, I don't tell her the truth: that many of the characters struck me as wooden, and that despite her supposed love of realism much of the plot seemed implausible and, worse—for all its carnage—dull. Instead, I mumble something about it being fun learning more about Enschell's fear of elevators. She looks at me blankly. Embarrassed, I tell her I didn't enjoy it as much as I did her others.

"Oh," she says. "Well, that's a shame."

Just then her assistant bounces back into the room to usher me out. As I'm gathering my things, she produces a copy of Black Water Elegy *and asks if I'd like it signed. Graceful to the last, Greene suggests that as I have a lot to carry, perhaps they should just send one on to me.*

When I'm almost out of the room, I turn back and wave. I'm sure she sees me, but she doesn't wave back.

That's it? That can't be it. What about the rest of it? She knew to expect the usual stuff. Her mother, Cazet. But this is different. Spiteful. What did she do to deserve it? Letting this girl into her home, indulging her questions, giving her tea?

When the phone rings, it's Nancy Bonchurch again.

"I've just read it. Do you want me to call someone?"

"No, it's okay. It's just—"

"I know. The bitch. But who cares? You know?"

"I know."

"You're sure you're okay?"

"Absolutely."

"If you're not, just say so. Please. Just say 'I'm not.'"

"I would."

"Okay. If you're sure."

"I am."

Lizbeth feels dizzy. The dogs are still protesting. But that's fine. It's all fine. She'll take them out, and then she'll start work. It's all under control.

Without even noticing she's doing it, she starts to reread the story. Fixes on her name. Lizbeth Greene. Lizbeth. Greene. The more she stares, the less it seems to represent. The letters blur and it slips all meaning. All sense of the person it refers to. What if this callow girl is right? If this is what Lizbeth really is? She turns away. Finds herself gazing at her hand.

Squirrel.

You know what? It's nothing. Doesn't matter. None of it. Everything is peachy. She's just going to sit here and watch the dawn and finish breakfast and then she'll take the dogs out, and when she gets back she'll go up to the study and start typing and keep typing and the ideas will come and take shape and the words will fill the page as they have so many times before. A morning as it should be.

She spoons up the fruit and bran. Lifts it to her mouth, opens and bites down.

And everything stops right there.

A juggernaut of pain rips through her teeth, her jaw, her skull. She screams and her right eye goes into spasm. Her hands up over her mouth. Her whole body in tremor.

Has she been shot? This is always how she pictured getting shot. Her breath a whisper, the life rushing out of her.

Only there's no blood. Just a pain she's never known.

All the pain in the world charged through her.

Until finally it narrows into her rightside front tooth. And now she feels something in her mouth: a foreign body, hard and injurious. What she must have bitten into.

She opens her mouth and it drops onto the table.

A plastic superhero.

One inch high.

His cape billows stiffly at his back as the dogs arrive to investigate.

TWO

"I T'S CAPTAIN FROSTO. That's who it is."
Nancy Bonchurch stands in the kitchen and gazes down at the tiny plastic figure, sticky with yogurt and spit. She holds it in her palm, tilts it into the light.

"They give them away in packets of Frostums. You know, the cereal? The one with the O in the middle? *Just milk and an O and a whole lotta Frostums!* That was the jingle. My little brother used to love them."

She shifts her weight to her other foot.

"I did too."

Lizbeth sits at the table, nudging her front tooth so gently she's almost not touching it at all. Moaning in pain when she does.

"Let me see."

"You already saw."

"So let me see again."

Lizbeth takes her hand from her mouth, just enough.

"There's a crack."

"I know there's a crack."

"This one at the front has a crack. A hairline. You're going to have to see someone. I'm going to call the dentist."

"Don't," Lizbeth says. "Really. Don't."

"You can't not see the dentist."

"It'll be fine. I'm sure it'll be fine."

All her life Lizbeth Greene has been phobic of the dentist. Just the thought of the chair makes her dizzy and nauseous. No actual experience ever served as a catalyst, no botched root canal work or bloody extraction. It's just a thing of hers. That's the phrase she uses: a thing. Like making sure the spoon rests in the bowl at the correct angle is a thing, or covering her hand with notes is a thing. So she brushes and flosses with military rigor, the purpose to spare her ever needing professional attention.

"I don't see how. It won't fix itself."

"Honestly, I just need something for the pain."

"Oh . . . you mean you—?"

"I just need a Tylenol."

And Nancy leaves Captain Frosto on the table, straight backed and puff chested. Lizbeth considers him with puzzlement and loathing.

"I just don't get how it happened."

Nancy returns with a Tylenol in one hand and water in the other. Lizbeth takes both.

"They must pack the bran in the same place as the Frostums. Lizbeth, you have to sue. Tell me you're going to sue."

But Lizbeth says no. There's too much hubbub around her already.

During most of the year, Nancy's role is limited to minor acts of general support: collecting Lizbeth's groceries, sorting her fan mail. Now, however, as always when a book's about to come out, her job is blooming into an epic panorama of scheduling and administration, sweet talk and go-betweening.

They move into the living room. Recap the signings she's due to attend, the cars that will pick her up and those that will take her home, the hotels, interviews, connecting flights, meals, the care of the dogs while she's away. The meat of her annual foray into the world.

There are moments in the the next two hours when she almost forgets her wounded tooth, glorious split seconds of complete absorption in the matters at hand. Then before she can even remember why, she'll be doubled over, flinching.

She skips lunch. Just watches as Nancy keeps talking through gluey mouthfuls of pasta. It's after two by the time they're done.

"So I'll see you—"

"Tomorrow."

"You sure you don't want me to come back and walk the dogs?"

"I should do it. They've been on edge all day as it is. Anyway, you've got your own stuff to take care of. So vamoose."

"But you'll call me if the pain gets worse?"

"I already feel so much better. Really I do."

As soon as Nancy leaves, she all but collapses. The tooth like a rusty tin can shard, buried in her nerves. She gazes in the mirror of her compact for the nth time since breakfast and sees it, the crack, snaking up the enamel, as fine as wire.

More tea. Another Tylenol. Captain Frosto stares at her impassively until she moves him to a shelf behind her, his face turned to the wall.

Upstairs in the study, from where you can see the trees stretch out to the farthest points of the horizon, her laptop is opened and switched on.

The room is empty save for a dressmaker's dummy in the corner, her chair and her desk, on which are her laptop and phone. Above it is a piece of card, a white square on which is printed: A Page A Day. This is her promise. An oath of productivity.

But nothing was written yesterday, and nothing the day before that. Nothing has been written for three months.

As of now, her next story has a title: *The Debtor*. Possibly *A Killing in the Market*. That's it. There was, at the end of summer, when she was vital and unwound, a brief description of a body being found in a Dumpster outside the corporate head office of a major bank. But that sat lonely on her screen until it got itself deleted and now, once more, there's nothing.

She shuts her eyes and tries to focus, blot out the pain. Raises her fingers above the keyboard like a concert pianist.

And stalls. Fingers rigid in midair. Until her tooth grabs at her attention again and without thinking she presses the tip of her thumb against it. Then it's mayhem. Double vision and she's screaming and the dogs are racing to the door.

It's an hour before she tries again.

This time, she just hits the keys. Doesn't think about it. Just lets it come.

It was 23 degrees outside as Enschell stepped into the night. Cold enough, he thought, that someone could die just from being out here.

Her fingers slow, then stop, and she waits for the next idea. A blackbird lands outside the window and a breeze sets the forest swaying, and she waits for the next idea. Keeps waiting.

She deletes it all. Starts over.

It was 102 degrees outside as Enschell stepped into the afternoon. Hot enough, he thought, that someone could die just from being out here.

How much Tylenol can you take in a day?

The blackbird dawdles by the window. Chatters at nothing. She looks back over at what she's written. One foot tapping the floor.

Remember first principles. The foundation stones. So:

There's been a murder. There's always been a murder. And with a murder comes a body; a corpse. Rich with secrets. Proceed from there. Identify the victim. The weapon. Deftly reveal motive and, in due course, the killer. Here are your precepts. Timeless, unfailing guidelines.

She sets to work. A zookeeper has been bludgeoned to death in the reptile house. No, the bear enclosure. No, not a zookeeper. A croupier. Shot through the head in a motel room. Better yet, a casino. Beside the roulette table. Killed by a gambler. Or so you might think. *Actually* killed by the casino's owners in order to frame a gambler. A gambler who got lucky but then—once his innocence has been established—turns up dead himself. Fingers sewn into his pockets.

It all seems familiar. Uncomfortably so. Then she remembers why. It's the exact premise of *A Losing Hand*. Her fifth Enschell mystery.

This happens all the time now. Old plots rising from the grave, beguiling her into welcoming them as new. She's never known a dry spell like it. For fifteen years, something—some obscure but trusty spirit—has fired her into action, into word after precious word. Now she just sits here. Stares out over the trees and waits. And so the days keep passing.

A writer has been found dead at her desk. She had writer's block. Had writer's block while trying to write about a writer with writer's block.

God. Has it really come to this? She stares down at her hand: *Squirrel*. Rodent. Vermin. Rat.

In a smidge under a half hour, she gives up. Returns downstairs. To her disappointment, there's no cleaning left to do. She's cleaned everything already.

She lines up her condiments and orders them by use-by date.

Most days she sifts through the paper for ideas. Today though, as yet, between the reporter and her tooth, she hasn't found the will. Now she looks again at the front page. Reads more about Congressman Mitchell Rieber and his plans to "exclude those who profit from crime from the benefits of society." But that could only be background. A subplot. The guy killed in Queens by the off-duty cop, that's better. A janitor named Ramon Carvajal, seemingly minding his business, shot twice leaving a bodega. Therein lies intrigue. Unanswered questions.

But even as she reads she knows it's futile. It's all too close to *Cold Reading*. (The eighth novel. Published between *Bad Blood* and *Blunt Instruments*.) And while her tooth rages she puts down the main body of the paper and finds the *Cultural Review* and, as it falls open at her photograph, she tears it into confetti.

30

The effort exhausts her. A lull on the couch bleeds into sleep. Again, she wakes to the dogs. Grousing at her elbow. They need their afternoon exercise. Their walk this morning barely got started. They've got energy to burn.

In the forest, her head clears. Watching the dogs roam around her, snuffling intently at damp leaves. All she can hear is their ambling progress and her own footsteps, advancing on through the trees as the rain subsides, petering back into drizzle as the sun goes down behind her.

The phone's already ringing when she gets back to the house. With the dogs underfoot, she can't make it before her machine cuts in. Whoever's calling hangs up.

A moment later they ring again.

"Hello?"

Lizbeth presses the phone to her ear. Hears the caller say *"Hello"* back. And as they do she feels her throat tighten and the air inside it stall.

"Hello?" she says. "Who is this?"

There's no reply. But just as she's about to ask again—

"Hello."

The same distracted tone. And the air still won't come. Because Lizbeth knows whose voice it is. She knew as soon as she heard it.

It's her own. Unmistakable.

Once more: *"Hello."*

Then the line goes dead.

She holds the phone away from her and stares at it. Puts it down, then picks it back up. Presses star 69 but the number's unobtainable.

Checks the line three times more.

She is certain. It was her. No one else.

It troubles her for the rest of the day. Evades reason. Everything seeming just a half inch wrong now.

Until her tooth crowds even that from her mind.

In the evening the Tylenol becomes irrelevant. The pain crashing through it. She needs something else. Starts to call Nancy, but remembers she's visiting her boyfriend tonight.

The nearest convenience store is in Simsbury. Twelve miles away.

The dogs are fed and then she's in the car, driving alone and in silence except for the *thuck* of the wipers as the rain starts up again. She gropes for music with one hand on the wheel, hits Play on the CD (I-Roy: *Sidewalk Killer*). Swings onto the expressway.

The clerk stares at her tooth. A woman buying lottery tickets asks for her autograph. Lizbeth finds the strongest painkillers in the place.

She has the bottle open before she's even in the car.

Back home, the dogs need one last excursion outside. They pad around the front of the house until it's time to corral them back in.

A message has been left on her machine. She gazes at the flashing red "1." Nervous to play it in case it's her again.

It's just her agent. Wondering how the new book's coming. She says she saw the paper and Lizbeth shouldn't worry. They're fags over there.

She's in bed by ten. The pillows, as ever, viciously plumped beforehand. The comforter yanked and smoothed, every last wrinkle harried out of existence. Only then can she sleep.

She lies on her back in the dark as the rain thrums at the window and, with no competition, her tooth becomes the absolute center of her thoughts. Gingerly, she lets her tongue roll over the crack, exploring it, a change in texture where there should be none, until the pain makes the exercise impossible.

As she turns on her side, it gets worse. On to her front is no improvement. The Frostums jingle squirms into her head and stays there, circling. The new pills aren't working either. She checks the time: 12:40. Then 1:21. 2:16. 2:48. 3.

On TV there's bad movies and creaking reruns. She watches *Quincy*, starts to doze, then, the instant she turns off the set, snaps back to consciousness.

Just milk and an O and a whole lotta Frostums. Just milk and an O—

And so on. She thinks of her voice at the other end of a phone line. Almost falls asleep a dozen times but never quite makes it. Twists onto her side again, then returns to her back.

It's almost five.

What if the day she knows herself is the day she finds there's nothing there?

The rain has stopped. The world is silent.

And all at once, her tooth soothes. The gnarl leaves her muscles. She hangs weightless, her eyes closing, going deeper, feeling warm now, deeper, warmer, deeper, warmer. To sleep.

At six-fifteen exactly on Wednesday morning, the dogs begin scrabbling at the door.

Between feeding and walking them—with her tooth more vicious than ever—she calls Nancy. Her tone in-passing casual.

"I need to visit the beach," she says.

And so, when her assistant comes at noon, she's holding a paper bag. Inside it there's another bag. Smaller. She takes that bag and hands it to Lizbeth.

"Thanks . . . listen, Nancy . . . this might sound weird, but . . ."

Lizbeth tells her about the call. The *Hello,* over and again.

". . . I thought maybe it was . . . I don't know . . . a prank . . ."

But Nancy thinks she's heard of this before. Happened to a friend in Winsted. It's electromagnetics, she says. A glitch on the line. Trapped and echoing. Strange but harmless.

"A glitch," Lizbeth says, unsure if she's persuaded. "Right. I just thought . . . I don't know . . . I don't know what I thought . . ."

Her eyes drop to the paper bag. Nancy follows them.

"Do you need to—"

"Uh-huh. You go. I'll be fine from here."

Upstairs, Lizbeth sits on the end of the bed. Carries out the ritual. Preps the needle. Throws one leg across the other and pulls apart her toes. The only place she ever does this. Finds the vein. And now at last she drifts free once more; her exhaustion dissolving into candy floss rapture. Only this time it won't be interrupted. It swaddles her tight as a midwife. Until her head droops grateful off her shoulders.

She's never met her dealer. Doesn't even know who he is anymore. But she knows the craving. It never changes. Neither does the high. Not when it's good. When every black dart of pain is sucked right out of you, when your soul fills with a bliss so pure that all you can do is wonder how you ever got by without it.

She first took heroin nineteen years ago. Let her boyfriend shoot her up in the cramped green bathroom of his mother's house. When he'd tried to fuck her earlier that night, he couldn't get it up; this was his consolation. He grinned as he watched her eyes roll up, and her jaw turned slack as she nodded beside him.

She's liked it ever since. Just now and then. An occasional pleasure. For when life gets too much. Some people fish, or do macramé. She's got this. It's just a thing of hers.

When she's clean she won't even take cold remedies. Now her chin's on her chest and her arms are dead by her side, and the last thing she sees before her eyes close is the back of her hand, and there's nothing written there at all.

Out of nowhere she mumbles, so low it's unintelligible. Then it gets louder, turns to speech.

"The light's on upstairs . . . Oh, God . . . the light's on upstairs."

Lizbeth jerks to, woken by the sound of her own voice. The darkness of the bedroom only relieved by the faint digital glow of her alarm clock. Her breath comes in flurries. An arm reaches out from beside her, then falls across her belly.

"What light? Where?"

The figure beside her has his eyes closed as he talks. Sprawled out, fair haired and slabbish.

"Go back to sleep, Ed," she says. "It was nothing."

"Is your tooth—"

"My tooth's fine."

But the opiate muffling is wearing off. She finished her supply last night. Three days after Captain Frosto, she still hasn't seen the dentist. Instead she's gone for the trauma-free alternative: permanent dope stupor. Getting lost in that ravishing fog. Unreachable.

Now she tries to get back to sleep before the tooth makes it impossible.

As the phone rings out from down the hall. The study.

She tenses at the sound. Unease ascending. But still she runs from the bedroom, ankles tottery. Only this time, when she picks up, she hears breath.

And not—she knows instantly—hers.

"Hello . . . ?"

Just the breath.

". . . Steven? Is that you?"

Steven Easter is Lizbeth's ex-husband. They married four years ago. She wore ivory silk, and he kept an orchid (her favorite) in his buttonhole. Within ten weeks they were separated. The divorce that followed was amicable. There was no emotional rancor. They were each wealthy to start with. Soon afterward, he suffered what his doctor termed a "cataclysmic" nervous breakdown. In the wake he made endless distress calls to her, nocturnal outbursts of inexplicable panic that would always begin, like this, with just the sound of breath. But he hasn't rung in, what? A year? He lives quietly on a farm co-op in Massachusetts now. So why would this be him?

She waits for a response. Still nothing. Then:

"Oh, you're kidding," she says, her voice abruptly caustic. "This is *you*?"

And down the line she hears the breathing, as steady as hers is ragged.

"*You.* I should have guessed. So was that you earlier . . . messing with me?"

There's no answer.

"I thought we weren't doing this anymore, Jessica. I thought this was done with."

There was a time when the woman Lizbeth thinks she's speaking to would call through the night, every night. Making accusations, threats. That woman's name is Jessica Brokenburr-Schaffer. Schaffer as in Ed Schaffer, the man now falling back to sleep in Lizbeth's bed. Brokenburr as in the catalog people, enduring giants of the mail order business.

Ed and Jessica were married eight years. Formally separated another two. Toward the end of that time Lizbeth met him. There was no overlap in relationships. The divorce, as bitter as Steven and Lizbeth's had been polite, took forever. Jessica kept his name.

The calls had begun within hours of the first time Lizbeth and Ed had dinner. They were maudlin, or violent, or both. Lizbeth's phone rang day and night with the dead echoes of two marriages. The wounded souls of Steven Easter and Jessica Brokenburr-Schaffer whistling through the cables that lay under Quince Hill.

Until, within a month of Steven's last call, hers stopped too. Just stopped.

Ed said she'd found someone else. That now he and Lizbeth could have a real future. Only Lizbeth's not convinced that she wants a real future. His underwear in her antique chest, dinner parties for his business friends.

He doesn't know about the dope. She always tells him she's working. Needs time alone.

There's still no voice at the end of the line.

"Okay, Jessica. I hope you're well. But I'd prefer it if you didn't call here again."

It's only when she gets back to the bedroom that she notices she's trembling. Ed lies on his front, face mashed into the pillow, one arm still laid across her side of the bed.

"That was Jessica."

And like hot ashes have been shoveled down his back he spins around and upright.

"Wait . . . fuck . . . I don't get it . . . I don't . . . *fuck* . . . What did she want?"

"She didn't say. Actually, she didn't say anything."

"But you're sure it was her?"

"Ed, if anyone's going to know, it's me."

Lizbeth can hear him rubbing his scalp as he sits up in bed. And again she thinks: What if the day she knows herself is the day she finds there's nothing there?

He leaves in the morning as she sets out to walk the dogs. Beyond these brief postscripts to the night before, it's still rare for them to see each other in daylight. Whenever they vacation together—impromptu weekends in old European cities, white sands in midwinter—it gets to nine A.M. and she finds herself baffled as to what he's still doing there.

He pushes a wisp of hair back behind her ear and with an unexpected urgency she moves to kiss him, pulling him toward her before he goes. She shuts her eyes and lets her weight fall into his. But her tooth is angry in her head again.

When she gets back from the woods it makes her shake. The pain so bad she could almost manifest it, make it real, wrest it from her body with the two halves of her tooth and hold it there, quivering in her palm.

Instead, she runs to the bathroom, and when she gets there she throws up. And then, with the mouthwash still fresh in her throat, Nancy appears at the door. Hours too early.

Isn't she?

Until, in halting stages, Lizbeth remembers. Today is Friday. Today is Friday, and as it's Friday they're being driven to New York. Manhattan. There's an interview. A radio show. It's been scheduled for weeks. Another stage in the Big Push.

She lets Nancy in, and then she tells her: "I need to visit the beach again."

"Today? But . . . we'll be in the city. The guy I use . . ."

"So he can drive in too. You can meet him somewhere. Just pay him whatever he wants."

"But Lizbeth . . . should you be doing this??"

"I'm in a lot of pain, Nancy. I don't think you know how much pain I'm in."

"I can see your tooth. I can imagine. It's just . . . you've got so much going on right now."

"Exactly. I do."

"But if you just—"

"Nancy, I am not going to the dentist. I can't. You know that."

So Nancy gives in and makes the call and sets a time and place, and then it's done and they move on like it was nothing much of anything. Chew over the schedule for the rest of the day, then those that lie ahead. Each fuller than the last with glad-handing sessions for bookstore executives and syndicated daytime talk shows that all blur loudly into one.

She takes the time she has until the limo arrives and uses it to make herself ready. Turn herself into the Lizbeth Greene of popular imagination. Black pencil skirt and single-breasted overcoat, Prada pumps, white blouse buttoned high. Makeup discreet but immaculate. Her hair, with its life-long tendency to frizz, is groomed into absolute order by fingers gummy with styling gel. Nothing is unattended to.

Music is grabbed for the drive, and then the front door is locked, unlocked, and locked again, the way it is whenever she's out for any length of time. Then unlocked and locked again.

The drive into the city glides by. Rush hour done with, the interstate half-empty. In the back of the limo she cues up a song (Yabby U: *Conquering Lion*). Cranks the volume. Nods her head, too stiff maybe, a little edgy, but enough to make Nancy smile. Through sheer familiarity, she nods her own head too.

As Lizbeth stares out at a drab bank of corrugated factory buildings.

"You know," she says, "I used to work in a poultry processing plant. I did the nightshift."

"You did?"

"It was just for a few weeks. The summer after my freshman year."

"I never knew that."

"I turned vegetarian the same day I started."

The traffic only curdles over the Bronx Kill, out on the Triborough Bridge. Inching into the city where she once spent a decade, that she visits now as rarely as she prays. Having the reaction she always gets here, even now, however faded; the adrenal pump at the cabs and billboards, the endless DNA strings of strangers with their unknown lives.

She has Nancy call the dealer in Midtown to confirm their meeting. He doesn't answer his phone. And Lizbeth knots up inside as the tooth nags at her.

When they get to the station, she realizes she's been here before. The same stocky building adjacent to a laundry and the same earnestly bearded producer.

The three of them smile inside the elevator.

"I'm trying to remember when you were here last."

"I was just thinking the exact same thing."

"Well, we're all still here. All the old gang."

In the producer's office, they make chit-chat over coffee and pastries that Lizbeth doesn't touch. Talk through her upcoming reading tour before the producer says he hopes she knows how pleased they are to have her here, and did her publisher remind her of the setup? Prerecording the interview now, going out on Sunday? Then:

"I've got to ask, you seem like you're having some problems . . . with your mouth."

So Lizbeth explains about the bran and Captain Frosto; her disabling terror of the dentist. And the producer gasps, fascinated, and holds forth on the phobias of literary icons: the lifelong dread of cattle suffered by Tennessee Williams, Kafka's fear of snow.

Across the room, Nancy holds her phone to her ear. Glances over. Shakes her head, then shrugs and mouths: No answer.

Inside the studio itself, Lizbeth sits with outsize headphones laid in front of her. A technician with a marker pen hung around his neck buzzes past, tutting enigmatically.

"I didn't know it was you today."

"Excuse me?"

"They never tell me who's coming in. If I'd known it was you I'd have brought that book for you to sign. *City Slicker*. That was great."

But by the time she thanks him he's left and the presenter's there instead. She's familiar too. A woman her own age, spry and professorial. She takes the seat opposite.

Through the glass of the studio partition wall, Nancy shakes her head again. And the technician reenters, raises his hand. Counts down from three with his fingers.

"Welcome to *The Written Word*."

The presenter's voice is rich and deliberate as she says that today she's privileged to be joined by a true doyenne of crime fiction. She canters through her guest's career by way of introduction: the birth of Enschell, the landmark works, the impending *Black Water Elegy*. Then she looks up and says: "It's been an extraordinary career, Lizbeth—and I guess what it has me wondering is what motivates you to keep writing?"

Lizbeth prepares to answer. Opens her mouth and lifts her tongue. But no sound emerges. She has, she realizes, no thought to express. Nothing to say.

Seconds pass. The presenter smiles in encouragement. Some more seconds pass.

"I'm sorry . . . could I get a glass of water? My mouth's very dry."

She hears the tape shut off, and the producer hurries in. The technician leans over. Asks if Lizbeth could make sure to speak up when they start again.

When they do, the presenter repeats her question. Lizbeth peers down at the plastic cup in front of her, the water inside it. Her expression as blank as the presenter's is baffled.

"I'll put it to you another way. What is it that gets you to the keyboard every morning?"

She hears the words. Individually, she understands them. She's just lost all sense of what they might mean strung together. Her confusion turns to the sheer-walled panic of losing every bearing she has, and the producer's voice booms inside her headphones.

"Is everything okay? Can we get you anything?"

"No, it's fine. I'm sorry . . . my tooth . . . I'm just having a little trouble . . . focusing."

"Let me ask you like this," the presenter says. "What is it you love about writing?"

Lizbeth feels like she's being microwaved. Her tooth the cruelest bully. She sits for an age before she speaks.

"I'm sorry . . . I don't think I can do this."

She pulls off the headphones and rises from her chair. In an instant the producer appears at her side. Offers urgent assurances that if she needs *anything* she only has to ask. But she says no. That's kind, but no. And eventually the producer and presenter nod, resigned.

When they leave there's just Lizbeth and the technician. He disconnects her microphone.

"Yeah, like I say, if I'd known it was you, I'd have brought that book. I thought that was great. Those first Enschell books too. I liked those a lot."

"Thank you, she says. "That's nice to hear."

"I guess I lost interest after that," he says, his tone unchanged. "I mean, my wife still reads your stuff, but she says you've been kind of samey the last few years."

Lizbeth picks up her bag and for the first time since she got here—for the first time in weeks—she knows exactly what it is she wants to say.

"You know what? Fuck off."

When they get back to the car, she bursts into tears, and nothing that Nancy says helps. Afterward, they spend a half hour driving in circles. Still waiting on the score.

At a set of lights by a newsstand on East 58th, Nancy's phone rings.

"They're here," she says, and tells the driver to make for a hotel by Carnegie Hall. There, she scoots into the lobby to meet them. Lizbeth stays in the car. Unseen behind tinted glass, she tracks the roaming tourists, observes the doormen in their tasseled splendor.

By the time Nancy returns, she's curled into a fetal ball across the backseat.

As they pull out into the traffic, she takes off her shoe and preps a vein next to her big toe. And then, from the depths of her swoon, she hears Nancy answer the call from the publicist. The inquest into this morning's fiasco.

It is, Lizbeth would agree, so very unlike her.

Her eyes are long closed by the time they reach the Triborough.

Back in Quince Hill, Nancy sees Lizbeth inside the house. Is thanked profusely and told to have a good weekend.

Alone, Lizbeth changes, makes tea, and winds up on the couch. Stretches out her limbs and basks. Until, as twilight sets in and the joy starts to fade, she reaches for the bag once more. Heads up to the bedroom and lets the warmth soak through her. Everything all right, forever.

It's dark when she comes to. The dogs slaver and huff around her. She doesn't remember letting them in. And the phone rings from down the hall, but even though her machine must be broken and it just keeps ringing she feels no particular urge to answer.

She has no idea what time it is. Can't make out the numbers on her clock. But there's a light on somewhere. She can see it under the door. She just can't tell where it's coming from.

Woozing to her feet, she checks every room upstairs. Finds them all un-lit. Repeats the process downstairs and still can't figure it out. The air feels staticky, and her vision is thick with stars and smears. The warmth gone now, in its place erratic waves of heat, then cold. She stands unmoving in the hallway and her mind fills with images of herself elsewhere in the house. Crouched in the shower; dawdling through the garden. And the phone keeps ringing and the light's getting brighter and it sounds like a mariachi band is playing in the distance as she finally sees the light is coming from outside. So she opens the front door, and the moment she does the music gets engulfed by a screeching industrial hiss, and the light is blinding now but then it fizzles and dies, like switching off an old TV; and there's nothing left but absolute blackness.

Then Nancy. The clear-skinned face of Nancy. Standing above her. Gazing down.

It's day. A vivid Quince Hill morning.

Lizbeth is on her back. Lying flat out in the kitchen. She turns her head to one side and looks into the utility room, the cupboard there pulled open, scattered piles of biscuit in front of it. The dogs staring at her, guilty, confused. Then Nancy again.

"Lizbeth? Oh, God. What happened? Are you okay?"

"I think so."

"Lizbeth . . . wait . . . what's happened to your tooth?"

Instinctively, her hand rises to her mouth. Finds an unfamiliar nothing. Just half her front tooth left now. The other half beside her. A flat white Tic-Tac.

And the pain she feels now makes the pain of before seem like a tease.

"Nancy . . . why are you here? What's happened? Has something happened? Why are you here on the weekend?"

Nancy stares hard at her employer's face, her pale bemusement.

"Lizbeth," she says, "it's Monday. Oh, God, Lizbeth. How much of that stuff have you done?"

But Lizbeth doesn't remember.

THREE

WILSON ULYSSES VELEZ hears the engine start first time. His whole body shackled, he sits bone cold in the cage of a prison van. A steel mesh box further secured by metal screens front and back, each fitted with a square of Perspex. It's the middle of the night. And they roll out through the gates of USP Essenville.

The suspension is nonexistent. With his wrists and ankles chained in place, even the slightest jolt has him lurching off the bench that runs down the middle of the cage. Two guards sit up front, one driving. A third rides in a separate compartment between them and the cage. They call it the buffer.

In the cage there's no air and no window either, but if he pulls himself upright and looks ahead—through the Perspex, past the guards—he can glimpse the road. He stares wide eyed at America. Almost forgotten since the last time he saw it.

A pothole sends him reeling into the sides of the cage.

Then a moment later the van finds a rhythm. A lopsided roll he can half anticipate, shift his weight and ride out. As ESSUSP recedes behind him. Down the hill that lies ahead, he can see the town of Essenville. The town the prison was named for, that now houses its colony of guards.

Its streetlights glimmer from the valley, stellar white and orange pinpricks. He starts to count them. Until the guard in the buffer compartment takes his baton and raps on the Perspex and gestures for Wilson to keep his eyes on the floor.

They hit seventy and stay there. A lonely speck traveling through a world without God. Taking Wilson Velez home.

There's no one unusual around as the van ends its slog through Manhattan. Arrives at Pearl Street. District Court. It coasts down into the parking lot that lies under the building. Into the blush of artificial light.

After hours of rodeo motion, Wilson's hands are numb in their cuffs and he can feel a bruise rising in the middle of his right thigh. He listens to the guards talk as they climb out, smoke cigarettes beside the van.

When they unlock the side panel, he starts to shake.

"Don't start that bug game shit, Velez. None of us are in the mood."

The guard from the buffer compartment steps up to open the cage. He and the driver pull Wilson out. And his feet touch civilian ground.

On the way inside he stumbles and the guards mutter blunt persuasions in his ear. Leading him to a sparsely furnished room, and a dapper, round-faced man who instantly ushers them outside. His name is Alan Ossery. In certain lights he still passes for younger than he is, but maybe not as often as he used to. Now he sups coffee and smacks his lips.

"You got my note?" he says. "You know about God?"

". . . I—I—I—I . . . didddddddddddd. Y—yyyessss."

"That's good. You know, I was phoning that bastard Sosa for a day before he took my call . . . and then he calls me back at six A.M. Anyway, forget that. He told you. That's all that matters. So anyway . . . how are you? Generally?"

"Mmmy—thigh—gottt hhurt—in—thhhe trrruck.—Andandand I—I—I—I still have—the rrrrrash on—mmmmy chestttt. But—otherrr—wwwise—I'mmmm o-o-okay."

Alan Ossery has been Wilson Velez's lawyer for the last nine years. His proxy and confidant.

"I'm glad to hear that, Wilson."

"Howwwww—are—yyyyou?   Dddddddid—yyourrr   ffffflu—clearrr uppp?"

"My flu? Oh, right. Last month. Yes, thank you. It's all cleared up now."

He pulls out a chair for Wilson Velez and one for himself.

"Wilson, I need to make sure you understand what's happening today. Today could be the most important day in your life. Do you understand that?"

"I—I-I-I-I—dddo."

"Good. So what I'm going to do now is talk through with you the arguments I plan to use today, and explain what I'm hoping they'll achieve. If there's anything you need me to clarify, ask me now. Once we're in court it'll be too late. Okay?"

Wilson says nothing and then, for the first time, he looks into his lawyer's face.

"Howww diddddd—it—happppppppen?"

44

"How did what happen, Wilson?"

"Gggggod . . . How—did he dddddddie?"

The star attraction is led inside as the press look on. They open up their laptops as they watch him. A shambling figure in an orange jumpsuit being steered in chains behind a low table, his guards maneuvering him into his seat.

And the reporters compose their opening sentences: *He called him God, but today Wilson Velez began life without the judge who condemned him to a solitary hell.*

Last night they reread their own archived stories. Reacquainted themselves with the events of six and a half years ago:

Wilson Velez, the infamous leader of the Latin street gang Sacred Incan Royals, was today jailed for life on charges of racketeering. The verdict promises to bring to an end what the prosecutor called "no less than a reign of terror" across the city.

For Velez, 27, his next residence will hardly be a culture shock— during various spells behind bars, he has seen the Royals become one of the most feared gangs in the prison system. But the streets of New York have always proved his most fertile recruiting grounds. From its birth in the early 80s, the gang spread from one run-down city neighborhood to the next, bringing with it an ever-growing criminal operation centerd on narcotics.

Ruthlessly violent in dealing with both rival gangs and his own members, Velez has always encouraged his members to take pride in their Latin heritage, a tactic dismissed as an offensive gimmick by mainstream Hispanic leaders but one which helped seduce huge numbers of followers. His orders were laid down in a manifesto given to all new recruits—a photocopied pamphlet treated less as a lifestyle plan than the word of a religious icon. Featuring instructions on how to dress, speak and deal with one's enemies alongside entreaties to take pride in their Latino heritage, it was another way for Velez to maintain control over a gang whose reach eventually extended from its base in Corona, Queens, as far west as Chicago.

But even the fiercest tyrant meets their downfall one day—and Velez met his last September when one of his soldados (soldiers) gave up their former leader to the authorities. Nine months later, their evidence has now proved enough to convict him. The jury took just fifteen minutes to reach guilty verdicts on all charges.

As Velez was led away, he saluted the gang members who had filled the public gallery throughout his trial. Now many wept, or screamed abuse at the judge and jurors.

"We're delighted," said Assistant DA Mitchell Rieber. "Hopefully now the city will be a safer place for all its residents."

Velez's lawyer Alan Ossery—who stood with his hand on his client's shoulder as his sentence was delivered—saw things differently: "Wilson Velez has been convicted by a system that hates nothing more than a young man looking out for his community. This is a dark day indeed for American justice."

Now the reporters turn and look back as Ossery follows his client inside, almost bouncing on his heels. He takes up a position next to Wilson. And Wilson just gazes at the floor.

The judge is last. A stout, skeptic-eyed woman in her fifties, she files in through a door behind the bench, robe like crows' wings, then begins talking as if she's in midsentence. Tells those present that court is in session to hear the appeal of Wilson Ulysses Velez against the conditions of his confinement as laid down by Judge John P. Aspera in the United States District Court of Southern New York.

Ossery clears his throat before he speaks, a phlegmless *hmh*. Just enough to make sure he's got the room's attention. He asks the judge if she needs him to recap the case.

But she knows the case already. She knows that in the wake of his imprisonment, Wilson Ulysses Velez remained—in spirit—the hub of the Sacred Incan Royals. That he clung to the world through the act of correspondence; writing letters, bales of them, messages that sprawled over as many pages as he had available. He would sermonize, vent, his tone wheeling from tribal elder to agony aunt and back in a single sentence.

And the judge knows what went on in his absence. The self-destructive fitting that convulsed the gang. The embezzling, the bloody squabbles over girlfriends and territory. The collapse of all discipline.

The deaths.

Detectives spoke off the record to reporters, telling them Wilson was involved in more than thirty counts of conspiracy to murder. Yet only two were ever brought to trial: the botched stabbing of a man named Felix Cruz and, two weeks later, the altogether more successful shooting of both Cruz and his failed assassin, Horace Gampas.

And last night the press reviewed their stories once more. This time from five years ago:

In a Manhattan courtroom packed with his supporters, the jailed gang leader Wilson Velez was today given the harshest sentence of solitary confinement in modern penal history.

The longtime head of the Sacred Incan Royals was found guilty of having ordered the killings of two of his own followers from his cell in upstate New York's Moxanie Penitentiary. Those orders, the court heard, were hidden in code within seemingly innocent letters.

Velez has now received a pair of consecutive life sentences to accompany the one he was already serving for racketeering.

But it was the nature of the conditions he will serve them in, as handed down by Judge John P. Aspera, that shocked observers—with even prosecutors calling them "unprecedented in their severity."

Currently ineligible for parole, Velez will spend the rest of his time in USP Essenville, Pennsylvania, a recently built high-security "supermax" facility an hour south of Pittsburgh, where he will be permanently segregated from his fellow inmates. But his isolation will not end there—he is effectively barred from correspondence, visits or phone calls from anyone besides his lawyer.

Moreover, any relaxing of the terms will be solely at Aspera's discretion. For any judge to take such absolute control over an inmate's confinement is believed to set a legal precedent. Yet Aspera told the court that his judgment was not intended to punish Velez—simply to protect potential victims.

He made no further comment as he left his chambers.

And so to an eternity in Ad-Seg ESSUSP.

Attempts were made to ease the hardship. Permission sought to enter poems and sketches into magazine contests, to get in touch with religious groups. But John Aspera said no. He always said no. Until Wilson Velez began to call him God, not with any sense of irony, just simple acknowledgment.

47

There were appeals to other judges. They referred the matter back to John Aspera. And Wilson's conversations with Ossery—the only ones he could have now—grew hopeless. Morbid. Fixated on his own longed-for death.

But God died first. In bed with the wife he had always loved, John Aspera suffered a massive hemorrhage in the posterior artery of his brain. Painless, and instant.

And now Wilson Velez's latest appeal proceeds without him.

Alan Ossery runs his palms over his notes as if imbuing them with voodoo powers. Then he looks up at the judge.

"In which case, I'll come straight to the substance of this appeal."

"That might be useful, counselor."

The judge purses her lips, and Ossery steps to the side of his desk. Speaks of his client having long since come to regard his time with the Sacred Incan Royals as a tragic waste of a life; how the gang itself has now all but forgotten him.

"Witness," he says, "the empty seats here today."

"I've witnessed the empty seats, counselor. Is there any other part of the court you'd like me to examine before you continue?"

"No, your honor. What I'd like to do is discuss the most urgent aspect of this case, which is, and always has been, the physical and psychological health of my client. Because both, your honor, have been routinely ignored and imperiled by the conditions he has had to exist in. Just under a year ago, for example, Mr. Velez found himself at the very edge of what a human being can endure."

With his index and middle fingers, Wilson pushes his glasses up his nose.

"Following Judge Aspera's rejection of a plea that he be allowed to speak with a priest on Christmas day, my client was left in a state of extreme distress. Yet despite his agitation, he received no medical attention. The following morning he was found unconscious in his cell. Each of his wrists was fractured, an ankle was broken, a number of ribs had been cracked and there was damage to his knees and elbows. In addition, the tip of his tongue had been bitten off, and a bloody welt almost an inch in width ran vertically down his forehead. A layman could only have assumed he had been viciously assaulted in the night. Yet every injury was of his own making. The wound to his forehead, for example, one that left a scar you can still see today, had been caused by my client literally beating his head against the walls of his cell until he passed out. Following the in-

48

cident, Mr. Velez was diagnosed as having suffered an acute breakdown induced by the years of solitary confinement that had gone before—"

"I'm familiar with the events of last December, Mr. Ossery. I'm not sure how productive it's going to be for you to spend today regurgitating them."

"I'm sorry, your honor, I should have come to the point sooner."

"It's never too late."

"Thank you, your honor. My point is that after this dreadful episode, my client was admitted to hospital for barely enough time to let his physical injuries begin to heal before being returned to Administrative Segregation. From then on he was given no further treatment. My *point,* your honor, is that my client never recovered. He was never *allowed* to recover. Instead, he remained tormented in both mind and body by symptoms that can be directly attributed to the conditions of his imprisonment."

With headwaiter fluency, Alan Ossery details the many physical afflictions of Wilson Velez. Barely draws breath as the list unfurls.

"But of course," he says, eventually, "the body is only ever half the story. Psychologically, I have seen firsthand the man beside me ravaged and destroyed. Reduced to cringing with fear when touched, terrified of what this world might bring him next. A person who spends weeks lost in catatonia, and whose time in Ad-Seg has been plagued with hallucinations. When he does speak, his speech is impaired to the point of incoherence. Moreover, on the one occasion a psychologist was briefly allowed to examine my client, he found his speech was simply a reflection of his thought processes. That his mind was turning, and I quote, 'to sludge.' Without human contact or external stimulus, his is a mind that is dying. And US Penitentiary Essenville is, to him, little more than a vast instrument of torture and—"

"Is there anything in your locker besides hyperbole, Mr. Ossery?"

The judge considers him with theatrical weariness.

"I'm sorry, your honor. Everything I've spoken of is documented in the medical evidence you've been presented with."

"I've read the medical evidence, Mr. Ossery. I don't recall any mention of vast instruments of torture. Shall we move on?"

But Ossery's almost done. Slowly begins to wrap it up. Until the point at which he says:

"So, if your honor feels you have enough information, I'll sit down. I would, however, like to say one more thing—"

"Just one, Mr. Ossery?"

"Just one, your honor. And that one thing is that while we are, of course, here to make a decision based on the application of law—"

"We, Mr. Ossery? Are you joining me?"

"—there is another aspect to my client's case. Humanity. My client's humanity, and our humanity. Because while we should never compromise our commitment to the punishment of wrongdoing, this is also a nation that cherishes compassion. And however much you abhor his conduct in the past, let us remember that Wilson Velez is human. Human, and all but broken by a sentence that, with due respect to the late Judge Aspera, is little short of barbaric. So today I urge you to release him not from custody—but from the misery that will otherwise continue, slowly but remorselessly, to destroy him."

In the mind of Alan Ossery, the room fills with applause. Everywhere else, all anyone hears is the stenographer coughing and the yowl of a chair pushed back too quickly. Wilson shifts his weight. His thigh still throbs from the van ride. As the judge retires, he hears Ossery's voice beside him. Turns and sees his lawyer's face inches from his own, ricked into apology.

"Listen, don't feel bad. The important thing is we laid the ground. Next time there'll be a different judge, next time this cunt won't be jumping on every word I say and, you know . . . I think we'll really have a shot at this."

"It'sssss—okay . . . Alllan. I—I—thought yyyyou . . . soundedddd—gggg . . . gggreat."

He stares down at his sneakers, their white almost luminous against the courtroom floor. Keeps his eyes there until everything else recedes. Until there's just the white. A pristine white. A white to be consumed by:

A blinding sun that fills the sky as he hurtles back out of the lime trees, blood still dripping from his face and his legs pistoning so frantically he half trips as he runs, scrambling on the balls of his feet for one, two, three, four, five desperate strides, so close to falling but somehow staying upright and in motion. Yet still unsafe.

"Jesus."

Ossery. Whispering, stunned.

"Wilson?" he says. "Wilson, do you understand?"

"Is there a problem, counselor?"

"I'm sorry, your honor. I don't think my client heard you."

The judge has returned.

"Fine, Mr. Ossery. Shall I repeat myself for his benefit, and you can try and ensure he's listening? The judgment of this court is that, given the present condition of the appellant, he poses a greatly reduced threat to the outside world. As such, his appeal is granted. At the discretion of the Department of Corrections and Warden Michael Sosa of US Penitentiary Essenville, Wilson Velez may be relocated to the main body of the prison facility, allowed a limited number of visitors, and permitted to enter into appropriate, vetted correspondence should Warden Sosa and the DOC feel it reasonable. I emphasize, however, that these adjustments to Judge Aspera's ruling will be kept under constant review, and that any sign of their abuse will result in their immediate withdrawal. There will be a formal review of this judgment at a date to be confirmed, at which time it will be decided whether the inmate is to be returned to Administrative Segregation."

And then:

"That's all."

Ossery discreetly pumps his fist. But when the reporters look over at Wilson, he's still staring at the floor, and none of them can see his expression.

FOUR

They play music at the dentist's. Delicate chimes sweetening the mood as you ease into the chair. Everything white or pastel, the air scented with herbal bouquets. A water feature murmuring beside the window.

Lizbeth grips the armrests so hard her fingertips squeal on the leather. Her eyes bugging and her body filmed with sweat. Hoping not to scream, or throw up, or both.

The last time she saw a dentist, a trolley stacked with savage tools gleamed next to her eyeline, and the only music was "Baba O'Riley" bleeding in from a car parked outside. Now the chimes are all around and there's a screen in the corner on which bold and curious patients can, if they wish, observe their own treatment.

Lizbeth is neither bold nor curious.

Before this, it took an hour for the dentist, the nurse and Nancy to cajole her inside. Eventually, a degree of force was used. Now the three of them are stationed around the room in such a way, Lizbeth realizes, to grab her at the door if she makes a run for it.

The exam's already been carried out. The forlorn nugget of pulp and enamel left in her mouth is to be—*has* to be—removed. Then, at a second appointment in the next few days, the surrounding teeth will either be filed down in readiness for a bridge, or (the choice is Lizbeth's) a metal implant drilled into the jaw.

But for now she's getting a false tooth. A "flipper," the dentist called it. Molded onsite. Ready in two hours. Purely—and this was stressed, then re-stressed—temporary.

In an attempt to make the process less agonizing, she's been hooked up to a drip that is releasing a sedative into her bloodstream. At any moment she will, the nurse explained, be overcome by a stunning calm. There will be no anxiety at where she is or what's about to be done to her; just carefree tranquility and, perhaps, vivid daydreams.

Now, however, her nails are gouging the armrests and her heart is a jackhammer in her chest. It's pathetic, she knows. So clichéd. Why could she not be scared of something less hackneyed? Because she has no imagination. That, she tells herself, is the problem. It always has been.

But it doesn't make this any easier.

The dentist steps toward her.

Lizbeth writhes back into the chair, but then—just at the point she expects to pass out, go nuts, explode—there's suddenly nothing but sunshine. A tsunami rush of serenity, like a monthlong vacation compressed into a second.

The dentist leans over her—so close she can see the pores on his cheek—and produces a slim metal cylinder that tapers into a hook.

"Okay, before we do anything else, let's get this mess cleaned up."

She relaxes with blissful intensity. Hands perfectly still, palms up. The dentist holds her mouth open as he slips the hook inside. A chip, then a scrape. Metal skins the gum.

Her eyes travel past him and she sees the nurse, smiling in encouragement, and Nancy's doing the same beyond that, and she tries to smile back at them as best she can with the hook lodged in her mouth and her tongue held down with a wooden paddle. It is, she feels, the least she can do. To thank them for making her so happy.

The dentist pulls away, and then he reaches for a second, larger hook.

"Okay, just hang in there . . . it's going to be a little trickier than I thought."

And Lizbeth stares up at the ceiling, hears nothing but the water feature's pretty babble, and knows she is in the most wonderful place on earth.

The sedative, the nurse said like an afterthought, could have a mild effect on Lizbeth's coordination.

At the surgery door, she duly careers to one side, staggers back and, in the attempt to right herself, lurches full-weight into the frame.

"Whoa there, Miss Greene."

The dentist and Nancy grab a shoulder each. Her brain feels like it's been dipped in warm chewing gum. She knows, in theory, what has just happened to her. She just can't relate it to what's in her mouth. She flicks her tongue across the place where the crack used to be and finds a perfect smoothness.

"So," the dentist says, "we'll see you again in a couple of days. I've given your assistant some pamphlets on both the bridge option and the titanium implant, so if you take a look at those and see which you think you might prefer, then next time you're here we can get that flipper out and fix you up with something more permanent . . ."

He pauses like he's not quite done. Stands in the doorway, staring rapt at Lizbeth as she sways in front of him.

"Miss Greene, I wanted to say what an honor it's been to treat you. I'm just a massive fan. I have been ever since *City Slicker*. I really hope I'm not being inappropriate. I'd have just kicked myself so hard if you'd left without me telling you."

Lizbeth stares at him blank as a week-old baby, until Nancy promises him a signed copy of *Black Water Elegy*.

Back outside, they sit for a moment in Nancy's car.

"How are you feeling?"

"I'm . . ."

The key turns in the ignition; Nancy puts the car into reverse; backs out of the parking lot; emerges onto the street.

". . . muzzy."

"I'll get you home and you can sleep it off. Oh, I nearly forgot. They gave me this."

With her free hand Nancy holds up a clear screwtop jar that holds the remains of Lizbeth's front tooth.

"We've got both halves now. You know . . . for when you sue."

In the wake of her treatment, her agent and publisher agree to pare back her schedule. Certain interviews are canceled; others converted from face-to-face meetings into phone calls.

She takes the dogs out the next morning and then she goes back to bed. Sleeps until noon. In the afternoon she walks the length of the house, just savoring not being in pain.

Pauses at the door of the study. Then steps inside.

There's a stale tang strong enough for her to heave open a window. She pulls out her chair. Switches on the laptop. A Page A Day.

Tea: she will need tea. She heads downstairs to make it. The jar from the dentist sits on a shelf next to Captain Frosto. She dribbles the honey into the cup. Feels the heat against her false tooth for the first time.

At the living room mirror, she stares at it. The exact same white as those around it, the surface ridged just slightly down the center. Under anything less than total scrutiny, no one would ever know it was fake. But she does.

She pops it out. Grins at herself so she can see the gap. A comic book black square. Slots it in again, like she's loading a video. Pops it out; slots it in; pops it out; slots it back in. Returns to her desk. Swivels in her chair.

She flips through the pamphlets from the dentist. Reads about the grinding process used in fitting a bridge, the length of time it takes the gum to heal after an implant.

The heroin she has left is in a jewelry box in her bedroom. Now she retrieves it. Takes it to the bathroom with the sure intention of flushing it away.

Stands there for drawn-out moments with the bag in her hand before returning it to where she found it.

Back in the study, the screen of her laptop comes to life as she types:

Enschell

Detective Frederick Timonon Enschell (his middle name was revealed in *The Hands of Angels;* her fans are given to debating its significance). Where are you, old friend? She closes her eyes to better locate him. He is—

On a boat. Or a horse. At the barber's. A funeral. A Weight Watcher's class. Having a shower. An appendectomy. Visiting the dentist.

Forget it. Find an image. Doesn't have to be him. Screw him. Just pick an image. An attention-grabber:

A plastic figure from a cereal box. A broken tooth in a screwtop jar.

So, bring him back.

She pictures him as she always has. Her trusty companion for fifteen years. His features as familiar to her as her own. More so. And then as always now he slips away from her. Dissolves. Turns faceless.

She breathes deep and types.

enschellenschellenschellenschellenschellenschellenschellenschell
enschellenschellenschellenschellenschellenschellenschellenschell
enschellenschellenschellenschellenschellenschellenschellenschell

And she keeps typing until she reaches the bottom of the page.

"So I pop it out . . . And I slot it back in again. See?"

"Oh, my God. That's . . . wild."

Lizbeth sits facing Ed Schaffer on the largest couch in her living room.

One last time she demonstrates the removal and replacement of her tooth.

"Isn't it just?"

"It truly is."

She grabs her wine from the table, twists around until her back's against his chest, her weight pressed into him, his arm slung around her. And with the remote control she hits Play on the stereo (Jacob Miller: "Who Say Jah No Dread").

"I'm think I'm suing."

"The dentist?"

"The Frostums people. Nancy says I can't let them get away with it."

He sips from his glass and then he lifts his hands to her shoulders. Kneads and massages.

"I'm still amazed they got you in there."

"They almost broke my arm doing it. Then they drugged me."

"They did?"

"Uh-huh. I was on a drip. Midazolam."

"God, really? They gave that to Tom Zwick during his root canal. He said he was bouncing off the ceiling."

"I don't remember a thing about it. I mean, I remember walking in, and I remember leaving. Everything else is gone. Nancy said most of the time I was waving at her."

She leans back into him, her head under his, mouth by his ear.

"All I know is I when I came to I was wet."

"Is that so?"

"It is."

With his fingers at her jaw, he angles her head to kiss her.

"So it doesn't put you off?" she says. "The tooth?"

"Me? No. I . . . I actually find it quite kinky. Maybe you could leave it out for a while."

"Are you serious?"

"You know, I think I am."

So she takes out her tooth, and five minutes later his hands are on her belly, head between her legs. She looks down and there's an inky bruise the size of a doughnut in the middle of her thigh from where she walked into the dentist's door. Something about it unsettles her. Keeps drawing her gaze. Until she grabs at his hair and starts to cry out and everything she was thinking of slips from her mind.

Ed Schaffer is a restaurateur. Sometimes she pictures him sampling ingredients in exotic locations; but she knows his actual role is the raising of funds before others more qualified do such things.

He calls her sweetheart right before he falls asleep, voice barely more than breath. She rolls the word around her head a while, wonders how he settled on it the first time he used it—as he does routinely now—why he chose that and not darling or honey, baby, sugar, angel. As her eyes adjust to the dark, she considers him. The placid sweep of his forehead, amiably canine spread of his nose. And her own breathing slows and deepens—

The phone rings out from down the hall.

By the time she gets to the study, the dogs are galumphing in circles outside the door. She negotiates around them through her daze.

But when she picks up there's no one there. Not even breath.

She says hello three times in succession, each more fractious than the last.

"Jessica, if this is you, then . . ."

Lizbeth trails off into silence as she gazes around the room. Moonlight between the undrawn curtains.

"Why are you doing this? If there's something you need to say to me . . ."

Apparently, there's not.

"Okay. You know what, Jessica? I'm going back to bed."

She hangs up, but the second she does it rings again. And now, when she picks up, a male voice talks fast and low:

"*Anoche soñé contigo. Es verdad! Como hago todas las noches.*"

Then a woman: "*Soy débil! Tú me haces débil!*"

Lizbeth's Spanish is barely rudimentary. She was lost from the start.

The man again: "*Soñarás tú conmigo también?*"

Then the line goes dead.

The number, as she expected, is unobtainable.

Back in the bedroom, Ed is sitting upright, eyes pouchy, manner anxious.

"It wasn't her," Lizbeth says, as she reassumes her place beside him.

The next day she sits at her desk and tells herself to forget it. Just a commonplace late-night crossed line. (Right?) Tries to focus instead on the string of phone interviews she has scheduled through the morning.

Their tone is innocuous. How would she describe a typical working day? Which of her books makes her proudest? Even then the answers flow like Vaseline.

And at the end of the last interview, the final journalist says:

"I just want to tell you I sincerely enjoyed the book."

Lizbeth thanks him before her attention is pulled toward the window. There, on the sill, a skinny gray squirrel cleans itself, slow and meticulous. A second later, it glances up. Notices its audience and stares back. Its paws twitch slightly as its eyes lock with Lizbeth's and, for a moment, neither of them moves; until, in the next, it scrams back to the trees.

"And also," the journalist says, "I really think the reviews have been incredibly unfair."

There is a pause as Lizbeth considers the squirrel. Another when she realizes what's just been said.

"Oh," she says, "well, I never read reviews. So I wouldn't know."

This is true. A thing of hers since forever: a preemptive defense of a lifelong thin skin. Instead, she has them read to her. Nancy collates them, then gives her the gist, filleted of ill will. Not that much ever needs to go. Even her less ardent reviews are unfailingly civil.

Nancy brings tea once the interview is done with, and Lizbeth turns and says as if the thought has just crossed her mind:

"Have any reviews come through yet?"

"Reviews? No. I mean . . . nothing substantial."

"Substantial?"

"Right. Papers from towns that people ten miles away have never heard of. Nothing stuff."

Lizbeth takes her tea and then she gets to her feet.

"You know, I think I'm going to try and get some work done."

Upstairs, she waits for the sound of the front door closing. A return to her own company. The only light in the room her desk lamp.

And with her laptop open a modem connects her to a world beyond Quince Hill. She searches for her own name, and the words "black water elegy."

Waterlogged, says the first document out of dozens. A review, like the rest. Taken from the second biggest paper in the Pacific Northwest. Published three days ago.

She leans in close to the screen as she reads.

The humble bow tie may not immediately strike you as the most lethal of accessories. For some, however, it apparently holds a dark and mur-

derous potential. Witness the latest thriller from Lizbeth Greene, Black Water Elegy—*a typically bloody yarn that begins with the neckwear in question being used to strangle a victim to death.*

Things soon get a good deal nastier. But sadly, the hard-edged realism that was once Greene's forte is nowhere to be found. Instead, the reader must make do with far-fetched plot twists and gory excess: a combination that will win her few new fans, and may see the old ones drifting away from her.

So it goes on. She stares at the words with her skin turning clammy like there's fat dead hands all over her. Until she reaches the end of it.

Then she starts the others. She reads them all. Such bile. Relentless. Every one a bomb under her ego and a knife in her heart.

She reads the *Times* last.

The critic begins with a lengthy anecdote about an unnamed distant relative considered by his family to be a rare beauty, she never having become a model or Hollywood starlet, a mystery despite the fact she was, with hindsight,

a plain Midwestern hausfrau *of advancing years.*

It was just that we had repeated the notion of her breathtaking good looks so often they became fact—until a young nephew blurted out in front of the whole clan that he thought our gorgeous relative was actually quite ordinary. And it was true. At once the spell was broken: the idea we had ever seen this woman as a small-town Venus now simply seemed bizarre.

Regrettably, this is what comes to mind when one reads Black Water Elegy, *the new Enschell mystery from Lizbeth Greene. In spirit, her work has perhaps always belonged with the trashy procedurals to be found on racks at dowdy supermarkets across the country—yet with the media and publishing industries besotted with her, she has instead confected a reputation as the consummate modern crime writer, a dainty-featured, raven-haired genre titan whose books also make safe bedside fodder for more high-minded literary types. As a sleight of hand, it takes some beating.*

Yet her self-conscious flourishes can have rarely made a less tasteful adjunct to the butchery she deals in. Moreover, the authentic is sadly AWOL from Ms. Greene's tableaux. While it was famously the real-life

*tragedy of her mother's murder and her own abduction by the notori-
ous Richard Cazet that inspired her breakthrough with* City Slicker, *the
irony is that her novels' reliance on ever more fanciful serial killers with
ever more outlandish trademarks has slowly pushed them from the
hokey into the outright laughable. At a time when a new, younger generation of crime writers is dragging the form into the harsh reality of
twenty-first-century America, her parade of cackling psychos now
seems painfully out of touch.*

*Reading this book, one can't help wondering when Ms. Greene last
actually saw a criminal, far less secured any insight into his or her behavior. No, the sad truth is that with only grand guignol set pieces
and froufrou prose to mask her shortcomings, this is a writer spent,
too busy spinning bloody variations on implausible themes to notice
her own redundancy.* Midway through Black Water Elegy, *the long-
suffering Enschell announces: "I've been doing this so long I can
barely recall the point of it." Frankly, by then, one can only think "me
neither."*

She doesn't leave the house for the next three days. Barely leaves the
bedroom. Nancy takes care of what needs taking care of. Says over and
again with palpable regret that she's sorry for lying about the reviews. But
Lizbeth's not angry. What else could she do?

The rain is an endless flat spatter on the windows and skylights. Lizbeth
huddles in bed and wonders what would happen if it never ended. Just
rained, forever. Which nearby towns would flood first? How soon would
the waters saturate the forest and rise above Quince Hill, sweeping up
small animals and cars as the land gave up its fixtures the way that Lizbeth
surrenders now to the serenade of neurosis?

Last thing at night she checks the safety of every plug in the house, pok-
ing at sockets on her hands and knees. Then she tests her locks.

The heroin she has left gets done, and afterward she buys more. She
burrows under the covers until there's no light getting in at all and then
she puts in earplugs.

And she sleeps on through the days.

She peruses herself one last time. Reapplies her lipstick. Deepens the color.
Fills out the corners of her mouth.

In a suite at the Manhattan Four Seasons, Lizbeth's agent stands behind her. Checks her own reflection in the same mirror. Taller than Lizbeth, older, groomed like a knife is sharpened. Her name is Inchy Burden.

"You're doing so well, honey. You're Inchy's bravest trouper."

She takes two steps back into the center of the room.

"You know, I almost thought we'd lost you back there."

"I know."

"But now all you have to do is get through tonight. One last big push."

"I know. What time is it?"

"It's seven."

"Oh, God—"

"Relax. It's your launch. Let the little fish wait."

Lizbeth runs a finger across each of her eyebrows and then, as she turns from the mirror, her agent takes hold of her arms.

"It's been rough on you, hasn't it, honey? These last few days? But it's going to have made you so strong."

"Oh, I'm a regular Charles Atlas."

"I wouldn't argue with you."

"You know, Inchy . . . when tonight's done with, I want to talk about the next book . . ."

"What's to talk about, honey?"

"The fact it doesn't exist. And I don't know if it ever will."

Inchy Burden guides her back to the mirror. Addresses her reflection.

"Here's what's going to happen. Tonight you're going to go to your party and you'll have fun. Tomorrow the book will come out and it'll be your best seller yet and a thousand times more people will read it and love it than will ever know this prick from the *Times* even existed. Then you'll rest up and then when you get back you'll write *another* amazing book that people will love even more than this one. Because that, Lizbeth Greene, is what you do."

Her gaze has, Lizbeth realizes, moved to the side of her head. Her earrings.

"Are those Cartier?"

And Nancy emerges from the bathroom. Says they need to go.

"Just let me make a call," Inchy Burden says, and above the conversation that follows, Nancy takes her place beside Lizbeth and says:

"Listen . . . your sister phoned. She can't make it. There's a problem with her youngest kid."

"Right. Isn't there always?"

"Also, she said to tell you she was going up to see your Dad on his birthday next week . . ."

"Right."

"And she sends her love."

The apology in Nancy's voice thickens as she gestures at her mouth.

"You've got . . . lipstick . . . on your tooth. The false one."

In the elevator, Inchy and Nancy stand on either side of her, flanking her as if she was a prizefighter en route to the ring. Outside, the limo is waiting.

The party takes place in understated grandeur on West 75th Street. Impassive young waiters in high-collared uniforms weave through the room beneath soft lighting, bringing trays of intricate canapes to knots of guests that form, swell, reach critical mass, shrink, break up, reform. A piano vies with the noise of the room: glass on glass and two hundred voices.

Every face turns to her as she enters. People who like what they are, who expect the world to like it too.

Inchy and Nancy bind themselves to her side but Lizbeth shoos them away. This must be done alone. And it can. The charm, the gracious dispensation of her time, it's a cinch. She gives it to everyone who wants it. The gushing women and unctuous men who cover her in spit-mist as they talk, the next in line already sidling up. No one ever comes at her head on.

No one except Nancy. With expert discretion she tells Lizbeth she shouldn't feel like she has to stay. That what with everything that's happened lately and the dentist tomorrow, she shouldn't work herself too hard. But Lizbeth says she's fine.

She just needs the bathroom.

When she gets there, a girl in a minidress is learning against the sinks. Nineteen at the oldest. Burgery complexion veiled under makeup. They half nod as Lizbeth washes her hands.

"I'm sorry," the girl says. "I'm kind of drunk."

It's true. She is. Brash. A little slurred.

"That's okay," Lizbeth says. "Sometimes when I was your age I was kind of drunk too."

The girl adjusts her position. Peers over.

"So," she says, "do you know Lizbeth Greene?"

"Excuse me?"

"Lizbeth Greene. The woman this party's for. I asked if you knew her."

Lizbeth considers the question.

"No," she says. "Not really. You?"

"Me? I don't know anyone. I started interning at her publisher today."

Lizbeth dries her hands. Waits for the moment.

"So . . . do you read her books?"

"Lizbeth Greene's? God, no. I can't stand that murder mystery shit. I mean . . . spending a whole book waiting to find out who killed someone you don't care about anyway, and then the answer's either completely pre-dictable or doesn't make any sense. It's so lame, you know? Do you have a cigarette?"

"I don't smoke."

"Oh, okay. Actually, though, I feel kind of sorry for her."

"You do?"

"Uh-huh."

She leans in close although there's no one else around.

"Right before I left to come down here the whole office was complain-ing about how bad her new book is. I mean, *everyone*. Apparently even her agent said it sucks. She was on the phone with the head of marketing and said the only way it would sell was if she got herself abducted again. That's how she got started, right? And tonight all those same people are here, kissing her ass. Isn't that awful?"

Lizbeth doesn't answer. Just turns and leaves.

Smiles as she hurries back through the party. Her mouth set in a tight glossy U worn half from habit and half from the need not to draw atten-tion to what, she realizes, will be her exit.

On into the lobby. Out to the street.

Her heels batter the sidewalk and when she finds the limo her knuckles rap on the chauffeur's window.

Inside, she gulps for air, her hand spread across her chest. She mea-sures out her breathing as the city's flux of light and motion falls away behind her.

She calls Nancy as they reach the Bruckner Expressway. Says she's sorry but she had to go, right then and there. Was suddenly exhausted. Over-come. But Nancy should take the suite at the Four Seasons. Enjoy herself. Order something extravagant on room service and charge it to the pub-lisher. Have them book her another limo home tomorrow.

"I'll get myself to the dentist," she says. "It'll be fine."

And with that she ends the call. Switches off the phone. Studies the back of the chauffeur's head—a ridge of fat around the base of his skull like a rubber ring—until her eyes get heavy from the drone of the engine.

She wakes up on the interstate, forty miles from home. The road empty in the darkness. Switches her phone back on and in seconds Nancy is calling. So Lizbeth tells her again that she's just wiped out, honestly, that's all it is; and no, there's nothing that she isn't saying.

But Nancy knows better than that. And finally, Lizbeth gives in. Explains about the girl in the bathroom, and as she does she hears anger in her voice. The sound of it alarms her. Displays of emotion have never come easy. (Pictures of her as a child show a round and unlined poker face staring noncommittally toward the camera.) But now she hears anger, and words—sycophants, cocksuckers—that sound strange to her coming from her mouth.

"And you know something? She's right. What I do *is* lame. Who cares who killed some corpse that always gets found on page five or what Frederick Enschell thinks about it? He isn't real. I made him up. It's all made up and and I don't even know why I do it anymore."

Nancy replies, and Lizbeth imagines what she's saying is wise and supportive, but the line's breaking up and her voice is fractured, distant.

She hangs up and it rings again. But this time the line is even worse.

"Hello?"

And as she tries to pick a voice out of the fuzz a man in a pale blue Nissan pulls away from the shoulder of the highway.

Earlier today, returning from his job as a manager at a data transfer center, he argued on the phone with his elderly mother over his mounting weight problem, then, in a fit of self-loathing, consumed a whole roast chicken directly before a long sought-after date with a female colleague. The evening was not, on any level, successful. He dropped the colleague home an hour ago. Ever since he's been parked on the shoulder, lost in a depressive fug. Now he drives, foot on the gas, eager to get home and to bed, so immersed in his own misery that he forgets to check his mirror as he changes lanes and thereby fails to note the presence of the only other car on the road.

"Nancy?"

The blue Nissan has reached fifty-eight mph as it swerves into the limo. The limo is traveling at seventy-seven.

At the moment of impact both drivers instantly lose control of their vehicles.

The cars scream across the tarmac like pool balls careering toward the same pocket, dying hulks of metal in a fountain of white sparks.

The Nissan flips onto its side before it stops. The limo skewed across the middle of the road with its hood wide open and passenger side caved in.

The silence only broken by the Nissan's horn, jammed and blaring.

Lizbeth quakes in the backseat of the limo, her legs covered in shards of tinted glass. She smells burned rubber. Gas. Meticulously, she flexes every part of her body. Just to be sure she can. Braces herself and nudges open the door. Creeps up to the front of the limo.

The chauffeur's sitting upright, facing forward. Hands fixed to the wheel. He turns to her and a patch of his scalp is sticky with blood. He rolls down the window and says:

"My head hurts."

"It'll be okay," Lizbeth says. "Just . . . stay where you are."

The Nissan lies wheezing on its side. She steps toward it.

The driver's door opens to the sky. A pair of feet appear, then withdraw, and then a hand takes their place.

The Nissan driver hauls himself out with just one arm and screams in pain as he does. Slumps down to the road, with the other swinging back like the elbow's jointed the wrong way. The bone jutting out.

He reels toward her and for a moment they stand beside each other. But neither speaks.

A hubcap from the limo spins on its edge down the road, fast and erratic, never quite tipping flat.

A motorcycle buzzes into view.

Lizbeth and the Nissan driver watch in silence as it speeds toward them, the rider veering wildly at the sight of the hubcap and being launched from the saddle.

The rider hits the ground and rolls three times before lying still.

The bike hurtles on.

It strikes the Nissan driver just below the waist, then crashes into Lizbeth. Pins in a bowling alley.

And nothing moves at all, for now.

FIVE

THE CHAUFFEUR SUSTAINED a concussion. The motorcyclist shattered his pelvis. The Nissan driver suffered breaks to one arm, a wrist, his collarbone and five ribs.

Lizbeth sits up in her hospital bed, supported by a wall of pillows. Her cuts have been bandaged and her bruises tended. She has broken her left ankle. Right now it's suspended in front of her, hanging doleful in a lightweight cast.

But that's all.

The doctor told her she was lucky. Crutches for less than a month, a cane for a few weeks thereafter. A fracture so clean, he said, you could eat a chicken dinner off it.

Nancy stands at the foot of the bed, sifting through bouquets. Even the most lavish are dwarfed by the spray of white orchids brought here last night by Ed. They stand in the corner, epic and unmissable.

He stayed until late.

"These are from Eileen Deschler," Nancy says, grappling with carnations.

"Who's Eileen Deschler?"

"I've no idea. I thought you must know her. I'll put them by the window."

Next, a vast array of gladioli. Nancy squints at the card.

"These are from Inchy."

"I don't want them."

"Really? I thought you loved gladioli."

"Do you want them?"

"No . . . They're yours."

"If you want them, take them."

But instead she moves on to the next bunch.

"These are from your sister."

"Oh, let me guess . . ."

"I meant to tell you . . . She called when you were with the doctor. She doesn't think she can make it today. She said she could get here Sunday."

"I'm not going to be here Sunday."

"I know. I told her that."

Lizbeth grabs for the chopstick she's been using to scratch under her cast. Says, to herself: "Well, isn't that just Mame all over . . . ?"

"Oh," Nancy says, "also, I'm getting you on the phone with Jeff this afternoon—"

"Jeff the vet? Why? Oh, fuck. What's happened—"

"Not Jeff the vet. Jeff the lawyer. He's giving us an update on the bran people . . . and he wants to talk to you before he files suit against the Nissan driver."

"Jeff the lawyer. Right. Sure."

"Lizbeth, you know, I'm so sorry about everything that's happened. You must be feeling so beat up—"

But, in fact—despite her ankle—Lizbeth feels good. She has, since she woke up here yesterday, been accruing some distance. Some much needed perspective. And now she gets it.

The problem is she has no more stories. There's not a word of fiction left in her. It's all used up. She has scooped out her imagination like a cantaloupe. Every grisly scenario and unlikely deus ex machina, they've been recycled and reanimated over and over again, until they're all one slicked-up churn of bodies, killers, motives, weapons, bodies and killers and motives and weapons and—

And she's not going to do that anymore.

"I've been thinking of getting a job."

Nancy trims the stems on a bunch of tulips.

"Really?" she says, carefully. "You have?"

"I could work in a bookstore. Or a library. I could use an assumed name. I could teach. It might be just what I need. I could get a job and it would inspire me. I could find something authentic. Something real. I won't find anything real in my study."

She sits up as straight as her winched-up leg will allow.

"How many signs do I need, Nancy? Ever since my tooth there's been this tap tap tap on my shoulder, telling me something has to change. Now this. What next? You know, maybe I should just take the hint. Get back to where I was when I started. When I was proud of what I did. Can you understand that, Nancy?"

"Of course," she says. And then: "I'm just going to see if I can borrow a vase."

As she leaves, Lizbeth falls back into the pillows. She feels at peace now, with everything dismantled. At last she can move on, weightless.

She hears a knock, and by the time she's turned her head, the doctor's already in the room. He smiles, and then he shuts the door behind him.

SIX

S HE'S PRACTICED HARD with her crutches. Quickly progressed from comic incompetence to a clattering technique that—while it could never be called graceful—gets her where she needs to be. She's almost used to the absence of balance, the redistribution of her weight. The way everything's slower now. Cumbersome. How *she* is cumbersome.

Lizbeth sits in her room in the hospital with the crutches laid either side of her and her bags packed at her feet. Today she's going home. Nancy's coming to collect her.

She leafs through a copy of *Time* as she waits. Comes to a roundup from the world of books. Sees a mention of *Black Water Elegy*. Recoils. Hurries back through the pages in search of something—anything—else to focus on.

Page nineteen. A picture of a convict. Slightly built, Hispanic. Standing in court with a lawyer beside him. Rounded shoulders lost inside a prison-issue jumpsuit. Tattoos on his arms and neck. Thick glasses and strange hairless patches on his scalp. A livid scar down his forehead. A chain around his waist; handcuffs; leg irons. He stares beyond the camera.

He is—to some—The One Eternal King Three Vee, Most Reverent Sapa of the People's Nation of Sacred Incan Royals, Devout Protector and Righteous Sovereign of the New York Tribe, First and Supreme Chapter. Others might know him by the meaning of the numbers tattooed around his wrist: 1.18.4.9.12.12.1—a numerical version of his childhood nickname—Ardilla, or squirrel.

Ardilla. Or squirrel.

And now she understands. This is it. What she was always meant to see. Where she was being led.

The answer. At last. Thank God.

But to the legal system in whose grip he's spent the bulk of his life he is simply Wilson Ulysses Velez—ultraviolent gang leader and latter-day Count of Monte Cristo.

And trying not to cry out in exultation she learns of the five years in Ad-Seg, the appeal that finally ended them. Immerses herself in the story as it leads her through what came before. Then back to where it started: Essenville. His ruin. Until, now:

Among the Sacred Incan Royals, still worshipful of their lost leader, his release from such brutal conditions has been greeted as a vindication. Since Velez's imprisonment, his successor Jose "Hurricane" Almanza has tried to reinvent the gang as a community-minded youth group—a move the Royals claim was begun by Velez, and would have been impossible without his blessing.

"Every positive thing the Royals are involved with is Wilson's doing," says Father Raymond Peres, a priest in Velez's old neighborhood of Corona, Queens, and an informal spokesman for the gang. "Even through the agony of unjust punishments his example has led the youth in the right direction."

Others, however, are less convinced of either the gang's transformation or the wisdom of allowing Velez out of Ad-Seg. For the high-profile Congressman Mitchell Rieber, for example—who in his previous role as Assistant DA secured both Velez's original conviction and that meted out for the coded letters—the appeal judges' verdict is a serious miscalculation:

"Wilson Velez is as big a thug as I have ever come across," says the famously hawkish Rieber. "While he is still drawing breath, he will remain a murderous felon and a threat both to his own followers and society at large."

Predictably, such a view finds little favor with Alan Ossery, Velez's effusive lawyer—for whom his client is, rather, a "deeply introspective man who presents no danger to anyone." Ossery's task now, of course, is to cement that portrait in the minds of the appeal judges before they meet again to review their decision.

For Velez, meanwhile, the process will begin by getting acquainted with the 1,100 convicts with whom he shares USP Essenville. Then will come whichever visitors Warden Michael Sosa lets through the gates. After enduring one of the harshest doses of solitary confinement the mod-

ern prison system has yet dispensed, what their companion will want to share with them will surely make for an intriguing conversation.

"Are you ready?"

Lizbeth looks up and Nancy's in the doorway, face shiny-raw under a white wool beret.

"You'll need to wrap up. It's freezing outside."

"I've found it."

"Found what?"

"The squirrel. Where all this has been going. What it was all for."

She reaches for her crutches.

"I'm not sure I know what you mean, Lizbeth."

But what she means is simple. She means she's found a platform from which to reclaim her credibility. She will tell the story of Wilson Velez. Of his crimes and his incarceration. And through that telling she'll find understanding, insight. Imperishable truth. It will be everything *City Slicker* was and more. The story of a life, just one American life, seemingly extraordinary but one that could, given a sidestep of circumstance, have been anyone's: how it was lived, and then scourged away.

"I'll explain in the car," she says.

And in the coming days she sits with her leg elevated on a mound of pillows and then roams the house on her crutches, and with every passing hour she just grows more convinced of it.

In the study, she pulls down the card that reads A Page A Day and replaces it with the picture of Wilson Velez from *Time*. Keeps it there while she researches him, combing old newspaper reports, each offering up the same neat strings of events and quotations but leaving their subject teasingly unknown.

She asks Nancy to measure the bathroom. Doesn't elaborate. Just waits outside as her assistant tallies the walls.

"So you really think it's a good idea?"

"I think it's an excellent idea."

"I just keep wanting to know more . . . about the letters . . . the code . . . what happens to the mind in that kind of place . . . I'm thinking of calling it *God's Lonely Man*."

"I think that's perfect."

Nancy guides the tape measure around the base of the sink.

"Lizbeth, I can't tell you how good it is to see you so . . . *energized*."

"I feel energized. I really do."

This is the blessing of focus. Something outside herself through which to order all the stray and awkward thoughts her mind swirls up. Make them useful. What doesn't fit gotten rid of.

"All done," Nancy says. "Twelve by fourteen feet."

"Oh. Really? That's far too big."

"For what?"

Lizbeth moves into the room, turning slow, then easing herself down until she's settled on the edge of the bath.

"It'll have to do," she says to herself and then, to Nancy: "Can I get a glass of water?"

When she has it, she sets the glass beside her.

"Now I need you to lock me in."

"What? Where?"

"Here. The bathroom. I need you to lock me in here overnight."

"But . . . why?"

"I need to see what it's like."

Lizbeth understands the look on Nancy's face. She knows it's absurd that this is the closest she can get to the torment of Wilson Velez. But then, what wouldn't be?

She makes sure she can maneuver with her cast and crutches. Asks Nancy to let her out tomorrow morning.

Her cooperation is not easily secured. Compromises are made, reassurances given. Lizbeth will keep her cell phone at hand; proper bedding will be laid down in the bath.

And so Nancy arranges pillows and leaves an ice pack in the sink. She's still not even vaguely comfortable with this.

"You're injured," she says, more than once. "You are an injured person."

But eventually, she leaves. Lizbeth hears the bathroom door being locked and seconds later the front door closes.

A thick pulse of unease shoots through her. A prickle to her skin. The primal urge to claw and butt her way out now. But that passes.

And as it does it leaves a glowing trace of satisfaction: it's working. She's experiencing.

Then she just feels alone.

It's dark outside. The blinds are down. She'll keep the light on all night, like she's read they do in Essenville.

Sitting on the edge of the bath she can see the top half of her face in the mirror above the sink. But no more than the top half. Just her hair and her eyes.

She plays with her tooth, spends the next few seconds popping it out and replacing it. One of the dogs huffs past the door. Then it's gone.

Upstairs, the phone rings. She waits for the muffled greeting of her machine, but it never comes. Whoever was calling hangs up.

It leaves her fluttery. She taps out a rhythm on her cast.

How much time has passed already? Two minutes? Five? She left her watch outside for the sake of authenticity. Her phone has a clock but she's keeping that switched off.

Her thighs are numb on the enamel. She straightens up. Grabs her crutches and lurches to the door. Pushes hard against it.

Just checking.

Back on the edge of the bath, she pulls her sleeves down over her hands. Leans forward, hugs herself. And she looks up into the mirror above the sink and watches herself stare back.

Nancy makes breakfast in the kitchen. The dogs lounging on the floor like sunbathers. The dinge of the morning outside just accentuates the warmth in here, the bustle and the cooking smells. Lizbeth sits at the table and feels as if she's trespassing, a small, pensive woman with a broken ankle and a false tooth who just spent the night in the bathtub.

Tea comes, then breakfast. Eggs and toast. Nancy takes the chair opposite, pours and butters. Lizbeth takes an egg, cuts around the yolk, moves it to the side of her plate.

"So you slept okay?"

"I slept through right until you woke me."

Lizbeth stares down at her plate.

"Nancy, I'm sorry . . . I actually feel a little sick."

There are repeated inquiries and then confirmations that she is—the leg and the tooth and, now, the nausea aside—okay.

"You want to lie down?"

"It's fine. It'll pass."

"You're sure?"

"I'm sure."

Nancy stands and takes her plate away.

"So . . . were you tempted to call and have me come and let you out? Be honest."

"Only once. About an hour in . . . I just . . . it got a little intense in there . . . what you find yourself thinking about . . ."

She thinks about discussing it further. Thinks not. And when Nancy asks if she wants to do it again, her no is categorical.

In the afternoon, she sits in the study and devotes herself to Wilson Velez. Collates what she knows of him, pinpoints what she doesn't. Sculpts her questions.

In the evening she calls a taxi. When it comes, she gives the driver Ed's address.

She phoned him a half hour ago. Got his machine. But this needs to be done now. There is no other option.

Ed lives ten minutes away, alone in a white colonial. She has the cab wait for her. Just in case.

There's no answer at the door but there's a light on inside. Music. Some old pop song she knows but can't place.

A pool sits at the back of the house. She edges around the building and sees the light garnishing the water.

She could be anyone. Planning anything. He should be more careful. She'll tell him that.

She follows the light to a ground floor window. Then she sees him.

Naked. With a woman. She's naked too. He fucks her on the floor to a hit from another decade. The veins in his neck like wire under his skin and his eyes bugged out in his head.

The woman is half hidden. Blond hair to her shoulders; legs around his waist, feet jerking in time with his lunges. He quickens and suddenly her face bobs out:

Jessica.

The more frantic he gets, the stiller she is, gazing upward, deadpan, one arm by her side, the other limp around his neck.

The music's head-by-the-speaker loud. He leans down to mumble into her ear, and then he laughs. Laughs like Lizbeth's never seen him laugh, with his head thrown back and his mouth wide open. Fevered. Transported. He doesn't stop laughing as long as she stands there.

She waits to be outraged or heartbroken. All she feels is puzzled. Bemused at how this could have slipped past her.

The cab takes her back to Quince Hill and there she calls him one more time. Gets his machine, again. Flatly informs it of the salient details.

"I stopped by the house earlier. I saw you. And I saw her . . . Anyway . . . I was there because I need to tell you something. So I guess I'll tell you now instead."

She is, she says, seven weeks pregnant. "It's yours. Obviously."

The doctor told her in the hospital. Then he moved straight on to the leg exercises she'll need to keep up once her cast comes off.

This is the first time that she's spoken of it. She has carried the information with her, sure that as long as she didn't acknowledge it, then it couldn't really be happening. But like the unread reviews that spell is broken now.

And she is faint and gasping and terrified.

Ed calls three times that night. Leaves three messages on her machine. Each more agitated than the last. She doesn't pick up.

The dogs form a cordon around her as she lies in bed. She lets them stay and their behavior is impeccable. The room fills with their snoring.

They only wake up at 4:33 A.M.

At 4:33 A.M the phone rings from the study, and her eyes wrench open. She lets it go unanswered, but it just rings again, and then again, until cursing she reaches for her crutches, and once she's rattled down the hall she says:

"I can't talk to you now, Ed. Maybe tomorrow."

But there's no reply.

"Ed, there's nothing I can say to you right now."

Still no response. And now she realizes.

"I don't believe it."

The phone goes down, but it just rings again.

"You're doing this now, Jessica? Why are you doing this now?"

—

"I thought you'd be happy. Aren't you happy now?"

—

"I'm hanging up now, Jessica."

And a voice at the other end of the line says:

"This isn't Jessica."

Lizbeth drops the phone and pulls the cord out of the wall.

Replaces it just long enough to call the police.

"And you're sure this was . . ." The cop in Lizbeth's kitchen sips at his coffee and thumbs back through his notes. ". . . Leon Slocomb?"

"I'm sure."

Lizbeth scans his face for signs of glibness, hostility. There's nothing like that. He's just young. Here at the end of a sapping night shift. And it was, she knows, years ago.

So she tells him about Leon Slocomb. How it started with letters. *He* started with letters: graphic threats and foul abuse, neatly typed with the occasional postscript added by hand, sent to her publisher before he got hold of her home address. Then the letters came with packages: animal corpses and worse. He sent audio tapes outlining his intentions.

People—Inchy, the police—assumed he'd randomly latched onto her. Turned out his grudge was specific. A character in the sixth Enschell novel, *Not Into Temptation,* had, he claimed, been based on him. Credit was overdue.

She was watching Augustus Pablo play at The Roxy on 18th Street. There was a steak knife in his hand. He was overpowered before he could use it.

"I can't believe no one told me he was out of prison," she says.

"They should have, Miss Greene. I can't honestly think why they didn't."

They sit in silence as he finishes his coffee.

"I hope you don't mind me saying this, but my brother-in-law is going to be so jealous that I met you. He's really a big, big fan of yours."

The cop leaves with a record of her complaint and a signed copy of *Black Water Elegy.*

By lunchtime, the same taxi driver that drove Lizbeth to Ed's house is carrying two suitcases out from the house to his cab. Nancy loads a smaller bag into the trunk.

"I talked to the police again, Lizbeth. You can have two cars guarding the house. The bastard won't get near you."

"I'm not doing this because of Leon Slocomb."

She slides into the backseat, brings her leg and her crutches in after her.

"I'm doing this because of Wilson Velez."

Her flight to Pittsburgh leaves this afternoon. It was booked half an hour ago. Once she gets there she'll fix up a visit to the prison. It is, apparently, just a forty-minute drive away.

And then she'll meet The One Eternal King Three Vee: Squirrel.

Nancy will look after the dogs and the house. This is the extent of the plan.

With the taxi about to leave, Nancy hovers at the passenger window.

"What do I say when people call?"

"Just tell them I'm away. That I'll call them when I can."

"Even Ed?"

"Even Ed."

"What about the dentist?"

"It'll have to wait."

"And your sister? Are you going to phone her, or should I? She's going to be so close, Lizbeth. I really think you should see her."

"Nancy . . . it's fine . . . it's all okay. I'll call you when I get there."

The taxi driver glances over his shoulder and Lizbeth tells him to go. The roads are clear all the way to the interstate.

Across the back of her hand she has written in fresh black ink: *Essenville.*

There's ice on the ground, ungritted, a scuzzy ring of frost around the concrete.

Wilson Velez stands in a corner of the yard surrounded by ESSUSP's general population. A sprawling mass of orange jumpsuits. Two thirds black, most members of the Five Percent Nation, zealous followers of Clarence 13X; a dandruff speckling of whites, prison-ink swastikas on the backs of their hands.

But even now he has a generous plot of space around him. His head stays down so he looks at nothing, sees nothing.

No one's close enough to hear the noise he's making. A vague low frequency rumble in the back of his throat. Were they to get nearer, scooch in real close, they might just hear him:

"Gggermmmmms—theyyyyy havve gggggerms—allllll ovvver t-t-t-themmm . . ."

A rusted hoop hangs above him, but no one has a ball. At either end of the yard is a low bench and a barbell, colonized by the prison's most gargantuan men.

The cold is a tranquilizer. All those not weightlifting reduced to hopping mechanically from foot to foot, blowing precious warmth into their hands.

Wilson Velez doesn't move at all.

He's still drained from the procession out here. Walking without restraints exhausts him. His body can't remember how it's done. Every few steps he lurches, half trips. Now he leans into the wall and stares at the ground.

". . . dddddddddon't wanttttt themm—on mmmmmmme . . ."

Since the appeal, he now spends an hour a day in the yard. (Unless an inmate is physically injured, he must go to the yard when instructed. Failure to do so means Ad-Seg.)

The guards stand at intervals in fur-trimmed caps and gloves. More of them in the watchtowers. General population guards are different from their colleagues in Ad-Seg. In Ad-Seg, they're clenched fists in riot gear, always ready—no, *eager*—for action. Here, they've learned expedience. Thin-lipped, headachey men with bills to pay, just counting the hours until they can nurse a beer, soak in the tub, take a day off, retire.

A bug cries out, unseen. Essenville's full of them. Bugs. Mental cases. Wilson looks up but he can't find this one through the crowd. Just hears him.

"I shouldn't be in jail, CO," he's screaming. "I am a man of great virtue and honor!"

As his eyes travel back, he sees the Hispanics. Two hundred at least. Clustered no more than ten feet away. Every one gazing at him. He tries to look through them, but then one kid steps closer.

Still in his teens. A downy mustache on his top lip, an ornate crown inside a golden sun tattooed over his neck. Wilson tries to work out what he might be intending. He can't read his face. Any of their faces. He peers at their expressions but they're a mystery. Speaking a language he's forgotten. He feels sloppy, old. Here in a place of quickness and ferocity.

There is—he can tell this much—something urgent in the way the kid nods at him, imploring Wilson to look down.

So he does.

The kid's hands are by his hips. He holds up three fingers on the left and two on the right. Crosses them over.

WV. Three Vee.

The gesture of deference taught to all members of the Sacred Incan Royals.

Wilson meets the kid's eyes. Acknowledges him. Then lowers his head once more and the kid steps back, buries his hands in his pockets. (In Essenville, open displays of gang allegiance are punishable with Ad-Seg.)

But the guards aren't looking this way. They're just waiting for the hour to pass. Chewing gum, allowing their minds to wander, grateful to the sedative cold. Nothing going down. Order, almost.

Wilson lifts his head again at the very second a burst of movement erupts on the other side of the yard.

Running and bawling. Inmates spilling in every direction from a single source of panic.

A prisoner is on fire. In flames from the waist up.

Wilson stares as he veers across the yard, weaving like a drunk. Half the inmates trying to get away, the rest craning for a better look. He flaps his arms maniacally, a thick column of smoke rising off him.

And it's only now that Wilson hears him scream.

The guards bawl unheeded demands, panicked themselves, randomly training their rifles. But a moment later they have control again. Batons out.

Wilson feels a blow between the shoulders propelling him back inside the narrow hallway that leads out to the yard. There the noise is seismic. Too many people in too small a space and more being driven in all the time. Spooked as cattle in an abattoir. He clamps his hands over his ears but it just gets louder, a living thing, swelling, brimming. Still more pushed inside here and he's crushed against a wall now as two guards charge past with fire extinguishers.

But he twists his head and through the bedlam he manages to look back out. Sees the inmate on the ground now, face down and motionless. The flames still lapping at the air as the smoke gusts up over the fence.

SEVEN

THE DOORS OF the hotel elevator half stutter as they open, threatening to jam. An unexpected glitch amid the routine opulence. Inside, two thickset men stand beside the button panel, twinnish in slacks and pastels, the backs of their heads reflected in the mirror behind them. They smile at Lizbeth as she navigates inside.

Since arriving at the Pittsburgh Airport Plaza, she's been getting reacquainted with the feel of strangers' eyes on her. Staring a moment longer than they do at each other. Most times she knows it's just the crutches. But then, one of maybe every dozen guests she sees—business trippers on cross-country stopovers, caffeine-buzzed and smelling of complimentary shower gels—will approach her and say: "So, tell me why I know you."

Now though, at the ground floor, the thickset men just hang back and wait for her to exit.

And the hotel doormen vie to find her a taxi as the sleet bullets down.

"Cold out there, right?" the driver says.

Everything starts today.

She's been busy since she got here. Calls have been made, meetings fixed. Her name, she has been reminded, is a thing of weight. She has hardly ventured into Pittsburgh itself, hobbled among its ferocious hills and artless courtesies. Instead she has stayed cloistered in the Airport Plaza, in a room overlooking the terminal. Ordered room service, used the spa, sat up in bed mapping out different opening chapters.

Now she is on her way to see Warden Michael Sosa of US Penitentiary Essenville. Visiting the town beforehand. She will, if this all works out, need a place there. A residence.

They drive south, skirting Pittsburgh, then curving beneath it. The road takes them through concrete nothing and a thin strip of exurbia and then, suddenly, the grand expanse of the Allegheny mountains rears up around them, the interstate just a gray-black groove between vast slopes of maple, walnut, hemlock, oak. The valley only widening at the banks of the Monongahela, flowing north back to the city; but then they turn onto a rutted highway that veers away from the river and carves again through madly inclined forests, less like a road than a tunnel. Lizbeth peers through the trees and glimpses disused smokestacks and trolley cars, the silhouettes of long-closed mines, ghost-traces of when all this was a fount of steel and coal, one massive factory, the debris like relics left among the trees to be chanced on by deer, and deer hunters.

The radio says it'll be -2 tonight.

They pass a stretch of cloudy water and then, just as the surface gets unbearable, there's a fork in the road, they swing left, and a half mile later a sign rises out of the ground to say:

WELCOME TO ESSENVILLE, PENNSYLVANIA:
PROUD OF ITS REPUTATION IN THE CORRECTIONS INDUSTRY
(POPULATION 33,057)

Around the next bend there's a mini-mall. A cinema. The largest bowling alley Lizbeth's ever seen. A rash of churches, golf course, high school, a smattering of condos and then, finally, an orderly sweep of new family houses with neat lawns and ample garages in which, assuredly, will be tools appropriate for every domestic need.

They drive on into the center of town. Three or four blocks in each direction, a sturdy regularity to every building, wide, clean sidewalks, the flag rippling outside a fire station.

She realizes she needs a bathroom. Has the taxi park and wait.

The street they're on is dotted with locals smothered in hats and scarves. A newspaper piled up in a vending box. *The Essenville Expositor.*

PIZZA RESTAURANT FINED FOR ILLEGAL DUMPING, says the front page headline. A few inches down, MORE NEW LANES FOR BOWLODROME?

She leans down on her crutch as she pulls on her gloves and buttons up.

A gift shop stands between a pharmacy and a video store. In its window there are mugs printed with cell bars, souvenir T-shirts that read (for instance): ESSENVILLE—WHERE THE CONS MEET THE PROS

Lugging herself inside, she finds an unstaffed counter. Shelves and tables laid out with yet more mugs and T-shirts alongside penal-themed baseball caps, mouse pads, bumper stickers.

"Oh, God."

Lizbeth swings around at the voice behind her. A man her own age, plain and heavy faced, wire-wool brown hair in disorderly retreat. Tall but out of shape in a sweater. Emerging from a stockroom.

"Oh, God," he says again, rooted in place. "Is this a joke?"

"I'm sorry . . ."she says. "I just wondered . . . do you have a bathroom I could use?"

"You're Lizbeth Greene."

"Oh, right," she says. ". . . Hi."

"I don't believe it. Lizbeth Greene. I'm sorry, it's just I'm a fan. I'm a huge fan, actually. I have been for years. There. I've said it."

"That's . . . wonderful. Thank you."

"I'm sorry. I guess I'm a little confused. This is just . . . I just . . . I don't understand why you're here . . . in my town . . . my store . . ."

So Lizbeth explains. She is, she says, in the early stages of a possible future project. Just traveling. Researching. And the gift shop owner nods excitedly before his gaze drops to her crutches. So she explains them too. Then she mentions the bathroom again.

"Hm. I'm afraid that's for customers only."

"Oh, really? Is there anywhere else that—"

"I'm kidding! I'm kidding! . . . Sorry. I just . . . sorry. It's right through here."

When she comes back out, the shop owner's standing at the door in a parka and ski hat. He looks anxious, but strangely hopeful. She tries to get a reading of the situation. Fails.

"Can you give me five minutes?" he says. "Not a second longer, I promise."

". . . I'm not sure I—"

And his face falls as he says: "You've got somewhere to be. Of course you do."

But her curiosity swells as he hovers there, and before she can stop herself she says: "I don't have anywhere to be. I mean, I do, but . . . I've got five minutes, I guess . . ."

"You do? Oh, that's incredible. Thank you. Thank you so much! Wait—"

He leans over to a switch by the counter and shuts off the lights and then, with no further comment, turns the sign in the door to Closed and dashes out. Sprints over to a battered red hatchback parked across the street and drives away.

She stands alone in the gloom. Moves toward the door, looks out and sees the cab still waiting. Gazes around her. Enough light from the street to see the print on the neat stacks of T-shirts—ESSENVILLE, PA: THE JAIL-HOUSE ROCKS—but not to rescue the back half of the store from darkness.

In front of the counter, she sees now, is a display stand filled with maps of the area, works of local history. By the register, a take-a-penny tray. And outside, someone bustles past every few seconds, their steps jet-heeled by the cold, face half buried in a muffler.

She picks up one of the history books. Reads that *after the successive waves of German immigrants who poured into the state from the Rhineland, by 1726 only the southwestern extremities of Pennsylvania were yet to be reached by settlers.*

And then, exactly five minutes after it left, the hatchback pulls up across the street again.

"Thank you!" the shop owner says. "Thank you so much for waiting!"

He has with him two leather bags in which, she sees now, are hardcover editions of every book she's ever written. With the lights back on, he heaves them onto the counter.

"I had to get these from home," he says. "I couldn't miss a chance like this. But . . . is this okay? If I've gone too far, please . . . just tell me."

But she tells him no, of course not. He let her use his bathroom. That's nothing to be sold short. So, beaming, he unpacks the books and hands her a pen; until, as she opens the first, she hesitates. Looks back at him.

"Oh, gosh," he says. "I didn't even introduce myself. I'm George Finer."

To the benevolent George Finer, she writes. *A Savior of Women.*

When he reads it, he looks as if he's misting up. Thanks her with such open sincerity she feels as if she could almost join him.

She just writes *To George* in the rest.

As she gets to the last of them, she asks which of the maps he'd recommend. Just something basic, she says. But by then he's already bent over the display stand, frantically detailing every one. This one's aimed more at the hunters. That one at Civil War buffs. Until—if only to snap him out of it—she says:

"So I take it you're a true . . . Essenvillian?"

"That's me. Born and raised. I mean, I spent a few years teaching high school in San Diego but you know how it is . . . relationships go bad, young hearts get broken. Blah. Then my mother got sick and I came back to see her through it. Once she passed away the plan was always to leave again, but . . . here I am . . ."

Finally, he pulls a map from the stand. A simple foldout.

"This," he says, "should be perfect." He pauses. Then: "Miss Greene . . . I know you don't like to talk about what you're working on, but I can't help wondering . . . could Detective Enschell at last be visiting the mighty Alleghenies? Is that why you're here?"

Lizbeth shrugs. Grimaces slightly. George Finer slaps a hand to his forehead. "I'm sorry. Jeez. Only I could meet Lizbeth Greene and ask her about something she never talks about—"

"It's fine," she says. "It's not a problem. Really."

"Really?"

"Absolutely."

"Oh, I'm relieved to hear that. I can be such a bozo sometimes. It's just that local history . . . it's a hobby of mine. Not the hippest pastime, I know, but that's the truth of it. So, if you ever did choose to go down that road . . . it would be my honor to assist you . . . and, of course, in a sense, the great detective too."

"That's a kind offer. So . . . how much do I owe you for the map?"

But of course he won't take her money. Just sees her to the taxi.

Laid up across the backseat, she tells the driver she needs the prison.

"Which one?"

"Excuse me?"

"Y'uns got a choice of four. Look—"

He gestures for her to pass him the map. Unfolds and jabs at it.

"Here's Essenville, right? *That* a mile east is ESSFDC. Medium security facility for women. *This* two miles further south is ESSFCI—low security, men. *That* to the west is ESSFCC. Men's medium. And five miles northeast of here is the daddy. USP."

"USP. That's where I need."

"So USP it is."

She had, she tells him, no idea. Then she turns and sees George Finer wave them off as they pull out from the curb.

They leave the way they came until they get back to the family houses, then bear right. Now the buildings drop away and there's forest again, but sparser, less imposing. Gradually it peters out and all that's left is a string of pylons before the road abruptly inclines.

Not another car in sight. Just the empty space on the map.

87

The taxi judders uphill. Already she needs the bathroom again.

And then, at the top, she sees it. A looming slab of beige, eighty feet high. US Penitentiary Essenville.

The driver skirts the perimeter. Two chain-link fences garlanded with razor wire. Both, a sign announces, are electric. Watchtowers rear up at metronomic intervals and between them there are floodlights.

The visitors' parking lot stands at the far end of the complex. She wonders if it was planned that way to ensure you grasp the full, monolithic sameness of the design. To be cowed. If so, it works.

Finally, the outer fence gives way to a security checkpoint: a set of twelve-foot-thick barriers operated by a guard in a pale gray uniform. He asks for ID from both Lizbeth and the driver.

"License, passport. Something with a picture and a signature."

The lot's almost empty. As she labors out of the taxi, the wind rises, gusting in her face as she bears down on her crutches and makes for the visitors' entrance. A steel gate in the center of the inner fence that runs along the side of the jail.

Beside it there's another checkpoint, and another guard. When Lizbeth tells him she's here to see the warden—instead of being ushered into some concealed private entrance—he just asks for ID again. Once he's seen it he reaches for a phone and says:

"It's her."

And then, beyond the gate, she's still 100 yards from the actual prison. Proceeding instead down a caged walkway, chain-link above and on both sides of her. It leads, eventually, to the steel door of the building; but not before it brings her to a semiopen holding area with a fixed roof and a clutch of guards at a metal table. Three more behind them with rifles.

Her driver's license is requested once more. She struggles with her crutches as she tries to hold it steady, but the guard checking it just notes down her details, picks up a camera and takes her photograph himself. Then he sends her down the table where—for the first time in her life—she is fingerprinted.

She worries she smudges the print by rolling instead of pressing down, but the guard doesn't seem concerned. With the ink still wet on her skin he directs her to a walk-through metal detector, and there a third guard holds out a Tupperware dish in which she is told to leave her keys, earrings, change and watch.

"Rings as well, ma'am," he says.

To her right, there's a tall booth draped in blue canvas. Pinned to it are federal guidelines for the performance of strip and cavity searches.

Lizbeth steps through the metal detector. The clasps of her false tooth fail to set it off. On the other side, her bag and its contents are pored over. Gloves removed and then she's patted down, the guard who took her jewelry now dispassionately clapping his hands over her thighs and ribs.

"We're going to need to check the crutches," he says, and leads her to a chair.

She passes them to him one after the other, waiting in silence as he peers, taps, spins.

"Going to need to check your shoes too, ma'am."

So she takes them off and they're turned upside down, shaken out and stared into. Until the guard hands them back and says, at last:

"Please follow me."

She scoops up her possessions as he passes his colleagues with the rifles. Faces the door and punches a set of numbers into a keypad beside it.

The door shudders open. He stands back, and she steps inside.

"At this time," he says, "I advise you to read the sign to your right."

The sign to her right says:

BE AWARE—SHOULD YOU BE TAKEN HOSTAGE THIS FACILITY DOES NOT NEGOTIATE WITH INMATES.

"Please follow me."

He strides down the corridor until they come to a ceiling-high gate fitted with another keypad. Then he punches in the numbers. Next, another corridor. Watched over from above by a security camera. Then two more.

There has been perfect, hermetic silence ever since she got in here. They could be in space. She looks across to the guard, but he just keeps walking.

"Please follow me," he says at the next gate, and as she passes through it she sees that they are, without warning, no longer in a corridor, but now, instead:

Out on the floor of the prison.

She looks up and it almost makes her swoon. Like standing at the bottom of a well. Five stories of walkways sheering up on every side of her, each one an endless strip of closed steel doors, of cell after cell after cell after cell after cell after cell.

But not a single inmate. No tiny figure up on a gantry, no passing shadow down here.

And still, even now, there is silence. She hears her own breath and the guard's. That's all. The only sign beside the walkways that this place is what it is the smell that hangs under the oceans of bleach, sour and invasive. It wraps itself around the fibers of her clothes, settles in her hair, and even as it makes her senses pucker, she tries—for the sake of future reportage—to break it down: bad food, stale smoke, sweat, piss, shit, cum. Hanging in unmoving air.

But the next gate takes them back inside the corridors, and this and those that follow have rooms off them, rooms and the sound of people, the working hum of administrative staff.

At the end of the longest is the office of Warden Michael Sosa.

His desk is a study in stripped-down order. In-tray, out-tray, framed family portrait, two Department of Corrections coasters on which rest his coffee and her tea. She admires that. Could have set it out herself.

His handshake is borderline painful. A face not built for smiling.

"So," he says, "you made it across the floor. Some people dislike that. They find it uncomfortable passing under the pods—"

He sees her confusion.

"Each twelve-cell unit is a pod, Miss Greene. Anyway, I'm sorry if you found it *oppressive*. But that's just how the place was built."

"It was okay. I guess I was expecting . . . more noise. And it was just strange, because I couldn't see anyone."

"I'd have been troubled if you had. Recreation isn't until noon."

"Right. It's just I wondered if . . ."

"You wondered what, Miss Greene?"

"I thought it may have been something to do with . . . the man who set himself on fire."

Warden Sosa's lips thin.

"Oh, you read about that? Well, it was an ugly thing. But this is a penitentiary. Ugliness is forever around the corner."

He pulls open his desk drawer and produces a small white plastic spoon, inlaid with prongs like a fork.

"This," he says, "is a spork. The inmates eat with them. Last August, one was smuggled into the yard. Then the inmate used it to publicly castrate himself. What's the answer? We clean up the mess. We crank up security. Then business goes on."

"I'm sorry. I didn't mean to suggest . . ."

"I know you didn't. I'm just explaining to you that horrible things go on in penitentiaries. Because of the level of security we operate at, fewer horrible things go on here than elsewhere. But I've got eleven hundred men out there, none of whom are serving less than twenty-six years. And we are not magicians. Now, I understand you came here to discuss one of my inmates."

So Lizbeth begins her pitch. She is, she says, intending to write the story of Wilson Velez. In doing so she aims—she *aspires*—to shine a light on his psyche. To unravel him. What made him what he is. It will be a serious work. Substantial. She emphasizes that. A cautionary tale. Salutary reading for those who might consider its subject somehow admirable.

But in order for it to be all that it could be—*should be*—she has to truly know him. Every atom of his character. And for that she needs to meet with him. Often, and at length.

And this, with all due professional regard, is what she's asking of Warden Sosa.

He takes an opened pack of mints from the same drawer as the spork and offers one to Lizbeth. She passes. He has it instead.

"Let me make something clear," he says, sucking on it as he talks. "I can't provide you with a bodyguard service whenever you might decide to drop by and chat with my inmate."

"I realize that."

"If this . . . *project* was to go ahead, it would do so on my timetable."

"Of course."

"I also think, given that you would be relying to no small degree on the cooperation of the staff of this facility, that in such a scenario you or your publisher might consider it appropriate to make a donation to, say, a local charity. Many of the COs here work very closely with a range of such organizations, and if a contribution was forthcoming, it would, I think, be looked on by them as a significant gesture . . ."

"Right," she says. "Okay . . . I mean, of course. That's only reasonable."

"Understand, Miss Greene, what I've just said is in no way an instruction, or a demand. It's only a suggestion. Mentioned in passing. Something that might help me secure the goodwill of my staff in the event that you do find yourself drawing on our resources . . ."

A moment passes.

"How much guarding am I likely to need?" she says. "I mean, I've read he's kind of . . . diminished."

"He couldn't tell you the difference between a skunk and a showgirl. I still assume you'd like a CO at hand while you're in the company of a man with no chance of parole."

And they turn to questions of editorial control. He would, at the least, want to cast his eye over any first draft. She needs, he says, to be realistic. And when she tilts her head in inquiry, he says that he can hardly give her license to produce something that makes him, the facility or the DOC look negligent, or incompetent.

"I understand that," she says. "And that's not my intention. I have an enormous amount of respect for the pressure that you and your staff work under."

He nods, just once. Tells her they're following the instructions of the appeal review slowly and with caution, and for that he makes no apology. That he knows the press made their usual hullaballoo, but the day-to-day of corrections is different. The appeal judges have given him a great responsibility. Not one he takes lightly.

"So have you actually let him see anyone yet?"

"No, Miss Greene, I have not. In terms of contact from outside the facility, all we've agreed to at this point is a request from the Christian Ladies of Western Arizona that they be allowed to write to him. They're a very well-established group. Devout. They correspond with inmates on Death Row, that kind of . . . endeavor."

There is silence. Then: "I'm at the Airport Plaza," Lizbeth says. "Could you maybe call me there when you've come to a decision . . . ?"

"About you? Oh, I've come to it already. It's fine."

"It is?"

"That's right. A sober portrait of the kind you've described, a lesson in the futility of a criminal life, executed by someone of your *status* . . . that can only be a good thing."

"That's . . . great! That's . . . I'm just . . . I'm blown away! Thank you so much. So . . . when can I start?"

"That's in no way my decision."

"But . . . I don't understand . . ."

"I can let you talk to Velez, Miss Greene. I can't make him talk to you. You need to speak with the lawyer. Ossery. And I need to consult with the Department."

"But if they're okay with it . . . and the lawyer's okay with it?"

"Miss Greene, I'm not what you might call a risk-taker. That's never been my nature. But you talk to him and I'll talk to them . . . and then let's see if we can't at least get you a visit." His tone creaks into something that she guesses is meant to be jovial. "Now before you go . . . I was hoping you might be able to do me a small favor . . ." He pushes back his chair and she sees heaped by his desk yet more of her books: hardcovers in mint condition, the occasional beach-worn paperback. "My wife's an avid reader of your work. She got herself pretty worked up when she heard you were going to be coming in today." He passes over a silver ballpoint and says her name is Joan.

When Lizbeth's finished signing, he offers his hand. Sees her to the door.

"I have to tell you," he says, "when you first explained your idea to me, I was perplexed. But I think I understand. You know, I was speaking with a friend of mine in law enforcement recently . . . he told me six in ten homicides currently go unsolved. Six in ten. And of those that *are* solved, the same number, the same *ratio,* are carried out by an assailant unknown to the victim. Now, that's no good for you, is it? As a writer? An office worker gets carjacked by a stranger in a ski mask, or that same stranger wanders out from an alleyway deranged on crack cocaine and stabs him to death. Not much in the way of a plot twist there, right? No grand whodunit. No, I can see why you might want to write something real. A true story. These must be hard times for a person in your industry. The days of the random and unsolved."

And he calls through for a guard to escort her back out of the prison.

She gazes at her crutches and wills the next three days to pass.

This afternoon, she left the Airport Plaza and took a cab into Pittsburgh. There, Downtown, at the foot of implacable hills, she visited a doctor. A specialist in sprains and fractures. He told her that her ankle was almost healed. Three days more and her cast will be off, her crutches gone. Three days and she'll be walking with a cane. Driving again.

So she left elated and the taxi carried her through bustling streets with ice on the sidewalks to another address, by the Duquesne Incline. A maternity clinic. Her first prenatal:

Now she lies on an exam table with her crutches propped up next to her, at once never more inside her body and its most rapt observer.

The cold in the room has her upper arms goose pimpled as the doctor, an Asian woman in her fifties with a voice even softer than Lizbeth's, asks if she's going to be in Pennsylvania a while. And Lizbeth says she thinks so. Hopes so.

They run through her medical history. Details of her cycle. Past operations. Her age and the risks it presents are discussed. The doctor calmingly matter of fact. There will be tests, she says, many tests, both now and in the future. As little left to chance as can be.

A clipboard is produced, and a list of symptoms offered up for Lizbeth to claim as her own (yes to skin breakouts, no—for now—to excess saliva). Fear is not among them. But fear she has. And when the doctor asks if there's anything else she should know, she straightens up and reaches for the words she's been practicing all day. But as she speaks she finds she has to look an inch away from the doctor's eyes. "I've used heroin for nineteen years," she says. "I last used it four weeks ago."

The doctor's tone is staunchly nonjudgmental. "Okay. But you're not still—"

"Oh, God, no. *No.*"

"Okay. That's good, Miss Greene."

Then comes the ultrasound. A chipper technician with her hair in a ponytail conducting an array of switches and buttons, confirming that Lizbeth's bladder is full, smearing colorless gel over her stomach. And when she presses the curved head of the transducer against Lizbeth's belly, she tells her to look at the screen.

A thumb of white fuzz. Tiny and cryptic.

Her voice is shaking:

"Is it . . . okay?"

"We'll be looking at the results in detail later," the technician says. "But sure . . . for now everything looks fine."

In the taxi, she thinks she's about to cry. It never quite comes. Then she feels the beginning of a heave of laughter; but that doesn't either.

Back at the Airport Plaza, she stands motionless at the window. The runways are visible on the horizon, lights winking in the dusk. A plane comes into land, and another takes off.

There's a copy of the *Times* on the bed. Complimentary from the hotel. Congressman Mitchell Rieber is demanding a thirteen-year-old Ecstasy dealer be sent to an adult prison. The cop who shot the janitor from Queens has appeared at an internal inquiry. He said he believed he was preventing a robbery. He may not even go to trial.

Above the dresser she has tacked up the photograph of Wilson Velez.

On her hand she's written: *Ossery*. Beside it: *Random/Unsolved*.

She turns and faces the mirror. Pulls off her sweater and unhooks her bra and stands with the same hand laid over her belly.

In the evening she makes calls. Nancy brings her up to date with her lawsuits and Leon Slocomb. The calls in the the night were, the police say, made from a stolen cell phone. Presumed since disposed of. Proof of nothing. They have, however, visited him. Reminded him of the conditions of his parole. He shouldn't trouble her again.

The conversation turns to the book. To Wilson.

"I still haven't seen him," she says. "I have to talk to the lawyer. I'm seeing him tomorrow . . . Right . . . Uh-huh . . . Right . . . So, how are the dogs? . . . Oh, that'd be great . . ."

So begins the ritual performed every time she goes away. Nancy holds the phone next to the dogs' ears and Lizbeth says hello to each of them in turn. Tells them she misses them and that she'll see them soon. Hears them pant as she talks. The sound, here, is the purest melancholy.

When Nancy comes back on the line, she asks if Lizbeth's seen her sister.

"I'm meeting her on the weekend. We're going shopping." She takes a breath and then she says: "Nancy . . . before I left . . . there was something I didn't tell you."

And her pregnancy is abruptly disclosed and then, as Nancy starts the questions, Lizbeth makes an excuse and hangs up.

She can't deal with anyone's questions. She has, as yet, no answers. All she knows is that—however unexpected, badly timed, fraught with possible trauma—this he/she is wanted. In theory, things might have been different; but theory is hardly relevant now.

The rest . . . who knows about the rest?

According to Nancy, Inchy Burden's been calling Quince Hill five times a day. Lizbeth phones her back on her own home number. She knows she won't be there. When she gets through, she says she's gone away to work on an idea and she'll be in touch when she has something on paper. She makes no mention of the baby.

The last call is to Ed. The phone barely connects before he picks up, and the instant he does she misplaces the tone of glassy neutrality she had planned to use. Instead she sounds jittery. Stilted. Like him.

"So where are you?" he says.

"Pittsburgh."

"Pittsburgh. Right. And you're okay?"

"I'm good. I'm coming off the crutches soon. I'm getting a cane."

"Down from four legs to three."

"Hoping for two again soon."

"I say be grateful for anything more than one."

The line echoes and spits between them.

"I'm sorry I haven't called."

"It's okay. But the baby? Is it—"

"I've had my first checkup. I need to have more tests but . . . you know . . . so far it's okay."

And he says thank God. Tells her that yesterday he bought a book. *Pregnant Fathers*. Sounds idiotic now, he says. "Do you know when you're coming back?"

"Not yet."

"Okay."

"So, are you and Jessica—"

"There is no me and . . . we're not . . . It's just . . . Lizbeth, I meant to tell you. I just . . . she'd call and . . . there's things she says that . . ."

"Ed, let's not. Let's just . . . not."

"Lizbeth, I'm sorry."

He is, and she knows it. It doesn't help. But the moment she puts the phone down, it all seems so distant anyway. Like none of it can touch her. She is somewhere else now.

She takes a bath with her bad leg propped up on the edge of the tub. Afterward she pulls the hotel robe around herself, puts on her headphones (Jah Stitch: *Bury the Barber*) and turns the bass up full.

Dinner is ordered from room service. She eats chocolate mousse in bed, the robe done up to her chin as she flicks around the cable. There's chocolate around her mouth, she knows, and her spoon slips down the bowl until it's almost in the mousse, but she doesn't feel the need to correct it.

She just keeps eating as her eyes get heavy.

As the last of the morning frost retreats, she opens the car door and puts her cane to the curb. Handsome dark walnut, fitted with a silver handle. She's had it two days now. Still relishes the absence of the crutches every time she uses it.

The car was delivered yesterday. Now, getting out—alone, unaided—she runs her hand over the curve of the trunk.

She could, of course, have chosen something plainer. But then, the dealership was just a mile from the airport, passed every time she left the hotel; and there inside, on a circular podium, was what she really wanted. A silver Porsche. Otter sleek and gleaming. The antithesis of the tanklike SUV she drives in Quince Hill, bought to accommodate the dogs.

Here though, it's just her. So now she has a sports car. The fulfilment of a want she never knew she even had until this week. Automatic to let her drive one-legged. She felt the call to indulge herself, and she did.

The result sits parked among scuffed-up Dodges and aging Mitsubishis outside the Venus Restaurant Diner, Main Street, Essenville. She turns and makes her way inside.

Bowling mementoes cover the walls: framed shirts, old photographs. Almost full with early lunchtime customers. Feels like a hub. A place of community. Two waitresses make graceful circuits. Lizbeth studies the menu, orders, sits. Sits some more. Until:

"Ms. Greene?"

A voice above her. Then opposite. A figure sliding into the booth.

"Alan Ossery," he says, and extends a hand.

As tan in winter as she is pale all year, he wears wire-framed glasses that were nowhere to be seen in the picture of him and Wilson in *Time* (which, she remembers, she later cut him out of). He calls out for coffee. Adjusts his wedding ring and talks fast about the awful drive over here, how he's a magnet for bad traffic.

She asks if he left Manhattan this morning.

"I just came from across town," he says. Tells her since Wilson was sent to ESSUSP he's sublet one of the condos north of Essenville as an alternative to Pittsburgh hotels. Just somewhere to put his head when he needs it. "Anyway," he says, "I've got to tell you, this is quite a thrill for me. I've had butterflies. Truly. Meeting someone of your . . . stature. It's . . . it's an exciting thing for me." His eyes flash across the booth. "I never knew you used a cane."

"I was in a car accident . . . Actually, I was in a car, *then* I was in an accident."

"But you're . . . okay?"

"It's getting there."

Their waitress arrives at the table. Puts coffee in front of Alan Ossery, then across Lizbeth's half of the table spreads an array of plates holding two eggs with hash browns, toast, pancakes and jelly, melon slices and coleslaw.

"Y'uns just let me know if you need anything else," she says, before she turns away.

Ossery leans in, lowers his voice. "It takes a little getting used to . . . the way they talk out here."

Lizbeth hears her at the counter, calling out to an unkempt figure behind the cook.

"Brian . . . y'uns mize well redd up the kitchen nah."

"It doesn't bother me," Lizbeth says. "I've got family around here."

"Oh, you do?"

"My sister's in Altoona. She moved down there a few years ago."

"Well, tell her if she ever needs the cash she can come translate for me . . ."

Lizbeth stares down at the expanse of plates in front of her. For a second she wonders what he must think. Then the smell of the food overwhelms her.

She presents the idea between mouthfuls. Explains how affected she was when she first encountered Wilson's story. How shocked by the pitiless nature of his time in Ad-Seg. Ever since, she says, she's wanted to document it. Tell the entire story, in fact—map his life and let the reader see the whole of the man before unveiling what the justice system did to him.

"Well," Ossery says, "that sounds very . . . intriguing."

"I can't tell you how much I want to do this."

"That's okay, Ms. Greene. You just did. So, let me tell you a little about where we are. As you know, Wilson's release from Ad-Seg is provisional. Subject to review. So my a priori duty during this time is to make sure that when that review takes place, I can demonstrate to the judges that my client is no threat to *a*, other inmates, *b*, the staff of the facility, *c*, any man, woman or child from sea to shining sea. That he can have visits and write letters and speak on the phone and nothing adverse is going to happen, then or in the future. But I don't want to *persuade* them of it. I want to give them no choice other than believing it."

He calls over to the waitress for more coffee. And then, he says, if everything unfolds the way he hopes it unfolds, there are other goals. Having

Wilson transferred back to a jail in New York. Jersey, even. Somewhere he could be out of his cell for more than an hour a day.

Ossery pauses as he gets his refill. "My point is that while it's heartening that someone like you is aware of Wilson's situation, I have to ask how what you're proposing can help him?"

And she tells him how many copies *City Slicker* has sold to date.

He gives the low whistle people do on the rare occasions that she mentions it.

"So," she says, "if everything works out, the book can be a springboard. And if it doesn't . . . that's how many readers will know about Wilson. About what he'll be going through . . . everyone with a congressman and a senator. Everyone as outraged as I am now."

She gives him the number again.

"I guess," he says, "that answers my question."

She wipes her mouth on a napkin. "May I ask you one?"

"Absolutely."

"It's just that, when you talked about your goals a moment ago . . . for Wilson . . . well, in the reports that I've read of his original trial, you seemed pretty aggrieved about the case and—"

"Oh, it was a terrible case. Flimsy as hell. Loaded with conjecture. A star witness who could barely remember his lines. But, you know, Mitchell Rieber . . . the guy could always juice up the press. Make the suburbs think he was personally swooping down out of the night sky to drag the bad men off to jail. Same way he does today. But if you're asking whether we'd ever try and revisit that judgment, the answer's no. We lost. We lost big. That's the reality. Everything else is so much folderol."

He shrugs before he goes on. "I mean, for a while there, sure, we hoped something might show up . . . evidence, testimony, some new piece of something. But it didn't. Then they got hold of the letters. So that was that. Now, like I say, what concerns me is keeping him out of Ad-Seg. Because it scares me to think of him going back there."

He sips at his coffee and his speech starts to quicken. "You know, we've never tried to say that Wilson led a blameless life. That would be absurd. The Royals were not people you or I would have wanted to run into. But please, hear me when I say this, Ms. Greene—my client is a repentant man. It's important you know that. What I'm saying to you is I don't want him becoming the next Hannibal Lecter in a *New York Times* best-seller. One, that isn't an accurate portrayal. Two, it isn't helpful to my goals."

"No. Of course. But that isn't what I want to do. There's no reason for me to do that."

He calls for another refill.

"Okay," he says, "so . . . let me outline an approach that might work for us. We would obviously need there to be a focus on what Wilson has suffered in Ad-Seg. To alert people to the damage it's caused to him . . . but it sounds like we're already in tune there. So, that aside, Ms. Greene, what your project would need to stress is that Wilson is acutely conscious of his mistakes. Which is why he's so qualified to act as a guide for the kids coming up now. To say to them, 'Here is the path I followed, and it was the wrong path.' Now, I know that kind of role would be close to his heart. Make this something we could *potentially* be supportive of."

The waitress fills his cup back to the brim.

"Now, of course, to realize that approach I know an element of candor will be necessary. And that's okay. In fact, that's good. But—and this is crucial—if Wilson was to commit to such a project, then what he tells you isn't to be tinkered with . . . paraphrased . . . interpreted . . ."

"I just want to tell his story," she says. "As honestly as possible."

"I know you do," he says.

"I mean, how much . . . candor . . . are we talking about?"

"Ms. Greene, neither of us are slow-witted people. We both know there's a limited function in putting something out there that no one can believe. I realize there's a certain . . . flavor you're looking for. And what I'm saying is that, as long as we retain some sway in that process, that's fine. I want people to know that Wilson is changed. Remorseful. That he sees the life he led for what it really was. And one of the best ways we can do that is to have him confront it, openly and sincerely. Although, naturally, I'm not going to have him incriminate himself over minor incidents that may or may not have happened *waaay* back when."

"So he'll be candid about the past . . . but he won't incriminate himself."

"You sound skeptical, Ms. Greene."

"No . . . it's just . . . I'm not exactly sure how that would work."

"Well, of course, if you have someone else lined up with a story like Wilson's who will incriminate themselves for you, then—"

"I didn't mean that . . . It's okay. I understand. It's . . . fine."

He breaks off for coffee. "You know, *my* only worry would be whether he could take part in something like this . . . in health terms."

"Is he still that bad? I thought—"

Ossery reaches for his wallet and takes from it a sheet of paper torn out of a notepad on which is drawn a stickman in the middle of what could be a circle of trees (although they could easily be streetlights or microphone stands). "He gave me this yesterday. He used to draw all the time. Then Aspera said everything he wrote or drew had to be destroyed. After that he took away his access to pens and paper. This is the first thing he's done since."

"It's very austere. Forceful."

"It sucks. He has absolutely no talent in this area. But at least it used to give him some respite. And if he's doing it again, that's a positive thing."

"So he's okay?"

"He's a mess. Physically. Psychologically. He can't tolerate noise. His eyes are bad. He's a raging hypochondriac. He can't focus and his memory's shot. His speech is . . . flawed. That place . . . it wrecked him. But he's getting better. I think. I guess we'll see."

He stares down at his cup, now drained, then up again. "Obviously," he says, "it could be problematic for Wilson to be seen to be profiting from an enterprise like this. But I think some form of financial . . . *acknowledgment* would still be appropriate. This is his story. Let's not forget that."

"I'm anxious that we do this fairly, Mr. Ossery."

"In which case," he says, and Lizbeth has a dead-on inkling of what's coming next, ". . . would you and your publishers be amenable to the idea of donating a sum to a charity or charities?"

"Absolutely," she says. "That would be . . . fine."

"Okay. Good. I know of several organizations around Queens that Wilson would be happy to see get some help. We can draw up a list pretty much immediately . . ." He checks his watch, then gets to his feet. Offers his hand again. "Okay!" he says. "So I'll be in touch."

"That's it?"

"That's it."

"Is that a yes?"

"It's not a yes. It's not a no. It's a 'When I've spoken to Wilson, I'll be in touch.' I can offer him my advice, Ms. Greene, but this would have to be his decision."

He's already halfway out the door.

"If you want to get on his good side, try sending him something. He's had no mail for five years, so that should make an impression. Talk to Sosa and see if he'll play along."

"What should I send him?"

"Try a magazine. Something bland. *National Geographic.* Otherwise, he's got a sweet tooth. He likes Mounds. Anyway—"

When Lizbeth looks back down at the table, she sees he's left ten dollars for the check. Then he's gone. She finishes her last pancake. Gazes out at her Porsche. Feels a nip of self-consciousness.

As she leaves, a pair of prepubescent kids, huge in matching red parkas, are staring transfixed at it. They whirl around at the sound of her cane and scurry away.

She stands at the curb with the keys in her hand until she realizes she's lost track of how long she's been there.

"Tell me if I'm being a pest."

A voice, beside her. Now it's her that jumps. She looks up, but the face means nothing.

"We met last week in the gift shop . . . the benevolent George Finer."

"Of course!" she says. "Where's my head? The benevolent George Finer. How are you?"

"I'm great. I was just on my way to lunch and I saw you out here, and I didn't know whether to say hi or not . . . and I thought I'd be bold . . . but I don't want to be a pest."

"It's fine," she says. "Really. How are you?"

"I'm good. Now, I'm not going to ask how your research is going—but I can't help noticing that you're off your crutches."

"*Ssh,*" she whispers. "Is it that obvious?"

He blushes at being in on her joke, and she leans forward to unlock the car.

"Oh, wow," George says. "This is yours?"

"I just bought it," she says, like an apology. "I don't usually drive anything so . . ."

Her voice trails off as a pair of ESSUSP guards wander past.

"God," she says. "I forgot the wheel lock."

"Don't worry," George Finer says. "We're big on the price of crime round here."

And as she drives away, she sees him wave her off once more.

They march through the shining heart of the Bemer Valley Mall like conquering troops. Mame Urkoff proceeding, as she always has, half a stride in front of her little sister, just enough for them to each appreciate the eternal differences between them: Mame's extra two inches of height, the strength of her calves. The product, it's implied with every forthright step, of a real life, significant years.

Lizbeth was born the day before Mame's third birthday. Now, they walk as they did to school, to church, around the neighborhood on Halloween. Half a stride apart.

The Bemer Valley Mall lies twelve miles from Mame's home in Altoona, ninety-five from the Airport Plaza Hotel. She and Lizbeth met in the parking lot ten minutes ago. The bulk of their time since has been spent in silence; Mame—blue jeans immaculate, hair definitively *styled*—occasionally stopping to peer in the window of Trade Secret or J. Jill, Lizbeth waiting for her to sate her interest and move on.

And as they walk parallel monologues rage in their heads. Fierce displays of point-scoring, the airing of pungent sibling resentments.

"Do you think," Mame says, turning to her sister outside Payless ShoeSource, "we could stop in here?"

Inside, Mame approaches Lizbeth with one of a pair of black stiletto heels. "Look familiar?" She holds it up, resting in her palm. "I had a pair just the same when I was . . . eighteen? So you must have been fifteen. And one of your little friends was having a party and you wanted to borrow them to impress that boy you had a crush on even though your feet were two sizes smaller than mine. And Dad wouldn't let you wear them, so you wound up stealing them from my closet, and he caught you and grounded you for two weeks."

"I remember. But he didn't catch me. You told on me."

"Lizbeth, I did not. I would never have done that. The number of times I used to cover for you with him . . . God. Anyway, you always liked being up in your room on your own, with your music and your black clothes."

Lizbeth holds herself in check. Considers the stiletto up close. "It *is* exactly the same, isn't it?" Mame tries a pair of leather mules, and they fit perfectly. Then she decides against them. And so they continue through the mall. Talking in brisk affirmations about the publication of *Black Water Elegy*—Mame thanks her sister for her customary free copy, says she hasn't read it yet—about Mame's job in corporate PR in Harrisburg and her husband Dave's role as a head of staff training at Sheetz, the state's leading indigenous convenience store. There are updates on the progress of the Urkoff children, Joshua (seventeen), Melissa (thirteen) and Kyle (nine). A wave of speech, nothing said.

"So," Mame says, "you like Essenville? Must be weird, out here with us hicks."

"Mame, you've been to my house. I live in a town of a thousand people."

"Oh, Lizbeth. How many of them do you even know the names of? You have your groceries delivered and Nancy runs your errands. Don't look so pissed off. I haven't seen you in a year and a half and you don't have two words to say to me. I'm just trying to elicit some kind of conversation."

"I fade out when you're next to me. You stand beside me and it pushes me off the end of the world. You fill the space that was meant for both of us." Lizbeth hears her answer in her mind. She doesn't say a thing. Just follows her sister into Old Navy.

"You know," Lizbeth says, "you're welcome to visit any time you want. You, Dave, the kids. You know this."

"Lizbeth, every Thanksgiving and every Christmas we ask you to stay with us. How many times do you ever come? But . . . okay . . . let's not get into this. Let's just have a nice afternoon."

"That's all I want to do."

They file between denim skirts and turtlenecks. Lizbeth pauses at a camisole. Holds the fabric against her. Sees Mame scrunch up her face.

"What?"

"Nothing. It's just . . . I'm not sure that's going to work on you. You're looking a little . . . *huskier* these days."

Lizbeth tries to keep her voice down, but it rears out of control.

"You know, some people have the right to make a comment like that. Some people might say that and it wouldn't sound like a cheap shot. A person who came to my book launch, for instance. Any of my book launches. Or a person who came to see me in the hospital when I was *in a car accident.*"

"Lizbeth," Mame says, her own voice rising to match her sister's, "if you ever thought about anyone but yourself you'd remember that Kyle is ADD and what that means is I can't always get away for what was—actually, ultimately—a minor injury. But then maybe if you'd ever once paid any of my kids, or indeed my husband, the tiniest modicum of attention you'd remember that. And don't even talk to me about your book launch. I know you only invite me to those things out of condescension. You really want me and Dave and the kids there? Really? Christ, Lizbeth, look at you, showing up here in a fucking Porsche. Pretending you'd buy clothes from Old Navy. What the hell is wrong with you?"

The clerk is looking anxious. A security guard's attention has been drawn.

"Mame, listen to yourself. This is insane. This is all in your imagination."

"My imagination? Oh, really?"

"What are you doing? You bring me out to the Bemer Valley Mall to prove to me how ordinary your life is and what a pretentious bitch I am? What is that? If you're unhappy with your lot, Mame, that's not my fault."

Mame smiles, sweet and wide eyed. "Tell me something, Lizbeth—are you still taking heroin?"

Lizbeth turns and, as quickly as her cane allows, rushes out. Hurries by another clutch of storefronts, frantically scouring for an exit. The best she can do is an escalator down to the next floor.

Getting breathless, all she finds there is another set of escalators and, through unmarked double doors, a corridor leading to the staff entrance of Radio Shack. She retreats and keeps looking. Slowing now. Struggling past an Amazon of potted plants. Emerging in the food court. By the counter at Taco Bell.

She stands there, exhausted. Grease in the air.

"There you are." Mame approaches from the other direction.

"I couldn't find the exit," Lizbeth says, and in that fleeting half second something like a smirk bats across both their faces.

"I can't believe we still do this," Mame says.

"I know."

"I just wish I knew why you hated me."

"I don't hate you. That's silly. I just . . ."

"Yeah. I know. Me too."

The blank-faced girl behind the counter stares up at them and they decide to stay. To order sodas. And even with the girl's back to them, their voices hush.

"About what you asked . . ." Lizbeth says.

"Betty, I'm sorry. I shouldn't have said that—"

"It's okay. But I'm not. Because—"

And she tells her sister about her baby just as the girl gets back with their sodas. Takes hers and sets off toward a table before Mame can react.

But when she catches up with her: "You're sure? You haven't just—"

"I'm past ten weeks."

"Right. Is it . . . ?"

"Ed's. Right."

"And are you—"

"We broke up."

"*Hoo* . . . I just . . . I don't know where to start . . . this is totally . . ."

"I know."

"I did say you were looking bigger."

"All I can think about is what I'll be like at six months. Already all I do is eat and pee."

"But is everything—?"

"I just got my first set of tests back. Everything's fine."

"Okay. Good. Now, listen . . . you *know*, if you ever need anything . . . practical stuff . . . advice . . . I have done this before."

"I know."

Lizbeth leans forward and pulls back her top lip. "Look. I've got a false tooth. I cracked the real one on an action figure in my bran."

"Oh, my God! Lizbeth! I can't believe you didn't tell me. When did this happen?"

"Before the accident. But it's fine." She gulps at her soda as proof. "By the way, for the record, I love your kids. And I think Dave's great."

They each cross their legs in turn before Mame speaks. "Have you been up to Mom's grave?"

"I went up on my birthday."

"We went up on Labor Day."

"You did? Why didn't you call? You should have come to the house. Stayed."

"It was a last minute thing . . . the kids wanted to get back . . . you know how it is."

"Sure."

"Have they taken care of the problem with the flowers?"

"Uh-huh. I talked to the caretaker."

A teenage boy passes by them gnawing a burrito. As he does a teardrop of sour cream oozes out. It swells on the edge of the wax paper wrap, poised to bleed down onto Lizbeth's arm. Lizbeth has her head turned the other way, but Mame sees it. Leans across and stems it with her finger; neither Lizbeth or the boy knows anything has happened.

"I saw Dad last week," she says.

"How is he?"

"The nurses say he's okay. He looked pretty wacked out to me."

"Did he know who you were?"

"Not a clue. But he wasn't, you know . . . distressed."

"I need to go see him."

"Well . . . I'm not going to argue with that. You know, at least while you're up here . . . it's only another hour's drive from here."

"You know, Mame, if you want me to get more involved, say so. It's just . . ."

"Yeah," Mame says. "I know."

Later, back in the Airport Plaza, she watches the planes and feels the presence of every guest that ever used this room. Transience preserved in each curtain thread and carpet fiber.

The phone rings as she's getting into bed. She picks up and the caller says: "Ms. Greene? It's Alan Ossery. I'm sorry for calling so late, but today's just never ended. Anyway, I talked to Wilson. And if you can get clearance from Sosa and the DOC, then it's good news. He's agreed to meet you. He'll talk to you this week."

A voice on the radio says: *"The things we wait lifetimes for go by so fast we don't even know how they feel."*

Although the drive out to Essenville takes place in lucid winter sunshine, by the time she reaches the prison the sky's overcast. The cloud a smothering lid on the world.

The guard in the visitor's parking lot ogles the Porsche. She passes through the ID checks and another guard picks up a phone and says, again: "It's her."

The same route is taken through the prison. But now, when they enter the administrative sector, they turn in the opposite direction. Continue down a single corridor until they reach a box room with a steel door, at the top of which is a porthole.

The guard tells her this is the lawyer's room. Gestures for her to go in.

She sees a low metal table set in the very center of the room with a bolted-down chair on either side. Cinder block walls. A camera, gazing down.

That's all. No window and, she realizes, no thick Plexiglas divide. Nothing between one side of the table and the other.

She takes her seat with her back to the door. The guard waits beside it, a picture of closed indifference. She glances over her shoulder at him, half smiles out of courtesy as he stares out from behind crossed arms. Taps his foot on the dull-gleamy linoleum. She reaches down into her bag. Pulls out a notepad, a pen. Keeps in the forefront of her mind the picture of Wilson Ulysses Velez still pinned up in her hotel room.

Speaking to Ossery last night, she ran through her preparatory questions. Tried to gauge what she could mention and what was best unsaid, for now. Inquired if there were certain colors she should wear or avoid. He told her to wear what she wanted.

"But," she said, "there's no chance of him being . . . hostile? Violent?"

"There'd be more violence with the Dalai Lama."

"So what do I call him? Squirrel? Three Vee?"

"Just call him Wilson," he said.

She glances up at the camera.

Ossery told her it would be there. There's one everywhere he sees his clients now. Sometimes they're not even recording. Just keeping you guessing. Maybe there's someone watching from a cramped and darkened room. Maybe they've gone home. Maybe they don't care about you. Maybe you're all they care about.

You just never know.

Now, her bad leg stiffens under the table as her fingers drum on its surface.

It's too cold for her to take off her coat. Her stomach feels knotted and unglued both at once. She looks back toward the door again, abruptly uncertain of what she's here for.

The second hand on her watch glides toward the minute. Closer. Almost. There now.

Past.

She sucks her bottom lip and looks over at the guard. He stares ahead. Puffs out his cheeks.

And it's now that she hears the sound beyond the door. Sudden, rising. Muffled speech. Footsteps, getting louder. Right outside and—

She spins around as it yowls open.

The room fills with bodies and it takes a moment for her eyes to focus.

He is here. In this room, with her. Wilson Velez. Dressed in a baggy orange jumpsuit. Pigeon-stepping to the other side of the table, manacled at his wrists and ankles, each cuff bound to a chain around his waist. A guard by each arm.

She'd put him at no more than five foot six. The irradiated clumps of hair she saw in the picture have been cropped down to a mostly even baldness. Circles of dry skin mottle his cheeks. His features in general look puffy, indefinite, overwhelmed by that vicious scar on his forehead. Under his jumpsuit she can make out the droop of his shoulders, and a doughnut of flab around his midriff.

His glasses, she notices, have a crack along one lens.

The guards lead him to the table. Raise their hands to his shoulders, pushing him down into the chair. She sees him wince.

Without even being aware of doing it, she presses back in her seat as he settles opposite. Until she feels the metal frame dig into her kidneys.

All three guards turn and exit. The one who brought Lizbeth here pauses at the door.

"I'll be right outside," he says, but she can't tell if it's a warning or a reassurance.

Then he leaves.

And it's just the two of them.

Wilson Velez sits unmoving with his hands clasped in his lap, legs splayed wide at the knees then tapering back to his ankles to form a perfect diamond. The light bounces off his chains. She hears him breathe, a broken wheezing. Estimates the distance between them. Twenty-four inches? Twenty-seven? Close enough to touch him if she wanted to.

The sleeves of his jumpsuit hang down to his elbows. From there down she can see his tattoos. One randomly snags her attention: a baroque arrangement of skulls and pistols, set around a flaming heart inside which is written: *100% LA REALEZA*.

And below it, around his wrist: *1.18.4.9.12.12.1.*

She finds herself peering at the texture of the skin beneath, hairless and parchmentish. The wrist itself bonily slender. The wrist, she thinks, of an old lady.

When she looks back up his eyes are locked on her face. But as soon as she meets them they skitter away.

"Thank you for meeting me today," she says. "I'm not sure how much your lawyer has told you about me, or what I wanted to discuss with you."

He says nothing. Just stares down.

"Did you get the parcel I sent you?"

He says nothing.

"The warden told me that he'd let you have it. There was a magazine. Some Mounds bars. Your lawyer told me you liked them."

Just stares down.

"My name is Lizbeth Greene. Did he tell you that at least?"

"I . . . I—I . . . ggggottttttt . . . thhhe pppparcel."

Wilson Ulysses Velez was asleep in his cell when the guards came. Dreaming, as he does now almost every time he sleeps, of the lime trees and the blood. Then the cell door was open and a baton was rapping on the inside wall, and he lugged himself upright so they could search him, chain him, march him out of the pod and down the walkways until the walkways became corridors and finally led here.

The chain around his waist feels tighter than usual. He lifts his head like it's on a pulley. Stares over at the woman. Dark hair. Maybe dyed. Pale skin; skin that gets cared for. Nervousness all over her face. Brown eyes. Plump lips. Small, obviously, but her coat makes it impossible to know much more. What's underneath. Pants, not a skirt, he sees. A shame.

He notices the cane propped beside her.

"Whatttttt's upp . . . witth yourrr . . . leggg?"

"I was in a car accident. It's getting—"

"Mmy hipp . . . is—aggony. Ittt alwwways iss—beffore . . . it rainsss, *ssssabes?* Hurtsss sssooo . . . badd. Whenn I—I ssit . . . ittt hurts. When I—I standd . . . itttt hurtts."

"Have you seen a doctor?"

But he just looks back down and says nothing. Until:

"How lllllong have I—I . . . beeenn here? Tttttttwo hourss? Three hourss?"

Lizbeth stares at him across the table. He's not, she is certain, joking.

"You've been here less than five minutes."

She should get this done now.

"Wilson . . . let me tell you in my own words why I wanted to meet you."

She wants, she says, to write a book about him. *With* him. His life, she says, has been important. Remains important. She has been moved, profoundly, by what she's read of him, those racking years in Ad-Seg, and she wants to know more. Has to know more. Feels a yearning for knowledge that while, yes, speaking to her as a writer, also addresses her as a human being. She wants to know who he was before. Is now. The nature of the worlds he has passed through. It's time, she says, that his experience was recorded. Understood. For his sake, and his people's sake.

She wants, she says, to give him the voice he's always been denied.

He lifts his head again, but this time his eyes flit around the room, landing everywhere—the walls, ceiling, camera, door—but on her. His lips look like they're moving, but he makes no sound. Then he looks back down and his whole upper body slumps in his chair.

This is not the response she was hoping for.

"Obviously," she says, "this would be a collaboration. It's your story, Wilson. I'd never forget that."

She thinks that he says something, but he could just be clearing his throat.

"I thought of *God's Lonely Man* for the title. But that's just an idea."

With evolutionary slowness, Wilson lifts himself off his seat. Pit-pats toward the door. "Thankkkkk . . . you forrr the . . . parcelll."

He calls through to the guards. "I'mm ddone . . . Lllett . . . mmmmme outtttt."

"Wilson? What did I say? What is it?"

He has the guard's attention, and now they're opening up.

"Please. Wilson, if I've done something to offend you, I apologize."

"IIII . . . don'tt wantttttt tto dddo . . . anyyy book."

She pushes down on her cane, gets to her feet.

"Wilson, at least think about what I've said. Just think about it."

And all three guards file back inside. The two who brought Wilson here reassuming their positions on either side of him. Conducting him out.

"Wilson! I mean you no harm!"

But he's through the door now. The third guard stands in front of Lizbeth, and raises his hand to say No Further.

She didn't even open her notebook.

Wilson Ulysses Velez moves down the corridor. He can tell the guards are angry with him. It informs their footsteps, shapes their breathing. They must have settled in for a long recess outside the lawyer's room, grousing and gossiping. Wouldn't have thought they'd be heading back to work already.

So USP Essenville reabsorbs them all, sucking them back into its pods and walkways, past locked steel doors and the men beyond them.

Inside his cell they unchain him. When he's down to just handcuffs, they leave and lock him in. Have him sit on the floor with his back to the food slot, extending his arms behind him to have the cuffs removed. Then he stands, and they watch as he strips, bends, shows them his armpits and the soles of his feet.

"Have a pleasant evening," one says as they turn and walk away.

Wilson pulls his jumpsuit back on. Flops onto his bed and spreads his arms. Lying flat he can almost touch both walls.

His new cell has the same dimensions as his old one: seven by ten. But other things are different now. In the corner are a toilet and sink, unaccompanied by a shower. (Now he showers three times a week in a purpose-built cell with five other inmates.) There is just a single door. No camera.

A pale vertical beam of natural light seeps through a never-washed Plexiglas slit three inches wide and twelve inches high, scored up by the ceiling.

A shelf is built into the wall above the bed, on which are five sheets of paper; a felt-tipped pen; his letter from the Christian Ladies of Western Arizona; the magazine. *National Geographic*. Censored, of course. Pages missing, pictures cut out, text blacked out with a marker.

He raises his hand and a sheet of paper flutters down beside him. Another drawing. Another figure in the lime trees.

The silence is more deceptive than ever. He lies here and feels every twitch of misery in ESSUSP vibrating through the walls like all that concrete was just plasterboard. The mood of the place restless lately. The bugs on edge. Guards putting rifle butts into ribs in the yard.

He pulls down the magazine and reads

the volcanoes that fume beneath Iceland's Vatnajökull glacier have been threatening

But the two lines after have been scored through.

His attention wanders. He thinks of Lizbeth Greene. Her neck. Her hair. Tries to imagine the feel of it against him. Brushing his skin as her head passes over his stomach.

He slides his hand between his legs:

Nothing.

This is not a recent development. Nothing's happened there since a year into Ad-Seg. But lately he's been trying again. Elsewhere, after all, there's been restoration. The rashes gradually clearing. The eternal congestion of his chest abated.

He pulls back his hand and his arm lies still beside him.

And that night, the coldest yet, Lizbeth drives out to the upscale houses on the northern tip of Essenville, over by the golf course. Their girth bathed in porch light. Finds the home of Warden Michael Sosa.

The invite to dinner was, she felt, nonnegotiable. Mrs. Sosa, the warden said, insists that Lizbeth let her cook for her. Call it a thank you for signing her books. She and her friends would be so thrilled to meet you, he said.

There are three more couples besides the Sosas. The deputy warden; the warden of the low-security Federal Correctional Institution; the sheriff of Essenville. Their wives. Homemakers all. Trim women with grown children who exercise and volunteer.

The sheriff and his wife, Joan Sosa says, were the first friends she and Michael made when the prison was built and they came out from Baltimore.

"And we're still trying to shake them off now," the warden says, passing around the drinks.

Joan is just as excited as he promised. She gabbles nonstop at Lizbeth, blushingly tells her how much she loves her work, gripping her arm for emphasis. Then she vanishes back into the kitchen.

In a glass cabinet in the family room there's a gleaming blood red bowling ball engraved with the warden's name in gold lettering. A gift, it says, from the Essenville Bowlodrome. Lizbeth peers at it as he wanders up to her. His manner relaxed here, almost avuncular.

"Between us," he says, "I bowl about as good as your average Girl Scout. But I have tried to use it to cement our place in the community . . ."

He stares into the cabinet.

"The town had got into a bad way before they built the jails. Like everywhere around here. When Joan and I first came out it was desperate. The whole place had died on its . . . rump. Pretty much all that was left was the people. And from what I know, bowling had always been a major thing for them, so ever since I've encouraged my COs to get involved. Had them shirts made up, that type of thing. Now there's teams, leagues, tournaments, so forth. It's become a real focal point of the town again. I like to think that's helped bond the old and the new in Essenville. Anyway, I guess I've sent enough dollars their way for them to figure they owed me a ball . . ."

Joan Sosa calls her guests to the table, producing from the kitchen a vast pot pie made—her husband reminds them—from the same recipe that has twice won her the county bake-offs back home.

So they eat, and between appreciative murmurs, turn as one to Lizbeth, seeking her opinions on news events, quizzing her over her creative life: when she first knew that she wanted to write, where she gets her inspiration. Twice, Joan Sosa reaches across the table and takes her by the hand as if worried she's about to float away.

Lizbeth does her best to satisfy them. But her thoughts have been consumed by Wilson. She just wants to know what she did so wrong.

What now?

Over coffee the other couples produce their books for signing. Then Michael Sosa walks her to her car.

"He said no."

"That's what I heard."

"So I guess that's it . . . already."

"Oh, I doubt it. He's just dancing. Teasing you. Being frank, Miss Greene, the man spent five years in a steel box. Even now the only visitor he gets is Ossery. I don't think he'll be turning away another candidate." He leans in the driver's window. Shivers. "Most of these guys . . . they love an audience. Attention. Now take that and multiply it by the value of yourself being that audience. Trust me. He'll come around."

He thanks her for coming by tonight. Says he hasn't seen Joan so aglow in years.

The next day, she calls him. Asks if she can send another parcel to Wilson.

He won't let *City Slicker* through—a real-life story is, he says, inappropriate—but three of her novels are okayed. She encloses the mini-biography that her publishers give to journalists. Then she calls Ossery, and then she calls him again, and each time he tells her that he'll talk to his client. See what can be done.

Then she waits for word. Kills time in the Airport Plaza. Orders room service and watches cable. Pulls out her suitcases and gets her clothes pressed by the laundry service. Lies on her bed and shuts her eyes and listens to the planes.

And so a week goes by.

It's eight in the morning when reception calls. Ossery's downstairs in the lobby.

"He's still thinking things over," he says. "But he wanted me to give you this."

He hands her a jiffy bag.

"There's a note in there. Some stuff dating back to before Aspera. Stuff he wanted me to pass on to you. Listen, I'd love to stay and chat, but I've got a humdinger of a day in front of me—"

"Does this mean he's going to change his mind?"

"I don't know, Ms. Greene. I'm not stalling you when I say that. I truly don't."

She opens the package back in her room.

There is, as promised, a note. The handwriting as erratic as his speech.

Dear Miss Greene. Thank you for your books and for sending me the information about yourself. I did know of your name before you visited me last week, but I'm sorry to say I had never read any of your books. I want you to know how impressed I was. Some words and passages had been blacked out by the prison censor (to avoid me being corrupted by them), but I never lost my interest in the story and Detective Enschell is an appealing character.

I remember the City Slicker case too and I was sad to read in your biography you had been attacked by Richard Cazet. (I am also sorry for the loss of your mother.) The cousin of a friend of mine was killed by him. Maybe you recognize her name—Gabriela Linares? I didn't know her so well personally but I remember the grief her demise caused like it was yesterday.

Anyway, I have asked my legal representative to pass on certain items to you that I hope as a writer you might find interesting.

I also hope your leg is not proving too onerous.

Despite the unsteadiness of the writing, his name is signed with elaborate detailing, the W and V towering over the other letters.

Then she finds a photograph. A hazy snapshot. At first she doesn't even know it's him. Just sees a grinning Hispanic boy leaning up by a fence in what looks like Flushing Meadows Corona Park. Dressed in a red and gold football top printed with a white 3. Then she notices his chin, the set of his eyes. And the gulf between this and the man in the lawyer's room at ESSUSP makes her say, out loud, sitting here alone:

"What . . . the . . . fuck . . . ?"

There's a stack of other papers.

At the top, a six-page pamphlet, neatly typeset and stapled. *The Eternal Righteous Manifesto of the Sacred Incan Royals,* it says on the cover.

Inside there's a standardized greeting:

I lay my right hand over my heart to show you my love for all Royal Peoples and with my left I make a fist to prove to you my honor.

Then a vow.

To Be Read by All Ascendant Soldiers of Royalty Prior to Checking In:
Almighty Father, allow me to embody the proud virtues of The People's Nation of Sacred Incan Royals, that I may shelter under its history and wisdom. May I bring glory to my chapter, to my tribe and to my People. Let the white that represents the holiness of this oath preserve my loyalty. Let the gold of my Incan heritage nourish me. Let the red that symbolizes my blood and the blood of all other Royal Peoples give me strength in my battles and trials.

Let me remember that the Royal People are the first and truest claimants of my faith, and that the Word of the Sapa is the one Word and the only Word, the Word that shall be followed without question or argument, His order the order that ranks above all others.

The manifesto proper begins on the next page. Long, florid passages in which the same central themes are aggressively stated and restated. Hierarchy is to be respected. Self-sacrifice is prized. Physical conflicts should be carried out one on one, unless the gang (never referred to as such) has collectively been insulted or endangered, in which case

the furious wrath of every People's Soldier across The Nation will be brought to bear on the perpetrator.

At the back a single sheet is tucked inside the cover. It reads:

Formal Request for Membership to The People's Nation of the Sacred Incan Royals: All information given in this application can be checked and any lies within it can and will be found out AND ACTED ON.

There's more yet in the jiffy bag. A sheaf of loose pages turn out to be journal entries dating back to the year and a half spent in USP Moxanie. Exhaustive records of his mood and state of health; vignettes observed in the yard or canteen; dirty-minded skits mocking guards. There are spools of free association and jagged bursts of poetry. A short essay titled *Incan Blood*. Another, *Amerikan Injustice*.

At the bottom of the pile is a collection of film reviews, seemingly written from memory. He is curt in his dismissal of *The Lost Boys*, enthused over *At Close Range*. Indifferent to *Freebie and the Bean*.

And all of it—the reviews, the journal entries—is perfectly spelled. Strung into neat sentences, arranged in grammatical paragraphs.

Wilson Ulysses Velez stares down from the wall above the dresser.

Ossery calls that afternoon. Wants to know what Lizbeth thought.

"I'm astonished," she says. "I honestly am."

"Well, you know, he wasn't always the way he is now. His mind was a lot more active back then. Stronger. He was always reading. Always coming up with stuff."

"I'm really very impressed."

"Well, in that case, be happy. I talked to Wilson and he'll give it another spin. He won't make any promises about the book, but he will talk to you."

"He will?"

"He will."

"Oh, God. *Thank you.* That's . . . wonderful."

"Let's just say it's a promising development."

"I'm just so relieved. I'm just . . ." She pauses. "What if I hadn't liked what he sent?"

"But you did. So why worry? Now, there were a couple of things we wondered if you might be able to help out with. He needs a new lens in his glasses. Also, there were some more magazines he's been asking for. If it's easier, I could just send over a list."

Three days later she's back in the lawyer's room at USP Essenville, with her cane up against the table and another guard tapping his foot on the linoleum.

She's getting to know the drill now. All but yawned through the pat-down search, the removal and inspection of her shoes and jewelry. Calmly looked on as the guard upturned her bag, scrutinized her compact, change purse, notebook, phone.

She doesn't hear them approaching until the door's already half open.

Wilson Velez again led up to the table bound at the wrists and ankles, seated opposite with his legs parted at the knee and his hands together in his lap.

And then, once more, they're alone.

"Thank you," Lizbeth says, "for agreeing to meet me again."

He looks up and she sees the broken lens in his glasses has been replaced.

"Nnnno . . . problemm."

"Did you get the magazines okay?"

"Uhh-huuh . . . Thankkssssssss."

"Sure . . . so, how are you?"

He shrugs. Peers up at the ceiling for an age but then his eyes flash back to hers.

"Sso . . . you knnnnnnnnnow who . . . who . . . Gabrielllllla Linares . . . waass?"

"Of course. She was Richard Cazet's third victim. I talked to her mother when I was writing my book. I did try and send you a copy of it after the last time we met, but the warden wouldn't let me."

He looks away again. Stares around the room.

"Ddo . . . you know . . . iiiif meningittttis always . . . sttttarts with a . . . stifff . . . neckkk?"

"Meningitis?"

"Rightttt."

"I think so . . . do you have a stiff neck?"

"No . . . butt I diddd . . . earlllierr."

Then he seems to lose interest.

"So," Lizbeth says, "I read what you sent me. And I thought it was amazing."

"Amazingggggg. Okay."

"The manifesto . . . that was what you gave out to your members, right?"

"To ourrr . . . *soldddddados*. It ttolddd themmmm everythingg they neededd . . . to know. Howw . . . to eat. Howw to drinkk. How . . . to walkkk downn the street."

"Sure. I mean, the rest of it was great too. The poetry. The film reviews. I had no idea—"

"Thattt I . . . I—couldddd write—myyy own nnnname?"

"No . . . that's not what I meant at all."

But it is.

"I alwaysss likedd . . . to write . . . Even whenn I—I was aaa little kid . . . I likedd . . . wordss . . . yyyyyou know? I lllliked . . . whatt . . . they coulddd do."

For the first time, when he meets her eyes they stay with her.

"I've hhhhhad a lott of tttime to . . . ffffind outt how ttto use . . . them. I-I firsssst went tto jjjail whenn I wassssss ten years olddd, you . . . know? Halffff my . . . life since hhhhas been in a *canttton*. A cellllll. Just me and wordddds. And I—I—IIII know thatttt I sound stupiddd . . . I sssounded stupiddd even when I tttalked okay . . . but with a pppaper and . . . pen . . . I coulddd prove I am nottt a stupid man."

"I never thought you were stupid," she says. "What you write has real power. I don't mean that to sound patronizing. I'm just talking as one person who likes words to another."

"Butttt thatt part of mme . . . is gone nnnnow."

He shuts his eyes and his head drops.

"Wilson, that's all the more reason for this project to happen. I want to be able to tell people about your creativity. Show them your inner life."

She thinks that he's fallen asleep right there until, in a snap, he looks back up.

"III have . . . bbbbbeen . . . thinkinggggg about it."

"You have?"

"Sssure. There's been . . . a lot of thoughts going through mmmmy . . . mind about it. Some badd but a lot . . . gggggood."

"I give you my word, if there's anything you want to ask me, to reassure you about my intentions, just ask."

Wilson Ulysses Velez shifts his weight in his chair to stop his thighs from numbing. Sees her stare at him in that eager way of hers. Who does she remind him of? Someone drifts through his thoughts whenever he sets eyes on her. But who? What white girls has he known? None this old. This starchy. He looks at her and it nags at him.

Lizbeth Greene watches him observing her. Almost tranquil, nearly detached. Like he knows things about her. She wonders how many people he ever gave that look to. What became of them. What he thinks he knows.

And then, without warning, she sneezes.

Wilson reels backward. Propels himself with such force he almost falls from his chair. Instead, he labors to his feet. Tries to bury his head in his chest.

Makes for the door in his leg irons.

"Wilson? What are you doing?"

"*Me vvvvoy. Mmme vvvoy.* I—I . . . I . . . I . . . can'tttt . . . stay here witthh a . . . sick personn."

"I'm not sick. It was just dust."

"Nnnno, you're . . . sssssick." He yells for the guards. "Lettt . . . me outt! Let . . . mee outtttt!" And when they start to open the door, he cajoles them. "Hey *jarabe*! Lett . . . me . . . outt offf—hhhhere! Hurrryyy . . . up . . . CO!"

"Wilson," she says, "I'm sorry. Can I see you again?"

She thinks that he nods as they steer him outside; but his head's turned away, so it's hard to know for sure.

EIGHT

A T SEVEN A.M. Ossery is waiting in an armchair in the hotel lobby, holding another, larger jiffy bag. As of waking five minutes ago—being woken, in fact, by the call from reception—Lizbeth has a blocked nose, pinkish eyes.

"I don't know what happened," she says. "With Wilson."

"To be honest, he was a little pissed off. He thought it was selfish of you to meet when you had a cold."

"That's ridiculous. I didn't even have a cold."

"You have one now."

"But I didn't then. At least I didn't know I did."

"It doesn't matter. Don't worry about it. He just fixates on things. It'll be fine. Anyway, he asked me to bring you this."

Upstairs, she orders room service before opening it. French toast and maple syrup. She clears her plate, then, instantly, is overcome with nausea.

This time there's no note. Just what she thinks must be a cold remedy. Instructions to mix sugar with water, then add whiskey, the resulting blend set on fire to burn off the alcohol. Lemon peel is added. Then onions. She gags just reading it.

Underneath there's a half-inch wad of paper bound with rubber bands. The pages typed. Single-spaced lines of text.

She puts it to one side and lies on the bed. Two pillows support her neck, three more are stacked under her ankle. Her belly feels swollen from breakfast. She stares down at it. Pictures what it's going to look like in a month; in three months.

The loss of control, that's what gets her. No, *theft* is what it is. Here in a suite at an airport hotel, locked into some freaky elemental process that got itself started without her even knowing, far less consenting. She had—however grudgingly—accepted the stodgy business of aging, the slow, brakeless irreversibility, the ever-accumulating sags and hitches. That was next, and she was ready. But now, instead—not instead, *as well, on top, in addition to*—there's this. Her body subject to God knows what strange, painful indignities, all leading to something she can still hardly—

No. She can't imagine it at all.

Wilson's papers are face down on the bedside cabinet, next to the phone and her keycard. She reaches out for them. Finds her glasses.

THE MONSTERS OF GRAMERCY PARK, it says. *By Wilson Ulysses Velez*. She sets aside the title page. Begins at the top of the next.

The night that everything went wrong, Hector and Edmond were happily watching over the city, dreaming of woe and anguish. This should not surprise you. It was how they always spent their days—perched beside one another, plotting and planning and scheming. Only at night could they put their plans into action. Because this is how gargoyles have always lived.

But wait. First you should know where they were, these monsters. Perhaps you should even note it down. Keep it safe in case you forget it. They lived right above the front door of an old building on a windy corner of Gramercy Park, New York, New York, carved into the fine gray stone. So when the city's gentlefolk walked past, they would see Hector and Edmond, and they would say to one another, "Sweetness, look at those ugly monsters" or "My, what perfectly horrible gargoyles."

Of course, they might have chosen different things to say if they knew Hector and Edmond could hear every word. But then how could they know what these gargoyles really were?

Because what gargoyles really are is ancient evil spirits, alive and well and hidden among us. Without a hiding place in the physical world, you see, these spirits will die—but when they have one they can spend all day feeding off people's negative thoughts, their anger and envy and selfishness and then, at night, fly free to stir up mayhem across the city.

In this way Hector and Edmond were just like every gargoyle—although in fact they were the very nastiest of gargoyles, the most mischievous of gargoyles, the most troublesome spirits transformed into the most vile of creatures. Indeed, had they not been so nasty and mischievous, they would never have had such a perfect home.

You see, the architect who designed this building to live in himself 156 years ago had no wish to have gargoyles on it. No—he just wanted a plain facade with perhaps a gold knocker on the door. But Hector and Edmond had other ideas (by the way, we will have to use the names they have called themselves for the last few centuries, as their ancient names are too dangerous to write down). They had been homeless for a long time, and their powers were starting to fade. They were weak.

Then, one black and stormy night, they heard a dreadful argument— the architect and his wife squabbling over his idea of a gold knocker for the door of the house. And when they stopped by the couple's apartment to enjoy the quarrel, the spirits saw the building plans. Hector and Edmond knew they had found salvation.

As the architect slept that night, they summoned up every last drop of vileness in their terrible bodies. They whispered in his ear. They pulled at his eyelids. And oh, the nightmares that plagued him as they did— ghastly horrors that left the poor man whimpering and soaked in sweat.

Yet come morning he couldn't remember one of them. Instead, he rose early, walked downstairs to his plans, and—as if in a trance— changed his designs so that now the building was covered with gargoyles. Foul gargoyles. Wretched gargoyles. Disgusting gargoyles with ears like bats and eyes like rats and tiny pointed teeth. And sure enough, when the house was built, a hundred spirits slipped inside the bricks and mortar and took their place over the spiked railings that ran along the front of the building.

But the best position of all went to Hector and Edmond. From then on and forever more they sat right above the front door on their own private ledge. And as word spread among the spirits and every new building in the area soon had its own hideous gargoyles, they all paid their respects to the first and wickedest monsters of Gramercy Park.

So there you have it. And that, if you hadn't noticed, brings us back to where we started—with Hector and Edmond watching over the city, dreaming of woe and anguish. Until finally the day turned into night. The kind of night the gargoyles adored, dark and freezing and wet. The people of the city were hurrying home, rushing this way and that. Some of them cursed. Some of them yelled. All of them were in a bad temper.

Hector and Edmond could not have been more delighted.

"You know something Edmond?" Hector said. "I love this city."

"Me too, old friend," Edmond replied. "The people are just so wonderfully awful!"

Just then a thin man in a long coat noticed them as he scurried by.

"Ugh," he said, under his breath. "Revolting." And with the next step he took he walked straight into a streetlight, almost knocking him-

self out cold. A trickle of blood ran out of his nose and a lump the size of an egg swelled up on his forehead. Hector and Edmond laughed so hard they thought they might fall off their ledge. Then they started planning that night's fun.

The phone bleats beside her. It takes two rings for her to snap to, place the sound. A third to pick up.

"My God. You sound terrible. Do you have the flu?"

Inchy Burden.

"Don't pretend you're not there. Lizbeth, I can hear you sniffing."

The conversation that follows revolves around two subjects: how Inchy discovered where Lizbeth was (she admits to bullying it out of Nancy); what Lizbeth might be doing there.

"I hear you're working on a new idea. Can I at least ask what it is?"

But Lizbeth says she won't discuss it. Inchy's baffled. Almost hurt.

"If you're unhappy with my performance while I've been representing you, Lizbeth, I can only apologize. I know things didn't go as well as we'd all hoped last time out, but you just need to put that behind you. All of it."

"I already have," Lizbeth says.

And as soon as she hangs up, she finds her place in the story.

Around them, an excited hubbub ran up and down the building. In the countryside, this chatter of evil spirits is what makes the trees whisper in the darkness. Here in Gramercy Park, it was more like a low hum bubbling under the noise of the city.

Then the old grandfather clock in the lobby of the building finally struck ten—the signal for Hector, Edmond and a hundred ugly, fiendish gargoyles to fly from their stone dwellings and take to the skies! If you could have seen them, you might have thought they were a huge flock of ghastly, black birds—but then they move so fast, you would probably not have been able to see them.

Hector and Edmond led the way, resplendent in their wickedness. By now the rain was so heavy the street below was full of umbrellas and the wind was so strong it was blowing half of them inside out.

"Ah," Hector said to Edmond, "what a marvelous night!"

As they flew over Penn Station, the gargoyles split up—spreading out all over the five boroughs. All of them wanted the same thing, to find people up to no good so they could feed off their badness and make mischief in their wake. Some went to Brooklyn, some went to Queens, some went to the Bronx and some even went to Staten Island. None of them had to wait very long.

Hector and Edmond stayed in Manhattan. High above Times Square, they saw their first bad person. Older gargoyles, gargoyles with much experience in the world, can tell such a person just from looking at them. They are never wrong.

This first bad person was a man dressed in an expensive raincoat. Under his expensive raincoat he had on an expensive suit, and an expensive shirt, and an expensive tie. The watch he wore was more expensive than his raincoat, his suit, his shirt and his tie put together. Even the man's socks were expensive. He was very pleased with himself, this man. He had spent all day on Wall Street making even more money to buy even more expensive things all for himself.

Hector and Edmond watched as he walked into a bodega. He bought a pack of gum and paid with a $5 bill. The store owner (who had been working since 4 A.M) was so tired and confused he gave the man change for $20.

The man saw what had happened, but instead of handing the money back, he just took it oh-so-quickly and left. Outside, he started to put the bills in his wallet, grinning to himself.

Hector and Edmond were thrilled when they saw such badness!

As quickly as the man had taken the money, they flew down to the front of the bodega where the produce was kept out on display. In the blink of an eye Edmond pulled open the pockets of the man's expensive raincoat, and Hector filled them with as much as they could hold—apples and grapes and passion fruit and two whole melons (it was a very large raincoat).

Just then the son of the store owner looked up from putting out oranges. The son of the store owner was nearly seven feet tall and happened to be a wrestler who trained by grappling with bears. He saw a pineapple sticking out of the man's raincoat.

"Hey you!" he shouted. "Did you pay for that?"

Before the man in the expensive suit knew what was happening, the store owner's son had lifted him up by his expensive collar and carried him back inside. Then he shook him.

"What's this?" he roared, as item after item spilled from the man's pockets. "A thief! Stealing from my father's store! I'll show you what happens to thieves!"

With that, still holding the man in midair, he took out his wallet and emptied it out onto the counter. Dollar bills, $5 bills, 10s, 20s, and 100s, they all fell out. Enough money to buy half of New York!

"That," the store owner's son said, "should cover it."

He put the empty wallet back into the man's pocket and kicked him like a football halfway down the street. When he hit the ground, the man got up and ran for his life, wailing with distress—and Hector and Edmond were filled with joy!

"I never get bored of doing that," Hector said to Edmond as they flew off into the night.

"Me neither," Edmond said. "I still love it just as much as I did back in 1923."

Then they flew up and across town, all the way to Harlem—where they saw the next bad person through the the window of a bar. A man sat with a drink in front of him, trying to impress every lady that passed his table. He whistled at them and told them how beautiful they were. He blew them kisses and asked for their phone numbers. Nothing worked.

Now, to you and me, this man might not have looked like a bad person—he may even have appeared a little sorrowful. But Hector and Edmond knew better.

Sure enough, as soon as he was outside, he stuck his hand inside his pocket and slipped back on the wedding ring that he had taken off and hidden in there earlier that night!

He trudged off down the street. Hector and Edmond followed him. As they passed a late-night drugstore, Hector darted inside—and when he came back out he was wearing shiny red lipstick! The effect was so horrible, even Edmond was revolted!

Then Hector crept up behind the man and quicker than a hungry cheetah planted kisses all over the collar of his spotless white shirt. Now there was bright red lipstick all over it—and the cheating man walked on unawares.

"We'll see how his wife likes that," Hector said.

They found their third no-good person of the night on Amsterdam Avenue. Two friends were about to leave a movie theater—the first, the gargoyles could tell, had just had her hair cut and styled. It looked so perfect—like a glossy black wedding cake on top of her head! Her friend, they could also tell, was jealous of the girl with the perfect hair. Her own hair was greasy and dull.

"Oh no!" the first girl said. "I forgot my umbrella! My hair will get ruined!"

"Don't worry," her friend said. "You can share mine."

So they huddled up together as they walked. But every so often, Hector and Edmond noticed, the jealous girl would tug the umbrella away from her friend, not enough for her to notice, but enough for her hair to get wet. By the time the girl with the perfect hair got back to her building, her hair wasn't perfect anymore—in fact, it was ruined.

The girl with the hair looked so sad as she went inside. But the jealous girl didn't care—in fact, she was pleased. Once her friend was gone she whistled a little tune to herself and knocked her heels together.

"Jeepers!" said Hector. "She is even more rotten than us!"

The two spirits followed the jealous girl all the way home. Then they sneaked inside and disappeared into the walls of her apartment as she changed out of her wet clothes, took a bath, made a tasty dinner and settled down in front of the TV.

It was only when she got into bed that she heard the gurgling noise above her. She opened her eyes right as the waterpipe that ran above the bedroom burst open—and before she even knew what was happening gallons of water were pouring through the ceiling and her bed was floating across the room!

Hector and Edmond flew away, and it was hard to tell what was louder—the screams of the girl or the laughter of the monsters.

All through the night they went on bedeviling the city until eventually the sun began to rise. Then it was time to go back to Gramercy Park. Hector and Edmond smiled horribly at each other as they made their return journey, two old friends happy after a good (i.e., dreadful!) night's work.

When they flew past Times Square again, all the other gargoyles rejoined them and fell into line behind them, back from their own mischief-making. The sight of their building, their home, made every one of them glad in their hearts.

Then just as they turned into Gramercy Park, Hector paused. A man named Louis Fung who had moved into the gargoyles' building last *week was standing outside of it. With a bald head and a long, wart-covered nose, Louis Fung was almost as hideous as Hector himself. He pinned a piece of paper to the wall next to the front door and then he went back inside.*

Hector and Edmond flew up to it.

"Petition to Clean Up Our Building And Our Area" it said, and fear spread through the gargoyles as they crowded round to read the rest.

"Are You Sick of Living With Ugliness?" it said. "Are You Fed Up With Trouble In The Neighborhood? If So, Sign Up Below—And Get Rid Of The Monsters of Gramercy Park Forever!"

Without looking away she turns the page, and begins the next chapter.

Ossery sounds like he's on horseback when she gets him on the phone. Every word accompanied by muffled snorts and hooves.

"Oh, yeah," he says, "he was writing that thing for months. He gave it to me for safekeeping right before he got Ad-Segged. Even then he was always freaking out about the guards deciding to trash it or burn it."

"I'm stunned. I had no idea it was a children's story. And it's good. I mean, it could use a little polish, but it's got a lot of . . . *zing*."

"What? Oh, yeah. Well, like I say, he got himself pretty wrapped up in it."

"Where are you? I keep thinking I hear horses."

"I'm up at a stable in Poughkeepsie. We're looking at a gelding for my daughters." Wistfulness drips into his voice. "You know, one of these days I'm going to have to sit down and write something myself. Like a legal thriller, maybe."

"I didn't know you . . . aspired to that."

"Oh, sure I do. Sure. I've always wanted something to get that absorbed in. That's the thrill, right? Giving every tiny detail a purpose? Making it all add up to something?"

Now he sounds glum. She hears a whinny in the background.

"Anyway, I'm hopeful he'll agree to meet you again soon. He's not angry about the sneezing thing anymore. So . . . let's take another run at this."

A rising crosswind whips the eighty-foot walls of USP Essenville.

Lizbeth sits in the lawyer's room and wonders how long this could go on for. The strip light hums above her. The door opens.

Wilson Velez sits opposite. Looks straight at her and doesn't blink.

"Howww's . . . the coldddd? You mmake up . . . that remedddy I—I sentt you?"

"You know, in the end I didn't need to. It pretty much cleared up on its own. But thank you. And you know . . . from now on."

"From nnnnnow on . . . Sure."

"So, anyway . . . how are you?"

A second passes. Then he launches himself toward her, feet still on the floor and hands in his lap, bent double from the waist so his chest lies flat across the table, head thrown back, jaws open. He stays that way, eyes on hers, like a seabass on ice.

One of the guards, she sees, is looming at the porthole in the door.

"Look at ittt," Wilson says. "Inssssside."

Lizbeth inches forward. Peers down into his mouth. Along the jagged range of his teeth. His tongue, flopped out obscenely. He opens even wider.

Past the tongue and the dangling uvula, his throat is a peevish red. Specks of inflammation dot the rear wall.

"It looks sore."

"Ittt is . . . Sssore as hell. I've been . . . tellingggg them ffor three ddddays."

Finally, he shuts his mouth. Sits back.

"I'm thinkingggg it's . . . strep. Feels like I can't evven swallowww. Fuckingggg . . . sttttrep andddd they're hhhhhappy to see me . . . suffffer. Ain't right."

He straightens up. Leans back into the chair.

"I gott a linctus. 'Cept you . . . need . . . honey. You think you . . . couldd get me some honey?"

"I'll try. I'll talk to Sosa. See if he'll let it through."

She thinks the groan he makes is frustration. Could be hostility. He does, she knows, hold her responsible.

"I'm sorry," she says, "if you caught it from me."

"You? Nnnnnah. You—didn't givvve me nothing. I gott . . . tthis ffffrom a Haitian *babiche* calleddddddddd Chantille coughingggggg all iiiiiiiin my face in . . . the yarrrd." He swallows, and winces. "Sssso, okay . . . ttell me . . . What didd yyyyyou . . . think of my story?"

"I thought it was remarkable," she says. "The language. The story-telling. It's really quite something, Wilson."

He nods, like he knew that already.

"So wwhat'ssss yourrr fffavourite . . . part?"

"Okay. Well, I loved that description of the first night after Louis Fung starts campaigning to have the monsters chiseled off the building . . . where Hector and Edmond fly uptown again to try and make mischief but—"

"But thissss time their . . . pppowers don'tttt . . . work!"

"Exactly! As if something's weakened them. And the other gargoyles fly back to Gramercy Park and they've all had the same experience."

"Anddd . . . when theyyy gettt back Louis Fung's already gottt . . . a hundred names on his petition."

"Right. That whole section really sucked me into the story."

Wilson Velez lets the praise keep coming.

"And the ending . . . the ending's great. Although I think it might be a little much for kids—"

"Kids," he says, "love thattt kind of . . . stuff. They wouldd love the . . . endinggg."

He is, she senses, not looking to debate this.

"So . . . how do you know Gramercy Park? Have you seen the real gargoyles on the brownstones there?"

"Sssure. I saw tttttthem . . . when I—I was . . . maybe nine yearssss . . . old. III useddd to . . . love the ones dddown in . . . Sunnysssside Gardens, *sabesss*? Then this . . . kkid said there wwwere some in . . . Mannhattan thhat were even better . . . So I tttook the seven all tthe way outttt to Granddd Centttral and . . . then I—I wenttt down there. And he wassss right. And I—I—I guess they just alwaysss . . . stayed with me."

"Well, like I say, I think what you've done is remarkable."

"Re-mar-ka-ble," he says, each syllable primly divorced from the rest. "So Lizbeth . . . III gggguess we are bboth remarkablllle people."

It's the first time he's called her Lizbeth. She's surprised how much it unsettles her. Feels like a trespass.

"Anyyyway," he says, ". . . I—I gave the issue ssome reffflection. Anddd the ansssswer is . . . yes."

"To . . . what?"

He glazes over. Stares past her. And one, two, three, four, five seconds pass. Then: "To yyyour . . . book, of ccourse."

Euphoria builds in her chest. A geyser of joy. She tries to keep it from becoming obvious but she almost cries out when she speaks.

"That's fantastic," she says. "That's just . . . wonderful."

"I—I . . . I'd shake yyyyyour hand," he says. "But . . . you know . . ." And he holds his wrists up as far as his waist chain allows.

"You've made the right decision," she says.

"I . . . know. That's . . . wwwhy I made it. But tttthere's some thinggggs you need . . . to do. Conditionsss."

Lizbeth's smile slips off her face. Could she not have held on to that simple yes for just a moment longer?

"One—ifff we ddo this, we do it . . . honest. Between tttthe tttwo of us andd in the bookkk. No bulllllsshit. No lies. *Verdad*. A hundred percent. You wantttt . . . me to beee honest with you, you be honessssst with . . . me. About . . . everythinggggg."

"That's fine. Of course. That's what I want too."

"Okay. In . . . thatttt case here . . . is the other conddddddition. My story . . . I want it publisheddddd."

"Your story? *The Monsters of Gramercy Park*?" She squints at him, and he nods back at her.

"Rightttt. I ssspent a long time . . . writingg itt and I'm proudd of . . . itt and I want itt . . . publishedd."

"Wilson," she says, "I can't tell you how pleased I am we're going to work together. And I think your story's great. But I'm not a publisher. I can't publish anything."

"Oh, bbbut . . . I'm sssure a woman who has sollld as many . . . booksss as you would hhhhave her recommmmendddation taken sseriously . . . Especially if her own . . . nextttt book dependeddd on itt. And esppppecially when . . . what she is recommending . . . is sssso . . . re-mar-ka-ble."

He leans forward and takes each word as slowly as he needs to. "For so lllong I have been cassst out of this world and not one parttt of me has livedd on in it. So now I want to make sssure I do. Because as lllong as one beatttt-up copy is on sssale for . . . twenty cents in some weirddd thrift store someplace, then I—I will be in the worlddd. I will not be . . . casttt out. Surely you undddderstand thattt, Lizbeth? So . . . what I am sayinggg is that I will helpppp you be . . . in the world, and you willll do tttthe same for me."

She hears the dry clack of her mouth. And, eventually, she says: "I can talk to people on your behalf. I can't make you promises on theirs."

"Talk to who you neeed . . . ttttto ttalk to. But it has to be dddone . . . right . . . So I don'ttt wanttt it coming out . . . unddder my name. You put Wilsssson Velez on the cover of a . . . children's book . . . nobody is going

to wantttt their kid to readd it. So I wanttt it publisshed . . . undder an-
otttther name. Clean of me . . . *sabes?*" He rises from his chair. "This . . .
is how it willlll work."

His eyes dim as if a switch has been flicked. A privilege withdrawn. Before she can respond, the guards are in the room. Hands at his back as he
shuffles monkishly out into the hallway.

"I'll see you nexxxxt time," he says. "If these . . . gentlemennn don't let
me . . . die first."

Outside, the wind has dropped now.

From her room at the Airport Plaza, Lizbeth makes a call to the office of
Inchy Burden and with that, everything is set in motion.

There are, in the days to come, frantic negotiations. Inchy dealing with
Ossery; Inchy dealing with the publisher. And in the hotel there is silence.
From New York, and from Essenville. Until, with Lizbeth half asleep in
bed, she calls.

Everything's taken care of, she says.

"For both?"

"For both."

A contract has been drafted for *God's Lonely Man,* another for *The
Monsters of Gramercy Park.* A payment has been made to the charities
nominated by Warden Sosa; another to those named by Wilson Velez. Significant expense already incurred by her publisher.

"But listen, they don't care about that . . . they know what they've got
here . . . If they need to speculate to make it happen, so be it. Same with
putting out the gargoyle book. It's nothing."

Anyway, she says, the kids' editor is crazy for it. Isn't that cute?

She tells Lizbeth she shouldn't feel bad for helping a man like Velez.
Great art, she says, often needs personal compromise.

"I know," Lizbeth says.

She orders champagne from room service. Pours herself a glass and dips
her finger into it, then brings that single drop to her lips.

There's the perfect house for rent in Essenville. Advertised in the *Expositor.* Set among the first few blocks you pass through coming into town.

She drives out the next day, and takes it.

The TV vans are arriving now. Cameramen staking claim to lengths of
curb, reporters making last-minute checks of facts and hair.

But the print guys, they've already got the story. Already on their phones, preparing to dictate it. Just waiting for someone to pick up.

A yellow tape cordon around the scene, battered by the wind sweeping in from Manhattan. Weary paramedics packing up the ambulance. The body on the ground left, for a moment, unattended. A blanket over the face.

The rest is cops and bystanders. No family yet.

And the print guys finally get through:

Violence erupted in Corona, Queens, again tonight as a man was shot dead near an all-night supermarket on Roosevelt Ave. Oscar Manzanares, 22, was mowed down by an unidentified assailant as he left the Fair Price Food Center at just after 10 p.m.

Police said the victim was shot three times, but that his killer fled before he could be identified or apprehended.

The homicide is the second in the area in the last 48 hours, coming after Tuesday's murder of 23-year-old Julio Diaz a block away on Junction Blvd. The shooter in that case also remains at large.

Corona has of course already seen its share of crime-related headlines this winter. Only yesterday, police officer Alan Managan was formally exonerated by an internal inquiry after the October shooting of unarmed janitor Ramon Carvajal outside a 53rd Ave bodega.

Area residents are hoping the neighborhood can now be spared any further turmoil.

NINE

THERE'S TEA FRESHLY made on the counter, a beacon of heat and revival in the kitchen of the rented house in Essenville. The place still cold after unknown weeks sitting empty. The whole place like a show home. Catalog spruce.

This morning she checked out of the Airport Plaza Hotel. Stopped on her way here at the mall. Bought an array of essentials: a bathmat, kettle, extension cords, stout brown boots in readiness for the snow that will, the forecasters say, be here any day now.

But she has, she sees now, no cups. Mugs. Anything to drink from. She considers the mall, the lights, the Muzak. Pulls her coat back on and drives, instead, toward Main Street. Her sense of the town becoming fuller now; which churches are most popular, where the kids go to smoke cigarettes, the locations where a cell phone signal is at its strongest and of the sad, skeletal factory buildings that lie out past "Old Essenville."

She parks by the gift shop.

Inside, the benevolent George Finer is busy with a customer. An angular middle-aged man in a padded jacket that says on the back: ESSUSP. He holds up a roadmap of Illinois.

"George, what I'm telling you is that because of a number of . . . uh . . . factors that I don't see the need to discuss right now, my trip to the state in question has now been canceled. So I just don't need this. And I'd appreciate my money back."

"But Don, you had me order it for you. No one else is going to want it."

The to and fro continues, but the moment George sees Lizbeth his weary features break into a smile. She gazes at the USP guard with the map. Wonders how he treats the inmates.

The guards are a constant here. A perennial current, forever passing through town to get coffee or a newspaper on their way to or from whichever facility they're payrolled at. And Lizbeth hears George give in. Agree to provide a full refund.

When the USP guard is gone she buys three mugs. Two with no slogan, just convict suit arrows running up them, a third that reads: *Essenville, PA—You Nail 'Em, We Jail 'Em.*

He exclaims as she tells him she's moved into town full time. Scribbles down his number and address.

"If you need anything," he says. "Ever. At all." And then he hesitates. Something stuck in his throat. "Miss Greene . . . I hope I'm not making an awful goof here . . . but if you haven't eaten lunch today, maybe you'd like to join me? The dippy eggs down at the Venus are something of a Pennsy legend . . ."

He doesn't move. Lizbeth keeps gazing up, examining him closer than she has before. Scans his face for a hint of the predatory. The look of a man in the throes of an advance. But she smiles at him and he smiles back and somehow she knows that's not the situation here.

With the yes hardly out of her mouth, he gives a Christmas morning grin of elation and steps out from behind the counter. Reaches for the Closed sign in the door.

Outside, half a dozen prisoners in yellow overalls are assembled on the shoulder at the far end of the street. Three guards watch over them, rifles cradled. ESSFCI, their jackets say. Male, minimum security. Each of the prisoners holds a refuse sack. Then an order is given, and they spread out across the grass and sidewalk. Start picking up trash. One can't be out of his teens; another looks like a grandparent. In seconds all six are bent double, never looking up, just filling their sacks.

"Once a week they take care of people's gardens," George says.

A bus rolls past, a passenger in every window. Headed out toward ESSUSP.

"Do they ever stop off in town?"

"The visitors? You know, not so much. I mean, people pass through. But I guess they tend not to announce themselves."

Lizbeth watches as the bus drifts on, its passengers facing front, eyes nowhere but the road ahead, while the inmates from ESSFCI keep busy with the litter.

When they get to the Venus Restaurant Diner, the place is already crowded. George finds a booth by the window. She watches his face as he settles in opposite. The stodgy features that will, she thinks, make sense on an old man. Will, by then, look sage.

As if in training for just that moment he says, with all necessary gravity: "Now, please trust me in what I'm about to do. You will thank me. I guarantee it." And he calls out to the nearest waitress: "Linda, honey, can we get dippy eggs twice?"

"What if I was allergic to eggs?" Lizbeth says.

"Then you'd be missing out on one of the most wonderful experiences of your life."

He shakes his head. Breathes in, breathes out.

"So, here we are. Me and Lizbeth Greene." His voice lowers. "It's funny, I keep catching people looking over here. They all know who you are."

"Well, they must all think I'm someone else."

"Oh, please."

"Really, I'm a lot less famous than I thought. You know, right as I was checking out of my hotel today this guy came up to me in the lobby . . . and he was asking how I was doing and saying how weird it was that he'd run into me here . . . and I was just getting ready to sign a book or an autograph or what have you when his face turned sour and he said Ken still missed me, and did I know I'd really done a number on him? Turns out he thought I dated his brother in Scranton fifteen years ago."

"Oh, no. That's awful. I just hope you don't think they put Stupid in the water down here. Ha! Listen to me. The man who sells T-shirts that say Alacatraz Is for Wimps."

Lizbeth cranes forward and peers down George Finer's shirt front.

"Actually, I think you have one of those on."

He checks, and then he groans. "Laundry day. Although I guess as an Essenvillian I can at least say I'm being civic minded."

She catches his eye across the booth. "You know, I heard you guys had a pretty rough time . . . before the prisons . . ."

"Oh, well . . . I kind of missed the worst of it . . ."

But he sees that she's curious. So he sighs, and leans forward: "When I was a kid, the town was all about rubber. That was what came out of here. What we were here for. Everywhere else for six counties was mines, but we were different. I mean, in reality, half of what we made was conveyor belts for the coal and tires for the shuttle cars . . . but we always *felt* like we were different. Like *Sesame Street*, you know? *One of these kids is doing their own thing.* Anyway, I left here in '82, and I came back in '91, and in the meantime it had all just disappeared. Shut down. Every last factory gone. Half the stores on Main Street were boarded up. There'd been a bowling alley right across the street from here—the Double J Strike-O-Rama—that was like the center of the universe. It was burned down for the insurance. While I was away I knew things were bad, that the mines were all closing, but . . . I guess I thought because we made rubber it wouldn't catch up with us. That we could get by without them. Asinine, I know. And, of course . . . well, I'm not a bowler personally but the best way I can put it to you is, you know how sometimes you'll see the ball hurtle down the lane and it'll slam right into the pins and they'll all go down except one . . . and it looks like that one is okay . . . but then, sure enough, it starts to wobble, and then it wobbles some more, and then finally it goes down too. That was Essenville. We wobbled on our own for a while there, and then we went down too—"

He pauses as the waitress reappears, laying down two plates of eggs sunny side up with home fries and buckwheat cakes. "Two dippies," she says. "Enjoy."

A picture of skepticism, Lizbeth ducks her fork into the yolk. Lifts it to her mouth.

"*Oh, my God,*" she says. "That is . . . so good."

"Isn't it?"

"Oh, my God . . . that's incredible."

She's not just being polite. Eagerly, she piles up a forkful of eggs and potato. George just smiles. Then he picks up the story. "I mean, they tried a lot of stuff. We had a billion different companies saying they wanted to set up here. They were going to build private jets, monster trucks. There was going to be a casino complex, a brewery, a racetrack. It was all hooey. People just kept leaving. What's now my gift shop was my mom's dry cleaners that was maybe six months from going bust. Then we found out the Department of Corrections wanted a site for a new supermax."

He takes a sip of water to wash down his own food.

"We were in competition with eleven other towns from across the state. So we put together a fundraising drive to buy up seven hundred and fifty acres of private land five miles northeast of us, and we donated it to the DOC. Got the contract. Now that land is USP Essenville. A year and a half down the line they'd built the others. And what they gave life to is the town you see before you. It was magical. Suddenly there were jobs . . . construction jobs, administrative jobs, jobs for guards . . . so many jobs for guards. More young families setting up home here every day. Brand-new houses. Condos. We'd never had condos before. We'd wake each morning to the wondrous sound of bulldozers and jackhammers. Now there's the golf course, the mall . . . the Bowlodrome. And down here in town we have stores open for business and sightseers that pass through who maybe stop in at mine and buy a mug and a T-shirt and pay for these delicious eggs—"

"Y'uns good over here, George?"

The waitress beams down at their table. He frowns like he's giving the question serious thought. Then: "Yes, Linda," he says. "I think we are."

She has Tuesdays, Thursdays and Fridays.

From now on one hour on each of these days has been set aside by Warden Michael Sosa to allow Lizbeth to meet with and interview Wilson Ulysses Velez. The warden has, he's told her, vouched for her at the highest levels of the DOC. He hoped, he said, she understood the significance of that.

She said she did.

Now she sits in the lawyer's room, and waits for Wilson Velez. There is, on the table by her notebook, a tape recorder. Walkman-style with a clear plastic window through which she can see the tape. Tape: a relic now. But dependable. Physical.

The door is opened.

As he's led inside he nods at her. Sits, hands together, legs spread.

She loses track of how long she just stares at him.

"How's your throat?"

"Betterr. Thank you for . . . the honey . . . I guess the warden mustt really like you."

Lizbeth reaches for the tape recorder.

"Do you mind if I switch this on?"

"I thoughttt . . . that was the point."

"Right," she says, but before she hits the button she pauses. "Oh. I meant to ask you—did you think of a name you wanted to use for the book? For *Monsters*?"

"I did. I wantt it to be . . . Jim Rockford."

"Wait. Like . . . *The Rockford Files*?"

"Verry good."

"You watched that show?"

"Whenever I could, you know? James Garner wasss a funny dude, you know?"

"I totally agree. My sister and I used to love that show."

"Well," he says, "it must have . . . been a show for re—mar—ka—ble peoppppple."

"I guess it must. Okay, Wilson, I'll pass the message on." Then she hesitates. "I'm glad everything was finally settled with the book . . . your book. You must be pleased. Are you . . . pleased?"

"Sure. I'm . . . ppppleased."

"Good. Then we're both pleased. Okay—" She presses Record. "So, what I'd like to do is just try and get a core of information down on tape . . . I guess I'd like that to be the format of these meetings . . . at least at first . . . to try and establish an overview of your life, and then revisit specific events . . . if that sounds okay . . . ?"

"Sssure."

"Great. So, I understand you were born in—"

"I wasss born in Panama. My vvvillage was . . . called Nolteros. It was a few milesss outside of Penonomé . . ." He trails off. Stares around the room.

"And what do you remember about—"

"Nolteros. It was like the very last point of . . . the counttttry . . . Attt the edge of the city, *sabes*? There was no water. No electricittty. We liveddd in a *bohio*. A hut, you know? It was strange . . . onnn . . . one side of us there was cornffields and grass that came uppp to your neck . . . but on the other you could look dddown the hill and see the . . . gas stations andd the buses on the Interamericana Highwway . . . like between two worldds, you know?"

He falls silent again. Then: "But I leftt there when I wass . . . very young. My memory of it is . . . hazy. A lot is probably . . . justt stuff I was tolddd afterward."

"Could you tell me something about your family? Your parents?"

"What would . . . you like to know?"

"Their names?"

"My father's name wwwas . . . Julio Velez. He was a drunk . . . and a *cabron*. Violentttt. Lazy. When he was sober enough he workedddd driving his shitty truck around Penonomé. Sometimesss . . . he would be in a bar there and get a jjjob driving to El Valle or Colón or Panama City. He'd be gone for ddays then come back with whatever money he had left. My mother's name was Nina. She wass a drunk too. My brother's name was Eduardo. He wass two yearrrs older than me."

"Was two years older?"

"He's dead nnnow."

"I'm sorry . . . I didn't know."

"It's okay. No probllllem."

"But I read you grew up in Queens? In Corona?"

"Sure. But ffffirst we were in Flushing. We left Panama . . . in '76. I had just turneddd five years old. We came to America and got a . . . place in Flushing."

"Okay. How did that happen?"

"From what . . . IIII know . . . my fatherr had been drinkinggg in Colón when he met this guy from Queens. René somebody. You know, I don't even remember his surname. He owned a sweatshopp on 39th Avenue. The kind of place no one knows isss even there unless they work there. It made shirtts and bedclothes. Tablecllloths for the—Italian restaurants down the block. Anyway, I ggguess they arranged together that the family woulddd move to New York anddd work there . . . and in trade we ggot this *jacal* apartment on Linneaus Place."

"I'm not sure I know where that is."

"No one ever did. Even in Flushinggg no one had ever heard of it. It was this alley lllike a horseshoe . . . a U-bend thattt came off—Prince above 35th. We had two rooms in the bbback of a rowhouse. I remember thatt the asphalt in the street was full of holes andd there were no lights out there so you would always . . . twist your ankle if you went out at night. No storm drainssss either so people always got flooded out. The place we were in wasn't heatedddd properly and the plumbing was all fucked up . . . I remember our mother screaming at our father when we firsst arrived, saying why had we come all thissss . . . way to live in a ppplace that was justt like Nolteros only freezing cold? And she was right . . . but then, outssside those two rooms everything was differenttttt . . . more different than I had evvver imagined was even possible. But you know, I got used to it all pretty quick. Kids lllearn fast."

"Did you speak English?"

"Sure. Our father had good English. He always had a hard-on for America, *sabes*? He woulddd come . . . back from Panama City or Colón and there would be magazines in his truckk. American magazines. I would look at the pictures and then at the words and that's how I learned to read."

"So as soon as you came to Queens both your parents worked at the sweatshop?"

"Right. Our fffather drove a delivery ttruck, and our mother . . . worked at the sewing machines . . . and my brother and I, we worked there too."

"Wait . . . when you were . . ."

"We workeddd as soon as we got there. I think that haddd always been the deal. That my father wouldd bring four pairs of hands to—work in exchange for those two shitty rooms in Flushinggg."

"My God . . . What did you have to do?"

"Mostly we workeddddd at night. Sometimes when there wasss a big order being filled we would bringgg coffee to the women on the machines. They would be working twenty-four-hour shifts, so without thatttt they would startttt to doze and their fingerssss would slip and they'd get blood on the fabric. Otherwise, we were only there when the place was—empty. We pppacked up the bedclothes and the tablecloths. Collected loose thread from inside the machiness and from the floor. Cleaned up the machines. Ittt needed someone . . . small. We were like two invisible children, workinggg in this invisible place . . ."

"And you'd sleep in the day?"

"Right. We had a bed made up in the corner . . . of the kitchen. My brother woulddd get so mad with me because I would . . . getttt out of bed and piss in the corner. Like an animal. I don'ttt know why. But I remember one time he pulledd back the flooring where I'ddd pissed, this cheap green . . . vinyl. It wasn't even tacked down. And the whole floor was lined with newspapers and—comics and pages torn outtt from books. That was the insulation. There wouldd be four pages from one story and a page of another and three pages of another . . . so we pulled them out and we would read what we could . . . which at the start was jjjjust a handful of words . . . but we would take what we could understand and out of that we'd carry them on ourselves . . . we'd take these little ppieces of stories and make them into something of our own."

"What were they about?"

"Oh, everything. I remember we had the first six pages of some science-fiction thing, you know, spaceships and shit. Then there wassss like a third-grade history book aboutttt the Incas. That one had a—a lot of pictures. We loved thattt Inca shit. We thought we *were* Incas, *sabes?* Then there wasss a spy thing. About Russians. And there was some stuff in there about codes, you know, so after thatt we got into makinggg up codes of our own . . . putting numbers in ppplace of words . . . so we could warn each other if—our mother came in dddrunk or our father looked like he wanted to let off some anger . . ."

"Did that happen a lot?"

"Sure. Of course. I got my jaw broke inssside a week of coming to New York."

He starts to glaze over, staring past her; and she tries to reel him back in.

"Did you have any school at this point?"

". . . We were at PS19 on Roosevelt. But we only really started to go . . . after my father left."

"And that was . . . ?"

"Maybe a year after we gggot there . . . a year and a half, I'm not sss-sure . . . anyway, he'd pretty much stopped showing up for—work or coming back to Linneaus Place . . . My brother and I would see him in the neighborhood, and he was . . . always drunk and with differenttt women. Then one day he . . . was gone. And somehow we justtt knew he wasn't coming back. My mother never ssspoke of . . . it, but some people saidd he'd gone to California with another woman. Other people said he'd made another man's wife pregnant and they . . . cuttt off his balls and threw him in the river by tttthe Triborough Bridge. Anyway we . . . never saw him again. And soon after that—we moveddd out of Flushing and into Corona. Xenia Street. This place belongedd . . . to René too, but it wasssss nicer. Still small but lllllike a real apartment, *sabes*? My brother and III . . . had a room tttto ourselves. And you know whatt else? My mother was now a U.S. citizen. René had friends dddown at the INS, you know? So me and my brother, now we were citizens too."

"Wilson . . . I hope this isn't too intrusive a question . . . but was your mother . . ."

"Sure. Of course. Why else would René have tttreated us that way? And that was fine. Now we had hot water and we dddidn't have to spend our nighttts over on 39th Avenue. After a while she pppretty much moved in with him fffull time, so we jjust . . . stayed there on our own . . ."

"You and your brother? On Xenia Street?"

He glazes over again and this time can't be brought back. She repeats, "On Xenia Street?" five times in a row. And then, abruptly:

"Rightt. Just me and him."

"How old were you then?"

143

"I guess . . . eight or nine."

"But how did you live?"

"We got . . . by. Our mother came by and gavvve us a few dollars. If something needed fixing we'd tell her and someone would come fix it. She just didn'tt want us living with her. But thattttt was okay. Now we coulddd make Corona our own." He stares at her from across the table. "You know Corona?"

"Well . . . I've been through it . . . obviously . . . I don't know that I've ever been there on foot."

"Ah, okay. It's just from the wayyy you were nodding when I was talk-inggg, I thought you must know it."

"No . . . I don't know it."

"Oh, you don't know it. Okay. Well . . . anyway, back ttthen I would gggo on the subway and journey all over the city. I was an adventurous kid, you know? And there were places all over that I loved . . . Coney Is-land, Pelham Bay—Park. I would ggggo to Manhattan and just the feel of life there would make my head spin out. That's why I put the monsters there, *sabes*? So much lllife in every direction. But I—I loved Corona most of all. I would ggget off the Seven ttrain again and the Unisphere would be watching over me and even the *air* tasteddd better. Because it was my air. My soul made iiiinto bricks and sidewalks. I would hear the planes coming into LaGuardia and to me it wasss like the sound of heaven. To be a kid in that neighborhood back then, it was ssspecial, you know? The Italians were moving out and in their ppplace were Dominicans, Salvadoreans, Ec-uadorians, Ricansss . . . it seemed like now every house had santos in the window, plastic flowers and candles . . . and the goombahs, they gave us shit, they harassed us and beat us, but we kids hungggg . . . together andd helped each otherrr. They calleddd us *perros perdidos*. Stray dogs. And if ever my brother and I were hungry ttthen Father Raymond Peres ddown on Van Cleef Street wouldd give us fruit and . . . condensed milk. From the goodnessss in his heart, okay? He was no fucking pervert, okay? Make sure you understand that."

"Of course. I understand." Lizbeth lets a moment pass before she con-tinues. "Can I ask you . . . the kids you were hanging out with . . . None of you had real homes? Families?"

"They all hadddd . . . families. But we all still hung outtt. The cops, they hated us. Picked on us, you know?"

"But did you . . ."

"Did we break a law sometimes? Well . . . sometimes even with the money from our mother and Father Peres's kindness we still needed food . . . and sometimes we needed clothes, or sodas or comic books."

"So you took stuff from stores?"

"Sometimes. Other . . . timesssss maybe five of us would go down intttto the subway and pick pockets. That's how I gottt my . . . name. Ardilla. It means squirrel."

"I know."

"Oh, you know that," he says. "I'm sorry. Well, this is how I gottt it. I was small back then, even for . . . my age. And so agile! So as soon as someone on tttthe platform noticed whatt was happening or a coppp saw us, I woulddddd run back to the street up the handrail of tttthe stairway, balanced there, *sabes,* and escape under the bbarriers. That's . . . why they callled me Ardilla."

She leans forward to check the tape's still rolling.

"Otherwise they calleddddddd me . . . Three Vee. From my inittttials, you know?"

She looks back up and he's staring at her.

"Didd you have a nickname when . . . you were younger, Lizbeth?"

"No. Not really."

"Not . . . really?"

"Not like you had one. Not one that everyone used."

"But you . . . haddd one?"

"My sister had a name for me. She called me Albino. Because I was always so pale."

"Ah! So, here we are. Ardilla and Albino. And what's *she* . . . called? Your sister?"

"Mame."

"Mame. And are you . . . clllose?"

"You know . . . we're sisters."

"And you're ffffrom . . . Danbury, righttt?"

"Well, we lived there a while. But only because my father's company relocated."

"So you weren't . . . born there? In Connecticut?"

"No, I was born in Connecticut. In Bristol. The Bell City. We stayed there until I was six."

Wilson Velez nods, and the tape rolls on.

"So," Lizbeth says, "this was how the gang got started? Picking pockets on the subway?"

"Nah. There wassss no . . . *clica* back then. We were just kids. None of usss even knew any *cholo*, any gangster, until Luis Palomo. And he was nothinggg special. Just some fucking druggg dealer with a spot on the corner of Apex Place. But he dressed cool, and we knew not tttto fuck with him. Then one day in springtime I'm walkingggg . . . south of the LIE and he calls out to me and says, 'Hey! Ardilla! You want to make—some money? Take this bag down to Elmhurst.' A brown paper bag . . . you know? So I didddd. And he gave me ten dollars and the next dday I took another bag up to Junction Boulevard and this . . . time he gave me twenty. Anddd from then on all through that summer I worked for him. Taking bags one place . . . picking them up from somewhere else."

"And how did you feel about that?"

"Are you . . . kiddingg? I felt great."

"Because you . . . felt like you belonged?"

"Becaussse I hadd money. Now I could drink and buy comics and cigarettes and Luis would give me enough *yerba* so when I wanted to get high I got high. But the bestt thing about . . . workingggg for him was that he gottt me a bike to do my deliveries. I never hadddd a bike before, you know, and this thing was high . . . class. Beautiful. Plus I wasss just starting to getttt . . . interested in pussy."

He lets the word hang there.

"When you were nine?"

"Ten. By now I was ten. And you know, I . . . didn'tt even know what I was meant to . . . dddo with it. I just knew I wanted some. And with me being so smalllll, you know, no *hina* was ever going tttto give it up. But with Luis I gott to go to parties every nightt—"

"Parties?"

"Sure. *Bailes*. Over at his place on Radcliff Avenue."

He leans toward her. "Do you like . . . parties, Lizbeth?"

"When I was younger, sure. Not as young as you, obviously."

"Whatt music do you like?"

"Reggae. I like reggae."

"Ah . . . reggae mmusic. Like the guy in your books. Okay. You know, they love reggae music in Panama?"

"I didn't know that."

"Well . . . that's what they tell me." He clears his throat; a noisy and protracted process.

"So how long were you living like this?"

"Oh, a few months, *sabes*?"

"Did your brother work for this guy Luis too?"

"A little bit. My brother was getting to be kinddd of a flake though."

"And were you going to school?"

"Sometimes. But it was . . . strange because I'dddd be there with kidds my own age and . . . at nightt I was with people ten years older."

He clears his throat again.

"You know . . . the firsttt person I shot was eighteen?"

"No. I didn't know that."

"Sure. His name was Juan . . . Alba. People called him Boost. He had owed Luis two hundred dollars for maybe a month. So one night everyone was talkinggg about him and someone . . . saiddd he needed to be embarrassed, right? Like he was embarrassing Luis. And someone else said 'What abouttt baby *cholo*? Squirrel?' They were all laughingg . . . but Luis, he came over and putt a gun in my hands. A .38. I remember itt was so big I haddd to use both—handddds to hold it. The next day he drove me up to 95th Street where—Boost hung outt. Saw him there on hisssss own. So Luis pulled over . . . and I got outtt of the car and walkked upp to this kid . . . anddd my fucking hands were shaking so bad I thoughttt I was going to drop the gun, *sabes*? So he turns aroundd . . . and sees me and he starts laughingg . . . I guess I must have looked kind of stupid, with this— *cuete* that was bigger than my two hands . . . So then I shot him in his belly."

"How did that make you feel?"

"I justt remember the gun felt so hot in my handss afterward and all I could think . . . was . . . that I couldn't drop it because then Luis would get mad. And I guess Boost must have been screaminggg but I was concentratingg so hard on not dropping the . . . gun that I don't even remember hearing him."

"How about afterward? When you were on your own?"

"Afterward, it made me throw up. But at the same time I felt so ppppproud. We heard that Boost was goinggg to be in the hospital for a month and that night Luis threw a parttty . . . and everyone there was sayinggg Squirrel is a man now. And this *hina* Annette Muniz . . . she was seventeen . . . she took me into the bbbathroom and we haddd a little fun."

"You lost your virginity?"

He hesitates. "I guess I—did. Anyway . . . people treatedddd me like a king for the next couple of days. Then Luis said . . . he wantedd me to do the same thingg again with this *vato* Tico Quesada who wassss selling *chiva* up in North Beach. Heroin, you know? Andddddd we all knew he was a true fucking *cholo, sabes*? But Luis said it was okay, we'd hittt him when he was by himself. So we drove out in the morningg anddddd waited and fucking sure enough the moment comes when there's no one else in sightt. Only when I . . . gett out of the car with the gun five of his fucking *clica* come around the . . . cornerrr. So I go to turn backkkk, but Luis is already driving away. Foot on the gas and . . . gggggone."

"Oh, my God. Did they—"

"They ssssssaw me. I ran but I caught a bullet in my thigh. Woke upppp the next day in the hospital in more . . . pppain than I'd ever felt in my life. Later that same morning the cops came and said they knew that—I'd shot Boost. I went straight from there to juvi. Spofford Juvenile Detention Center. In the Bronx, *sabes*? It was November 1981. My first bitch. First time I heard metal doors slam on me. But I was alive. So I guess nothing was so badd, huh?"

He rises. "That'ss enough for one . . . day. My throat is still . . . sore."

"I'm sorry. I didn't realize."

"That's the kind of thingg you wantt, right?"

"Sure. I mean, that was . . . fascinating."

He nods and then he moves toward the door. Shouts through to the guards that he's done. And when they're in and on either side of him, he looks down at her.

"You ever thoughttt about changing your . . . hair color, Lizbeth?"

She stares up, thrown. "Not lately. Why do you say that?"

"I justttt . . . think maybe you might look better with a lighter shade. Something softter. You wear so much black all the time . . . it makes you look kind of . . . severe."

As the tape shuts off he calls back to her: "Just somethingg," he says, "for you to think about."

Next time she comes with the regular visitors. Arrives at the prison when they do. Before interviewing Wilson, she'll see the visiting room in use. Then she'll tour the rest of the prison.

After another dinner (this time with Joan Sosa's parents in attendance), she told the warden she had to. That the book would be nothing without that insight.

The most senior CO in the place will be her guide. He shakes her hand at the visitor's entrance. Tells her his name is CO Brink.

Once she's through her own searches and rigmarole, she watches the others who follow her. Some emerging from cars, dented old stagers, others from the bus. Here at the end of journeys begun in distant states a day or two days or three days before. Mostly women. Wives, pulling their wedding bands off for the metal detector; the occasional girlfriend, their numbers thinned out by the years. Mothers. Many mothers.

Two minutes in, a drawn, fiftyish woman in a windbreaker and jeans is pulled aside and led into the canvas booth at the side of the metal detectors.

The rest wait barefoot for their shoes to be inspected.

"You'd be amazed what people try and get in here," Brink says.

One hour twice a week is set aside for regular visitors. There is an average waiting period of fourteen weeks for each visit to be approved.

The visitor's room could pass for a high school gym. Thirty pairs of facing seats set out in five rows of six, ceiling-high Plexiglas dividing them, perforated to allow audible speech. Twenty guards are already stationed round the walls, dressed in full riot gear as the visitors pass by. Until finally everyone's seated, and the place is silent. Then the inmates are led in.

Lizbeth gazes at them as they file through in handcuffs, a tottering line of orange jumpsuits. One guard for every three of them. Still more batons and rifles. Some trying to strut, others hunched and faltering. But all with the same stricken eyes.

Sinking in quicksand. Almost under now.

Her hand finds her belly, and she leaves it there.

The inmates find their visitors. Guards at the end of each row.

At some points of the room, neither the inmate nor their visitor speaks. One seat along, both might be talking at the same time, fervent words spilling into and over each other. Elsewhere the visitors might have their hands pressed to the Plexiglas, solemn and unmoving. But the inmates' cuffs mean they can't reciprocate.

She turns to Brink and makes sure her voice is flat as she says that she's ready to see the rest of the facility.

Wilson Ulysses Velez stares across the table, and the tape recorder is already on.

"So, last time we talked, we got as far as your first time in—"

"Spofford. Rightttt. They gave me a two-year bitch in Spofford. I did fourteen months. That pppplace was a dungeon. Like a hundred years old, you know? I thought I was going to die inside there. Every kid there was older . . . tthan me. Bigger than me. There was . . . war every day. But that was nothing. I would fight as nasty as I had to fight. It was . . . having no one there to ttttalk with. And . . . hearing thattt metal door. I never cried, not once, butttt . . . on the inside I was weeping."

"Did anyone visit you? Your brother or—"

"Sure. And Father Peres too. He came once a week with books. Not religious stuff . . . stuff that would help with my schooling or that was justtt fun. They let pretty much anythingggg into Spofford. I guess they thought no one there could read."

His gaze narrows as he stares at her. "Lizbeth, I need to—ask you a fffavor. It is of ggreat importance to me. Please, I beg you, can you ttttalk to Warden Sosa about me being permitteddd to meet with Father Peres? Or even just to write him? It wouldddd mean so much if I could jjjust write one letter to him."

"I . . . I could mention it to him. I guess . . . Has your lawyer not spoken with him about it?"

"Of course. But they will never let me have any contacttt with anyone from Corona. If you were to ask them on my behalfff, though . . . Lizbeth, it would mean so much to me."

"I doubt it. But . . . sure . . . I can ask . . ." She stares back. "Have you been getting mail from—"

"The Christian Ladies of Westttttern Arizona. Sure. And it is nice to be written to. But at the same ttttime . . . not to sound like I am ungrateful but . . . sometimes I don't know if they're writing to me or just some *vato* from Panama doing life in USP Essenville . . . *sabes*?"

"How about your mom?"

"Huh?"

"Did she visit you in Spofford?"

"Nah. Her and René, they were down in Florida a llllot now. He had a place in Miami. I mean, she talked to the social workers aboutttt me and said she was living with us and that she was sorry and everythingg would be okay . . . but then she went back tto the sunshine . . ."

"And you went back to Xenia Street?"

"Right. But my brother wasn't around so much anymore. He was seeing this *hina* Christina up in Jackson Heights, so he would usually be out all night. But that was okay . . . By now I thoughtt I was a man, you know? *El mas chingon.* So thattt was . . . nothing. Then I found out I really *was* a man."

"I'm . . . not sure I know what you mean."

"It turns out the *hina* I had been—with the nightttt before I got shot . . . Annette . . . she had gotten pregnant. First time I hadddd . . . even kisseddd a girl and . . . *Boom.*" He shifts his weight in his chair. Re-settles. "She'd lost it though. I guess it was not . . . tttto be. But what I also heard was that Luis Palomo haddd been seeing Annette too and was mad at me for what me and her had done, and that'ssss . . . why he took me to get—killed."

"Was that true?"

"Who knows? I . . . I guess it makesss a nice story. Personally, I think . . . he just ffigured if thinggs went well he could get ridd of Tico and if not then it wass only Squirrel who would be gone. Like I was ex-pendable, *sabes*? But that was okay. Soon he . . . lost his business."

"What do you mean?"

"He came to harm. Physically. Andddd he . . . lostt his business."

"You harmed him physically?"

"He came to harm. That's how I'd puttt it. He came to harm with a two-foot lead pipe. And then he lost his business. Andddd the . . . funny thing was not one of his ffriends defended him or even stayed at his sssside. He didn't have one true *camarada.*"

"What did it feel like to attack him like that?"

"Well . . . I guess if *someone* was to do something like that . . . then what they would say to you is that mostt people have it in them to throw a pppunch or swing a bat or maybe even a leadddd . . . pipe. But that once they've swungggg it a few times their anger dies and . . . they see the per-son they are violating and think of them with their kidddds or at their jjjob. But then some people jjjjust see all the shit they ever took from the worlddd . . . so even when the other person's face is pulp and . . . everyone around is screamingg they keep swardinggg that pipe . . . they swing and they swing and keep swinging."

"How badly did you beat him?"

He doesn't answer.

"How badly was he beaten?"

"He livedd. But he wasss in a wheelchair. He was pretty . . . fucked up. There was some—brain damage. A few months later he killed himself."

The tape rolls on.

"So then you took over his business . . ."

"Right. I took over his spot on Apex Place . . . I sold some *yerba,* some blow. Some *chiva.*"

"Sure."

"But I never diddd that shit. I saw the *tecatos* come around, *sabes,* and that was enough to know never to touch it. No crack either. I justttt smoked *yerba.*"

He stretches out his neck. "Do you smoke *yerba,* Lizbeth? When you're listeninggg to reggae music?"

Her eyes dart up to the camera. "No, Wilson. I don't. I mean, I used to . . . a little . . . when I was younger. But not now."

"Oh, not now. Okay. I see. So . . . anyway . . . I guess you coulddd sssay . . . thatt was how the *clica* got started. By now I had a name around Corona . . . but I still needed strength at my back . . . and the kids I'd hung with when we were *perros perdidos,* they were olddder now. More capable. So I gathereddd up the ones that I knew I could count on."

"How did you know who they were?"

"You jjjust know. You jjust know who is real and who's not. It's nottt . . . even something you think about. So there wasss Hurricane—José Almanza. As wide as he was—tall. Not fat. Just big, *sabes?* Then there was Ignacio Solis from 59th Avenue. I called him Ojos. Eyes. He knew every-thing that was going down, everywhere, every hour of the day and night—"

"Wait. Ojos is—"

"Right. Ojos is who I sentttt the letters to. The letters I am here for. You want to talk about that shit now, or letttt me carry on with whatttt you asked me about first?"

"I'm sorry. I just wanted to make sure I had the right . . . details."

"So, now you know you do." He takes a breath. "And of course there wasssss my brother . . . he could be a pppain in the ass but—we would still have diedddd for each other. And I used the name Sacred Incan Royals be-cause that was what we had calledddd ourselves back in Linneaus Place, *sabes?* So right at the start I guess it was us four andddd—from there we picked uppppp another six kids that we knew were a hundred percent reliable in every situation, and those were the first—Royals. Other kids would come to us wanting to join but back then it was jjjjust us. Exclusive."

"And then?"

"Then we jjust looked out for each other, *sabes*? Watched each other's backs."

"But you were still selling—"

"We sold what we sold and we made thatttttt corner our own. And sometimes thatt needed hands to be lifteddd up in anger. But I didn'ttt want itt to only be about that. I wantedddddd it to be something more."

He looks down at the tape recorder as he talks.

"You know, I remember the day we each gottt our ink done. All ten of us went uppp to this . . . tattoo artist that worked out of the back of a discount electronics ssstore on 104th Street . . . and each of us hadddd the same thing put on our chests . . . a crown insside a sun with the numbers 19.9.18 beneath it. From the code me and my brother had used as kids. 19.9.18. S.I.R., *sabes*? And we all came out of there laughingggg like crazy, because it hurtttt real bad but none of us wantedddd to let the others know we felt it . . . and that nightttt we threw whiskey on the tattoos and drank the rest and ate *yucca con chicharrón* and watched Roberto Duran fightttt live from Madison Square Garden. Fists of stone, right? *Manos de piedra*. And thattttt is what they called me too . . . because although I—I wasss so small I could put a kid a foot taller than me down with one punch . . ."

She's about to speak when she realizes his eyes are full of tears.

"I'm sorry," he says.

"No, please . . . do you need anything?"

"No," he says, and he blinks until his eyes are clear again. "It's just hardddd for me to think about that life. Memory is a bitch ssssometimes. Anyway . . . with a spray can I puttt the— . . . name Sacred Incan Royals everywhere in Corona, and with my heart I madddddde sure no one woulddd ever take what was ours."

"The business?"

"Not just that. Not jjjjust that. Although, sure, I will not—lie to you . . . that was part of ittt. I told you, having money wasssss nice. You know, we even had this *vato* Ruben who drove us around Queens in his '58 Impala . . . like it wasss a private taxi. That was fun." He stares over the table. "So, what kind of car do you have, Lizbeth?"

"Back home, I have an SUV. I have dogs. I need something big for them.

But here . . ." She stalls. The next words heavy on her tongue. "Here I've been driving a Porsche."

"A Porsche? *Hijole!* I would nottttt have—guessed that . . ."

"Oh, really . . . why not?"

"To be honest? A Porsche . . . to me . . . thatttt is what a business guy from Westchester drives on his way ttttto his office . . . to make him feel like somewhere at the back of his closet he mighttt possibly maybe still have a pair of balls . . . it just doesn't seem like you. *Sabes?*"

"I guess I was just curious to drive one . . ."

"Oh, you were curious. Okay."

Seconds pass.

"So . . . you know, everything we have been talking aboutttt . . . this was all happeninggg at the same . . . tttttime as City Slicker."

"Right. I guess it must have been."

"One of the kidssss we knew back then . . . Freddy Linares fffrom Saultell Avenue . . . it was his cousin who wassss killed. Gabriela. She was a few years older than us . . . I can barely even recall what she looked like. But I remember her family crying outt in the ssstreet when they found the body like I'm watching them now." He catches her eye. "So tell me, Lizbeth, what is it like where you live? What'ss the name of tthe place again?"

"Quince Hill."

"Right. Quince Hill. So tttttell me about . . . Quince Hill."

"It's nice. I live a mile or so outside town. It's pretty much just woods. It's not too far from where I grew up."

"Bristol? Or Danbury?"

"Bristol. You know, we really weren't in Danbury too long. We left after my mother died."

"I'm sorry. Thattt was dumb of me to . . . bbring uppp."

"It's fine. I just don't remember a lot about the place."

"Diddd you go back to—"

"Bristol. Yeah, for a while. Then my father changed jobs, and we moved to New Haven. A couple of years later he met a woman there and got remarried."

"Mussstt have been difficult . . . for you, I mean."

"Not really. I was kind of messed up when I was a kid . . . but she was actually a very good-hearted woman. She died twelve years ago. Cancer."

"But your . . . father is stttill alive?"

"Right. He has Alzheimer's. He's in a nursing home."

"I'm sorry to hear thatttt, Lizbeth."

"My sister's taken most of the strain. She's moved him around with her for the last few years. It's been a lot harder for her than me."

"Lizbeth, can III ask you a questttion?"

"Sure."

"Do you stttill think about your mother?"

"Sure. Of course. Every day." A beat. "Just maybe not the way people think I do."

"Oh? And how isss that?"

"I don't know . . . I just think people assume it's this unbearable burden that I never found out who did it. And it was. That's true. For a long time, it was. It got jammed inside my head. But it's like . . . when you stare at something that long, it just blurs up. And the older I got, the more it felt like it didn't matter anyway. What difference would it make? Knowing who killed her? She'd still be gone. So when I think about her now, I'm not thinking of some unsolved murder. I'm thinking of my mother."

"But you still like to live around there? Where it happened—"

"I'm comfortable there. It feels like where I should be." She leans forward to check the tape. "Anyway . . . you were telling me about the first few years of the gang."

"Righttt. So . . . I guess in a lot of ways those were the best years too. The most fun. But then I got sentt back to Spofford. And from there things moveddd to a whole new level."

He seemed, at the very moment he finished speaking, to lose his train of thought. Sat motionless and silent, staring past me. His mouth hung open. Even now, this still happened every few minutes, a strange and uneasy punctuation to our meetings. After a while, I learned there was only so much to be gained by repeating the question. You just had to wait until he came back from wherever he was, whether that took a second, or five, or ten, or sixty.

Lizbeth lifts her hands from the keyboard and reads back what she's written.

The house feels more like hers now. Finally warm. Tea and fruit beside her on the kitchen table where she's working.

This is the night after his fourth interview. She has been in Essenville almost two weeks.

It's late, and she's been writing most of the evening, but she won't stop now. She's in flight. A routine has been established. Nights spent trawling her notes, listening back to the interviews, typing up their contents, blending them on screen, blocks of text to be set in order, crafted, sculpted. She looks over the transcripts piled beside her, gravitates toward those quotes already highlighted, sips her tea and her fingers drub the keys again.

Then, eventually, he found his mental place again, talking at length of how he used his second imprisonment in Spofford to bring to life his idea of the gang—the clica—*as more than just a vehicle for low-level street crime and thuggery.*

He was serving a twelve-month sentence for battery after a Dominican cocaine dealer attempted to take over his spot on Apex Place. But this time, he said: "I didn't cry even on the inside. I just let the guards take me to my cell and I fought when I needed to fight and I spent as many hours as I could each day writing."

With paper and pens brought to him by Father Peres, Wilson got to work. But he wasn't simply killing time. His was as serious in intent as any literary project could be. If the fledgling Sacred Incas were to survive without being preyed on by adult rivals, he knew he would need the very smartest of plays—a way of expanding their numbers while cementing his own authority.

What he emerged with was his manifesto. It was, he told me, just a first draft. Sloppy. But it already contained the central themes that would transform the Royals from a bunch of delinquent kids selling black tar heroin in a Queens alleyway to the fastest growing gang in the country.

Written in the extravagant language of comic books, it told its readers to take pride in their heritage as "spiritual descendants of the mighty Inca" and draw strength from their collective power—to "rise above those who would seek to destroy you through the embrace of the Royal beside you." For many young Hispanics in early '80s Corona, frequently harassed by those Italian teenagers who remained in the neighborhood and eager for their own sense of identity, the message would prove hugely seductive.

On his release, however, the first thing he had to deal with was more prosaic—returning to Xenia Street, he found his apartment being boarded up. René had sold out. He had, Wilson learned, abandoned New York—his own apartment, the sweatshop—to settle permanently in Miami. Nina Velez had left with him.

With his brother, Eduardo, staying with a girlfriend back in Flushing, Wilson was obliged to spend the next few days sleeping on couches and floors until the tenant of a cramped apartment above a 47th Avenue pet store was persuaded to sublet to him.

But down on Apex Place, things came together instantly. Reassuming his old spot—safeguarded along with his drug connection by José "Hurricane" Almanza—Wilson put the word out he was now accepting new members. And, by the following morning, a steady procession of applicants was filing across the Long Island Expressway to the shabby corner where their new leader would hand them a manifesto from the batch he'd just had photocopied at the copy shop on Calloway Street. Come back tomorrow, he would tell them. Make sure you've read this. Be ready to do whatever is asked of you.

They did. In the months that followed that procession became an explosion—one fueled by a grasp of marketing that would have served the adolescent boy wielding it well in the chrome and glass meeting rooms of a Madison Avenue ad agency.

Branding and ritual were all. A color code was adopted: red, white and gold, their use imbued with emotional and spiritual significance. Tattoos became compulsory, public and permanent oaths. Numbers, of course, featured heavily: 19.9.18, or the gang member's nickname (often conferred by Wilson) rendered numerically, significant dates in the Royals' calendar, even the Corona zip code. Often they lay within larger designs, each approved of for use by Wilson. Some were generic gang motifs (the "happy/sad" theatrical masks that had long symbolized gang life); some specific to the Royals (variations on the crown inside a sun). Others were both—the three black dots Wilson himself bore on his fingers represented both the traditional gang maxim of Mi Vida Loca and Corona's 111th Street subway station. Among new recruits, it became popular to emphasize loyalty by having at least one design on the face.

The manifesto, meanwhile, was read, absorbed, copied, passed on.

And soon, the same slogans and designs that covered the bodies of ever-growing numbers of Latino teenagers were inescapable on neighborhood walls and the cars of the Seven train.

They were both commercials and communiqués, delivered in a private language. More everyday messages, meanwhile, were expressed in hand signs, complex arrangements of fingers crossed, brandished or hidden. It took me until my third interview with Wilson to persuade him to show me any used by the Royals—the prison rule that displaying such signs would lead to Ad-Seg was enough to spook him to the extent that, when he finally agreed, he twisted in his seat so that his hand was shielded from the camera watching over us both.

Even the gang's speech was filled with code—ever-evolving Hispanic street slang. For me, the confusion I felt when he spoke of soplons (informants) or claveros (thieves) was a blunt reminder of the gulf in our backgrounds. Once, I half seriously proposed that he write me a slang dictionary to accompany the Spanish phrase book I kept beside me when transcribing our interviews; glumly, he told me it changed so fast that his knowledge of it would be hopelessly outdated.

Most of the time what the hand signs and the slang were signifying, of course, was violence. A reference in the manifesto to "checking in," for instance, puzzled me: I learned it described the gang's initiation ceremony, in which a new Royal had his hands tied before being beaten by three existing members for forty-six seconds $[19 + 9 + 18]$. The process was meant, Wilson told me, as a test of resolve. For him, nothing toughened you up like a beating with fists—giving kids guns before they could fight was, he said, like letting them use calculators to teach them multiplication.

Within the gang, violence was routine. Failure to attend a rally would be punished with a beating, as would verbal disrespect to a senior member. The real ferocity, however, was reserved for those who committed the cardinal sin of asking to leave the gang. "Checking out" made "checking in" look genteel. Instead of three assailants, there would be up to ten; the only time limit when Wilson said he'd seen enough.

Few Royals checked out. Instead, their numbers just kept swelling. Before Wilson, most Hispanic clicas in Queens were semiactive chapters of gangs based in distant California. Now, inspired by Wilson's marriage of branding and brutality, a tsunami of red, white and gold engulfed the borough, sweeping through Elmhurst, Jackson Heights,

Astoria. Soon it crossed the East River into Orchard Beach, the "Rican Riviera" of the Bronx, and Manhattan's Washington Heights. In the south it reached Brooklyn: Williamsburg, Bushwick and Red Hook, its progress marked by spray-painted demands for the locals to Dé el Amor Al Real (Give love to the Royals).

If Madison Avenue had provided the blueprint for the Royals' ascent, then as the '80s went on, its rapacious takeovers of rival operations seemed inspired by nowhere so much as Wall Street. "Acquisitive" was how Wilson himself described the era, though he pronounced it a-kwysee-tiv. I realized then he must have known the word only through seeing it in a book or magazine and had never actually heard it used.

She stops typing. Peers at her words. Presses Caps Lock as she always does when making notes to herself. Writes: IS THIS TOO JACK HENRY ABBOTT? SURE I READ SAME THING IN *BELLY OF THE BEAST*—CHK! Then returns to where she was:

Yet theirs was not the figurative savagery practiced on the trading floors. With a ruthlessness made all the more shocking by the fact those involved were too young to legally buy cigarettes, the gang simply rolled over the opposition. Sheer force of numbers prevailed. "No one called us perros perdidos *anymore," he said. "Now they said we were* las hormigas—*the ants, you know?"*

Assaults with pipes or bats were the first step; an attack with a razor or perhaps a bullet to the knee the next; if further resistance was encountered, the results were more grisly still. Almost matter of factly, Wilson mentioned the time a rival gang member had a two-inch nail hammered partway into his skull or another his throat cut with the tongue then pulled through the wound.

She stops typing again. Cracks her knuckles. Reads it back. Maybe it's a little overcooked. It doesn't matter. Everything written can be rewritten. She sips her tea again, sees the words *LEMON ICE KING* on the back of her hand.

Yet even as he masterminded this ascent much of his life still resembled that of any teenage boy in Queens: summer days spent poring over vintage Chevys; lounging in Flushing Meadows with the Unisphere above him watching Frisbee and drinking frías *(cold beer); visits to* 108th *Street's Lemon Ice King of Corona (peanut butter his favorite flavor); the irresistible rhythms of salsa and hip-hop twisting in the air; girls. There were, he told me, many girls.*

But of course, he was not any teenage boy in Queens. Lazy after-noons in the park were liable to be interrupted by a desperate tecato *looking to cop, dates in the evening followed by a late-night battery of an errant Royal or stubborn rival.*

Maybe in acknowledgment, as time passed the gang—or Wilson at least—began to let much of the riskier or more onerous gruntwork fall to his soldados. *There were surely enough of them to cope. By the dawn of the '90s, thousands of young Hispanics across New York were sport-ing crowns in suns somewhere on their bodies, their loyalty pledged to this slightly built figure in his anonymous garb of outsize jeans and Chuck Taylor All Stars.*

It was, without question, him *they were loyal to—because the gang simply did not exist outside of Wilson Velez. He was* the Royals. *That was how it had always been. That was how it stayed. While the* clica's *relationship to the rest of the world had taken its cues from the corpo-rate temples of Manhattan, its rigid hierarchy and absolute deference to its leader owed more to the Incan palaces of Cuzco.*

Supported by the lieutenants who had been with him since the start—his brother Eduardo, Hurricane, Ojos et al.—Wilson was the object of his followers' adoration, even of their prayers. And while much of the gruntwork was now delegated elsewhere, internal discipline remained his preserve alone. The Royals' ultimate sanction, for instance, could only ever be carried out by direct order of King Three Vee.

"When a Royal had betrayed the clica," *he told me, "they would have our ink cut from their skin. They would have shown themselves not worthy to bear it. But that was never for anyone but me to call for."*

I looked at the man opposite, this man not much bigger than me, and wondered how he had ever held such power in a world like his. There were, it was true, glimpses of a charisma that must have been quite something before the years in Ad-Seg. When his speech held up and his eyes stayed focused, there was the slightest trace of something mes-meric. But still—

A question sat in the back of my mind throughout every one of our meetings. Until, eventually, I asked him. When had he first killed someone?

There was almost a minute of silence.

"I remember this vaina [thing]," he finally said. "I guess maybe it was '85 or '86. We were having troubles with other clicas trying to steal our members . . . and one time I watched this vato who was caught up in that walking through Flushing Meadows Corona Park. It was twilight, you know? Out by Meadows Lake. He was wearing pale blue All Stars you could see had come straight from the box. I followed him a while until he was past the snack carts and the picnic tables and he came to the underpass there . . . and I watched him walk down into it . . . I watched every step he took in those blue All Stars . . . and I asked myself if he would walk out through the other side . . ."

It was left to me to interrupt the pause that followed. So, did he?

"You know . . . now that I think of it . . . maybe I remember it wrong. I think maybe I just saw that scene in a movie one time. So your question . . . it's not one I have an answer to."

When I checked police records, I found no homicide in the underpass by Meadows Lake at any time during the '80s.

Mostly, the failures of his memory seemed only too genuine, his inability to summon a name or date leaving him cursing. At other times, I wondered if it didn't all feel a little forced. Equally, although many of his stories of nocturnal ambushes or revenge attacks found him center stage, others would be couched with a vague "I heard that . . ." or "This vato that this kid we knew knew, he did this vaina . . ." But the one time I cautiously asked him whether he himself was involved in an episode, he snapped at me: "If it had been me, I would be telling you the story with 'I' in it, not 'he.' I am not keeping anything from you, Lizbeth. I promise you that."

The next few stories he told me each cast him as the protagonist. As he told them, I studied him. Sometimes, I thought I saw a sparkle in his eyes as he described the violence, a glimmer of relish at a certain bloody detail. Sometimes, in fact, I knew I did. There it was. There it was again. But then, a moment later, he seemed so distressed that I could only put that glimmer down to the strip light above us bouncing off his glasses. The shame that filled his voice did not sound coached. It sounded raw; like someone torn up by his past.

"You know," he told me, "every fucking time that I spilled a person's blood . . . once it was done with . . . I threw my guts up, just like that first time."

Already, just in the course of these five meetings, I had seen a spectrum of moods emerge from the flat suspicion of our first encounter. They swept in without warning, settling just long enough to register before another overtook them. The mention of an insult from a guard that morning would bring a flash of anger; a moment later, he was almost playful.

Yet whether he was furious or wry, titillated or sorrowful, his stories were never less than engrossing. Whenever a one-word answer gave way to a narrative, his sense of how to keep a listener snared was expert. Even the most mundane events gripped—at one point he held me enthralled for minutes with what was, I had to remind myself, an account of buying Q-Tips.

Throughout his life, he told me, he had always recorded the yarns that would come to him at random moments, honing them in tattered notebooks. At fourteen, he said—with his own formal education in ruins—he gave a story he wrote "in the time it took to smoke a joint" to a Royal then in the eleventh grade at Elmhurst's Newtown High School. He wanted the student to claim the work as his own to see what grade it received. It was, he said, given a commendation by the principal, having moved the English teacher to tears.

"Sometimes," he said, "I made it so what I wrote meant something personal to me. Sometimes, I forgot all that shit and just let the story have its own mind. Its own heartbeat."

He read, widely and constantly. He enjoyed movies too, even if my assumption that he would be a fan of Brian De Palma's gangster opus Scarface was greeted with a shrugging comment that he preferred the director's earlier Dressed to Kill. But books were his first love—and his idol was Poe, the dark lyricist of the Bronx. He wrote short gothic vignettes in tribute. There was, he told me, a raven tattooed on his shoulder.

I could tell he expected me to be shocked, to be nonplussed by the thought of a man like this spending his time with novels and notepads. But though I tried my best to keep it from him, I wasn't. A child is hooked young on the power of storytelling to make sense out of a *threatening universe, preferring the sagas they build in their heads to the chaos outside of it. Later—using their own semicoded language, no less—they create a world around them where events are theirs to dictate, characters directed. To me, it didn't seem so strange.*

But that wasn't all he assumed was beyond me. To Wilson, no matter how many hours we spent here together, I could never hope to fully understand the pressures that had made him what he was. He told me he admired my writing. He said he respected what I'd gone through with my mother's murder and Richard Cazet. But for all that, he said, a person "like me"—a reference I took to mean my color and social background—would never truly fathom him. The best I could do was record his life and leave the rest to the reader.

Maybe he was right. After all, no matter how much of a connection I felt we'd made by the end of an interview, we each knew that when the hour was up, I would be exiting the lawyer's room and driving back to Essenville—but for Wilson, there was only "the pods."

Lizbeth's fingers quicken now, trying to keep pace with her thoughts.

As well as providing the location to our interviews, ESSUSP was their constant subtext. I was, after all, listening to his story from inside its ending.

But it was also prison that gave the Royals the biggest success of their seemingly limitless recruitment drive. For Wilson, there were two spells in jail as an adult, the first in the Bronx's Fulton Correctional Facility for possession of a quantity of marijuana, the second in upstate Auburn for carrying an unlicensed firearm. What he found in each jail was that the manifesto he had written back in Spofford was as widely read as the Bible or Hustler. *For much of the East Coast's Hispanic prison population, the strength in numbers that the Royals offered had been gratefully accepted. There were thriving chapters in each facility—and Wilson was treated as a visiting god.*

Such prison chapters of the gang ensured a constant supply line of new members, converting to the Royal cause while inside, then taking their loyalty back out on the street. By the middle of the '90s, the gang had established a wide-ranging portfolio of criminal activity across a dozen states with a membership of almost sixty thousand: ID numbers *were issued to Royals as a means of keeping track. The hierarchy remained in place, but the dizzying increase in new soldados, reinas (female members) and pee-wees (children under fifteen) saw it added to by a strata of what were essentially middle-managers. The changes didn't stop there—after being checked in, every Royal was now expected to pay between $20 and $150 dependent on age as a registration fee. Further dues were payable monthly.*

The pinnacle, he knew, should have been somewhere here: the highest point of the Ferris wheel, the peak of the arc. Only I heard little nostalgia in his voice when he said it. Living under the watchful eyes of federal gang intelligence units meant his daily routine was severely curtailed. There were still girls; but most of them just wanted free drugs, he said. There was more money than ever before; but the bulk was given over to legal fees for senior Royals. When he might have been expected to be living the ultimate vida loca, he spent much of his time playing dominoes with Raymond Peres in the barely furnished two-room apartment he was renting on 47th Avenue.

Yet the gang just kept on growing. Not even membership of la raza (the Hispanic nation) restricted candidates anymore—applications to join local chapters were received from Vietnamese kids in Buffalo and white teenagers from the Jersey suburbs. Corona, however, was where its roots remained, and where Wilson would always stay. To him, it was simple:

"Peopppple . . . I knew and loved died building the Royals in that neighborhood. So how could I betray their memories by leaving itttt? That was never . . . even a choice tto me."

Lizbeth leans forward and pauses the tape. "I'm sorry. I need to use the bathroom." She puts her weight on her cane and rises from her seat.

"You need to . . . do somethinggg about your . . . bladder."

"I know. Sorry."

When she's in the bathroom down the hall, she can hear the guards outside.

"That kid's an accident waiting to happen," one says.

"As long as I ain't around when it does," says another.

They stand aside as she steps back past them.

Wilson keeps his eyes on her.

"You know . . . a lot of this . . . stuff I never really tttttalked with any-one about before."

"Well . . . I'm glad you feel you can with me."

"But . . . you know something? We've been talking aboutttt . . . me for a long time. Maybe we can talk about you for a while? Lettt my voice . . . recover."

"Sure," she says. "If you want to."

He hesitates. "So . . . How are you . . . setttttling in to Essenville?"

"Good. So far it's been good."

"Yeah? Me personally, I couldn'tttt live in a town full of *jarabes*."

Jarabe means syrup. And syrup, she has learned, means guard. Even when they're kicking you in the head, Wilson said, they move so slow you want to scream at them to hurry up.

"So you getting to know anyone dddown there? Anyone you like to hang out with?"

"Ah . . . not really. I mean, there's a couple of people I say hello to . . . but that's all."

"So . . . it really is jjjjust me you are here for."

"Of course. For our project."

"So, your husbandddd been out to see you yet?"

"I'm not married, Wilson."

"Shit. All this time I thoughtttt you were married. Kids?"

"No kids."

"A boyfriend?"

"No boyfriend. No husband. No kids."

"Ever been marriedddd?"

"Sure. One time."

"What was his name?"

"His name was Steven. It still is."

Wilson nods but doesn't speak. Lets the silence gather.

"He's had some problems . . . some psychiatric stuff."

"And that is why you . . . broke up?"

"No, we'd already broken up."

"Oh, okay. So what wenttt wrong?"

"It was just . . . it didn't work out. That's all."

"So you broke upppp and that's why he got sick?"

"No. That's not how it happened."

"So then I don't gettt why you sound like you feel guilty."

"I don't feel guilty." Her fingers find the handle of her cane. "I don't know. Maybe I do."

"Why? Whattt . . . did you do . . . to him?"

"I didn't do anything to him. I just didn't make him happy."

She runs her thumb along the silver curve. Sees him gaze across the table. Waiting for her to go on. For a moment she wavers, and then: "I remember going to the theater. Some weird off-Broadway thing that this friend of my editor was involved with. Anyway, there was some half-funny line about ten minutes into it, and Steven started laughing. Really laughing hard. I mean, howling. Which was fine, because so was everyone else. But then he kept on laughing. And everyone else had stopped, and the actors were trying to get back into it . . . and people were getting pretty uptight, muttering, giving him these filthy looks. But he just kept laughing. He just laughed and laughed. Until finally, the actors just stopped . . . and the director came over, and he was a pretty big guy . . . it got kind of ugly. And I was so mortified by the whole thing I just got up and walked out. I left him there. Now I know that was the start of it. Then all I wanted was for someone else to deal with it."

"That is what . . . you are beatingggg yourself up over? That's . . . stupid."

"Maybe."

"Do you wanttt to . . . tttalk about me again?"

She says that she does. Leans forward and unpauses the tape.

"Okay, so, one thing I've noticed, Wilson, is that the longer we've talked about the gang and the bigger it's gotten the less *enthusiastic* you've sounded . . ."

"Oh, you know how it is. Just because something looks gggood from . . . the outside, that doesn't mean you're enjoying it. *Sabes?*"

"Right."

"I mean, I was just tired. That's what I remember most. *Huesos molidos*. I was twenty-seven years old and all I wanted to do was sleep. And sssure, we had love from our own people but there wassss always someone wanting to pull us down. I know in all the newspapers you must have readddd before you came here they mmmade out like we were the only *clica* in New York, and maybe for a couple of years it was somethinggg like that . . . but there's always some new set coming up . . . people wanting their own *vaina* . . . and every few weeks there'd be a funeral, and there wouldddd be tears and grief . . . And I guess when my brother died too it gave me cause to thinkk . . . about whatttt direction we were . . . headed in."

"That was how he died? Another gang?"

"No. For a long time my brother had been into *chiva*. That was all he cared aboutttt. And so one night he OD'd in Spaghetti Park. They found him face ddddown the next morning."

"I'm sorry."

He shrugs.

"*Tecatos* die. It was no big surprise. But—ittt made me think about what the Royals was meantttt to . . . be when we started out. And how the bigger we had got the further we had moved away from thattt. And I felt like a *clavero,* a fucking hypocrite, takingggg twenty dollars from some Pakistani kid in Michigan and telling him he was a part of the gggreat Inca nation. That's why I wanteddd—to change the organization. To give it back to the people in Corona. To help them better their . . . sssituations. You know, everything I had written in the manifesto, about our people standing as one together . . . I believed it. Or maybe I came to believe it. So I talkedddd to Father Peres, and we set outttt a program for us to work for the community. I see the look on your face, Lizbeth. That's fine. I understand. Seriously, have my lawyer puttttt you . . . in touch with Hurricane and Father Peres. Have him arrange for you to go outttt to Corona. They can sssshow . . . you whattt the Royals have done. I want you to see thatt."

"You know," she says, "I did ask the warden again about letting you write him . . . Father Peres . . . but he's not giving an inch . . ."

"It's okay. You don't need ttto ask him again. But it wassss kind of you to try." He shifts in his seat. "Anyway . . . a month after my brother died they arrested me. The FBI came with twelve men and smashed down my door and tttttttold me I was a racketeer."

They can each sense the passing of the hour. The impending guards.

"Lizbeth, you remember when we were talkingggg about your mother . . . and you mentioneddd stuff getting jammed inside your head . . ."

"Right . . . ?"

"I have this fucking dream. Every fucking night I have ittt. Except it's not jjjust a dream. I see it all the time. Whenever I close my eyes or jjjust looking at the wall in front of me."

167

And he tells her about the lime trees. Racing down the dirt track as a child. The heat on his skin. The mask of branches and the blood, sprayed across his face. Sometimes it feels so real, he says, that he finds himself raising his hand to wipe it away.

"So then I look up," he says. "But it's like the sun has blindedddd me."

The guards file into the room and lift him from his chair.

"I see this shit so many times," he says. "And I don't know what any of itttt means."

They stand on either side of him and then they take him out.

George Finer stands in Lizbeth's kitchen and it sounds like the world is ending.

Earlier today, they met for lunch at the Venus Restaurant Diner. There was a mention—just in passing—of her wanting to make smoothies for a houseguest. That was all it took. He said he had the perfect thing: a top-of-the-line blender that would turn out the most awesome smoothie she had ever tasted. Would ever taste. Then came the pause. The pause as he waited for her to say: "That sounds great. Could I maybe . . . borrow it?"

Now, he stands with it over by her sink and runs through its features and attachments and the noise is making her eyes bounce in their sockets. He pushes a button and shouts across the room.

"What?" she says. "I can't hear what you're saying."

He nods and gives her a thumbs up. Hits a second button and the noise shudders off.

"So," he says, "did that make sense?"

"Absolutely," she says.

He has been at a barely controlled pitch of excitement since he came through the front door. Just seeing her laptop made him flustered.

"This," he said, "is just so incredible for me. To be here. With you."

But now, with palpable regret, he tells her he's got to go. Tonight, he says, is the creative writing class for adults that he teaches up at Johnstown Community College. It's a lot of fun, he says. He still likes to flex his educator's muscle.

"Do you ever teach up at the prison . . . at any of the prisons?"

"Oh, no. There's nothing like that at any of them. But the DOC pretty much keeps the college in business wanting vocational courses for COs, so I guess it kind of balances out."

As she sees him to the door, a Jeep pulls up outside. They watch as the driver's window rolls down. And Nancy Bonchurch leans out in a matching green hat and scarf and asks: "Am I okay to leave this here?"

She has driven from Quince Hill to bring Lizbeth those possessions she has decided she will need from now on. Her bedding, a trunk full of CDs, her thesaurus.

Nancy and George are introduced, and between them they unload.

Right before he leaves, he warns her the first snow is definitely coming in tonight. The stores are almost out of bread and milk, he says. The surest sign there is.

When it's just Lizbeth and Nancy they stand with Nancy's overnight bag at her feet and hug, only a touch uncertainly.

"You look amazing," Nancy says. "Seriously. You look so good."

"I'm so fat. I had to get all new underwear."

"Lizbeth, really, you look great." And then she says: "So, come on . . . let me see the car."

Inside the garage, she stares ahead of her. "Where's the Porsche?"

"I took it back yesterday," Lizbeth says.

There is, before them, a dark brown Volvo.

"I don't get it," Nancy says.

"Oh, you know . . . it's not going to be much use in the snow . . . and anyway . . . I'd started to feel so self-conscious driving it. Around here . . . up at the prison . . ."

She steers Nancy back into the house. Makes tea. Settles in the lounge and asks to see the photographs that have been brought here in lieu of the dogs.

"So they're okay?" she says. "Tork's ear hasn't flared up?"

"He's fine. They're all fine. I mean, they miss you, obviously . . . But they're fine." She gestures out of the window. "So that guy . . . ? The guy that was here just now . . . ?"

"George? Oh, he's a fan. He has a store in town."

She sees the way that Nancy looks at her.

"Oh, it's not like that. *Really.* I don't actually think I'm his *type.*"

"Oh? As in—"

"I'm not sure. Anyway, he's sweet. I like him. And it just struck me the other day the only people I know here are the warden and his wife. And they can be . . . well . . . I told you about these dinners, right? They make me feel like I should be wearing a fez and banging a little cymbal."

"But the people down here have been okay? They haven't pestered you?"

Lizbeth gets to her feet and passes Nancy a copy of the *Essenville Expositor*. On the front page, beside the headline BENTLEYVILLE BITES THE DUST AT THE BOWLODROME is another that says: STAR AUTHOR SETS UP HOME!

"The editor lives right opposite. He was over here the same day I moved in."

Nancy reads aloud: " 'Although Miss Greene has no plans as yet to relocate permanently from her home in Connecticut, she says she is delighted to be here in Essenville as she develops ideas for her next book.' "

"You know, that really ticked me off. I told the warden I'd appreciate it if the guards that dealt with me kept it just a little quiet what I was doing . . . so that it didn't get in the local paper for some stringer in Pittsburgh to see and then the next thing it's on Page Six . . . but, of course, as soon as the editor shows up he's all 'So, the notorious Wilson Velez' . . . I had to promise I'd come back and give him an exclusive when the book's out in exchange for him keeping it out of the story."

Nancy turns her gaze to the picture by the text. "You look kind of . . . sleepy."

"I'd been napping on the couch when he came to the door." Lizbeth's tone is suddenly urgent. "So, did you read the story yet? *The Monsters*?"

"Sure. I read the whole thing last night."

"And?"

"I see what you mean."

"You liked it?"

"I liked it a lot. It's just so weird it's written by someone . . . like *that*. But you know what was funny? I was in bed reading it and I got to the chapter where Hector and Edmond find out Louis Fung's got five hundred names on the petition, and they discover it was him who's been stopping them from making trouble—"

"Using a hex to protect the bad people . . ."

"Right! And that he's an ancient spirit too . . . and there's that scene where Hector says, 'He wants to take it all! The whole city! All of it for himself!' And he pulls out the one straggly hair on his head in panic . . . Anyway, for some reason that really tickled me, and I realized I was laughing, and all I could think was 'Thank God I'm single.' Because otherwise I'd have to tell whoever I was with I was laughing at this story about talking gargoyles."

"How about the ending?"

"The ending? I liked it. It's just dark enough. Why, did you—"

"I just wondered if it might be a little much for kids. A little strong, you know?"

"Oh, no. Kids love that kind of thing." Nancy sips her tea and asks: "So how are you finding it? . . . Him?"

Lizbeth opens her mouth to answer but the words aren't quite there yet.

"It's actually kind of a rush. It is. When he's talking, it's like I can see the words on the page already, and it's incredible. I'm getting more and more out of him every time I go up there. I guess he's getting better. I mean, he's still pretty fucked up, but . . . for some reason he's really getting pretty talkative . . ."

"Well, you're obviously bringing it out of him."

"I don't know about that. I think he just likes talking about himself."

That night Lizbeth cooks eggplant linguine. She didn't even used to like eggplant. It must, they agree, be hormonal.

"So," Nancy says, ". . . have you thought of names yet?"

"Nothing my conscience would let me burden them with."

"I like Mackenzie. For a girl."

"Too prep school." Lizbeth slops the pasta into the skillet. "Listen . . . there was something I was meaning to ask . . ."

"Uh-huh?"

"Do you think my hair makes me look . . . severe?"

"Severe?"

"Right. I mean, do you think I should dye it? Lighten it?"

"Lizbeth, I told you, you look great. You don't need to change a thing."

The food is ready, and outside the snow has started falling.

TEN

S O WHERE IS your . . . cane?"

Wilson Ulysses Velez stares across the table.

"I don't need it anymore," Lizbeth says.

Yesterday, with the snowplows having cleared the night's fall from the highways, she drove up to Pittsburgh and got the okay. Ever since, she's been rediscovering the joys of free movement. Back inside the house with the curtains closed, she danced to Jack Ruby and The Black Disciples on the ninety-dollar CD player she bought at the Essenville mall. Later, in the bedroom, just for a moment, she hopped.

"Congratulationssss."

"Thank you."

"I wish the dddoctor had good news . . . for me."

"When did you see the doctor?"

"I haven'ttttt."

"Are you sick?"

"I could be. I feel kind of . . . fuzzy. I hadd a headache lastt night that felt like the veins in my temples were jjjjjust going to . . . pop right open."

"Okay, listen . . . if you get sick and they won't let you see a doctor, let me know. Okay?"

"I will, Lizbeth. Thank you."

She hits Record. "So . . . the last time I was here, we'd just started talking about your final arrest. I was hoping we could pick things up there."

"Sssure. Okay."

"Now, let me make sure that what I know is accurate. You were charged—"

"With racketeering."

"And, specifically—"

"Specifically—loansharking. Extortion. Possession and distribution of narcotics. Robbery. Trafficking in stttolen . . . ggoods. Obstruction of jjjustice. Twenty-seven counts of assault and . . . battery. Incitement to murder."

"Right," she says. "Could you maybe tell me about the circumstances of the arrest?"

"What is there to say? They put me face down and the cuffs were so tighttt my hands were . . . numb for three ddddays afterward. Then someone stamped on my—back as they were putting them on me. What more can I ttttttell you?"

"Well . . . what evidence did they have?"

"One of my *soldados* went over to them. Turned *soplon*. His name was . . . Mauricio Jiminez. From Elmhurst. People calledd him Slinky. I hardly even . . . knew who he was. I don't tttthink I was ever even in the same room as him."

"And you've no idea why he turned against you?"

"Why does anyone do that shit? He must have gottten . . . himself pulled in and thought he coulddd save his *soplon* ass with . . . fairy tales."

"Fairy tales?"

"Sure. Conversations I had with him, orders that I gave him, stuff he . . . saw me do. It was . . . bullshit. I mean, okay . . . lettt's be clear. Some of what he was talkinggg about may have happened. But never how he saiddd it did. Because he had never . . . been there. He was jjjust some little *puta* I would have never let get that close to me. So insteaddd he took stories he'd heard about me and put himself in the middle of ttthem."

"Are you saying you weren't involved in those . . . activities?"

"I'm not trying to . . . mislead you, *dulzura*. At different times in my life I had done many of those ttthings. What I'm saying is I didn't do them how this *conejo* Slinky said. He knew nothinggg. So maybe in one way I was guilty. But not of whattttt I was convicted of. To convict me they had to use bullshit. You understand?"

"I think so."

She clears her throat and he winces.

"We told Mitchell Rieber we would cut a deal. Take a plea, *sabes*? But they had this *puta* telling them everything they ever dreamed of so they weren't interested. Nine months . . . later I came to trial. There was trouble every day inside and outside court. I remember sitting in the dock . . . and you could hear the people chantinggg *Justicia para Three Vee!* One day they set a fire and burned an effigy of Mitchell Rieber. Ittt was chaos. The police killed a kid. Fifteen years oldddd. Later the same day Father Peres gave evidence on my behalf. He called me a prophet. It didd no good. They put me . . . down all dday. Life without parole. And that night they took me to USP Moxanie."

He starts to glaze over before he snaps back. "But even then I still felt hope for the future. I knew these storiesss of Slinky's were bullshit and one day they would have to crack apart. Anyway . . . ttthen he showed up."

"Right . . . ?"

"He had disappeared straight after the ttttrial. A year into my bitch, they found him in a motel outside . . . Jerome, Idaho. He was in the . . . tub. His head was missing."

"Oh, God."

"They found it in a trash can in . . . the next room. Ittt had been set on . . . fire." He shuffles forward as far as he can. "Lizbeth . . . I will tell you now thattttt this was not by my order."

"It wasn't?"

"It was not. Ask me a thousand times and . . . you'll have the same answer. No. I wantedd him alive. I wanted him to take back his bullshit. But the gang was crazy back then. Hurricane was supposed to be in charge now but Royals from all over were . . . trying tttto take his crown. It was chaos. And I guess some fucking idiot thought they could win my favor by endingggg Slinky. So that was that."

He stares at her and his foot is tapping. "Lizbeth, there is nothing in this world lower than a *soplon*. Nothing. So if I had ordered this then I would have wanted his tongue pulled out and his lips taken off. *Then* they coulddd have cut off his head." He rises up in his chair, tries to straighten out his back. "Not now, you understand. I'm not that person anymore. But can you truly sayyy you wouldn't have wantedddd to do the same? Not even for a moment?"

"I couldn't kill anyone, Wilson."

"Even someone who had jjust taken your own life? Then you are—a very noble person."

"I wouldn't go that far. I just couldn't kill anyone."

"You can't know thatttttt."

There is silence.

"So, anyway . . . I got the cover for the . . . book this morninggg. Sosa let me have it through the mail."

"Isn't it great? I thought the monsters looked fantastic . . . looming up over the city—"

"Oh. How come you saw it?"

"Inchy . . . she e-mailed me a copy a few days ago."

"She did? Well . . . then I guess you also know they've askedd me to . . . write somethinggg else. A sequel."

"They have? No. I didn't know that."

"Oh, I thought Inchy would have tttold you. Well . . . I guess Jim Rockford really must be an author in his own righttttt now, huh?"

"I guess he must be."

And silence, again.

"So, have you got any ideas for it?"

"I think—so. I've been playing with some thinggggs in my head."

"Well, that's the good part," she says, and she sees that his foot is still now. "Just don't get bored with your own imagination."

There are new exercises to learn at her next antenatal. Pelvic tilts and waist twists. Inevitably, the doctor raises the subject of Kegels.

She feels trained hands laid on her belly and she thinks of Wilson and it makes her jolt with unease.

These checkups, she thought, would be traumatic. Invasive. In fact, she finds them reassuring. A calm accounting of her body's latest quirks and transformations. Her fractured sleep over the last few nights is, she's told, a common complaint. The lapses in short-term memory that have gone on for a week now—toast left to burn, purse misplaced—they too should only be expected. It is, the doctor says, perfectly normal to be distracted. Forgetful.

"I haven't felt it move," Lizbeth says. "Nothing at all."

"You probably won't," the doctor tells her. "Not for a while yet."

When the doctor asks if there's anything else she wants to know, she asks if she can dye her hair. If, she says, she wanted to. "You know . . . with the chemicals."

"That should be fine. There's no reason for you to grow it out."

"Grow it out? No, I mean . . . I don't dye it now."

"You don't? Oh, I'm sorry. Well, no . . . as I say, it should be fine."

Back at the house, she phones Ed. She has a mass of things to say, sudden, vital insights about the future, their relationship, this child; all of which vanish from her head as soon as he answers. But that's okay. He talks enough for both of them. Pleads with her to go back to Quince Hill. To meet him, face to face. He wants, he says, for them to try again.

She can't even think about that. And she won't be leaving Essenville. Not yet. But they will speak again, she says. Soon.

That night she stands in the video store, gazing at kaleidoscopic racks of DVDs.

"So what are you in the mood for?"

George Finer stands next to her. Points straight ahead.

"Oh, God, no," she says. "I can't stand him."

"But it got such good reviews."

"I know. I just . . . ugh. But George, listen, it's up to you. Your house, your call."

It takes ten minutes for one of his suggestions to be accepted. She waits outside while he deals with the clerk. Looks out at the charcoal sweep of Essenville at dusk. The dark banks of hemlocks sloping down to the road. The high school band in a yellow bus driving either to or from an out-of-town performance, tuba and cello cases propped up in the aisle.

"They're out of popping corn," George says. "The real stuff. We'll have to stop by the Foodline."

So together they walk to the Foodline Savers Mart at the far end of Main Street. What she believes to be the town's only drunk hovers outside.

As they pass him, he mutters at Lizbeth: "You do not exist."

Before he stumbles away.

Inside, the heating has blown. A harried manager yammers at an engineer as two exquisitely bored young women shiver on the checkouts. "La Isla Bonita" plays over the speakers.

Lizbeth and George take their place in line and as they do, an ESSUSP guard peers out at her from the produce aisle. Stands there for longer than she feels entirely comfortable with, then turns and strolls away. He doesn't look back.

They pick up George's hatchback from outside the gift shop next door. Driving off, he waves at an elderly couple. Old Essenvillians, he says, then adds, In every sense.

His house is five blocks south and three east of hers. The same size and basic layout, but worn in, cared for. Where her place has a storage cupboard, he has another room, lined—she sees on entering—with bookshelves. On them she reads the names of her every peer and forebear: an exhaustive library of crime fiction. The unravelings of mass poisonings in Edwardian London, bloody slayings in modern Scandinavia, sniper rampages on the streets of Los Angeles, any number of macabre rituals in countless rustic cabins. Assassinations and child murders and crimes of passion, densely packed shelf after shelf of them.

"Don't worry. Enschell's still my favorite."

George is beside her.

"Thank you, George. He'd be touched."

"No, I mean it. I always find myself coming back to him. He's always had that . . . inexorable quality."

She sees her books, signed in his gift shop, taking up a shelf to themselves, and then, as her eyes track across the spines of those below it:

Settlers in a Misty Place: A History of the Towns of the Southern Alleghenies
GEORGE MacDOUGALL FINER

"Oh, my God, George. Why didn't you tell me?" She pulls it out; it's slim and pristine.

"Oh, that . . . really, it's just . . . I wrote it years ago. It's completely out of date. Please. For you of all people to be seeing it . . ."

She turns and sees his cheeks are authentically flushed. But she can't resist flicking to the author photograph.

"Ah," he says, "the days of hair."

"So what's with the MacDougall?"

"My mother was a MacDougall. I guess I just thought it sounded more . . . authorly."

She leafs through the pages. "Why don't you have this in the store?"

"Oh . . . I wouldn't feel right taking people's money for it . . . there's better alternatives out there . . . so those are the ones I stock."

"That's the silliest thing I ever heard."

So she tells him she's borrowing it, that's final; and he winces but doesn't snatch it from her hand.

On the wall of the living room there's a framed photograph of him clipped from the *Expositor*. He stands in a group of half a dozen men in shirts and ties, that group at the head of a crowd of maybe a hundred more people. They are, she realizes, in front of ESSUSP.

"That was the night they opened the place up to the public," he says. "A week before the first prisoners arrived. Everyone was up there. The kids had a riot. There was a celebratory buffet in the canteen."

"But they don't have a canteen."

"They mocked it up. People got dressed up in uniform, the old striped suits, and the local circuit judge came down and sang prison songs. The guys from Murray's Sporting Goods paid two hundred dollars each to spend the night in a cell. For charity, you know?"

"Everyone looks so happy."

"So they should. They just got their town back . . . even better than it was before."

"And these guys you're with . . . you were the fund-raisers?"

"Uh-huh. I mean, everyone chipped in what they could, but I guess the business community led the way. By then us six pretty much were the business community."

The men in the picture beam proudly through their camera-shyness. One, however, stands at the edge of the group, unsmiling. Pole-skinny, arms folded.

"This guy doesn't look too happy," she says.

"Oh. That's Lloyd Dreiz. He owns the photographers' studio down on Hudurden Street. He's a bowling guy. Grew up here same as me."

"George, the temperature just went through the floor. Is there some kind of . . . history here?"

"History? With Lloyd Dreiz? He's just not the sweetest grape on the vine. That's all. I mean, look at the picture. Tells you everything you need to know."

They take care of the popcorn in the kitchen. George keeps singing the same two lines from "La Isla Bonita" as he stands watch. "I've got that ridiculous song stuck in my head now. Jammed right in there."

"George," Lizbeth says, "I'd prefer it if this could stay between us . . ."

He turns, schoolboy attentive. And she tells him exactly what she's doing here. About the nature of her project. About Wilson Velez: *God's Lonely Man*.

"Oh, wow," George says.

She only needs to glance at him and: "You knew already, didn't you?"

"I guess I did hear something . . . You know, word tends to get around. But thank you for trusting me enough to tell me. I'm really so flattered."

"It's okay," she says. "It just seemed a bigger deal ten seconds ago."

They take a couch each in the living room, the TV between them. The lights are dimmed. Dry warmth from the radiators. Through a gap in the curtains she can see another snowfall getting under way. A half hour into the film she finds she's curled up on her side with a cushion for a pillow.

George pauses the machine and lays a blanket over her. Brings the lights back up while he refills the popcorn bowl.

She calls through to him. Asks if he thinks she should lighten her hair.

"Maybe," he says when he comes back in. "But then you wouldn't be Lizbeth Greene, would you?"

And he turns the movie back on and the room is filled with sound and color.

"Put the paper down on the table."

The guard to the left of Wilson Velez has his baton cocked while the one on his right is speaking. He does as he's told. Takes the scrap of paper in his hand and lays it in front of Lizbeth.

"It's fffffor you. You always reminded me of her."

A pencil drawing. Crude but instantly recognizable.

"*The Bride of Frankenstein?*"

"Right. Not the hair, though. The face. The actress's face. That's who you reminddd me of."

"I do?"

"Sure. I always thoughttttt she was very . . . beautiful."

Seconds go by and Lizbeth can't place her response. Finally: "Thank you, Wilson."

"That's okay, Lizbeth. So, how have you been?"

"Good. I've been good. And you? Are you okay? Last time I came you'd had headaches . . ."

"Well, I got the Tylenol you sent me, and they have helpedddd. So I'm still . . . alive. And you know, I've been lookinggg forward to talkinggg with you again."

"Great."

"You've been looking forward to it . . . as well?"

"Of course."

"Tell me something, Lizbeth. Do you think that if we had met in—normal life, we would have been able tto talk to each other the way we do now?"

"I don't know, Wilson. We've had very different lives."

"I know. I jjjjjjust mean—"

She leans forward to check the batteries on her tape recorder.

"Oh, I'm sssssssorrry," he says. "I'll stoppp ttalking so—you can asssssssssssk me . . . the real quesssssssstions."

"I just wanted to check the machine. We can talk about anything you want to talk about."

"It'sssss okay. Realllly. I know why we're . . . here."

"Honestly, Wilson. I didn't mean to be rude—"

He stares at her. Both feet start tapping wildly. Then he turns away. "It's okay. No problem. Can you remind me where I—I haddd gotttt to with the—story?"

She tries to gauge his tone. "Well . . . the last time we talked, we were discussing your trial. Your conviction."

"Right. When they tttttook me . . . to Moxanie."

"I guess we haven't talked much about your experiences in prison, even though—"

"Even though it's whattttt you always . . . wantedddd to talk about."

"No . . . that's not—"

"It's okay, *dulzura*. I'll gggggive you what you need." He turns back. Straightens up. "Tell me, you've been comingg . . . here a while now. Have you figured out what is in the . . . air yetttt?"

"I'm not sure I understand."

"It is dead time. Time withoutttt purpose. Time that has—nothing inside it but sadness. Until the place is choked with it. And there's more day after day after day after ddday after . . . day."

Dead time. To Wilson, the phrase had a practical connotation. In ES-SUSP, he said, the silence that still unnerved me every time I came here may have been a product of soundproofing—but it would be a mistake to assume the inmates were raging in their cells. Instead, he told me, most of those up in the pods would simply be asleep. You could just as easily be in a graveyard, he said, passing row upon row of steel mausoleums. Sleep was the best, most painless way of getting through the time. The higher security the facility, the more it was clung to and sought after. A Puerto Rican Royal from Orchard Beach named Stoopie slept for a minimum of eighteen hours a day through a seven-year stretch in Attica, he told me. Six months from release, he died of a stroke.

Lizbeth gets up from the keyboard. It's late. From the window she can see the lights are out in every house on the street.

She leaves the kitchen table and sits on the floor to carry out her stretches. Raises her arms over her head in turn with her legs crossed beneath her. Continues for ten minutes before returning to her laptop. The table covered with transcripts now.

Throughout his various stints in prison, however, Wilson's own urge to sleep away his life had been overcome by his ardor for language. Communication. Ever since his time in Spofford, he had read insatiably: textbooks, magazines, pulp thrillers. When he wasn't reading, he would write—composing his own stories just as he did on the outside, sending countless letters to friends and followers back in Queens. Although José Alamanza had once more taken over day-to-day control of the gang, Wilson remained the Sapa, the one true king: his exile did nothing to diminish that. So it was only to be expected that the Royals would still turn to him for advice and guidance.

Besides offering counsel over the correspondent's love life or his taste in clothes, the letters he sent back evolved into an ongoing portrait of life inside the prison system. Often, the details of each stretch were interchangeable. The daily routine was, for example, powered by the dual engines of commerce and contraband, the latter most often available through "hooping" (smuggling material anally). "In prison," he told me, "everything is for sale"—even if all one party was offering was not beating or stabbing the other. Back in his first stay at Spofford, he had peddled "smut books." Masturbation, he told me, was as much a staple of life in jail as head counts and weight lifting. "It kills the time when you can't sleep," he says. "Guys jerk off until their dicks bleed."

He shook his head when I asked if he'd ever witnessed a prison rape. "Heard a few, though," he said. More common in adult facilities, he told me, were consensual arrangements where one inmate became another's "wife." Had he had a wife? "I don't do that shit," he said, curtly. Then the machismo left his voice. "I'd be scared of catching the blickey (AIDS)."

If barter and sex were routine, however, violence was inescapable. A glance misinterpreted, a way of eating that another inmate took exception to, these were all it needed to end up in the hospital, or the morgue.

That was when there were reasons at all. For any inmate who valued his safety the answer was, of course, the succor of a gang—and for Latino prisoners in and around New York, that meant only one thing.

The loyalty demanded by the Royals' prison chapters was more ferocious even than that out on the street. Wilson told me of a member in the Sing Sing Correctional Facility who confessed to the leader of his chapter that he'd given away secrets to a rival gang. Stabbed forty-six times in the back, his last words were to tell the guards his injuries were self-inflicted.

But things were different in Moxanie, Wilson's first residence as a convicted racketeer. An aging maximum security facility fifteen miles from Saratoga racetrack, its structure may have been decrepit—but its adoption of "permanent lockdown" was entirely state of the art. In his time at Auburn and Fulton, lockdown—the confinement of all prisoners to their cells for twenty-three hours a day—had been used only in response to a crisis. In Moxanie, as in a growing number of prisons across the country, it was the norm.

With only an hour a day in which inmates could mix, watched over by dozens of guards, gang life was barely liveable. Among the locked down, meanwhile, were ever-swelling ranks of "kids and bugs"— teenage drug users and the mentally ill. There was a suicide every week. And out of this dark pool of frustration a war of attrition with the guards developed.

Wilson held them all beneath contempt as a professional body. Most of them, he told me, "just flat out hate their inmates. The ones up at Moxanie, you could see it in them straight away. Everything they hated about their lives they made us pay for."

Pay they did. By Wilson's account, inmates who incurred the displeasure of their guards would be handcuffed, then dropped face first onto concrete floors and kicked in the "ribs, kidneys, nuts, head." I asked if this had happened to him. "Of course," he said.

He had, he told me, suffered other assaults by the guards at Moxanie. Burning paper would be thrown into his cell to give them a pretext for attacking him with fire extinguishers; alternatively, they would come at him with Taser guns; he was forced, he said, into scalding baths, and held underwater until he passed out. His food was tainted with body waste.

But by his own account, one positive emerged from his time there. "My eyes," he said, "began to open." What he meant was a growing political consciousness.

The "corrections industry" no longer aspired to the rehabilitation of inmates—this much was common knowledge. But to Wilson, its function had moved beyond mere warehousing into something more sinister. Alongside the kids and bugs at Moxanie were men whose profiles were more radical: leaders of campaigns for the rights of Native Americans, founding members of militant African-American pressure groups. And the discipline they were subject to was, in essence, behavior modification—using violence and punishment to destroy their will much as you would a dog's.

"It all slotted into place," he told me. "When I first got to Moxanie, I remember thinking how fucked up it was that I was getting locked away just when I was turning away from the life I'd been living. Then I realized that suited the system fine. They didn't want a person like me giving my people a strong, peaceful role model. I had been exactly what they wanted me to be—an idiot. The people with power, they want the dispossessed high every day and taking their anger out on each other instead of bankers and politicians. So then no one will rise up when the cops next come to take us into their jails to die or be prison labor."

At times, his tone was melodramatic. At others, he just sounded paranoid. There were, he assured me, the bodies of inmates murdered by guards buried under ESSUSP. More than once, he said he knew he would also die at their hands. "Like George Jackson. They will switch off the cameras one night and come for me. That will be the end of my story."

But for every moment of hyperbole, there was another of clear-headed logic. It was hard to argue when he lamented the ongoing prison boom as providing jails for a generation of inmates not even born yet—or not to be affected when he described his experience of growing up Latino in America: "Pushed to the margins of your own existence, lost in a place where no street or school or federal building will ever be named after any one of your people . . . facing adulthood without self-love or knowledge or the belief there is anything for you besides a life of craziness or tending to white people's lawns."

My head filled with the inmates of ESSFCI, sent out to pick up the trash and prettify the gardens of Essenville.

So while his letters dealt with the minutiae of his members' lives, he also made sure to encourage those reading to help José Almanza transform the gang into a positive force in the community. Returning to the imagery he had chanced upon as a child in Linneaus Place, he talked in typically grandiose terms of the "new" Royals being like the Incan city builders who packed the vast stone blocks of their temples so tightly a razor blade couldn't fit between them—the gang bringing the same, seemingly impossible fortitude to its good deeds in Corona.

When Wilson was in full flow, it was almost possible to forget the bloody nature of his past. Certainly, he seemed keen to embrace his new identity—that of a political prisoner, a staunch and fearless revolutionary. I could tell he liked that version of himself.

"But, you know . . . it's funny . . . without prison I don't know if *The Monsters* would have turneddddd out so good." Wilson Ulysses Velez rocks back and forth in his seat. Just to get the blood moving.

"Why not?"

"Because now every last shred of power I had over my life was gggone. Ripped ffffrom my hands. So I put everything into—my other one. You must understand that, Lizbeth?"

"Of course," she says.

"I thoughtttt you would. So . . . tell me something about the worlddd."

"Anything in particular?"

"Just . . . something about the world. What it felt . . . like to turn off your bedroom light last . . . night. What your coffee tasted like this morning."

"I don't drink coffee in the morning. I drink tea."

"So . . . how was your tea?"

"My tea was good, Wilson."

"And the drive up . . . here? How was that?"

"The drive up here was fine."

"Are you enjoying your Porsche?"

"Actually . . . I got rid of it."

"You did? *Hijole.* Why didddd you do that?"

"Oh, you know . . . with the snow getting worse and everything . . . it just seemed dumb. Impractical. So I got a Volvo instead."

"A Volvo? Shit. I never drove one of those before. You thinkk I can borrow it?"

"You want to borrow my Volvo?"

"Sure . . . you can just bust me out of here and I couldddd cruise down . . . into Essenville."

"Okay, Wilson. Sure. Just bring it back with a full tank."

"You seen any good movies lately? Anything I can catch this weekend when I'm out in your . . . Volvo?"

"Not really. I saw this thing a couple of nights ago. Rented it. What was it called? Damn . . . you know, I don't even remember."

His foot taps, just once.

"Did you see it alone . . . ?"

"No, I saw it with someone else."

"Oh, okay. Who didddddd you see it with?"

"Just someone I know. They run a store in Essenville."

"Oh? You do know someone down there, huh?"

She holds back her answer, and a second later he relents. "So it suckeddd? The movie?"

"Pretty much."

"Well, thank you . . . for the tip. I'll make sure notttt to waste my time." He waits until he's caught her eye.

"You know whatt's a great fucking movie? *Out of the Blue.* Linda Manz. Dennis . . . Hopper. Before he turned *manajado.* Now *that* is a great movie. You ever see that movie?"

"Actually, I saw that when I was sixteen. A midnight show at Cinema Village. I thought I was the coolest thing on two legs."

"You were sixteen and hanging out at midnighttt shows? And your papa was okay with that?"

"Not really. Like I told you before, I was a little wild when I was that age."

"How wildd is a little, *dulzura*?"

"Oh, I wasn't so bad . . . I just got bored easily . . . so me and my friend Ingrid, we'd go into the city on the weekend and hang out and get drunk on wine and just be . . . kids. It was fun. For a while it was fun."

"You never gott in trouble? Sixteen . . . year-old girls from Connecticut playing out in the city?"

"You know, I think back now and it terrifies me. But at the time we were indestructible. I'd waltz around town with this fake ID this boy in my French class made for me, and Ingrid and I would sneak into these crummy bars, go see midnight shows, go see bands."

"Always inttttto music, huh?"

"Oh, yeah." And a grin slips across her face.

"What's . . . funny?"

"No, it's just . . . I don't talk about this very often . . . but I used to play. In a band."

"No shitttt."

"It was a couple of years later. In college. I played bass. That's when I got into reggae for the first time. I could hardly play a note, so I just went and bought a bunch of reggae records 'cause the guy in Bleecker Bob's told me they had cool basslines. Anyway . . . my boyfriend at the time was the guitarist. There were five of us. All dressed up like what we thought New York starving artists looked like. It was that kind of time, you know?"

"So what . . . was the name of the band?"

"Oh, God. It was so pretentious. We were called . . . Suburban Diaspora."

"*Hijole*. That *is* terrible. And . . . what kindddd of music was it?"

"I don't even know that we got that far. We just used to fight a lot and walk round St. Marks smoking cigarettes. I guess we thought we were punk rock . . . or new wave . . . or something. I wanted to be like Tina Weymouth. You know . . . from the Talking Heads?"

His face is blank.

"Well, anyway . . . there you are. Some of my oldest friends don't know that about me." She glances down at her watch. Then back up at him. "Sorry."

"Nah. That's . . . okay. I know you gottt stuff you need . . . to do. So what do you want to ttalk about next?"

"I guess . . ." Her voice is sober now. ". . . maybe we could move on to what led up to your transfer here."

There is no reaction.

"The letters."

He stares past her in silence. Keeps staring. Then: "When they took me . . . into the lawyer's room at Moxanie, Ossery was already there. Sittingggg—across from me like you are now. Nothinggg weird. Nothing out of the ordinary. But then I saw his face. And I knew someone was dead. Someone in his family. Or no—maybe it was someone close to *me*. Father Peres or Hurricane. But all he said was 'They found them.' So I say 'Found what?' That's funny . . . now, right? 'Found what?' And he says,

'The letters. The fuckinggg letters to Ojos. They found every one of them.'
He said they knew all about them. That they were . . . kites. Full of code.
And Mitchell Rieber was going to prosecute me again. And all I couldddd
think was 'What? They . . . found that shit *now?*' "

"What do you mean?"

"What I mean is the last time I'd written a . . . letter like that had been
in Auburn. Four years before. I hadn't sent out one kite the . . . whole time
I was in Moxanie."

"But you told me you were writing letters every day."

"Letters, sure. I was writinggggg letters. But there were no kites. No
code. No fucking orders to beat anyone or fucking kill anyone. None of
that."

His face is expressionless. The tape rolls on.

"Lizbeth, I saiddd when we first hooked up I would give you the truth
and that is what I'm givingggg you. *Verdad.* Point one, every piece of mail
they said was a kite had been written in my first year at Moxanie. My first
year . . . at Moxanie I did nothing that might dirty up my record because
back then like an idiot I—I still thought I—would be able to get out of
there. Point two, Hurricane knew what . . . needed to be done. He knew
how to run the organization without me sending little notes to Ojos. And
point three, I didn't want the Royals to be spillinggg blood anymore. I already told you thattt. This was meanttt to be a new chapter."

"But you'd written kites from prison before?"

"Of course. Ever since I firsttttt went up to Spofford."

"And what kind of thing had those kites . . . pertained to?"

"They *pertained* to . . . any shit you didn'ttttt want the guards to read
about. What you wanted hooped in the next time someone visited. Who
the—person you were writinggggg to should talk to if they needed a gun."

"Who you wanted beaten up?"

Nothing. Then a shrug. "Sure. Maybe. Why not?"

"Can you tell me what kind of code you used in those letters? Was it the
system you'd developed with your brother? Numbers?"

"At first. But then . . . the guards open your mail and see what looks
like a fuckinggg math paper, they're going ttto look twice, right? So things
moved on." He speaks matter of factly. "To start out with there was noth-
ingggggg too complex. All I did was move the alphabet forward on the
words I wanted hidden. So instead of the alphabet being ABC, I might
move everything forward so that it started BCD. You understand?"

"I think so."

"It's simple. Every letter you wanttt to use is now the . . . letter after it. So you don't write dog D-O-G anymore. You write it E-P-H. Your cat? Your itty-bitty kitten? That's cat, D-B-U. Right? And you can move shit forward as many times as you . . . want. So now there's twenty-six alphabets you can use. Alphabet One starts ABC. Alphabet Two, BCD. Alphabet Three, CDE. Alphabet twenty-one, UVW. Rightttt?"

"Sure. But how did whoever you were writing to know which one you were using?"

"The . . . date at the top of the letter. Not the month or the year. Just the day. I write the letter on the twelfth, I'm using Alphabet twelve. First letters LMN. So now dog is O-Z-R and cat is . . . N-L-C. Very old technique. Caesar made up . . . that shit. A five-year-old could use it. All the same it worked. You'd be amazed how much stuff IIIII sent out that way. But there were alwaysss problems. First thing, you end up . . . with nonsense words. DBU, OZR, XPTUIVG. It looks crazy. After a while even the dumbest *jarabe* is going to know something's up. So then the trick . . . is to make it look like part of a normal message. And the way you do that is to . . . space the letters out in a message that has nothing to do with what you're really sayinggg. Bury them inside other words."

"Okay. But how would the person reading know what they were supposed to be looking for?"

"The date. Always the date. If I'm writing on the third, then every third letter is what needs attention. On the twenty-fifth, every twenty-fifth letter. I'll give you an example. Say I want someone to hoop in a Mounds for me. Because I do love Mounds. Now let's say I'm writing on the seventh. That means Alphabet Seven. That means M-O-U-N-D-S is actually S-U-A-T-J-Y. You see?"

"I think so."

"Right, so now all I need to do . . . is come up with something where the first letter and every seventh letter after that spells S-U-A-T-J-Y. So . . ."

He gazes up to the ceiling for no longer than it takes her to recross her legs.

". . . what I'm goinggggg to . . . write is this. 'Dear friend, I need to tell you something that is of deep importance tttto me—Soon I must see a bird, a tree, or just anything.' Okay? Now, the person reading knows that because it's the seventh they're looking for the first letter and then every seventh. So he reads that and what he sees is capital S, and then the seventh letter after that is U, seven more A, then T, J, Y. Translate thattt back out of Alphabet Seven and you got M-O-U-N-D-S. 'Dear friend, I need to tell you something thatttt is of deep importance to me—Mounds.' And then he knows whatttt the Sapa wants next time he comes up to visit."

Lizbeth scrawls down the words in her notebook.

SOONIM USTSEE ABIRDA TREEOR JUSTAN YTHING

"Test me if you like."
"Okay. Say it's the fourteenth."
"Right."
"And you want to have someone called Joaquin beaten up."
She sees his lips purse. "No problem. In that case I would say, 'Dear friend, there is something I must tell you that has to be dealttt with— When I can remember the past I'm unhappy and soon despair is in my heart. I cannot ever give in but sadness fills me.' "
She notes down the words again. Translates herself.

WHENICANREMEM BERTHEPASTIMU NHAPPYANDSOON DESPAIRISINMY HEARTICANNOTE VERGIVEINBUTS AD- NESSFILLSME

WBNDHVA.

Alphabet 14 = JOAQUIN.

" 'Dear friend, there is something I must tell you that has to be dealt with—Joaquin.' "
"That was very quick."
"I've . . . had a lot of practice. But there was still another problem. People got confused over what was code and what wasn't. They would search through my letters for stuff that wasn't there. Then when there was something they woulddd miss it. So from now on if I was writing just an ordinary letter I always wrote in black ink. If there was somethinggggg else in there, I usedd blue. And then to . . . make clear what part of the letter they haddd to decode, I had trigger words."

"Trigger words?"

"Signals that whatever came . . . next would be the real message. Again, it all came from the ddddate. Whatever the date was, you would count in that many words from the start of the letter and there would be the trigger word. And the nexttt time you saw it used, you knew what came after was code. So if you get a letter from me in blue ink and it's the sixteenth, you count sixteen words in and you see 'Sunshine.' Then later I might say, 'I would love to be outside now, walking in the sunshine'—and you know you must pay attention to whatever I say nexttt."

"Okay. I understand."

"With that system, no *jarabe* would ever know what I was saying. It was all down to me. A test. If I could make what I was writing seem like unre—mar—ka—ble enough, then they would never even know there was anythingggg to look for. Let alone where to find it."

Pride has bled into his voice.

"Anyway, that was the system. Of course, I played aroundddd with it. Strengthened it. Adapted it. Maybe instead of the date, I'd let them know what alphabet I was usingggg with the first letter I wrote on the page. Later I had all these crazy random alphabets. I gave copies of them to the people closest to me and memorized them for the nextttt time I was sent away. I had a rule that if I ever . . . wrote three words beginning with V that was always a trigger. Three Vee, *sabes*? I threw all kinds of shitttt in there. Initials. Area codes. Birthdays. Fuckingggg slang and weird dialects. I even played around with the way I wrote the characters so that differentt kinds of As or Bs or Cs meant different things . . . you know, like the Inca with their quipus."

"I'm impressed."

"Thank you."

"So in the letters you were charged over, what code did you . . . did they *say* you used?"

"That was just it. It was a . . . mess. One letter they said I'd used the ID number of some *vato* who got shot up down in Red Hook, like I could . . . walk round with sixty thousand numbers in my head like fuckinggg Rain Man. Another time they said I'd coded the maiden name of the mother of some kid I never even met who died in . . . Chicago. Fucking *Chicago*. This kid's mother's maiden name. How fucked up is that? And more than that, *more than that,* when you actually looked at the letters, none of it even workeddd. That shit didn't even—work, *sabes*? But they'd just hold up something I wrote and make up some crazy way that it meant I was talking about some shit that—wound up happeningggggg six weeks later." He shakes his head. "You know, if you want to, you can say anything is code for anythinggg else."

The tape comes to the end of a side. He pauses while Lizbeth flips it over.

"Anyway . . . most of what they came up with still couldn't stick. They tried to charge me with thirty-two counts of conspiracy to murder. *Thirty-two counts.* Insane. By the time I . . . came up for trial all but—two had fallen apart. Even the greattt Mitchell Rieber knew he couldn't get anywhere with . . . the rest of it. But they still had these two homicides."

"Can you tell about them?"

"*Dulzura,*" he says, "I know what you know. They had a letter I'd written to Ojos where they said I toldddd him to have this *vato* Horace Gampas kill this—other *vato* Felix Cruz. Only Horace Gampas fucked up, they said. So then I'd written to Ojos again to say now I wanted Felix Cruz *and* Horace Gampas killed. Now, of course, they know Ojos didn't kill either of them, because he was being introduced to his *hina*'s parents the nightttt they died. But what Mitchell Rieber says is 'Oh, in that case, he must have just passed the order on to another Royal. So he is still guilty.' So Ojos gets life without parole for the crime of receiving a letter from me and meeting his *hina*'s parents. And I tell you, that *vato* has a fuckinggg lion-heart because not once did he try and save himself by telling those *cabron* fucks that I ordered those murders."

"So who did?"

"*No sé.* I have not one idea."

"Okay," she says. "In that case, let me clarify something. Have you ever sent a letter from prison in which a murder has been ordered?"

Aside from the tape rolling, there is silence. Then: "I have dddone a million things. Most of them . . . fill me with regret. I have told you time and again, Lizbeth, that the life I led was a useless waste."

But nothing more is forthcoming.

"Wilson, I don't mean this to sound confrontational . . . but I find it hard to believe you developed your own private code for twenty years so you could have Mounds bars smuggled in."

She feels his gaze harden.

"I have told you that in the past, I . . . ggggave some terrible orders. I wanted bad things done. But in the letters Mitchell Rieber used against me, in those I didn't order shit. You need to ask yourself why I would lie about this."

She doesn't have the answer.

"Anyway, I knew as soon as I set foot in courtttt that Mitchell Rieber would win. I knew it like I knew my own name. All I was . . . unsure of was what they would do to me—afterward. And then I found out."

He slumps in his chair. "I'm exhausted. You think we can . . . stop for today?"

"Sure. Of course. That's fine."

"You look kind of tired yourself, Lizbeth. You didn't sleep last nighttt?"

"I slept. I just didn't sleep well. I've been getting this recurring dream too, like you—"

"Shit. Not the lime trees?"

"No, not the lime trees."

She slides her pen into the binding of her notebook. Puts that into her bag. Sighs.

"I'm at my desk. Back in Quince Hill. And I'm typing, maniacally. Far quicker than I can actually type, you know? And it feels amazing. But then I realize that no matter what keys I'm hitting, I'm really just typing the same thing over and over."

"So whatttt is it?"

"I don't know. I didn't even seem to know in the dream. I know it's the same word or the same series of words . . . but when I actually try to read it back, it doesn't even look like English. But in the dream, I didn't seem to care. I just started typing again."

She leans forward to switch off the tape. And after he's gone, she too rises from her seat and walks back through the endless hallways with her escort guard, a giant redhead who has recently progressed from absolute silence to hello and good-bye. She's familiar with each of them now, the half-dozen-strong roster assigned to her visits. Knows which she feels at ease with, and which put her on edge. Who talks, who doesn't.

The redhead leaves her at the visitor's entrance, and she carries on alone into the empty parking lot, where she curses out loud as she finds that she's left the Volvo unlocked.

The Urkoff house looks wholly unchanged since the last time she visited. That, she remembers, was three Thanksgivings ago. Painted white and blue, the structure patched up but robust. Stubborn icicles above the front door.

She can already hear the noise inside. The jangle of childish excitement.

"So you made it," Mame says. "I wasn't sure you would."

Lizbeth feels her neck tense as she follows her sister inside. Heads for the source of the noise. The family room.

When she gets there every sixth-grader in Altoona appears to be clustered under a banner hung from the ceiling that declares them to be celebrating the tenth birthday of Kyle Urkoff. The family's youngest son.

He stands in the corner with a pack of other boys. With Mame beside her, Lizbeth approaches. Prepares to stoop down and greet him before she sees he's an inch taller than her. He was, the last time she was here, still talking to imaginary friends.

His real ones scatter.

"Happy Birthday, Kyle," she says, and hands him a gift-wrapped parcel. He tears it open. Finds inside deluxe editions of *Moby-Dick* and *The Hound of the Baskervilles*.

"Thank your aunt," Mame says.

"Thank you."

"You're welcome," Lizbeth says.

He stares at her. "Why does it say 'Judge' on your hand?"

"Because I wanted to remember it."

"It looks weird."

There's no insult in his voice. Just observation.

"You're the one who looks weird, Kyle," says a voice from beside Lizbeth's shoulder.

Lizbeth glances down and what she sees terrifies her. There, as if plucked whole from history, is Mame at thirteen. The same prim snub to the nose, the rod-straight posture. Every last detail just how it was.

Lizbeth takes a second to realize it's her niece.

"Hi, Aunt Lizbeth. I'm sorry about Kyle being such an idiot."

The voice. God, the voice too.

"Hello, Melissa. How are you?"

"I'm fine, thank you."

A disembodied hand holds out a plastic cup in which sits a red, viscous liquid.

"Traditional Urkoff fruit punch. Strictly nonalcoholic. *For now.*"

Dave Urkoff, husband and father, epically affable. He turns and calls across the room.

"Josh, get your ass over here."

A towering figure in plaid hulks up beside the rest of the family. Joshua. The eldest child. He smiles warmly, if vaguely. His eyes are a little red.

So she stands with her hands cradled at her waist, encircled by Urkoffs. Kyle taps his foot and hums, eager to return to his friends.

"It's uncanny," Dave says.

Mame peers at him, suspect.

"What is?"

"You and your sister. You're like twins. You even tilt your heads the same way. It's hilarious."

Mame and Lizbeth turn to face each other, staring, making sure to keep their heads straight, but even as the children fall about laughing, neither of them sees it.

And as the afternoon passes, there are conversations with Dave about the new stores Sheetz has opened up in Virginia, much time spent having the rules of computer games unsuccessfully explained to her by Kyle's friends. Later, those party-goers not yet driven home by their parents crowd around the Urkoffs' TV to watch loud and dazzling movies.

She looks on as they gape in the darkness before she retreats upstairs. Hears guitar music from behind one door, phone chatter from another.

"Hey you."

At the end of the hall Mame sits cross-legged on the floor of the guest room, hunched over a storage trunk.

"Hey yourself."

Lizbeth joins her. Sits adjacent.

"Listen, were the books okay? For Kyle? You said he liked to read."

"They were great. They were perfect."

"It's just he seemed a little . . . underwhelmed."

"Oh, don't worry. He's on his own planet most of the time."

She forages in the trunk, picking through the contents: old postcards and school reports, photo albums, ticket stubs.

"He says he wants to be a writer."

"He does?"

"That's what he says."

"Wow. What happened to astronaut?"

"Yes! I knew this was in here!"

Mame exclaims in triumph as she pulls out a torn yellow notebook. Its cover says, handwritten in capitals: *THE CASE OF THE LONELY ICE SKATER MYSTERY.*

"Oh, my God," Lizbeth says.

THE CASE OF THE LONELY ICE SKATER MYSTERY was, as far as either Greene sister can remember, Lizbeth's first completed story. Written at ten in an August heatwave.

"God. I thought this must have been put out with the trash when we went to New Haven."

"No. I had it."

Lizbeth just shakes her head.

"This is . . . *whoa*. Too much."

"You know, it's funny . . . because I spent that entire summer screaming at you for making stuff up. Do you remember? You'd disappear off on your own and come back two hours later and say you'd been to Lake Compounce on your own and everyone'd get all freaked out . . . and really you'd just been down at Patty Twine's house. Just those dumb lies that always got found out. Then one night you knocked on the door of my room and left this outside for me. And I always thought that was the bravest thing, 'cause you must have known I was going to rag on you with no mercy without even reading it."

"Which you did."

"Which I did. But I guess you knew that I'd read it eventually. See how good it was."

"I never knew you had."

Lizbeth gazes down into the trunk.

"Shit. Are those the comic books?"

They are. Mame's collection of Monkees comic books, ritually purchased for seventeen issues between spring 1967 and fall 1968, their covers now faded and battered, dog-eared pages filled with cartoons of Peter Tork dressed as a sheikh or Mike Nesmith relaxing at home. Borrowed from Mame after she grew bored with them, freshly cherished, then returned to her custody when Lizbeth too found new fixations.

Now, once again, she shakes her head.

"Anyway, look where it got you."

"Huh?"

"Making stuff up. Your overactive imagination. I could always see it, you know? I knew you were going to do something great."

"Really? I always thought it'd be you. You were the one with the grades and the prizes. And the friends. And the boys."

"Well . . . I thought things might go that way for me too. But you know . . . I met Dave and . . . I just wanted something different from what we'd had at home, you know? Something that was mine. That was simple . . . I guess I thought I could get to the other stuff later. So now I commute five hours a day to organize promotional days for Saran Wrap . . ."

"Mame, I'm sorry. I must have made things a thousand times worse back then. Going AWOL . . . coming home drunk."

"You were just a kid. It wasn't your fault. The only thing that pissed me off was the night you disappeared in New York. It's hard to have much of a prom when your sister's been picked up by the police sleeping on a bench at Grand Central."

"Oh, God . . . when I think of it . . ."

"But it wasn't your fault. I should have been . . . stronger for you . . . when you were younger. Anyway, fuck it . . . I wouldn't change anything I've got now." She stands and stretches out her legs, then returns to the floor. "So . . . how's the baby?"

"According to every test known to science, it's fine."

"And you?"

"Oh, me too. I mean, I can barely remember to put my shoes on before I leave the house, but I'm fine. It's just . . . I still can't picture it, you know? When it's all . . . *happened* . . ."

A door slams down the hall.

"Joshua!" Mame screams. "Would you please stop destroying the house?" She turns back to Lizbeth. "I won't lie to you. Everything from your old life is gone now. *Pfft.* Finished."

"That's okay. I was getting tired of it anyway."

They stare into the trunk.

"You know," Lizbeth says, "it's been so long since we talked like this. We used to talk like this all the time."

"We did?"

"Of course we did."

"Betty . . . honey, I love you . . . but you and me . . . we've never done much but scratch at each other."

"Oh, shit," Lizbeth says. "I just remembered something. Wait there."

She gets to her feet and hurries downstairs. Then out to the car. When she returns, she hands Mame a paper bag.

"I wanted Kyle to have this, but I wasn't sure you'd think it was suitable. Maybe you could take a look at it and, you know . . . if you think it's okay, pass it on to him. It's a kids' story. But the ending might be a little strong."

Mame tears open the package.

"*The Monsters of Gramercy Park*. By Jim Rockford."

"It's something my publishers are doing."

From downstairs, they hear whoops and applause.

"I thought he might enjoy it."

Ossery sits across from her in the Venus Restaurant Diner, speaking like he's been tranquilized. Lizbeth stares around. Recognizes faces.

The waitress takes their order, and he asks for decaf. His doctor, he says glumly, has told him he's in bad shape. He's having to make some life changes.

The timing, he says, couldn't be worse. He looked in his diary this morning and counted off the weeks until the review of Wilson's appeal. So close now, he says. Crept up on him.

"So," he says, "you wanted to talk?"

And she enthuses over the progress of the book. How excited she is about the way it's taking shape, how compelling his testimony has been.

"I'm glad," he says. "And from our side, I really think you've been a huge part of his improvement. Just having someone he likes to talk with showing him that level of interest . . . his moods are better . . . his focus. You must have noticed how his speech has cleared up."

"I'm pleased if you think I've helped," she says.

But there's a problem.

"We've been discussing the letters," she says. "The kites. It's just that—"

Ossery sighs before she's even finished. It's just, she says, that it's crucial to the book—to the success of the book—that the bond of honesty between her and Wilson remain intact. That his *candor* remains as vital as ever. Anything else can only undermine their relationship, she says, the same way it will undermine her readers' faith in the story.

"So I take it he's said he didn't order any murders."

"Not the ones he was convicted of."

"I really hoped he wouldn't do this," Ossery says, and he takes a desultory sip of his coffee. Lizbeth waits until he's stopped making faces afterward.

198

"Do you believe him?"

"At this point in time," he says, "I couldn't tell you with any degree of confidence."

"You must know if you believe him."

He closes his eyes and hums. Then: "I believe Wilson's original conviction was heinously flawed. That is a matter of record. *Conversely* . . . given that Wilson admitted to sending out kites in the past and that Mitchell Rieber could draw a pretty straight line between phrases that were written and events which took place . . . it's always been difficult for me as Wilson's legal representative to remove the impression of guilt. Speaking colloquially, you could say the *impression* the case gives is of a kid getting his hand caught in the cookie jar. Oh, my head . . ."

He stares bleakly at his coffee cup, then calls to the waitress to take it away. To bring him another one. A real one. When she does, he gulps it, still steaming. Visibly revives.

"He told me," she says, "there was no code. Not in the letters to—"

"The letters to Ojos. Right, right. Let me tell you my feeling at this point. My feeling is that however much energy Wilson chooses to devote to the subject, the actual details of which set of orders he admits to and which he doesn't is not all that relevant. What is relevant is keeping him out of Ad-Seg and making sure his future lies in a less oppressive environment. I *thought* that was the whole purpose of our involvement with you . . . for him to show some damn contrition."

Half his coffee is gone already.

"But, you know, welcome to Wilsonworld. Where the guy in charge likes to keep the staff dancing. It's nothing new. It's also not helpful for those of us working on his behalf. Which, frankly, is enough of a struggle already. You know Mitchell Rieber's already campaigning for reelection? So God help us if he wants to drag Wilson into a few speeches to remind everyone what a gunslinger he is . . ."

Lizbeth gazes around the diner again. The collective shudder of those nearest to the door as frozen air gusts in every time it opens. A stately figure in a ESSUSP parka wanders past the booth, and when she looks up she sees it's another of her escort guards. CO Sherwin Baines. A man whose clothes, brush mustache and Groucho eyebrows are in the *Expositor* almost every week, whose fame and kudos in Essenville exceeds hers by some margin: the captain of the town's bowling team on the battlegrounds of the Southwestern Pennsylvania Bowling League. On Main Street, that makes him a sports legend in the body of an overweight fifty-year-old chain smoker. With his wife and teenage daughter beside him, he notices Lizbeth. Nods in acknowledgment and finds a table.

She turns back.

"I guess what worries me," she says, "is that if he keeps denying any involvement with the letters, it could damage the book. Make the whole thing seem . . . implausible. It just stretches your belief so much . . . and it turns the story into something else . . . something different from what I thought I was writing."

"I'll take care of it. Make sure he understands. When are you seeing him next?"

"Now," she says. "Right after this."

"Fine. As soon as you're done, I'll get word to him."

He summons the waitress, and asks her for a refill.

"So you know, I've got this interview tomorrow . . ."

Wilson Velez lifts his hands in their cuffs and scratches above his eye.

"Interview?"

"Right. With the *Times*. They want—to talk to me aboutttt my life. Ossery arranged it."

"He did? He didn't mention that to me."

"When did you tttalk to him?"

She takes a moment.

". . . We talked today. I needed to . . . clarify a few things."

"You sound irritated."

"I'm not irritated. I just didn't know there was anything like that planned. But you know . . . it's your life. You can talk about it with who you want."

"He said it would be good for me. Show the public I am a thoughtttttful person."

"I'm sure he's right."

"It was jjjust . . . I was wondering if you could give me any advice . . . About what I should say to them. How I should be around them."

"You need to be direct. Unequivocal."

"Unequivocal. Okay."

"If it seems like you're hiding something, they'll know."

"Like the cops."

"Right. But at the same time you can't be as open as you have been with me. About your past. What you tell me, I can contextualize. Explain. Reporters won't. So be wary."

"So I should be direct and unequivocal . . . but I can't be open and I needddd to be wary."

"Right."

She brings out the tape recorder.

"You know what? Forget it. It doesn't matter. They'll have written it before they get here anyway."

"They will? I never knew it worked like that."

"Wilson, can we get started?"

She unwraps a new cassette.

"Of—course we can, Lizbeth."

"By the way, I'd prefer that you didn't mention that you and I are working together."

"Sure. If you prefer."

"I do," she says, and she slips the tape into the machine. "So . . . I was hoping that today we could pick up from last time."

"John Aspera. Okay."

Record.

"You know, right before he sentenced me he just sat there playinggg with his robe. Fussing with the sleeves, *sabes*? Like maybe they didn't fit right, or his maid put too much starch in them. And then finally he looked dddown at me." He stares past Lizbeth, eyes fixed on the wall behind her. "He said he had thought very deeply about my case, and thattt he could only see one course of action. Then he tttttold me of the kind of confinement he had . . . conceived of. Everythinggg that would be strippedddd away from me. And only he, Judge John Aspera, could ever change this. At first I thought I must be hearing wronggg, *sabes*? I said to him, 'You mean thatt I can no longer be part of the human race? That I will live my life alone like this until I die?' He didn't even look at me. He just wenttt back to his robe. And then he said, 'I have not come to this decision to punish you, Mr. Velez—but to protect others *from* you.' He said arrangements should be made so thattt I was far from New York and the people I had corrupted could live free of my shadow. Then he got to his feet and walked away."

His head drops but he keeps talking.

"They brought me here that night. Drove seven hours. When we arrived it was pitch black. Other places, the guards spit at you when you arrive.

Kick you, curse at you. Here, they said nothing. Did nothinggggg. Just the place was enough. Then in shackles they took me to the cell that would now be my everything."

He breathes in through his mouth. Holds it. Lets it go.

"I was used to cell doors being locked on me. That was nothing. But my first nighttt here I whimpered and I sobbed and I threw myself against the door and begged to be let out."

"What was different?"

"I will try to explain."

The more Wilson talked about his experiences in Ad-Seg, the more it distressed him. Hunched over the table, he seemed to almost physically shrink in his chair. His voice, barely a mumble.

Lizbeth looks back over her last sentence. Grabs the mouse.

His voice was barely a mumble.

The place of his confinement was, in essence, no more sophisticated than the "holes" prisoners had been cast into since men first began jailing one another. Barbed by technology, however, the Ad-Seg Unit of US Penitentiary Essenville was a hole like few others. A windowless, almost entirely soundproofed box rendered from concrete and steel, it resembled nothing so much as a sensory deprivation tank. Prisoners who spent the customary periods of two to six weeks here emerged dazed and depressed. Wilson, of course, would stay five years.

The deterioration began immediately, and worked fast. Throughout his first twelve months, he found the traditional refuge of sleep all but impossible to reach under the strip lights that stayed on in his cell around the clock. Hours were spent weeping or screaming. With the delivery of his meals through a slot in his cell door the only way of marking time, he became disoriented. Attempts to talk with the guards were ignored. He lost his voice yelling through a tiny air vent above his bed, trying to contact the inmate in the next cell. Weeks later, his lawyer told him he'd learned it was being kept empty to prevent him doing just that. Occasionally he was given a pen and paper; but anything he wrote would then have to be destroyed.

Slumped in his cell, he found his moods narrowed into one—despair. "A blackness oozed into my soul, flooding it with sorrow. All I could do was try to think of nothing, because every thought I had was agony. Every day that passed was carved into me."

He fell back on a quotation: "The rigid embrace of the narrow house . . . the silence like a sea that overwhelms." I recognized it as Poe— later, I realized it came from his short story "The Premature Burial."

Slowly, the few noises he was exposed to—the automated flushing of the toilet, the motion of the security camera positioned by the ceiling— began to seem deafening. His body started to turn on him. Muscles withered; his skin broke out; his hair thinned and fell from his scalp.

When he met with his lawyer, Alan Ossery, meanwhile, his speech was so fractured as to be unintelligible. The stammers and losses of concentration were becoming more extreme. Words he once knew disappeared from his memory. Language, his solace, was abandoning him.

Day to day, his only representatives of the world outside were his guards. They were, he discovered, a slightly different breed from those at Moxanie. There, violence was meted out near randomly in an atmosphere of simmering chaos. Here, the COs spent their days in a sterile control booth 100 yards from the nearest cell, venturing out only to deliver and collect meal trays.

Yet were there any breach of discipline, if just one of the unit's countless rules was breached, the response was instant and unforgiving. The result was an "extraction"—the all-purpose name for the removal of an inmate from his cell, but which in this case meant its charging by up to six guards who then disabled the inmate with pepper spray before knocking him off his feet with "stun plates" (plastic shields similar to those used by riot police). If an inmate was especially aggressive, an attack dog could be sent in to subdue him. He would then be removed from the cell using

She checks her notes from her tour of the facility.

"all necessary force"—before being taken to a specially designated room until he was deemed sufficiently cooperative.

She remembers the unmarked door that CO Brink told her led to that room. How when she asked if she could look inside, he told her he didn't have the keys. That it would take an age to locate them. So they may as well keep moving.

But incredibly, there were times when Wilson's sense of isolation became so acute that he deliberately provoked such confrontation. It was worth the pain, he said, just to know his actions still had consequences—that he still existed in this world.

"Without that I had no proof," he said. "In Ad-Seg I learned that you are only alive when others can see you. When you can see yourself in their eyes. All we are is what is seen. What is thought of. So that meant I was dying."

Beset by "perceptual disturbances"—hallucinations of dead Royals and movie characters, the sound of numbers being chanted—he swung between torpor and frenzy. By his fourth year in Ad-Seg, he found a refuge obsessing over the rashes and spasms that wracked his body—his fantasies of exotic diseases a distraction of sorts from the grinding reality of his decline.

But not one that could hold.

"I felt like I was about to be swallowed up," he said. "Like something from below me was trying to devour me."

Eventually, it did. On December 15th of that fourth year, Ossery told him the result of a plea to John Aspera to be allowed a half-hour visit from Father Raymond Peres over the holidays as "spiritual comfort." It had been rejected.

Now, in the lawyer's room at ESSUSP, he remembered little if anything of the night that followed—only "being seized by a terrible power."

The next morning, when the guards came to deliver breakfast—they later said their monitors had "malfunctioned" in the night—he was face down on the floor of his cell, naked, the result of what was assumed to be a psychotic episode. Bite marks covered his skin. Many had drawn blood. A gash as thick as a middle finger was scored down his forehead like some gory tribal marking: the product of butting his head against the cell walls so often and with such force that he knocked himself unconscious.

I gazed at the still livid scar as he talked. He remembered coming to, he said, thinking he was being moved, passing out again and then finding himself in the hospital, "shackled everywhere that wasn't broken." Once his fractures had been set and wounds bandaged, he was transferred to the prison infirmary. Then, three nights later, he awoke to find himself being moved again—back into his cell in Ad-Seg. He screamed until his throat gave out.

And then, he said, he just closed down. His access to pens and paper was withdrawn by John Aspera. They had, the judge said, "obviously encouraged dark thoughts." It was debatable whether Wilson could have used them anyway—now for the most part he just lay still, near catatonic, his eyes open but unseeing. He still worried about his health—but only because all he wanted was "to see out my time in this body free of pain." Now, he said, he had finally come to understand the nature of Ad-Seg. It was limbo.

"My soul was already gone. It left me the day they took me back there. So I was just waiting for my body to join it. Wilson Velez? He was a speck of dust. A puff of smoke who once dreamed he was a man."

As Wilson talked, I thought of John Aspera—the man he knew as God. He was, from what I'd read, some way from the wrathful zealot his treatment of Wilson implied. Rather, he was famous for his independent-mindedness, an opera lover and family man. Popular among his peers, his career had been informed by an almost philosoph-ical bent.

I wondered if he thought of Wilson Velez while attending La Travi-ata; *whether the specter of Ad-Seg ESSUSP troubled him as he played softball with his grandchildren. If it did, it never persuaded him to re-vise his judgment. Despite a series of appeals backed by a raft of civil liberties watchdogs, he remained unmoved. Until, on a blustery night toward the end of last October came the intervention of the massive brain hemorrhage that killed John Aspera in his sleep.*

And now Wilson Velez was here with me in the penitentiary lawyer's room.

The day he was taken out of Ad-Seg, he told me, he stared from the window of his new cell and the light fanning through the watchtowers looked like a Pacific sunrise. But what he had lost would not be easily retrieved. Part of me doubted it could be at all.

"Nothing that happened in that cell made me stronger," he said. "All that happened there was evil. To be taken from the world like that . . . it can never be undone."

Finally, he looks back up. His eyes red rimmed.

"And these kids here with Royal ink on their arms and their faces, they stare at me from across the yard . . . But what they think they see . . . is just not there."

"What would you do," Lizbeth says, "if you had to go back?"

His voice is as clear as she's ever heard it: "I would die before that could happen."

There is a fierce propulsion to the woman's steps as she advances down 108th Street. Hurrying home in the twilight, past Manny Mayi Corner, the Corona Sewing Center, approaching Alfano-Queens Plumbing.

Her name is Silvia Benavidez. She is twenty-two years old and tonight she has a million things to do. Her mother has the flu, her father's out at work, her sister and brothers are going to need dinner. She should have been back an hour ago.

The 7 rumbles by as she turns into Roosevelt Avenue. Stops at the crosswalk on the corner. Sees a guy she knows across the street. Rafael Ferrer. Tee-O, they call him. Used to hang out with her oldest brother. He sees her and he breaks into a smile. Thinks he's such hot shit. He isn't, she silently concedes, so wrong.

She sees a man in a black do-rag sprint up behind him, then stop.

Reach into his coat.

A glint.

Tee-O's still smiling when the first shot rings out. It only drops from his face with the second, as his legs collapse underneath him.

There's no one behind him anymore.

Silvia Benavidez stands mute and rooted as she hears the first screams around her. Looks down, and sees the beads round Tee-O's neck snap from their chain. And red, white and gold spill across the sidewalk.

ELEVEN

The last of the sun sank behind the Hudson River. At the same time, a cruel wind picked up, howling as a stray dog with only three legs and an empty belly howls. The monsters of Gramercy Park watched the night draw in. If you were to walk past them and listen closely, you might have almost heard the dreadful creak as they stretched out their hideous stone claws.

Perched above the front door of their beloved building, Hector turned to Edmond.

"So here we are again, old friend," said Hector.

"Indeed we are, old friend," said Edmond.

"We have seen so many glorious, terrible nights since coming here, haven't we?"

"Oh, yes. Such marvelously ghastly years they have been!"

Hector looked closer at his fellow gargoyle. "Edmond—I have to tell you, there is something disgusting stuck between your fangs."

"Really? There is?"

"Yes—and it looks magnificent!"

The two grotesque creatures cackled repulsively. But in their laughter was sadness too. Because they knew that Gramercy Park might not be their home much longer. Every day, Louis Fung—or the ancient demon they knew him to be—had more names on his petition to remove the monsters from their building. Soon, he would have enough to get his way.

But that was not all. Ever since Fung had arrived, not one of the gargoyles had been able to so much as cause a person to step in gum, leaving them weak and tired and ailing. So when the old grandfather clock in the lobby at last struck ten and the time came to seek out the most horrible people in the city, their mood was gloomy. (There had also been an outbreak of mold on their scales that only made things worse.)

Yet still they took to the skies, this army of ancient spirits. And over

Penn Station they split up as they always did, spreading out across the city to feed on the badness they would find below.

As they soared above the Chrysler Building, Hector and Edmond looked down and saw Greasy Joe the hot dog vendor, leaning up by his hot dog stand. This made them delighted—because they knew they always could rely on Greasy Joe to be mean and miserly. Although he was famous across New York for his skeezy hot dogs, there were always enough tourists around to keep him in business.

Sure enough, in no time a man on vacation from Sweden passed by and asked for a hot dog. Greasy Joe quickly produced a prewrapped hot dog already in a paper napkin and handed it to the man. Then he charged him $5!

The Swedish tourist thanked him and walked away. But after no more than three steps, he took a bite and made an unhappy face. He walked back to Greasy Joe. "This hot dog has no ketchup in it! And no mustard in it! And no onions in it!" Greasy Joe just shrugged. "You never said you wanted no ketchup or mustard or onions."

"But of course I do!"

"Then you shouldda ordered the super deluxe. The super deluxe comes with ketchup and mustard and onions."

Greasy Joe took back the hot dog and opened up the bun and over the wiener he squirted some watery ketchup, some flavorless mustard and a spoonful of onions so small you would need a magnifying glass to see it. Then he handed back the dog.

"That's another $2," he said.

The tourist shook his head but handed over the money. Then he looked down. Now that the hot dog was out of its napkin he could see the truth!

"This is the smallest wiener in the world!" he cried. "Look at it! It's no bigger than my thumb!"

And he was right. It was exactly *the same size as his thumb. But Greasy Joe just shrugged again. "You shouldda said you wanted the extra large!"*

With that he took the world's smallest wiener out of the bun, scraped off the ketchup and the mustard and the onions, and replaced it with a regular-size wiener.

"That's another $3," he said. And by now the tourist was so hungry

that he just handed over the money. But when he bit into the hot dog it was all he could do not to spit it out again.

"This hot dog is stone cold!"

Greasy Joe wagged a greasy finger in the Swedish man's face. "Listen, buddy, take a look around! D'you see anyone else complaining?"

The tourist threw the hot dog to the sidewalk before he turned and marched away. Greasy Joe bent down and picked it up. Without further ado, Hector and Edmond appeared beside him to see what havoc they could cause.

But nothing happened.

They tried putting holes in Greasy Joe's buckets of watery ketchup and flavorless mustard so they would leak all over him. But nothing happened. They tried letting off the brakes on his stand so that it would roll off down the street. But nothing happened. They even tried knocking Greasy Joe's wig off his head so that everyone would see the huge red birthmark on his big bald head.

But nothing happened. No matter how hard they tried, none of the monsters' plans succeeded. Until finally another tourist walked up to Greasy Joe's stand, and Hector and Edmond could only watch as he handed them the same dirty hot dog he had just picked up from the sidewalk!

With frustrated scowls on their hideous faces, they took to the skies again. They flew north as far as Inwood Hill Park and east as far as the Lincoln Tunnel, as far west as the Williamsburg Bridge and as far south as the Statue of Liberty. They saw old ladies and movie stars and Wall Street bankers and Sunday school teachers and all of them were doing some kind of badness. But, to the monsters' dismay and confusion, no matter what kind of chaos they tried to create, nothing at all, in any way, shape, form or fashion, happened. Their trouble-making powers had deserted them—and with every hour that passed, they grew a little weaker.

Which is not to say that nothing bad happened in the city that night. In fact, plenty did.

Just as it chugged away from Battery Park, the Staten Island Ferry sprang a leak and everybody on it had to jump overboard and swim back to land. Across Manhattan, the subway had a power cut and everyone on their last train home got marooned in dark tunnels with the rats. But this was not the kind of mischief the monsters made—this was made by a much more dangerous spirit.

Long before dawn, Hector and Edmond turned back. When they rejoined the other gargoyles above Penn Station, not one had carried out any act of mischief or mayhem themselves—although they had seen many others.

Then, as the monsters glumly flew home, they came upon the most awful vision of the entire night! But this was awful in a way that made none of them glad!

There, on the corner of Gramercy Park, the grand old house that stood opposite theirs was ablaze. Orange flames danced in the windows, and thick black smoke enveloped the roof.

The people who lived there ran out, waving their hands in the air and screaming. The monsters didn't like to see this—these people had never done anything bad at all. Indeed, when Louis Fung had started his petition, they had put up a sign in their window that said "Save the Gargoyles!"

But now they were losing their home too. Then the monsters saw Louis Fung standing in front of the grand old house, stepping up onto a wooden crate to address the crowd that had gathered in their nightshirts and pajamas. And what he had with him was an even more awful sight than the fire.

There, on a leash like a Chihuahua, was Pulga—the very smallest of all the gargoyles that lived in Gramercy Park. Hector and Edmond gasped in horror. They had not even noticed he was gone!

Louis Fung waved the leash in the air and pointed at Pulga. "Friends!" he shouted. "I, Louis Fung, have apprehended the grotesque creature that started this terrible fire! It is, as you can see, one of the vile monsters from the building opposite."

Without further ado, Hector and Edmond ordered the monsters to get ready to rescue Pulga. But another of the building's smaller gargoyles flew up beside them—and whispered the worst and most horrendous thing they had ever heard.

"Pulga is there on purpose," the tiny gargoyle said sorrowfully. "Last night, Louis Fung told him that if he took the blame for the fire and said we had all started it, then he would save him when we were torn from the face of the building. He asked me too. I said no. I never thought Pulga really would do it . . ."

Hector and Edmond were full of woe. Never had they imagined that one of their own spirits would do such a shameful thing. Mournful, they watched as the fire blazed and the people in the crowd got angry.

"We must put an end to these monsters!" yelled Louis Fung. "I ask all residents of the neighborhood to sign up now to have them removed! Starting with this one!"

Hector and Edmond looked at Pulga. Suddenly, he was scared. And then, oh, so slowly, Louis Fung bent down and put each of his hands over the treacherous creature's ears.

Every one of the monsters shuddered with fear and with disbelief. For they all knew what it meant when a gargoyle in spirit form has a person's hands put over its ears.

For a second nothing happened. Then, in a flash, Pulga turned back into the rough gray stone of a gargoyle. And then, *with the monsters unable to bring themselves to look, he crumbled into a thousand pieces that fell to the sidewalk and then blew away in the wind.*

Another mighty cheer went up from the crowd. As it did, the siren of the fire truck finally rang out. And while the firemen tried to put out the flames, the people of Gramercy Park ran to the monsters' building to add their names to Louis Fung's petition.

George Finer looks up from the page at Lizbeth's kitchen table. Puffs out his cheeks and exhales.

The two of them ate lunch here an hour ago. The plates now cleared away but still unwashed on the counter, the Sunday afternoon outside benignly damp.

"Well, that's . . . intense . . . I mean, for a book for children."

"Take the rest home with you if you want," she says without looking up. "I'd be interested to know what you thought about the ending."

She has laid out in front of her the *Times.* The story about Wilson. "THE SURVIVOR," the headline calls him. A recent picture taken in ESSUSP, slumped and mongrel eyed, beside a photograph from the first trial.

Ossery is quoted at length. There is discussion of Mitchell Rieber's use of the case in kindling his political career, the effects of long-term Ad-Seg: the damage Wilson suffered there and how he reemerged, broken but radicalized, "a fiercely persuasive critic of America's obsession with prison as a tool of social control." *Cogent and insightful,* the reporter calls him.

Anyone concerned with the health of the justice system should, the story says, watch for the impending review of his release from Ad-Seg.

Reading it feels like watching a stranger sleeping in her bed.

"So is he really called Jim Rockford?"

"Huh? Oh. Apparently so."

Putting the loose pages aside, George leans over. Glances at the paper. "Hey! It's your guy!"

"That's my guy."

He props his elbows up on the table. Scans the first few lines. "So tell me," he says, "how do you *talk* to someone like that?"

"We just talk. And it seems to tick along, you know?"

"And the project? Is it . . . coming together?"

"It's getting there. It definitely is. I feel good about it, you know?"

George shakes his head. Tells her it's the most amazing thing to be around a talent like hers. To see it at work, extending itself. He has, he says, embarrassed now, tried so often to write at her level. Produce something so compelling. "Only it turns out there's nothing that compelling in my head. You know? *Tsk,* listen to me. George, this is Lizbeth Greene. Of course she doesn't."

And she almost replies; but not quite.

"I just hope you know," he says, "how much it means to me that you'd talk with me about your work. I know I don't have that creative *gift* myself, so this . . . it's really special to me . . ."

"George, I've been reading *Settlers in a Misty Place.* So you can quit that nonsense."

"Lizbeth, please . . . don't make me feel like even more of a boob."

"I mean it. You write beautifully."

She pats his arm. Gets to her feet. Takes a handful of jelly beans from the counter. "You want some?" she says.

"Oh, no. There's a spare tire I need to shift before I'm allowed jelly beans."

So she gets back to the *Times,* and he returns to the monsters. She glances up at him as he reads. Someone to be silent with. And then: "I've been thinking about Lloyd Dreiz." He has his elbows on the table again.

"Lloyd . . . Dreiz. I might need something more here."

"Lloyd Dreiz. The town photographer. In the picture I have at home . . ."

"*Lloyd Dreiz*. Right."

"Well, I've been thinking about him . . ."

"You're sounding a little demented, George."

"No, it's just . . . there's something about him I wanted to talk about . . . with you. I wondered what you might make of it . . . with your expertise."

"Sure. George, I have no idea what you're talking about."

"*Okay*. Here it is. For a long time in Essenville, there have been rumors . . . there have been *theories* . . . that Lloyd Dreiz killed his wife."

Lizbeth's hand is clapped over her mouth. "George, I'm shocked. An upstanding man like you trading in such awful gossip."

"I didn't say I believed it," he says. "If you'll stop laughing, I'll tell you the story. I've known Lloyd Dreiz since grade school. He was always rotten. Mean spirited."

"Mean spirited. *Whoa*. George, are you sure he only killed once?"

"Mean spirited was the least of it. He was a bastard of a kid. A gun nut. We never got along. He left for Pittsburgh the year I went to college. Came back six months after me. He'd been working as a photographer up there. Still just as much of a creep, and now he'd started drinking too. Only somehow he'd got himself married. And she was an angel! A lovely woman called Gina. Who knows what brought the two of them together? Anyway, she had money. Family money, I guess. So when they fetched up back here she pretty much set him up in business. Rented him a studio, bought him a bunch of equipment. Of course, back then the town was pretty much dying, so there was nothing much to take pictures *of*, but she kept paying the rent anyway. Then the prisons opened up and the town came back to life and suddenly Lloyd had a business after all."

He leans in close. "Gina had a heart condition. Some kind of problem with a valve. Chronic. She had pills she took. Kept them with her all the time in case of an emergency. Except one weekend, maybe a year and a half after ESSUSP was built, she was at the back of the house tending the yard and she had an attack. A nasty one. And for *whatever reason,* she didn't have her pills. The poor woman fell to the ground right there, gasping for breath and crying for help. But Lloyd, *apparently,* didn't see her. Didn't hear her. He was down in the storm cellar cleaning his guns. So Gina died where she lay."

There is a moment's silence.

"So what do you think?"

"What do I think? I think you've just told me a sad story about a man whose wife died."

"Oh, come on! You, Lizbeth Greene, are just being coy! You know something's wrong here. A woman with a lifelong condition goes out without her pills. Why would that happen? Where were the pills? Huh?"

"Why are we talking about this, George?"

"Because you've spent your whole life dealing with this kind of thing. You must be thinking what I'm thinking. It was Lloyd! He hid the pills!"

She loses the struggle to keep herself from laughing. "George, I hate to remind you of this, but . . . I make it all up."

He sighs and rises, ambles over to the jelly beans.

"Can you leave the watermelon?" she says. "They're my favorite."

The phone rings out from the living room.

"Right," she says when she answers. And then: "Excuse me, how did you get this number?"

Warden Michael Sosa takes a mint from the packet on his desk and holds it in his mouth without sucking or chewing. Beside him is a young black woman in a fitted blue suit. She looks to Lizbeth like she runs. Lean; stoic.

Her name is Alicia Mapp. She offers Lizbeth a seat, and the warden starts to chew.

"Thanks for coming in today," she says.

"I didn't know if I had a choice."

"As I told you on the phone, Ms. Greene, it's an entirely voluntary thing for you to be here. But we're obviously grateful you decided to stop by."

Lizbeth studies Alicia Mapp and expects to find smug disdain. Sees only painstaking courtesy.

"Let me tell you why I asked you here."

Alicia Mapp is, she says, employed within the national Gang Intelligence Unit. "Our mandate extends both in and out of the prison system. We try and keep track of who's killing who. Periodically, we try and stop them."

Anyway, she says, she really just wanted an opportunity to introduce herself.

"Obviously, we are aware of the project you're working on here, and I can assure you that no one at the unit has anything but the best of wishes for that, Ms. Greene. But I did feel that you and I should at least meet . . . to let you know that if you need any assistance with research or fact checking, then you shouldn't hesitate to approach us . . . and also, so you would feel comfortable if at any stage we might approach you in the same spirit. In case we need to copter the situation."

"Excuse me?"

"I'm sorry. I forget I'm not in the office sometimes. Copter the situation. Monitor and assess. As if we were looking down at events on the ground from a helicopter. Honestly, Ms. Greene, it's nothing to be alarmed about. I shouldn't have even mentioned it. By its nature intelligence needs a broad frame of reference . . . that's all." Alicia Mapp smiles. "How are you finding him, Ms. Greene? In general terms?"

"He's been very . . . civil. I mean, he's still not in great shape, but . . ." Warden Sosa chews a little louder.

"Are you having this conversation with the *Times* as well?"

"I hope to, Ms. Greene, yes."

And she smiles again. "Ms. Greene, have you been following events out in Queens while you've been here?"

"Which events?"

"In Corona?"

But Lizbeth is no wiser.

"There's been what looks to be a flare-up of gang activity there, Ms. Greene. Several young men have been killed."

"God . . . I didn't know . . ."

"Oh, let be me clear—there's obviously no suggestion of Velez having any influence over that. We're very aware that Warden Sosa and the DOC have been vigilant in deciding which situations are appropriate for him to be involved with. I really only mentioned it in the event that you did know and maybe it had come up during your interviews?"

"I didn't. It hasn't. Wait . . . are you asking me to bring it up with him?"

"No, Ms. Greene, I'm not asking that. As I say, I'm really only here to introduce myself. And to let you know that if you ever need my assistance, you should feel free to call me." She passes Lizbeth a business card. "And I hope the same would apply if at some future date we need to consult with you."

"Copter the situation."

"That's right." Alicia Mapp stands. "Thank you for your time, Ms.

Greene." Then she reaches down into her bag and pulls from it a copy of *The Hands of Angels*. "I've always been a fan," she says, as she passes it over.

There's a pen already tucked inside the title page.

CO Sherwin Baines escorts her down to the lawyer's room talking about bowling all the way. Lizbeth doesn't hear a word.

". . . so when ttthey're taking us out into the yard, they bring the twelve of us in our pod out from the cells onto the gallery . . . then they lead us down through the restttt of them. And at every pod we have to stop and collect another twelve *vatos*. Allllways more, more, more, more."

Wilson's feet drub the floor of the lawyer's room.

"So from my cell to the yard ttttakes forever, *sabes* . . . and the—whole way I always have this fucking bug Rinser from my pod walking right beside me. Always. Every time. And this *vato* is fucking fried! I mean, insane! The entire way, down through fourteen pods, he wails and bawls and he yells in my ear, screaminggg like the place is on fire, 'I am a man of honor! Let me out of jail! I am a man of honor!' . . . and he is right there at my shoulder, writhing, shaking his fuckinggggg head . . ." He grimaces. Rolls his tongue around his mouth. ". . . So anyway, yesterday, by the tttttime I get to the yard not only has Rinser left me half deaf but hissss spit is all over my face. It is dripping from my ear! *Ay coño! Sabes?* Disgusting! And I will be truthful, at that moment all that I could think was how much I hoped some serious misfortune befell this *cabron* . . . that although I tttry to wish no harm on any soul, I might not protestt with too much vigor if this individual were to come into harm's way . . . *Hey*. Are you even listening to me?"

Lizbeth glances up at him. "Sure," she says. "Of course I am."

"Oh, okay. It's just you seem very distracted today, Lizbeth. Still, I guess now you have your llllife in Essenville, your friends down there, it's going to keep you busy in the head." He rises off his seat, twists, then sits back down. "So, you going to keep your hair that way? You're not going to lighten itttt up?"

"Not at the moment, Wilson."

"Oh, okay. I guess it's upppp to you. So, anyway . . . you see my interview?"

"I did," she says.

He lifts his chin. Waits for more.

"I thought you came over well. The political stuff was . . . compelling."

"Oh . . . the stuff I see your eyes ggglaze over when I—talk about it. Okay." He whistles through his teeth, and the sound cuts through the room. "You know, the reporter . . . she was nothinggg like as bad as you said she would be. And in any case . . . I'm not—sure you are a persson who can talk so badly about other writers."

She peers at him a notch harder. "Why do you say that, Wilson?"

"Because you are—someone who talks behind my back about the thinggggs I tell you."

Her heart shudders. A plunge in her belly. *He knows? How could he know already?* "I haven't told them anything," she says. "I only just talked with them."

He tuts, and then he shakes his head. "Ossery said you talked to him righttt before you came here last. And I know thatttt you told him a lottt."

"*Ossery.* Right. I talked to Ossery."

"And he talked to me on your behalf. So now I know you were un-happy with what I told you about the letters. The truth. The truth you didn'ttt believe. So now I know I should only ever tell you things you wanttt to hear."

"Wilson, I never said I didn't believe you. I just felt—"

"Please. It's fine. I would never want to get in the way of your story, Liz-beth. After all, who am I to tell you about my own life? So now, for you, I am guilty of everything."

"Wilson, that's not what I—"

"Please. I understand now. It's okay. I would rather we jjjust kept on until the end."

To anyone else, he would look expressionless. But she knows what's there in the set of his face, gripped in the skin cells and muscle: the fury in his lips; the rage at the corners of his eyes.

He rocks back and forth just once.

"So what would you like to talk aboutt today?"

She tries to find the remedy. The formula of words that will correct this. Appease him. It doesn't come.

"I thought," she says, "perhaps we could talk more about the . . . early days."

"The early ddays," he says. "Fine."

She reaches over to start the tape recorder.

"You know, Wilson . . . I'm sorry if you're disappointed in me. If you think somehow that I've betrayed you." *Betrayed*. The word sounds so absurd in her voice. So overheated. "Will you at least let me explain?"

But he just stares ahead. Until finally she sighs and hits Record.

"Okay . . . so, maybe we could clarify a few things about the period when the Royals were first active across the city . . . details I'm blurry on."

"Sure," he says. "You go right ahead."

"Well, a while ago you told me about the time . . . I think it was around '85 . . . when other gangs were trying to coopt your members?"

"Not this shit with the *vato* in the underpass at—Meadow Lake again . . . we already talkeddd about this too many timesss, Lizbeth . . ."

"No, I actually meant . . . there was an incident with—" She checks her notes. "The Latin Sixers? From the Bronx?"

Still no response. Then: "Oh, that. Right."

"Right. It's just I remember you started talking about them in particular one time, and then the hour was up and—"

"The Royals," he says, staring past her, "were getting bigger every day. All acrossss the city you would see *Dé el Amor Al Real*. The Sixers were just some fucked-up *tecatos* from Hunts Point. But I ggguess they looked at us like we were weak, *sabes*? Just kids. So they thought they could steal our pee-wees. They would get them drunk andddd try to recruit them. When they said no, they would put a *cuete* in their mouth and make them paint broken crowns over our graffiti."

He stretches out his neck like a turtle. "Two days before Christmas, Ojos told me this kid fffrom Elmhurst had been playing in the snow when the Sixers grabbed him. Nine years old. They took him up to the Bronx and poured gin down his throat. When he still refused to join them they took a scarf of red, white and gold and made him piss on it. Then they burnttt his clothes and threw him naked into the street with just the scarf wrapped around him . . . I knew I would have to act. And when I did, I would need to put an end to this. The *vato* that led the Sixers was called Pluto. They hung out by this barbershop on Hunts Point Avenue. Right next to Drake Cemetery. Never less than twenty of them. I had Hurricane drive me up and waitttt for me. Everyone knew Pluto had a fucking artillery up there. More *cuetes* than the army. So I guess they thought I was there for some kind of duel. Like a western, *sabes*? But instead I just walkedddd up to him. Kept my eyes set on him and walked until we were nose to nose. And all I said was '*Que honda?*' And then from out of

218

nowhere I threw one right hand cross at this *pendejo,* and he was out cold on the sidewalk."

"You just hit him?"

"Right. I just hit him."

"That was it?"

"That was all it needed to be. One punch and everyone couldddd see he was a *maricón.* We never had problems with the Sixers again."

"But did you actually have a gun?"

"There was no reason. *Manos de piedra,* remember?"

"You weren't afraid he was going to shoot you?"

A shrug.

"Okay . . . there was another detail from the same period that I'm hazy on . . . You mentioned to me once that after you came out of Spofford for the second time you wound up staying with an older girl—"

"Rosalinda Pena."

"Right. And she was . . . twenty-one? twenty-two?"

"Something like ttthat."

"You said she was nothing to do with the Royals."

"That's right."

". . . So I wasn't clear how you came to know her."

"I used to see her up by Linden Park. She'd take her kiddd up there in a stroller. It got so we might nod at each other. Just say Hi. And sometimes she looked so happy, but other times you'd see her with bruises all over her. Her boyfriend, *sabes?* And one time I was makinggg faces at her kid and I noticed her lip was all busted up and something jjjust snapped in me. I asked her where her boyfriend was at, and when she told me I found him and I beat him until he couldn't even beg me to stttop. 'See how you like it, *puta.' Sabes?* A week after that he moved out of . . . Corona, and from then on Rosalinda and me were friends. We were never . . . together, *sabes,* but I coulddd stay with her when I needed to."

Lizbeth nods.

"You look surprised. Has somethinggg that I've said surprised you?"

"Not at all. It's a very impressive story." And then, although she nearly pulls back, she says: ". . . It's just that I remember you telling me most of the girls that gravitated toward you from outside the gang were there for drugs. I wondered if . . ."

He glowers across the table.

". . . I just mean—"

"No, I am sorry, Lizbeth. I should have remembered thattt you knew my life better than I ever could. *Dios mio,* these last few weeks must have been so frustrating for you, listeninggg to me tell you all this shit you knew already. I am such a fool. Imagine, forgetting you were there the whole tttime. Shit, you *were* there . . . weren't you?"

His voice is hardening. "I guess all I can do now is apologize once more and ttttry to tell you some stories that you might like better. Okay, so . . . how about the time I put a knife into a man while he was singingggg lullabies to his baby son? Do you like that one? Or maybe I should tell you a story about a *soplon* whose heart I cut out and fed to the puma in Queens Zoo? It might not be the truth, but I'm certain thatttt you would find it exciting."

The rage billows off him. She is, for the first time since coming here, aware of his shackles less as restraining him than protecting her.

"I should have remembered that you don't want to know the truth. You just want something with the ttttaste of blood. Something visceral."

He says it vi-*scer*-al. Like feral. All but spat across the room.

She hears herself speak before she can stop herself: "It's visceral," she says. "That's how you pronounce it."

The room falls silent. Stays silent. Then: "Thank—you, Lizbeth," Wilson says. "Now next time I say it I won't sounddd so stupid." He makes sure to catch her eye. "You know, the reporter and me . . . we talked abouttt you."

"You did?"

"Don't worry. I didn't tell her about the book. But when she asked me what I liked to do now I was outttt of Ad-Seg, I told her I liked to read your books. So then we talked about you a little. And it turns out there's something you never told me about. Something she tttold me about you that you never did."

He waits. Lets her hang there a moment longer.

"You never told me abouttt Leon Slocomb."

She feels herself wince. Just the name is enough. "It never came up."

"Oh, it never came up."

He lurches forward until his chest is jammed against the table. "I thought that we were being honesttt with each other, Lizbeth. You complain behindd my back about what I have told you, and then I find out you kept a thing like that from me. Now whattt kind of example is that?"

"I never lied to you, Wilson. I just didn't . . . tell you. It has nothing to do with what we're doing here."

"Oh, okay. When you sit there hour after hour with your shitty tape recorder, expectttting me to tell you about every last momentttt of my life. So then you can laugh about it with your friends in Essenville and decide what fits into your book and what doesn't? But something like this . . . you decide it's not important."

"I didn't say that . . . it's just . . . not something I enjoy talking about."

"So, you'll talk about the City Slicker. You'll talk about your mother. But this is not for me to know?"

Her arms draw in to her sides, then across her. "So what did they tell you? The reporter?"

"Only that for years you had a stalker named Leon Slocomb. That he senttt you letters and then he tried to kill you."

She watches the tape spin, the teeth of the spools like cars on a Ferris wheel.

"The first letters went to my publisher. They sent them on to my agent like they did with all my fan mail. Then my agent sent them on to me. My assistant had to open them. She was the one who actually had to read them." Her voice is a whisper. "They were hard to get through. Things he wanted to do to me. That he was *going* to do to me. It's amazing what people walk around with inside of them. He sent one a week for six months until he got my home address. Then there were more of them. But at least he finally told us why he was doing it. One of the books. *Not into Temptation.* He said I'd used him as a character. Stolen his life. That was how he put it. Crazy asshole."

She clears her throat before she continues. "He sent dead rats by FedEx. They'd been cut open. He said that was what he was going to do to me. There were tapes. They'd tell me how he was just waiting for the right time to drop by. I had to hire a bodyguard. Get all this security for the house. Sensors. Cameras. Alarms. Endless meetings with the police. And then he just disappeared. The letters stopped. Everything stopped. Like none of it had ever happened. It was like that for a year. Then I went to a show . . . a club on 18th Street . . . he finally came for me . . . sprang out of the crowd and tried to slash my throat . . . the guy behind me managed to bundle him over and pin him down . . . otherwise . . ."

Wilson is quieter now. Pacified. "You were okay?"

"He barely broke the skin. It was later things got rough . . . It spun me out for a while . . ." She lifts her hands to her mouth. Closes her eyes.

"What was it . . . in the book . . . that mmmade him so crazy?"

"Back in 1980 . . . maybe '81 . . . Leon had been acquitted of murdering an old lady down in Tallahassee. He was working as a pool cleaner. They said he'd been putting urethane in the water . . . but at trial the case just fell apart. Anyway, ten years later, eleven years, whatever, I write a story where the killer poisons his mother's pool . . . and Leon gets hold of it. Becomes convinced that it's all about him. And that I've filled the story with all this other stuff from his life. His childhood. The whole thing was just . . . nuts. Groundless. But, you know, we said we'd give him some money . . . just to try and get him to leave me alone. It didn't interest him. He just kept on sending his letters and telling me I had to suffer because I'd—"

"Stolen his life."

"Exactly."

"But you hadn'tttt?"

"No. Of course not."

He nods. Says nothing.

"I mean . . . ideas . . . they come to you in different ways. Something passes and you grab it. It could fall out of the sky, or it could be on *60 Minutes*. That happens. Sure. But even when it does you change it, break it down, pull it inside out . . . make it yours."

"So that's what happeneddd with Leon Slocomb? You made the story yours?"

She looks everywhere but in front of her.

"Maybe you read about him and it got stuck in the back of your mind and you didn't even realize you were usinggg it?"

"No. I'd remember if that had happened."

"I've done it."

"Done what?"

"Used real people in a story. I even diddd it in *The Monsters of Gramercy Park*. Back when we were kids, Hurricane's landlord was Mr. Fung. That guy was a prick and a *clavero* . . . and he had these fucked-up warts all over his nose and chin . . . so as soon as I thought of the character I thought of him. Or maybe it was the other way arounddddd."

Lizbeth can't help smiling. "I named the killer in my first book after the first boy I ever made out with. I was thirteen and he told the whole school I'd gone the whole way with him."

Wilson shakes his head. *"Cabron."* Then he stares across the table and slowly bends side to side from the waist. Easing the stiffness in his bones. "See, I don't understand why it is such a big thing anyway. Takingggg something from a newspaper, something you heard, that someone told you. What is the problem? That shit must happen every day."

"I'm sure it does."

He keeps flexing from side to side. "Anyway, I like that idea. Something terrible in the pool. I can see why you woulddd have been pleased to have . . . struck on it."

From side to side.

"It is a tribute to your imagination, Lizbeth."

Side to side.

"I mean . . . an idea like thatttt . . . it is that kind of idea that makes you the writer you are."

Now he's perfectly still.

"But it *was* Leon Slocomb? Right?"

She feels her mouth dry out and then: ". . . Right," she says.

Wilson leans back in his chair and she exhales. Then silence.

". . . I found a mention of the case in Tallahassee when I was reading up on poisons. It just went from there . . ."

There is silence again. A minute of it. Until: "Well . . . like I say . . . it's no big thing, right?"

But she doesn't answer.

"So where is he now?"

"Leon? He got parole right before I came here."

"Hijole. I didn't realize."

He inches forward. "You know, Lizbeth, I'm sorry if you feel I have been . . . hostile. Mean spirited. I did not mean to appear mean spirited—"

And something snags. But her head is full of Leon Slocomb, and Wilson is still talking.

"I just felt so foolish listening to this reporter ttell me all about you and your life like I was just ssome ignorant *pendejo.*" His shoulders slump and his head drops.

"I'm sorry," she says, "if you felt that way."

"No, I should not have been so harsh with you. I'm just all fffucked up today. I can still feel that freak Rinser's spit on me . . . and every time I shut my eyes all I see is that shit with the lime trees." He starts to bend again, and as he does his voice brightens. "But I will figure it out soon, *sabes*? And once I have, I know I will feel attt peace."

The boy knew his fun would be over soon. Any second his mother would break from her chores and summon him inside the thatched bo-hio *they shared with his father and brother, briskly cajoling him to stop his play and help build the cooking fire. Just another afternoon in the village he had never been outside of in the five years of his life thus far. Five miles from Penonomé, each to him a journey to the moon.*

And so he slipped away, not yet ready to give up the adventures of the day. Barefoot, he ran from the bohio *and turned down the narrow powder-muddy path that twisted off the main drag through the village. Just him now, only him in the world. Running because he wanted to run, joyfully ignorant of the frailty of things.*

He was breathless by the time he reached the lime trees. Barely older than him but twice his size. Their branches sagging with fruit. He threw out his arms and lifted his head and reveled in the sun.

Until in an instant everything changed forever.

First, from somewhere close, there was a moan, high and plaintive. Then another sound, a different sound: heavy, unechoing. The boy real-ized he was not alone out here in the trees.

And a moment later, a warm spray of blood spattered his cheek.

He was afraid, yes. But in that moment his fear was overwhelmed by curiosity. The simple need to know who or what had caused these sounds, sent the blood across his face. So the boy looked up to where the sun beat down on him, and through its blaze he saw

Her wrists are swollen. Lizbeth takes her fingers from her laptop and stares at them, bloated and puttyish.

The doctor warned her this might happen in the fifth month. Just one among the ever-morphing circus of symptoms that grip her body and then release it. And all the while she keeps getting bigger.

She focuses on the screen once more.

to where the sun beat down on him, and through its blaze he saw

What?

She closes her eyes and puts herself there. Takes the last few steps down that pinched dirt track and stands among the lime trees. Beckons the heat onto her skin, and then the blood, as she too gazes up.

But she, like Wilson, sees nothing past the sun.

She opens her eyes and returns to Essenville. It is two minutes before seven A.M. She saves the file and closes it, then opens another.

"I'm going out to tidy up the yard, honey!"

Lloyd Dreiz stared at Gina as she left through the back door, turning back to wave at him as he reached the bottom of the stairs. Gina, his wife of just over a year, forever smiling that full-beam smile of hers. Always so damn perky.

He thought of the day ahead, the shuffling line of customers visiting his studio to have their picture taken. Badly matched fiancées, ugly babies, squabbling families. At least in Pittsburgh he didn't know them. Could pretend he wasn't one of them.

He searched for the Q-Tips in readiness to clean the endless racks of rifles in the cellar, their contents assembled with such passion down the years. Watched Gina as she strode by the window, brandishing her shears. Usually the sight of those shears made him wince. But not today. Today they didn't trouble him at all.

Because today he was going to kill her.

She shuts down the machine. And in one unbroken sequence of motion she pulls on her coat and picks up her bag and walks from the house. Takes the car and leaves Essenville. Drives north. Onto the highway.

The traffic there is sparse, truckers and salesmen caught in rewind as she flashes by. Her foot only nudging the brake at the exit that will, a few miles later, deliver her to:

Pittsburgh International Airport.

Through the wall-thick glass of the departure lounge she gazes out past the runways to the Airport Plaza Hotel. On the plane, she pulls out the *Newsweek* she bought at the airport. Finds within a short piece on the rise of Mitchell Rieber. The congressman's ideas on crime are, it says, setting a national agenda. His reputation swelling accordingly. Even as he gears up for reelection, the informed debate is what will come next for

the onetime assistant District Attorney whose snarling law-and-order rhetoric has proved so seductive to scores of Gotham voters

She stares at his picture—seasoned crag and stern resolve—and the plane starts its descent. In the moments before they touch down she fixes on her breathing. And then:

LaGuardia.

Her cab driver vaults out to open the trunk, expecting a plump fare to SoHo or Central Park West. Looks surprised—aggrieved, even—at where she tells him she needs to go.

The entire journey takes six minutes. When they get there, he looks back at her, incredulous.

"This is it?" he says.

It is. Now that she's here, part of her wishes it wasn't. But it is. The drab concrete vista of Waldron Street, Corona, and a gutted house. The top story burnt out. A half-perished iron gate lolling off its hinges and from the steps beyond a dozen Latino kids of maybe eleven to maybe seventeen staring at her dryly as she gets out of the taxi. Watchful boys in jeans big enough to sleep under with weights-pumped arms theatrically folded, girls whose hair has been scraped back so fiercely their eyelids are like Mc-Donald's arches, lips lined in plum and expertly curled. She stands before them and feels less threatened than freakish.

"Miss Greene?"

She spins to her right and there—as Alan Ossery promised he would be—is José Almanza.

"I'm Hurricane," he says. "It is a pleasure to meet you."

He can only be an inch taller than Wilson, but broad like a vending machine. The backs of his hands gloved with tattoos, the rest of him engulfed in a spotless white down coat.

"Thank you," she says, "for meeting me. It's so good to be able to talk with you . . . to see where Wilson came from."

"If it helps Three Vee," he says, slow and gracious, "then it's an honor. May I take you inside a moment and show you what is being done here?"

The kids stand and clear a path as he saunters up the steps, their fists knocked twice over their hearts in salute.

Inside, it's just boards and joists. The glass out in all but one of the windows. Yawns in the walls and floors where the copper pipes have been ripped out for scrap. There are more kids here, adults too, eleven people that she counts in total, spread out, working. Some paint, others drill, saw, hammer. All with beads around their necks of white, red and gold.

This, he says, is just one of the buildings the Royals are renovating in the neighborhood. It's important to teach the pee-wees teamwork, he says. To nurture a sense of pride in achievement.

"There are," he says, "many wrong paths for them out there."

He leads her through the interior, and talks about how, when it's finished, they will give the place to the community.

"So that no more families with four kids have to pay their *cabron* landlord eight hundred dollars a month to live in one shitty room with no hot water."

As they leave, the kids on the steps rise and pound their chests once more.

"*Real por vida,*" they call out.

Lizbeth and José Almanza walk side by side. A block in, she turns: "I understand there's been violence here recently."

He sighs. And then he says it's true. That the problem is kids new to the neighborhood, forming *clicas* and stealing guns, wanting to be men, trying to start a war with those whose peacefulness they see as frailty. But that, he says, will not be allowed to happen.

"Because every time someone dies, I do too. You understand? Not just because of the lives we have lost. Also because now every politician and reporter who ever said, Oh, the Sacred Royals, they have not changed, they are still drug dealers, they are still killers . . . now those people will say, You hear *la noticia*? *Has oido?* These Royals, these animals—we were right all along. Please, will you follow me?"

They step around the corner and he gestures to the flat-roofed annex of a stout brown church. Inside is a lobby the size of an elevator car, its walls smothered with pamphlets in Spanish on adult education, photocopied flyers for child care providers. A lawyer, she sees, comes every third Wednesday to give free advice. Alternate Fridays it's a nurse.

At the end of the lobby there's a door, and when José Almanza calls out, a man in his early fifties with a cloud of white hair and a darker beard bustles through it, arms outstretched. The two embrace, then turn as one to Lizbeth.

"Miss Greene, this is Father Raymond Peres."

"I have read your books," he says. "You have a wonderful mind."

In the tiny reception that lies behind the door, Father Peres makes coffee, atomically strong. Lizbeth sticks with water. Just listens as Hurricane and the priest talk over each other, detailing the Royals' work in the borough. Wilson's legacy.

"The older Royals—" Peres says.

"The *vatos* Wilson hung with—"

"Many of them are involved in after-school programs—"

"Teaching sports and—"

"Educating the young people in—"

"Safe sex. Living free of drugs."

"You know, any kid that wants to be a Royal now must first show a clean attendance record at school."

"The most important thing is that *los mancitos* stay in school."

"Because then we have a chance of—"

"Building a brighter future for this community. Something lasting. That is what every Royal is working toward."

They talk themselves to a standstill. And then the priest's face rumples. "Miss Greene," he says, "may I ask you . . . how is Wilson?"

"He's . . . okay," she says. "I mean, he's better. Just in the time I've known him he's gotten so much better. But . . . you know . . . he's been through a lot . . ."

The priest shuts his eyes and shakes his head. "It grieves us so strongly that even now we cannot see him, cannot write to him. It is an outrage to our sense of justice. You know, Wilson has suffered all his life because of the world he was brought into. Because in that world he had no choice but to do things you or I might find beyond us. But surely he has made recompense for them already."

"He told me there were no orders in the letters to Ojos," Lizbeth says. "No code . . ."

"In that case," Hurricane says, "he told you the truth."

"Wilson was a great man," the priest says. "An honest man. I knew him when he was eight years old, and you could already see the greatness in him. I would never doubt his word. So to see him judged on lies and left to rot in their dungeon . . ."

"The way he speaks of you, Father," she says, ". . . I know you still mean so much to him."

"And I still feel the anguish of his being torn away. But in another sense I know that he is still here. Every good thing that has taken root in this neighborhood has done so through his inspiration—so for those who were too young to have even heard his voice but who now want to become Royals . . . this way he will always be with them."

Hurricane pulls out his wallet. Hands her a photograph from inside it: Four teenage boys in wifebeaters and red trackpants strike rowdy poses on a sunny day. In the middle of them are a smooth-cheeked Wilson and, she realizes, Hurricane himself.

"That's Ojos," he says, as he points first to the fair-skinned kid to his left. Then the straggle-haired figure next to Wilson: "That's Three Vee's brother. Eduardo. This picture was taken on this very street back in the summer of '85. I wanted you to have it. To see us when we were *la realeza original* . . ."

He gazes at it in her hand, his voice giving way. "It breaks me up just to look at that shit."

She listens to them reminisce about the days of Three Vee; still like mourners even now.

They each shake her hand as she leaves, and tell her they wish her every good fortune in telling the world about the real Wilson.

And then, with a street map tucked inside her bag, she walks alone through the low-rise jumble of Corona, the ashen streets. Finds Apex Place. Stands on its weed-clogged and deserted corner, a circle of crowns painted on the facing wall. Stays there a minute and a half, balming her lips against the cold, and then keeps on. To Xenia Street: twin lines of tightly packed walkups with pigeons convening on their roofs and a male voice calling out, repeatedly, *Carmello—levántate! Vamos!* Wilson's, she knows, was the last on the block. Outside it, she pauses again to breathe and observe, before a harried woman with a stroller labors out and glares at her with such crabby suspicion she instinctively turns and moves on.

Up Junction Boulevard. Traffic sludging on one side of her, a string of parking lots on the other. Makes her way to 44th Avenue and continues as far as the old Tiffany glass factory. Waits there in front of its weathered brick and consults her map. Turns into National Street, where a large-framed musician flails at a requinto guitar outside a tiny café. She registers everything, everyone; on the wall beside her another bold swirl of graffiti, demanding that she *Dé el Amor Al Real.* A clutch of middle-schoolers barrels past, and on the corner of Roosevelt the din of the 7 train clashes with a snatch of hip-hop quaking from a passing car.

There is, at 108th, a poster tagged to a streetlight. An appeal for witnesses in the shooting of a man named Rafael Ferrer. She gazes at the picture, the blurred contours of his face, his pupils dissolved into grainy pixels. Then she heads south, past the grocery stores with their green plantains and vast cans of turtle beans, Dominican flags in the window, the long-distance phone centers offering cut rates to Peru, El Salvador, Ecuador, Colombia above handwritten signs that say *Pagamos En Dolares*. Still taking those brisk, observant steps, she passes the other end of 44th Avenue and cuts into the park. Ahead of her a ring of Asian men with belted robes over heavy sweatshirts practice karate moves on the hard ground under the trees. And the Unisphere seems to take up half the sky. She stops. Just breathes. Tries to feel all this how Wilson did.

Then off again. Past the men doing karate, down to the edge of Meadow Lake before crossing into fume-choked west Flushing, its mosaic of Korean supermarkets and Chinese pharmacies. She checks her map by the Luck Joy Restaurant Number 1. Stashes it inside her bag again and advances up Prince Street. Until she sees Linneaus Place:

A horseshoe alley, just as he described it. Pockmarked tarmac, row-houses that look like they'd go over in a wind. There are, however, street-lights now. *Wilson? Wilson Ulysses Velez?* She tries to summon him, to conjure him beside her.

But finally, she gives in. Hauls herself exhausted to the subway as the sun goes down over Queens.

Back at LaGuardia she's checked in and waiting for a gate when her flight vanishes from the departure screen. When it reappears it says DELAYED.

The hearty woman at the check-in desk shrugs and grimaces when Lizbeth asks her how long it's going to be. It is, she says, a security thing.

A half hour goes by in the departure lounge. Then another. Parched, she gets to her feet and wanders in search of water. Finds every store has its lights off and grill down.

There is, eventually, a bar, or its airport likeness: gleaming dark wood, pictures of '40s ballplayers. Nothing else in sight. Her ankles beginning to swell now. So she orders and sits in a booth near the counter with a single glass of water. The men dotted around—a riot of khakis and loafers—look too zoned out for anything lecherous.

She takes Hurricane's photograph from her bag, stares at it, then replaces it.

The TV in the corner shows stock footage of office workers, and she finds herself sinking into the colors, her head getting heavy until she snaps back to the now. Blinks into focus. Now there's a commercial for Rogaine.

And then, once more, she drifts away.

This time when she jerks back upright there's a female news reporter. Standing in front of the Tiffany glassworks.

Baffled, Lizbeth rises. Leaves the booth and steps up to the counter, close enough to hear the reporter talking to the camera.

". . . that's right, Ted, sadly it looks like we're witnessing another tragic night here in Queens."

A cop walks through the background of the frame, and a disembodied male voice asks: "Can you tell us what happened, Marcia?"

"Ted, details are scarce," she says, "but we do know that around thirty minutes ago a Hispanic man was shot dead by an unknown assailant here on Corona's 44th Avenue."

"Do we know the victim's identity, Marcia?"

"Ted, what we're hearing is he was a twenty-three-year-old male called Armand Pichardo. Other than that, we're still trying to piece things together."

Lizbeth turns to see the reaction of the other customers, but none of them are watching.

George Finer turns the sign in the door of the gift shop to Closed.

The sun is out for the first time in weeks, and even though it brings no warmth Lizbeth is glad to be under it, to be in Essenville, headed to the Venus Restaurant Diner for dippy eggs. Today there are no sad-faced prisoners filling refuse sacks on the verges, just the ambling to and fro that passes for the lunch rush.

"So," George says, "I finished *The Monsters*."

"You did? And?"

"And I liked it. It's got pep."

"George, are you just being polite?"

"No, if I was just being polite I'd say it was spunky. Although I see what you mean about the ending."

"Too much?"

"Yeah, but kids have strong stomachs. It's not like it's one of yours."

Inside the Venus, a hugely pregnant woman and what looks to be her mother ease into the adjacent booth. She and Lizbeth smile at one another as they both reach forward for the menu.

The waitress says, *What y'uns in the mood for?* and for the first moments after their dippy eggs come, Lizbeth and George are too busy eating to speak. Then:

"So you know the first *real* snow's on its way?" he says. "It's supposed to be coming in next week. Not this *talcum* we've had so far. The real stuff."

"I heard," she says. "Every time I switch on the news there's a story about plows."

Then, abruptly, he leans across the table and taps the back of her hand. "Look out of the window."

"Huh?"

"Look out of the window. But don't make it obvious."

Lizbeth turns her head ninety degrees as if it's on a rotisserie. Talks out of the side of her mouth. "Was that obvious?"

As George tuts, she sees a gangling middle-aged man on the street outside bend down and pull a copy of the *Expositor* from a vending box.

"What am I looking at, George?"

"What you're looking at, Lizbeth, is Lloyd Dreiz."

"Oh, for God's sake," she says. "Would you just get on with your eggs?"

But even as she scolds him she knows she hasn't actually turned away, not yet, not while she's still taking in Lloyd Dreiz's sunken cheeks and hatstand frame.

When she does finally look back, George's eyebrows are halfway up his forehead.

"Okay," she says. "Fine. What's the motive?"

"Gina was going to leave him."

"Oh, George, that's terrible. If your writing class could hear you now."

"It's true. She'd been spending a lot of time with an ex back in Pittsburgh . . . and although I have no idea whether there was any kind of romance there, Lloyd obviously thought so. You'd see him following her around the supermarket with drink on his breath, you know, picking at her. The way that kind of man gets. I heard she was about to call it quits. And of course Lloyd knew that if she did, the house went with her and the business too."

Lizbeth turns back to the window and watches him spindle away, the *Expositor* under his arm.

"You're intrigued! I can see it in your face!"

"That's right, George. In no way at all am I just humoring you."

"No, I can tell. You are intrigued."

"Okay, George. So tell me why he wasn't arrested."

"Well, some people might find it noteworthy that Lloyd went hunting with several members of the police department on a regular basis. Or that he was the only Old Essenvillian who kept his place on the town bowling team when the guards reformed it."

"No one gets away with killing his wife because he's on a bowling team, George. It's just implausible."

"But what could anyone ever prove? A person forgets their pills or her husband sneaks them out of her pocket? Who's ever going to know the difference? And anyway . . . the town was just getting back on its feet. Young people were coming. Families. We were in bloom again. No one wanted anything like that to have happened. So no one looked too closely."

"Ah . . . shit."

"Excuse me?"

Lizbeth's hands cover her face as CO Sherwin Baines ambles through the door.

"I'm supposed to be at the prison," she says. "Ossery left me a message. They changed my days around so he could see the doctor. I'm supposed to be there now. Oh, God. Oh, *fuck*."

The pregnant woman's mother scowls, and asks that Lizbeth refrain from that kind of language in front of her daughter.

Warden Sosa lets her come the next day. As she pulls into the parking lot, her nerves are already crackling. Her hands damp on the wheel.

It's Baines that escorts her. Chatters as they walk, oblivious. As they cross beneath the pods he says: "You know, there's been a weird atmosphere up there since the morning . . ."

An inmate, he tells her, took a fall from the top of a ten-foot stairway as the men were being taken to the yard. Went down face first.

"We tried to see what happened on the tape," Baines says, "but there were too many bodies in the way."

Lizbeth paces on behind him, only half listening.

"We're assuming someone decided to trip him up when they knew they could do him the most damage. He got kind of . . . *trampled* when he hit the ground. Didn't leave him in the most attractive condition."

He leads her into the administrative corridors. Toward the lawyer's room. Says, casually: "One of life's victims, Inmate Rinser."

Lizbeth stalls midstep. Remembers Wilson's podmate. The screaming bug. It hits her now. *He must have . . . Could he really have—*

Baines is opening the door.

And then, belatedly, she is facing him.

He stares past her and says nothing.

"I'm sorry about yesterday, Wilson."

He stares past her.

"It just went out of my head." And says: "All I can do is apologize."

Nothing.

Then his eyes lock with hers.

"So where were you?" he says. "When you shoulddd have been here?"

"I was in Essenville. I was eating lunch with a friend. Then I remembered."

"What friend?"

"What friend?"

"What friend were you eatingg lunch with?"

"Just a friend."

"Oh," he says, "just a friend. *Claro*. I understand. I see now why you treattt me with such discourtesy. Like a dog you keep tied up in the street and then call to heel when you remember ittt." His feet tap as his voice sours. "You know, Lizbeth, if there is somethingggg I have said or done which has aggrieved you, have the grace to say so. Do not act this way toward me. Do not ttttease me. Do not share yourself with me . . . and then discard me as if I was something you found atttttt the back of the refrigerator. Do not insult me. Do not come to this place and say yes, Wilson, you are of greatttt importance to me and then disprove that with your aaaaactions. Do not do that, Lizbeth. Because I will not stand for it."

"Wilson, it was a mistake. I just made a mistake."

"But maybe it was not a mistake. Maybe your frienddd is better company than me. Maybe you justtt didn't want to come because you want to spend your time with him in the Venus Diner? That's what it's called, right? Is that where you go with him? Where the *jarabe* hangggggg out? You know, it just hurts me, Lizbeth. I give you everything I can, everything of me . . . and you don't even remember I'm here waitingggg."

"Wilson, I messed up. That's all. And I'm sorry."

But he turns his head, and keeps it turned. Until:

"I went to Corona. I met Hurricane. Father Peres."

He doesn't turn back, but in profile she sees his lips part.

"How are they doing?"

"They're good. They said to tell you that you were missed beyond words. They said it in Spanish, but you know . . . my accent . . ."

"*Más allá de palabras,*" he says. "Back at the start of the Royals thatttt was how we expressed our love for one another. *Amor más allá de palabras.*"

For a moment, she debates telling him about the killing at the Tiffany glassworks. Then, instead: "I saw Linneaus Place. They have streetlights now."

He doesn't respond.

"How was the doctor, anyway? Did they know what the problem was?"

Nothing. More in ritual than expectancy she sets her tape recorder between them. Unwraps a new cassette. He has, she sees, closed his eyes.

But the moment she presses Record, they open. And he spins back to face her:

"Lizbeth, there is something I need to tttttalk with you about. I've been thinking maybe I should be the person who writes my story."

He leans forward until he's all but speaking into the machine. "You know, when you first talked to me about the project, I thoughtttt I had to have a real writer portray me . . . but now I'm a real writer too . . . and you obviously have other things in your life that interest you more . . . So maybe you and I should just forget this and I should tttake over from here."

"Are you serious?"

"Sure. Although I guess it will be difficult right now . . . I have so many demands on my time. I have to make sure everything is correct with *The Monsters of Gramercy Park* before it is in the stores, but also I needddd to focus on the—sequel. I have all these ideas I need to work on, *sabes?* Plus there are always more people wanting to claim my attention. TV shows wantttttting to interview me. More newspapers. *Don Diva* magazine, they want me to write a column for them. Crazy. Then there isss the Web site—"

"The Web site?"

"Right. For a while me and Ossery have talked about it . . . creating somewhere that people can learn about my case, and where perhaps merchandise could be sold to raise money for the work the Royals are engaged in . . . T-shirts, dogtags, a CD maybe . . . And of course, most important of all, the appeal review is so close now . . . and that needs so much of my energy . . ."

Then he pauses. ". . . So now that I think of it all . . . the time it will take . . . maybe I *do* need someone to help with my story. You know, I just cannot decide. Maybe you can help me decide, Lizbeth. I know what would help me decide—you could remind me why you believe you are the right person to tell my story."

"I don't think so, Wilson. We're through the audition stage."

"But Lizbeth . . . all I'm asking is that you remind me why you are here. Why you wanted to write aboutt Wilson Ulysses Velez?"

He gazes at her with mocking wide eyes and the second that follows rings with wills in collision. Each waiting to see who blinks first. Discover which of them could end this now and forget they even met the other, let the tape be stopped and never restarted, exit the lawyer's room in the certain knowledge that will be that, forever.

"For the same reasons I want to write about you now."

Her voice is so quiet he has to crane his neck to hear her.

"Your story's important. What you've been through shouldn't go undocumented. People need to hear about it. And I thought, with my name . . . my readership . . . that I could make sure they did. I still think the same thing now."

"Thank you, Lizbeth," he says.

His eyes are shining.

"And all this time I thoughttttt it was because your books weren't selling anymore and you were all out of ideas."

She can't get her breath. She hears her windpipe open, but nothing comes through.

"Oh, I've always seen whattt you are, Lizbeth. It's obvious. *You* are obvious."

He leans in and whispers theatrically. "Like I know whattt you like to put into your veins."

Then sits back and stares at her.

"Oh, don't look so freaked out. You don'ttt think I've met enough *tecatos* to know when one is in front of me? I see the twitch you make every time I mention *chiva*. Like you could feel it run through you just thinking of it. Let me guess, you started when you were eighteen? nineteen? You'd go up to Central Park and score in the tunnel under Bethesda Terrace . . . And even now you put the spike between your toes so thatttt no one knows about you, or at least you think they don't . . ."

"I don't know how you . . . think this is appropriate . . . or where . . ."

"Relax, *dulzura*. I am not judging you. How could I jjjjudge you? I just hope you are not doing that shit anymore now you have your baby."

Her breath comes now in one fluttering rush.

"Oh, Lizbeth, please, I know you think I'm stupid, but how stupid do you think I am? You've been bigger every week you've come here. Look attt you in your baggy clown clothes. Still, at least your hands have stttttopped swelling up now, right?"

She stares down at them as she speaks. ". . . It was never meant to be a secret."

"Oh, okay. I guess it just turned out that way. So tell me, the friend you were with when you should have been here, is he the papa? Oh, no . . . of course . . . because you're not with the papa, right? Because if you were then you wouldn't look so *infeliz* when I ask about him. So who is he? Some rich ggguy back in Quince Hill?"

But he just keeps talking. "Ah, don't worry, Lizbeth. There is still one side to you that is a mystery to me. Maybe you can explain it to me. Because I see the way you look when I tell you about the things I used to do . . . so *excited* . . . so *thrilled* . . . but I am sure if, let's say, your new friend in Essenville or the papa of your baby were to do those things, then you would not be thrilled at all. Right? You know what it reminds me of? What you reminddd me of?"

Again, he doesn't wait for the answer.

"You remind me of these girls from up in Jackson Heights thatttt used to come down into the neighborhood when I was sixteen. I would see them hanging out by the playground on Alstyne Avenue. There were five— of them, like a year younger than me, right? Rican princesses. *Muy alzada*. They wouldddd walk past me in their little *clica* swinging their asses and I would call out to them to come and have some fun, *sabes*? And they would jjjust keep walking, too high class to even look at me. But then—every weekend one of them would call me up and say, 'Oh, Three Vee, Three Vee, my parents have gone out and I am feeling itchycoo . . . can't you come over, baby?' *Sabes*? So I guess to them I was dirt, but that is why they wanted me. Now, is that what it is with you too, Lizbeth? Maybe you can explain thatttt shit to me. Is that how you feel? Do I make *you* itchycoo? Is that it? Are you a little itchycoo for Three Vee?"

She feels the chair frame in her back.

"Oh, I don't mean to single you out, Lizbeth. Please understand thattt. I know people like you get itchycoo thinkinggg about people like me. They want us in our barrios and their jails so they can forget we are even real people . . . and then they creep back wanting to know how we live, how we talk, wanting thattt taste, *sabes*?"

He shrugs as much as his chains allow.

"And the stories you write, the novels, they're all bullshit too, right? All your silly murder mysteries, they all say the same thing, right? That there is someone out there who can make sense out of even the most tttterrible, lonely death, a good person who cares enough to come and find the reason behind it, and there will always be a reason, and that reason will be found and the death explained and jjjjustice done. And that is a lie, right? Just a filthy lie. So I guess now that I think of ittttt I can see why you would not want to tell that lie anymore. Why you came here thinking you could understand everything I am with an afternoon stroll in Corona and a fuckingggg dictionary of slang."

"That's unfair," she says, but her voice is quieter than ever.

"That's unfair! That's unfair! Listen to you. It's pathetic. Your whole life is built on bullshit and lies and if anyone tells you thatttt, you start whining. That's unfair! That's unfair! *Wah! Wah!*"

"Fuck you." She is perfectly still. But louder now. "Fuck you. You think I'm such a fraud? What does that make you? You spout off to reporters about your people. Your community. Hey, Wilson! You know the thirteen-year-old kid whose tattoos got cut out of his skin after someone said they saw him talking to a cop? That's your people. The fiancée of the guy you had shot in the knees at their engagement party? She's your community."

And her anger carries her onward.

"The families you speak up for so movingly, Wilson . . . you know, the ones I saw all over Corona trying to get by on six dollars an hour . . . maybe you could remind me when they asked to have a violent drug dealer represent them in the *Times*?"

His eyes don't even flicker. "And maybe you could tell me why if they interesttttt you so much, you're not writing a book about them?" But then the scorn leaves his voice. "I have told you many times, Lizbeth . . . I ttttturned my back on that life. And you have seen yourself whatttt the Royals have become."

"Sure. What they've become after six years with Hurricane."

She isn't, she realizes, quite done yet.

"By the way," she says, "I heard you got your wish with Rinser. He certainly came into harm's way, right?"

He doesn't speak. Just gazes at her placidly. Then: "I saw that, yes. A horrible accident. Seeing somethingggggg so dreadful . . . it made me realize that I didn't wish him harm at all." He sighs and looks down. Takes a second before he looks back up. "You know," he says, "what I said to you earlier . . . it was unfair. I know that you have suffered loss, and fear. And thatttt they live on in your stories."

A beat.

"Tell me, was it hard for you to go back to Queens?"

"Why would it be hard?"

"The City Slicker. Was it not hard for you to go back where he tttttook you?"

"I've been through Queens since then, Wilson. It's not an issue."

"It was Queensbridge Park he took you to, right?"

"Right . . . the waste ground next to it. By the Terracotta House. On the waterfront."

"But he picked you up in Manhattan?"

"Right."

She sees his head tilt to one side, and she's just grateful normal conversation has returned.

"My boyfriend and I had a room on Varick Street. I was just trying to get back there."

"The boyfriend you were in the banddd with?"

"The boyfriend I was in the band with. The place on Varick was mine. He'd just stayed over and never left. My dad paid the rent but I waitressed between assignments to keep us functioning."

"Were you—"

"On dope? Yeah."

"You were high thattt night?"

"Not that night. I'd just been at a friend's apartment, you know? A girl I worked with. She had this weird place up in Bridgemarket. And it was late . . . two in the morning in the middle of February, so cold it stung, and I came out of her front door and I just wanted to get home, you know? So I started walking, and a block and a half later this guy comes at me from a doorway. And before I can find my Mace there's something metal in my ribs."

Wilson says nothing. Just listens. Face rapt.

"Then I heard a voice. His voice. He just said: 'The van.' Not even 'Get in the van.' Just 'The van.' It was parked around the corner. That yellow van we'd all read about."

"Shit. The yellow van. Every girl I knew was so scared of seeing thatttt van."

"Right. Well . . . there it was. And the next thing I remember I'm waking up in the back of it."

She sees Wilson nodding.

"It was pitch in there. I couldn't even see the rest of me. All I knew was my head felt sticky and I was inside that van and I was going to die. But that he wasn't there. Right then, he wasn't there. So I groped around until I was sure where the doors were, and then I whaled on them like I'd never whaled on anything in my life. I kicked at them and kicked at them again and I kept kicking until one of them came open . . . and then suddenly I was outside, and I was running . . . I couldn't even see right because of the concussion, but I could see the lights up on the bridge and I made it that far, and a car came past me . . . they just drove right by me and all the time I was waiting for him to fucking catch up to me . . . and then I saw another coming . . . and this time I just stood screaming in the center lane until it stopped."

She gazes up to the ceiling. "I watched the news that day and they were calling me the luckiest girl in New York. Then they found out about my mom, and that made the story perfect, didn't it? And I remember sitting there with my head bandaged, thinking it was weird, because until now every time I met someone new there'd be this point where I had to tell them about my mom . . . and now they'd want to talk about this instead."

"Your boyfriend must have been relieved."

"I guess. He was pretty much the world's biggest asshole . . . but, sure . . ."

"And then the next day the City Slicker puts a gun in his mouth and ends himself . . ."

"Right."

"Tell me, did you nottt feel like he had gotten away from justice?"

"I was just glad it was done with."

"It's good you are at peace with it, Lizbeth. I guess writinggggg your book helped, right?"

"I guess so."

He sucks on his bottom lip.

"But the thing I don't get is this—what the fuck you were doing walking on your own through Bridgemarket at two in the morning? That is fffucking crazy."

"Sure. It was. But, you know, I'd been over to my friend's place a bunch of times before, and there were always cabs. Always. Even in the dead of the night. It was right by the bridge, you know? So if they'd taken anyone out to Queens, they'd be coming back right through there . . . So I guess I thought I'd find one right away . . ."

"*Hijole.* That is so fucking stupid, Lizbeth. I just cannot imagine even the dumbest girls I knew doing that. I mean . . . it is just incredible."

"Well, you know . . . I was kind of dumb back then. We've talked about that."

The bottom lip is sucked again.

"So . . . why do you think he picked a white girl? Because he only ever went for black girls and Latinas, right? And then you."

"He'd had white girlfriends in the past."

"He had?"

"He had."

"Oh, okay."

And then he shakes his head. "So . . . how come he left you in tttthe van?"

"I was out cold."

"But that is a fucking idiot's mistake to make, right? *Qué pendejada.* That is even more stupid than you walking through Bridgemarketttt on your own in the first place. You put some girl in the back of your van, and then you park and leave her . . ."

"The cops said he always smoked a cigarette right before he . . . finished up. They thought he'd probably run to a store to get some."

"*Whoa.* What a fucking moron."

"Well, you know . . . he was taking risks . . . every time he attacked a girl he was leaving himself more and more open to get caught. It's pretty common."

"Sure. That's in all the TV shows, right?" He raises his hands in their cuffs and spreads his fingers like starfish. "I swear to God I'm going to die of a fucking blood clot, *sabes?*"

Stretches them out five times in succession. Then lowers them back to his waist.

"Lizbeth, please don't feel like you have to talk about this if it makes you uncomfortable . . . but can I ask—what you were thinking as you were runninggg from the yellow van?"

"I was thinking of the view out over my fire escape on Varick Street and how beautiful it always looked right before the sun set. I was thinking of eating Popsicles and picking out clothes and dancing to songs on the radio and . . . just everything I'd never know again if that bastard caught up to me."

And Wilson's sucks his lip now for one, two, three, four, five—

"Okay, Lizbeth, I will tell you what I think. Because it would be false of me not to. I think that what you have said about this night is bullshit. I think itttt never happened. None of it."

He lunges forward. "When we have spoken about your mother, I can see your pain is true. It is the same when you talk aboutttt Leon Slocomb. I have seen enough people who have felt great fear to know what it looks like. But this? The way that you talk about this? 'I was thinking of sunsets and eating Popsicles.' That isn't real. That is just some pretty trash."

"Okay, Wilson, you know what? I listened to your shit earlier but this is . . . too much."

"Right, Lizbeth, it *is*. To lie about *chiva*, Okay . . . but to pretend to share the agony of the families of those girls who really were taken by that freak . . . *Dios mio,* that is low. Gabriela Linares, Okay, the things her cousin told us that were done to her . . . But of course you know all that already, don't you? From your book? The book thatttttt made you what you are."

She switches off the tape and gets to her feet. "I'm not . . . indulging this anymore."

"It's a shame that you had to say he left you in the van. That is whatttt really fucks up the story—right?"

She stands unmoving.

"But then how else is it going to work? Somehow he has to attack you—without actually doing all those things that he did to the other girls. The real girls. He needs to take you, but then you have to be okay. It is a problem. So I guess he *has* to leave you in the van. Not tied upppp, of course. Just lying there."

She still hasn't left.

"But people take shit at face value, right? If they want to believe something, they believe it. Just ignore what doesn't add up. And anyway, before anyone looks too close at what you have told them, the *pendejo* puts his gun in his mouth. Ha! It's perfecttttt! You must have been so happy!"

And he shouts now. "All those girls dead and you must have been so happy. Were you happy, Lizbeth? Did it bring a smile to your face? Did it make you feel like you were ssssso much smarter than the world? Was that how you felt? Special? Special and happy and all those other girls dead but you with your idea for a book—"

"That had nothing to do with it."

She stands with her face turned away from him.

". . . It was a stupid mistake . . . a stupid mistake that turned into something else . . . something it was never supposed to."

She sees a guard peer in through the porthole in the door, but she gestures that everything's fine.

"Bridgemarket was where we used to cop. Me and my boyfriend. The girl I worked with, her roommate was our dealer. So that night we were both up there, me and him . . . me and him and the girl I worked with . . . only her roommate was missing. He was supposed to have been there at nine, but he never showed . . . so we just sat there, all night. Waiting. They were both drinking rum and Tab, but it made me feel sick, so I was the only one sober. It just got later and later, and more and more obvious nothing was going to happen, and I had classes the next morning, but my boyfriend wouldn't leave . . . I kept asking him to but they both started laughing . . . they were so drunk by then, like cuddling up together, you know? . . . and I kept saying, 'Adrian, let's go. I want to go.' Until finally I just stood up and started to walk out . . . And he called out to me, and I thought, 'Thank God,' you know? Because at least he's not going to let me leave alone with this fucking psycho out there . . . but then he just asked me to make sure I left enough hot water in the tank so he could take a shower when he got home . . . And I left and I was so fucking angry . . . *wrathful,* you know? . . . I just walked down and stared at the river and I thought, I'm going to make him sorry."

Without looking at him, she sits back down. "So I walked the whole way across the bridge and the cold stung my face and I was more and more furious with every step . . . and as soon as I got into Queens I walked down to the shoreline and I found a concrete wall and twice I smashed my head against it. Just as hard as I could, you know? And it scared me so much, because I thought I'd really hurt myself, I was staggering and I could feel my hair was wet from the blood . . . and I waited there until I could see okay . . . then I ran back up to the bridge . . . And the guy who stopped for me took me to find a cop, and all I could think was how my boyfriend was going to feel knowing what had happened . . . And it was only when I was giving my statement to the cops that I thought 'oh, fuck.' You know? That nausea? Because I knew it was already too late. Everything was moving. And what was I going to do? Tell them? So I just stuck with it . . . with the cops, the reporters . . . And I just remember thinking the whole time 'what if they arrest him and he confesses?' You know, to everything. And then he'd look at me and say, 'Who the hell is that?' So when we found out he was dead, my sister held me in her arms and told me, 'You're safe now.' And I knew I was . . ."

She looks up just long enough to catch his eye before she gazes down again.

"And in time it just becomes part of you. It's not like you start believing it. It's not that at all . . . it's just that it gets easier and easier to tell it. Or you think it does. And when you've spent two years writing your first novel and it sells twelve hundred copies . . . and Inchy says, 'Honey, have you ever thought of writing something more . . . *personal* . . . ?' Well . . . here we are."

Wilson stares across at her and almost calls the guard, because her whole body's shaking so badly now that he thinks she might fall from her chair.

TWELVE

THE DOCTOR SMILES down at Lizbeth and says: "Have you decided?"
"I have," she says, and then, a moment later: "I don't want to know."

So that statement is duly passed on when the ultrasound technician comes, before she starts to rub the gel over Lizbeth's bump, her hands like fish in a tank.

Lizbeth stares up at the ceiling and thinks of nothing until they lift away, and she feels the strange pressure of the transducer in their place.

"Okay," the technician says, "now if I see anything that's going to indicate the sex, I'll make sure you have the chance to look away. Now, let me get this image as clear as I can."

Lizbeth's eyes settle on the monitor, where—in place of the indistinct lima bean it has always shown until now—there is a head, half imprinted with a face. Arms, hands, fingers, fingertips.

Nothing in the world but her/him.

"Oh, God," Lizbeth says.

The technician draws the transducer up over her belly. "Did you feel that?"

"What? Did I feel what?"

"It just moved its head."

"It did?"

"It's okay if you didn't feel it. It was just a fraction of an inch. The fetal ear picks up the soundwaves, and sometimes it moves in response."

Lizbeth feels a smile taking hold of her mouth and it's only now she realizes there are tears flowing down into its corners.

She flicks through her notes with the tape recorder idle in front of her. Stares at the tangles of her handwriting. Flicks back and starts again.

Lizbeth and Wilson have been in the lawyer's room six minutes. In that time she has neither spoken to nor looked at him.

Just hearing him move in his seat makes her jitter. Then: ". . . I thought perhaps we could use this session to talk in more detail about your first year in Moxanie."

He doesn't answer, and she doesn't look up.

". . . Alternatively, I have some holes around the time the Royals first expanded out of New York . . . if you preferred we could revisit that era . . ."

"I can help you." He taps his feet in emphasis. "I can help you with the ssshame of your lies."

And now she looks.

"Tell me, Lizbeth . . . when did you lllast do something illegal?"

"Wilson," she says, ". . . please. I can't do this . . . not again . . ."

"Not like a—traffic offense. Something real, *sabes*?"

". . . I have no idea."

"It can't be that hard to answer. You mustttt know when you last took *chiva*? But no, wait . . . maybe that is not what I am looking for. Okay, so . . . when did you last *buy chiva*?"

"I don't . . . actually buy it. Someone else does that."

"No! Shit! Lizbeth, that is so fucked up! You have someone do thattt for you? *Dios mio*."

He tuts and as he does he shakes his head. "Okay, the way that I see your problem is this—you are a fraud. Your life is built out of shit and you write without knowing the truth of your characters. Yes? So, let me give you my idea. You should recognize it. It came from one of your stories. *Night Blind*, right? You sent it to me when we first met? I'm thinking of chapter eight."

There is no response.

"Lizbeth, please. It is your story. Chapter eight. Where Enschell's mind has grown so clouded that he no longer believes he can ssssolve the case. The Atlas Killer has claimed another victim and Enschell can see no logic. No pattern. He is beaten. And he is so distressed that he gets drunk in that *jacal* bar and steals that *vato*'s Beamer and joyrides through the city in it—and *then*, then he sees the answer!"

He clears his throat. "Now, to be honest with you, itttt struck me like a cliché. The cop solves the crime by becoming a criminal and blah blah blah, *sabes*? But last night with that *puta* Whitmore banging on my cell door I thought of it. And of you. So, here is my request—"

He leans in to the table.

246

"May I uuse . . . your pen?"

She stares at him and he repeats the question, eyes darting up to the camera by the ceiling. So she holds it out to him and with his wrists held rigid by the cuffs he closes his fingers around it. She pushes her notebook into the middle of the table, and he nudges forward. Writes with stiff deliberation on the page in front of him:

BREAK A LAW

She turns the notebook back around to face her.

"It's okay," he says. "I don't expect anything unrealistic. Just something small. Lizbeth, I truly believe that doing this will bringggggg the thing that you need mostt to your stories. Some heart, *sabes*? What you came to me looking for . . . well, here is your chance to find it."

He drops the pen. She retrieves it.

"And this way my conscience will not trouble me. Because I will know you are trying to make amendsssss for your lies. So there isss no reason for me to tell anyone about them."

"Wilson, I can't—"

"Please understand me, Lizbeth, I'd never wish ttttto harm your reputation. But I don't like secrets. They are bad for the spirit. And remember, it is me who has tttold his whole life to someone who is not what they claimed to be. So I would think you would want to prove to me that you were sorry. Thatt you wanted to regain my trust."

She gazes down at the page, his awkward characters. He leans back in his chair.

"So . . . what do you ttthink you could do to prove that?"

And exits for towns she's never heard of blur past the window as she drives west in the slate early evening; foot down, fifteen minutes out of Essenville, state line ahead. A CD playing (King Tubby: *Tubby Get Smart*). More than once she changes lanes ready to turn off before something says *Not yet*. So she keeps driving, and the miles tick by.

Not yet. Not yet. Not yet. But then:

Finally, she picks an exit. Doesn't even notice the name of the town. Just a half mile of ticky-tacky butting into the forest. A slow fidget of traffic through the streets.

A convenience store on a corner. Not, she sees with relief, a cheery red-fronted Sheetz, its staff trained by Dave Urkoff, its profits helping raise Lizbeth's niece and nephews.

Just a Unimart.

She parks out in front of it. Pulls her coat around herself and hears the soft clip of her steps across the lot.

I shoplifted, she said. In my teens.

So there we are, Wilson said.

Inside a pair of kids skulk near the counter as two pudgy clerks trade eye rolls. Down one wall is a cooler filled with sandwiches. An elderly man stands transfixed in front of it, staring up at a poster-size photograph of a turkey sub.

One of the kids fumbles in his jacket as Lizbeth passes him, and she hears the first clerk tell him there's no smoking in the store.

Do it today, Wilson said. Do it, then come back and tell me how it felt. But don't lie to me. If you lie to me, Lizbeth, I'll know. And we'll be finished.

She walks past the first aisle, stacked to brimming with chips and salsa. Makes for the second. The candy. Looks up to check on the clerks as the old man by the sandwiches calls out to them to ask how much for coffee and a muffin.

She can't tell which is greater, her fear or her sense of absurdity. Candy bars. She stares across them. Which one? Her gaze falls on a Mounds. Wilson's favorite. Should that matter? Her hand twitches at her side.

The headlines, she knows, will be unsparing. FAMOUS AUTHOR NABBED AS SHE GRABS. There will be a statement read by Inchy Burden outside a local courthouse, blaming stress and misunderstanding. Her name will ring through the opening monologues of a thousand late-night talk shows. Her life exposed and then picked clean.

Three forty-eight, the second clerk says.

But this is just a question of nerve. The blotting-out of consequence. Just like swimming in the sea or getting on a plane.

She stands as close as she can to the display, and her hand extends out to a Mounds. She feels the wrapper in her palm before closing her fingers around it. Then she pulls back and slips it inside her pocket. Exhales.

Up at the counter the kids do something, or say something—Lizbeth's too far away to know what—that has the first clerk threatening to throw them out.

Lizbeth moves into the next aisle. Household essentials. This time she doesn't even pause. Just plucks a citrus air freshener from the rack and thrusts it into her pocket.

The old man at the cooler says *Y'uns goddany choclit chip?*

Now she's at the fridge. A foot taller than her. More exposed than any of the aisles. The clerks would only have to look down here and she'd be in full view. But she's baited now. Feverish with breaking from the script. She couldn't think of leaving without trying.

So she slides open the door and without looking round takes a 7UP and jams that too into the now bulging pocket of her coat.

The second clerk says *Nuh-uh. We just sold out.*

And she's done. Turns toward the exit and strides past the old man and the picture of the turkey sub, beyond the loitering kids, and as she passes the clerks they glance at her like they hadn't even noticed her come in. She leaves and walks back across the lot and no alarm shrieks and no hand falls on her shoulder.

Until, once more, she's in the car.

She sits for a moment before emptying her pockets. Lays out what she's taken on the seat beside her. Stares as if she's never seen any of it before.

Then she whoops. Punches the air. Screams with glee so loud that at first she doesn't hear her phone ringing inside her bag.

"Oh, hey."

She holds it to her ear.

". . . Sure I am . . . Sure . . . This weekend's fine . . . No, really . . . I want to. I said I want to see him and I do . . ."

She glances over at the Unimart. Starts the engine.

"Sure . . . I can drive over to you on Friday night then we can go up to-gether on Saturday . . . Okay . . . Sure . . . That's fine . . . Oh, you fin-ished it? . . . Oh, you did? That's great . . . Well, let me know how Kyle likes it—"

She takes one last look at the store as she pulls away.

"Listen, Mame, I got to go . . . Uh-huh . . . You too."

In moments, she's on the highway again. And it's only when she's halfway back to Essenville that she has to pull over to the shoulder.

George orders lunch at the Venus Restaurant Diner, and when the waitress has his order he turns to Lizbeth and tells her he drove by her place last night. Almost called in before he noticed that the lights were off.

"Right," she says. "I was having dinner at the Sosas."

"Ah," he says, "Joan Sosa's mythic pot pie."

She turns her head. Gazes out at the street. Lost in the faces of passersby.

"That good, huh?"

"Sorry," she says. "I'm a little . . . off center today."

"But you're still okay for tonight?"

It means nothing.

"Movies and popcorn. My place. Tonight."

"Movies and popcorn. Your place. Tonight. Of course. Sure. I'm there."

"Although I should warn you I told some old San Diego friends of mine about you being here, and after ten minutes persuading them I hadn't gone completely nuts, they mailed me their books and—"

"I'll make sure my signing hand's nice and supple." Then her voice is pensive: "George, have you ever lied . . . in your job?"

"You mean at the store? To a customer? I don't think so. Absolutely not . . ." Panic spreads across his face. "Why? What did you hear?"

"Nothing," she says. "Forget it. Really."

But just when she thinks she's going to have to elaborate, salvation pulls up outside.

Lloyd Dreiz waits at a red light in his silver Hummer, elbow on the window, cigarette between his fingers. He drags on it and flicks the ash into the street. Radio blaring.

George's face hardens in contempt. Lizbeth turns back to him.

"So where do you think he's headed? A lunchtime tryst with a mystery lover? The shallow grave of another victim?"

"I'd guess he's going somewhere to shoot guns and drink himself insensible." He leans across the table. "See, you're pretending you think this is all so much hooey. But deep down you know there's something in it."

"You think?"

"I do think. Uh-huh. I do."

She turns back to the window. Stares out. "Maybe."

"I knew it! I just knew it! So, do I have your permission to be interested in this now?"

"Yes, George," she says. "You have my permission."

The waitress returns with their orders but neither of them notices her. They're too busy watching the light turn green and Lloyd Dreiz speed away.

*   *   *

250

He has grown a mustache in the time since she last saw him. A flawless black surgeon's stroke that runs across his upper lip, then curls down each side of his mouth, flaring to conclusion an inch below it.

"Are you listening ttto me?"

She looks up and Wilson is staring across the table.

"Oh, Lizbeth. It seems like your mind is somewhere else. Again."

She grabs for the first thought she can.

"I see you've grown a—"

"You like it?" he says.

"Sure. I mean . . . it's . . . distinctive."

He nods, shuts his eyes for a moment. Shoulders relaxed.

"Thank you. You know, a very close friend of mine had a mustache llllike this, back in Corona. When he was maybe eighteen years old. *Sabes?* It was kind of a signature. A trademark of this *very close friend.* You understand me?"

"Sure."

"It's funny . . . I remember, one afternoon my close friend was crossinggggg 99th Street when he saw this other *vato* . . . a kid named Miji . . . a Royal . . . and this kid was wearing the exact same mustache. Now that— alone is fucked-up, *sabes?* An act of insolence. But my friend thought, No . . . he would give this idiotttt the benefit of the doubtttttt. Thought maybe he was fucking retarded or something, right? So he just called him over and explaineddd the situation. That this was *his* mustache. His signature. And Miji got the message. Said he was sorry. That he'd turn around righttttt there and then and go home and shave."

Wilson tuts to himself at the memory. "But he didn't. A couple of days llllater, my friend sees him again, and he still has the mustache. My friend was obviously very unhappy. He tttttold him, as a matter of extreme urgency, to get riddd of it . . . but it didn'tttt work . . . because a week after that, this *hina* Edita thattttttt my friend had been dating, it's her birthday party. A huge *baile* up on 38th Avenue. And Miji shows up—still with the mmmmustache! He stands there caressing it! So finally my friend knew he had to express his displeasure in the strongest ttterms."

He swivels from the waist in his seat. "The next morning, Miji answers his door, and my close friend is waitinggg there. And he stepped inside and shaved off Miji's mustache for him. He used a hunting knife. Of course, not beinggggg a trained barber, it ended up a little messy. An unkind person might even say ugly. But one thinggg was certain . . . Miji never grew another mustache."

Then he smiles. Not for long; but long enough. A cool smirk of amusement.

Lizbeth feels queasy as she watches the tape roll.

He lowers his voice to a whisper.

"Anyway . . . forget that . . . let's get to the importantttt stuff . . . tell me whatt happened."

She glances toward the door, and then the camera. Writes the answer in her notebook. Turns it around for him to see.

"You never told me you liked Mounds, Lizbeth. You are always ssssso full of surprises." He waits until she looks up again. "So how did you feel afterward? Was it as gggood as it used to be?"

"Better," she says, her voice a whisper too. "It was a blast."

He nods and grins.

"Then I had to pull over on the highway because I was freaking out so badly I thought I was going to drive into the median barrier. I sat there for an hour and all I could think about was having my baby in prison—"

"Oh, Lizbeth, please. Be serious now. What jjjudge is going to send a famous white lady with a *bebé* on its way to jail for stealing candy? Don't be so dramatic. Your head is all messed up with hormones, right? You apologize to everyone for making such a silly mistake and it will never happen again, right? And—anyway, you're sitting here now, aren'ttt you? So after we are done here you can go outtt and have a blast again."

"No," she says. "Absolutely not. I will not."

"But you just said you had enjoyed it?"

She says nothing. Just shakes her head, fierce and adamant.

"You think one time is enough? Lizbeth, no. You need more than one time to learn abouttt what you're missing. And if you just gave up this afternoon and tttonight for your studies—"

Her head lowers, but keeps shaking.

"Okay. *A la chingada.* You and I can go no further. I am sorry that you feel the way you do, Lizbeth, and that things have not worked out how we hoped they would. So I wish you gggood luck with whatever you choose to do next."

He turns toward the door, parts his lips, about to call out to the guards.

"I can't do anything tonight."

And he turns back. "Why not?"

"I've got plans tonight."

"So unplan ttthem." He pitches himself toward the edge of the table. "Tell me, who is it you have plans with, Lizbeth?"

"Just . . . someone I know in town."

"So tell me his name."

"Who even said it was a him? You know, it is possible I know more than one person."

"So maybe you joined a religious cult, Lizbeth? Is that ittt? Are you going to be showing up here in a white robe from now on?" And from its hush his voice abruptly rears into a bellow. "This is making me so tired Lizbeth! So very sick and tired! You have lied to me and misled me and I have gggggiven you a chance to make amends and to prove that you are sorry—but you will nottt even make the smallest effort! Not the tiniest effort!"

His feet yammer the floor, one after the other, one after the other. "You need to ask yourself why you are here, Lizbeth. You miss our meetings and when you do come your mind is elsewhere. And itttt confuses me because I thought you were here to write a book that would tell people important things. But it seems like maybe the real reason is to spend time with these friends of yours. So let me say this, as another friend—it is my strong conviction that you should go from here and have another blast."

He pulls back from the table, and as quickly as it rose his voice drops again. "But it is up to you, Lizbeth. It is all up to you." He turns again, and now he does call out to the guard.

She drives north from the prison without her eyes once leaving the road until she sees the saw-toothed Pittsburgh skyline. When she gets Downtown she finds a parking lot by Heinz Hall and leaves the Volvo there. Then she heads for the streets around Market Square, passing through stores in which—among the glut of shoppers—no one pays too much attention to the small woman with the gray woollen hat pulled down over her hair.

Every time it's the same. An adrenal tremble and then a strange absent calm as her hand reaches out. Then afterward, the thrill and the dread both together.

She steals a canvas tote bag from a rack outside a luggage store. With it over her shoulder, she slips into a baby store and takes a rattle in the shape of a monkey's face and a pair of elastic bootees. A block down at a cramped boutique she waits until the clerk is busy with a phone call, then grabs two pink T-shirts and a pale blue scarf. In Eckerd Drugs she steals eyedrops, tea tree oil, cortisone cream, an unscented deodorant.

Then she hurries back to the car. Throws everything inside. Drives across town to the Strip. There she parks again. Wanders through the produce markets with the smell of fresh trout in her nostrils and ducks into a used CD store. Emerges a moment later with the tote bag stuffed. Paces toward the USX Tower, and in its shadow she finds a spotless diner where she drinks tea and picks at a slice of cheesecake and, before the waitress can bring her the check, quietly gets up and walks out.

It's dusk when she leaves the city. Speeds back the way she came across the dappled Monongahela.

Five miles outside Essenville, she spins east, past the signs for the women's prison. Drives for another ten minutes, then takes the next exit to present itself. Another valley. Another town. Another Unimart. Laid out just the same as the last one.

She makes for the candy. Repeats her previous routine exactly. Slips a Mounds into her pocket, then moves on to the air freshener. At the fridge a slouching dude with a six-pack under his arm catches her eye and for one cold moment she thinks he must have seen her. Then his face settles into a leer and she all but sighs with relief.

She waits for him to get bored and then, once the clerks are busy, she grabs a 7 UP.

The next store in the next town is a Sheetz. But the one after that is perfect. Thronged with customers, haste and disorder. A lone teenage clerk. She roams the store and fills her pockets.

Outside she empties the lot across the backseat: a candy landslide.

Then she drives east again with the heater on full. Stares at the road and thinks, What if she just kept going? Spent the night in a fifty-dollar motel and drove on in the morning, rolling through Gettysburg, past covered bridges and Amish orchards, on toward whatever?

Instead, she exits again. Finds a 7-Eleven in the next town she gets to, and from there steals more candy and a fruit punch Gatorade. And then she turns back. Shaking, nauseous. Listening for sirens.

She only sees she needs gas ten miles out of Essenville. Debates trying to make it home on what she has left but no longer feels in the mood for taking risks.

She's filled up and turning the key in the ignition when a figure appears at her window.

"George . . ."

"I thought that was you."

His car is at the next pump. He has, he says, been visiting a student from his writing class. That when she canceled on him earlier, he thought he'd make use of the evening anyway.

"I don't get it," he says. "You said you were too tired to do anything but sleep . . ."

She gropes for an answer, but he's already staring at the backseat. The candy and the baby shoes, the CDs, eyedrops, cortisone cream, the T-shirts with their price tags still hanging from their collars.

"Lizbeth . . . is everything okay?"

She sees the concern in his face and it makes her put hers in her hands. And she sits that way for an age, still and unspeaking.

"Lizbeth, what is it? What's going on? Is this stuff—"

And without meeting his eyes, she lifts her face just enough to be heard as she tells him what she did tonight, and last night too. She doesn't get into why.

When she finally looks up, he's nodding. Troubled but wanting to understand.

"How long have you been doing this? I mean . . . is it something you do . . . regularly?"

"No, no. Not at all . . ."

"Are you . . . I mean, if you're having . . . psychological problems . . ."

"It's nothing like that, George."

And he starts to nod as if now he gets it. "You're an artist," he says. "Artists go outside of the conventional. It's . . . research. Right?"

"Right," she says. "It's research. That's what it is."

He squats on his haunches, reaches out and lays his hand on hers. And on the glacial lot of a gas station at night loomed over by tilting banks of walnut trees, he tells her how in tenth grade there were rumors about him. About his lifestyle. Baseless but persistent, he says. So in order to stop them, to save his family hearing them, he asked out a girl from his drama class. Karen Kelly. Sweet girl. Popular. Sister still lives in town. It was, he says, enough to stem the whispering. And on the night itself he got dressed up in the clothes they make fun of now but which back then made him feel like John Travolta in *Saturday Night Fever*, and his parents beamed from the front door as he left. Then, as he strolled with Karen into town for hot dogs and soda, a red T-Bird cruised by, and Lloyd Dreiz leaned out of the window and aimed a pistol at his chest.

It wasn't loaded. Just—as the sheriff told the Finers later that night—boys having fun.

But George reacted as anyone would with a gun pointed at their heart. *Physically,* he says. *Primally.* And even now he can see the look on Karen's face.

"I have such respect for you," he says. "And whatever reasons you have for *this*—" he gestures at the backseat—"I respect them too. But I hope you can respect me when I say I want to see Lloyd meet with the consequences of his actions. Not because of the pistol. Because he has something wicked inside him. And I want people to know about it. I want him to pay for it. And for that to happen I might need to . . . go outside the conventional too."

Lizbeth feels clammy as he talks.

Gina Dreiz, he says, died in her yard while Lloyd was in the cellar cleaning his guns. Right? Didn't hear her. Couldn't see her. Right? Except he could.

"My parents had friends that lived in that house. They moved up to Pittsburgh when I was seven, but I must have played out in that yard a dozen times before then. And sure the window was just this tiny dirty square in the wall, but I *know* you could see into that cellar from outside. So anyone in it could have seen out too. So Lloyd's alibi . . . it's a crock."

It just needs exposing. And George is ready to do that now.

"It's the state playoffs at the Bowlodrome Monday night," he says. "Lloyd's bowling for the town. He'll be gone until eleven."

"Ms. Greene? It's Alicia Mapp. Gang Intelligence."

Lizbeth holds the phone to her ear. Outside, it's so bright she has to squint just to look out of the window.

"How are you Ms. Greene?"

"I'm okay. How are you?"

"I'm good, Ms. Greene. Thank you for asking. Ms. Greene, I'm sorry to contact you at home like this but there is something I wanted to check in with you about. I'll get straight to it. We've watched the last couple of tapes of your interviews with Velez—"

Lizbeth all but reels. Feels her legs wilt and her head wooze at the thought of everything said in those sessions. She has to press her hand to the wall just to stop herself from falling.

"—and it's come to our notice that in those interviews, both you and Velez have been exhibiting some pretty . . . *quirky* behavior."

Lizbeth knows she shouldn't answer until her voice is sure to be calm and composed.

"Ms. Greene? Are you there?"

". . . Quirky?"

"That's right, Ms. Greene. For instance, we noticed on the tape of your last meeting that much of it was conducted in whispers between the two of you . . . inaudible whispers . . . followed by an outburst from Velez, after which he asks the guards to return him to his cell . . ."

But she makes no response.

". . . In addition, in each of your last two meetings at least one of you has written in a notebook that they have then shown the other in lieu of speech. Could you tell me why that was, Ms. Greene?"

There is a pause.

"A lot of Wilson's conversation in that last session became overtly . . . sexual . . . He was asking me questions about that . . . area of my life. I guess he whispered because he wanted it to seem more intimate . . . or more intimidating . . ."

"I see. And the note writing? Was that also sexual in content, Ms. Greene?"

"Right. It was."

"Including the one you wrote for him?"

"No . . . That wasn't . . . I mean—"

"Ms. Greene, if I wanted to, might it be possible for me to see your notebooks? It could be very useful for me to get an idea of the tone of your interviews with Wilson . . ."

"I . . . ah . . . sure . . ."

"And your audio tapes, Ms. Greene? If I wanted to hear those, would it be possible to have access to them?"

"My tapes?"

"Right. I thought we could possibly listen back to some of those points where you're whispering . . . clarify what's being said . . ."

"Wait . . . are you telling me to turn over my notes and my tapes?"

"Not currently, Ms. Greene. I'm just trying to find out whether it would be a problem if it did become appropriate to go down that route?"

"No. I mean . . . of course not . . . I . . ." Then she gathers enough co-
herence to ask: "How long have you been recording . . . I mean, everything I've talked about with Wilson . . . has it *all* been—"

"Ms. Greene, I couldn't possibly go into that with you. But let me say
this—nobody here is trying to *scoop* your research. I guarantee that. And
please be aware we have no interest in anything . . . anything that isn't re-
lated to our investigation. That's all we're listening for here."

The sun's so brilliant now she has to draw the blinds.

"I understand you visited Queens recently, Ms. Greene. Spoke with José
Almanza and Raymond Peres."

"That's right. It's not a secret. For the book, I need to—"

"Of course, Ms. Greene. Of course. Can I ask what you discussed with
them?"

"We talked about the work the Royals are doing . . . the building reno-
vations . . ."

"And did you find that aspect of the gang plausible, Ms. Greene?"

"I guess. I don't know. I . . ."

"Did you talk about Velez with them, Ms. Greene?"

"I did."

"May I ask in what context?"

"We just talked about . . . his health . . . the letters . . ."

"The letters that had no orders in them?"

"That's what he says . . ."

"And do you believe him, Ms. Greene?"

"I don't know."

Alicia Mapp lets a moment pass.

"I take it you heard about the boy being shot in Corona the same day
you were there. Armand Pichardo."

"I did. It was a horrible thing."

Again, the line is quiet. Then: "Ms. Greene, please understand, we're
not suggesting there's anything sinister going on in your meetings. It's just
that in a scenario like this we have to look at everything that may help us
find an answer . . . And it simply occurred to us that he may have said
something to you . . . or written something . . . that while not *seeming* important could prove to be exactly that. And when we can't hear what's being said, it makes that kind of difficult . . ."

"But you're not suggesting . . . that I—"

"Ms. Greene, of course not. As I said to you when we met in Warden Sosa's office, we're not even suggesting that Velez himself is involved . . . frankly, it's not something we feel is particularly credible. We just feel it's possible that his release from Ad-Seg may have undermined the *equilibrium* of the neighborhood. And also . . . between us, Ms. Greene, even if we were to look in that direction, there are any number of easier channels for someone like Velez to use than you."

"There are?"

"Of course, Ms. Greene. If an inmate is smart enough, it's almost impossible to stop information getting out or coming in. Inmates talk to other inmates. Other inmates have visitors. Prison employees can be less than ideally scrupulous. And Ms. Greene, it's not even as if you're the only civilian Velez is in contact with. There's mail going back and forth between him and the Christian Ladies of Western Arizona on a weekly basis . . ."

She trails off. Pauses. "But this is so hypothetical as to be ridiculous. Ms. Greene, at the present time all we're trying to do is see which routes might potentially be open to us. We know you're simply here to write a book, and speaking personally it's one that I'm greatly looking forward to. Just as long as you understand that we also have a job to do."

"Of course. Of course."

Lizbeth thinks of the interviews, the whispers. The tapes. ". . . Are you coptering the situation now?"

"Goodness no, Ms. Greene. We're not coptering the situation." Alicia Mapp clears her throat. "This is just two people having a conversation on the telephone."

The snow she has heard spoken of with such reverence ever since she came to Essenville—the real snow, Pennsy snow—is finally due tonight. The first major fall of winter. A steady cascade already under way, a prelude to the coming blizzard that will, by morning, have demanded a train of plows and salt trucks.

George sits restless in the passenger seat of the Volvo. Clicks his fingers, whistles, pats his knee and hums. He wears a black leather jacket she's never seen him wear before that's making the whole car smell musty.

Lizbeth drives replaying every word of her last two meetings with Wilson. The others before it. Her head full of people she has never met hearing everything's she said to him. Until George starts flipping through the radio. And the noise drags her attention back.

They pass through Essenville in the deserted mid-evening. The whole town bunkered at home or gathered at the Bowlodrome.

George turns to her by the Foodline Savers Mart.

"Thank you for coming with me. It means the world. You know, I've wanted to do this ever since Gina . . . passed on. I just never thought I could. But then, I never thought I'd be hanging out with Lizbeth Greene."

He brushes off the sleeves of his jacket, shakes the tension from his hands and neck.

"With you . . . I just feel *realized*. You know?"

She has tried to talk him out of this. It didn't work. Seeing her at the gas station, he said, reminded him that sometimes a noble goal is more important than the letter of the law. She has inspired him. And he can't be uninspired.

He'd do it alone, he said. If he had to. But this way at least she can look after him.

He pulls a small square camera from the bag at his feet, then spins through the radio once more. Settles on what sounds like a mariachi band; enough to make her wince with irritation.

"George, what are you actually planning to do with the pictures? You're breaking into the guy's house. They don't give you the little tin star for evidence they can't use."

"The pictures are going in the mail. When they see them they'll have to do something. Especially when they find out the papers have them too."

On the radio are wailing trumpets, frantic guitars.

"I just don't think you've thought this through, George. There has to be another way to do this. I mean, maybe you could just . . . look around . . . from the back of the house . . . ?"

But he just sits beside her, silently patting his knee until her temper gives.

"George, will you get rid of this fucking music?"

He switches off the radio and turns to her. "I don't see why you're mad. You did what you did because of something that was important to you. And that's all I'm doing too."

She stares at the road ahead as the wipers bat away the snow. "Where am I going?"

They have crossed into the southwest of town. Old Essenville. The un-lit husks of factory buildings and, beyond them, a string of shabby detached houses, the roads wider now but potholed.

"Take a left, then keep straight on."

As the wheel turns through her hands, she feels an out-of-nowhere urge to tell him: "George . . . I'm pregnant."

"Right," he says, and tinkers with the camera. Then he glances over. "Sorry . . . I thought you were about to say something. I'm pregnant *and . . .*"

"But I never told you."

"Huh?"

"I never told you."

"You thought I didn't know? Oh, my God. Lizbeth, look at you. You are *with child*. It's obvious. Maybe not when we first met, but now . . . ?" He shakes his head, incredulous. "I just assumed you didn't want to talk about it . . . You never mentioned the father, so . . ."

"I'm not with him. Self-evidently I'm not with him."

There is silence.

"Do you want to be?"

"I don't think so. I don't know."

He gazes at her as she drives. "I wish I had something to say you might find useful. Everything I think of always sounds like it came off one of the T-shirts at the store—" And then his voice turns urgent. "—*Okay.* That's it."

Lloyd Dreiz's house stands sideways on to the road. Set back ten yards with a curving path to its front and back doors. Three storeys painted gray and white, lawn and garage out front. A zigzag of black guttering. The snow starting to thicken on the sills and roof.

They are at the exact point where suburbia gives way to countryside. The nearest house barely in squinting distance, the woodland between them wild, not ornamental.

And no signs of life beyond a porch light.

She drives past the back of the house and pulls into a half-veiled nook on the other side of the road.

George steps out. Zips his black jacket, straightens his black pants. "I can see why you like dressing this way," he says. "You feel so . . . funky." He reaches back into the car for his bag. Takes out a balaclava. Yanks it down as far as his eyes. "I still can't believe you thought I didn't know," he says, and shakes his head. He has, she is certain, never so much as been late in paying a parking ticket. Now he taps the ball end of a screwdriver into his hand to rehearse the breaking of a pane of glass.

She feels no pride when he says:

"You know, last night right before I went to sleep I reread the chapter in *The Hands of Angels* when Enschell breaks into the doctor's apartment . . . it almost felt like homework."

He steps around the front of the car. And for the first time he looks afraid.

She tries to pinpoint what it is she wants to say, but the best that comes out is: "George, you really don't have to do this. This is . . . unnecessary."

He stops and closes his eyes and his breathing steadies. "Do you know if it's a boy or girl?" he says.

"I haven't found out yet."

And then he crosses the road. "I'll be five minutes," he says.

She calls after him to wish him luck. Watches as he steps toward the back of the house. Approaches the door.

When he reaches it he seems to hesitate, until she sees he's just putting on his gloves.

Then she loses sight of him.

A moment later, glass breaks.

After that it's quiet.

She feels the suedelike plush of the driver's seat against her skin. Looks out at the road, the woods. And there is, unexpectedly, a peace here.

The snow getting heavier.

"Oh, God."

The flutter of nerves in her stomach is not, she realizes, the flutter of nerves. It is the baby's first kick. Gentle but unmistakable.

One hand covers her mouth, the other falls across her belly.

"Oh, God."

And then: "*Oh, God.*"

From the second story of the house, a light comes on. And a stick-thin silhouette appears.

Lloyd Dreiz rises to his feet and moves across the room.

"Oh, fuck. No. Fuck."

And he carries on through it, then he turns the light back off.

The pale gleam of a flashlight in its place.

There is no plan for this. Their one emergency plan—to call George's cell phone with the horn a last resort—was designed only for the distant appearance of Lloyd Dreiz's Hummer.

Not this.

What is this?

"Oh, fuck. Oh, God."

She grabs her phone from the dash and her fingers feel as if she's never used them before.

It doesn't even ring out. Just: "Hi, you've reached the cell phone of George Fi—"

"Oh, God."

Her eyes fix on the house as her heart batters. And then, downstairs, she sees the flashlight's beam by a window, then Lloyd Dreiz's shadow, and she watches in mute but blossoming horror as he passes through, then pauses. Half crouches, then continues.

Into the next room. Toward the back of the house. And the phone again yields nothing but: "Hi, you've reached the—"

"Hi, you've re—"

"Hi, y—"

In the last room at the back of the house, she sees the shadow of Lloyd Dreiz again, stooping and waiting before every step, but when he takes them moving fast, moving onward.

Until he's gone:

Out to what must be the cellar door.

The house returned to darkness.

She slams the heel of her palm against the the horn. One sharp blast that does nothing. So a moment later she pushes it again, weighing down on it in the hush of Old Essenville with the snow beginning to swirl around her.

Then she wrenches back her hand.

"George . . . oh, please . . . George . . ."

But George does not come running.

There is only silence.

Then a gunshot.

The TV is on downstairs, and the sound of it carries through the house. Kyle Urkoff lies in bed with the lamp beside him illuminating the dirty clothes that layer the floor, the crammed shelves of toys and board games and books.

He turns onto his side, scratches at his leg through his Stone Cold Steve Austin pajamas. Finds his place in the story his aunt gave his mother to pass on to him. She didn't write it. Some guy wrote it. His mother said it was going to be a real book soon, and Kyle was lucky to even be reading it.

He's been getting through a chapter an evening. And now, in the last precious minutes before one or other of his parents bawl up to him to turn out the light, he checks how many pages are left, and reads:

The rain poured down over the city, making puddles like rock pools in the middle of the sidewalks. But in Gramercy Park, it was heaviest of all—each raindrop big enough to soak you to the skin.

It seemed to the monsters as if the heavens themselves knew what lay ahead. Because tonight was the last in which they would ever be able to call their beloved building home.

Their fate had been decided. Louis Fung had collected more than a thousand names for his petition, and given it to the Mayor. And when the Mayor saw all those names—every one a voter!—he had no choice but to order in the workmen with their hammers and chisels. They were coming the next morning.

Oh, but it was a scene of such woe and sorrow! Even the largest, most hideous of the gargoyles—the ones who most people would faint away at the mere sight of—were now so weak from having gone so long without mischief that all they could do was huddle together, coughing and sniffing and waiting for the morning.

Hector and Edmond looked out sadly from their perch above the front door. They started to reminisce but stopped after the first wonderfully terrible memory. They knew it would break their foul hearts to continue.

"I think this is really the end, compadre," Hector said.

"Yes, old friend," Edmond replied. "I fear that you are right."

The two gargoyles agreed they could not bear to see this tragedy unfold. Together, without speaking further, they abandoned the perch and crept away, hoping that the other monsters would not see them.

Just then the front door swung open. And out of it came Louis Fung and a pair of businessmen as fat as walruses, or maybe sumo wrestlers, or maybe walruses who sumo wrestle.

"Yes, yes," he said as he showed them out of the building, "once

these terrible ugly gargoyles are off the building for good and all, then we can replace them with something far more useful."

"Like a billboard," one fat businessman said.

"Or TWO billboards!" said the other.

"This is the beauty of the situation, gentlemen," Louis Fung said. "We can do what we like! After all, who will raise their voice against the man who rid Gramercy Park of its monsters?"

The two fat businessmen waddled away under huge umbrellas. Then, as Louis Fung turned to go back inside, he looked up at the gargoyles' perch ready to gloat.

"Well, well," he said when he saw that Hector and Edmond were gone. "Too cowardly to even see through the night. So much for the famous monsters!"

Then, from above, he heard the most disgusting noise you could ever hope NOT to imagine—the sound of an out of tune violin being played with a bow made of rusty nails while a hundred stray cats howled along with a hundred screaming babies. He slapped his hands over his ears and yelled: "Where is that noise coming from? It is abominable!"

Running back inside, Louis Fung scoured the building trying to find the noise. Higher and higher he climbed, and as he did it just grew louder.

Finally, he stepped out on the roof. And there he found where it was coming from.

Shivering on a ledge was Hector. It was he that was making the loathsome noise—it being the sound all gargoyles make when they are almost at their end. He was indeed a pitiful sight: his scales flaking off, his fangs yellow and crumbling.

"I should have known," Louis Fung sneered. "Look at you cowering up here. How pathetic!"

He jabbed a bony finger at Hector.

"Just think, by tomorrow you and your gargoyle friends will be gone from this building forever—and I will claim it as my home and headquarters. Then I will make sure that the people of New York forget all about your silly troublemaking—and find out what it's like when a REAL demon makes trouble!"

By now Louis Fung was shouting—shouting so loud he didn't notice that the residents of the building had come to the roof to see what all the noise was.

"You should have known you could never beat me!" he yelled at

Hector. "I am the most ancient and powerful evil spirit of them all! Did you really think I would let a bunch of gargoyles run a place this full of badness forever?"

He took a step toward Hector.

"I know! Why don't I just push you off this ledge now—that way I don't have to listen to your mewling and I can get on preparing some fun for tomorrow! I tell you, that fire I started is nothing compared to the havoc I've got planned!"

Then, as he cackled, his true demon face took over—as red as a flaming chile and dripping with clear gloop like Vaseline. The residents of the building gasped in horror. Louis Fung spun around and saw them.

"Oh, darnit," he said, sarcastically. "Now you know what I truly am. Oh, wéll! Tomorrow you're all going to die anyway!"

He turned back to Hector and just as he was about to push him from the ledge, he paused. "Wait," he said. "Aren't there two of you stupid creatures?"

And at that very moment, using the very last of his strength, Edmond swooped down from the rainy gray sky and with a mighty flap of his wing knocked the demon that was Louis Fung clean off his feet.

For a second, he swayed back and forth—and then, with a shriek that sent shivers up the spines of all who heard it, he toppled over backward and fell from the roof.

"You left that late, old friend," Hector said.

"Sorry, compadre," Edmond replied. "Still, it seems like the plan worked, right?"

They looked down over the ledge. There, Louis Fung was stuck on the spiked railings that ran around the front of the building. One spike had pierced through his demon tail, another through his demon throat—and the third straight through his demon heart.

As he squirmed, he opened his mouth and his tongue flopped out—it looked like a flat salami with a fork at the end like a snake's. It was so long it almost touched the sidewalk. Because of this, a passing mongrel dog saw it there and thought it would make a tasty snack. So he bit down on it and ran away with it between his teeth, and as he turned the corner out of the square he pulled the demon inside out!

That was the last anyone saw of Louis Fung.

The residents of the building knew they had made a grievous mistake. They gave Hector and Edmond their apologies and first thing in the morning, the Mayor was told what had happened, and the workmen were canceled.

The monsters of Gramercy Park were saved.

That night, it rained again, even heavier than the night before. And with the rain there was now a high and gusting and blustery wind.

Hector and Edmond looked out from their perch above the front door of their building on their corner of Gramercy Park and then they turned to one another.

"What an awful night this is," Hector said.

"Indeed it is, old friend," Edmond said.

"You know, I think this could be the most horrible night in all the time we have lived here."

"You know, I think you may be right."

"How marvelous!"

Just then, a stuffy-looking man in a wide-brimmed hat hurried past and saw them. "Ugh," he said. "Repellent."

And with his next step he tripped over and fell face first to the sidewalk. When he got back up, there was a bump the size of a golf ball on his chin.

How Hector and Edmond laughed!

Then the old grandfather clock in the lobby of the building struck ten—and with every ounce of badness in the whole of New York waiting for them to feed on, the famous monsters of Gramercy Park took to the skies, their scaly wings lifting them far above the city and their watchful eyes ablaze.

And tonight, I can promise you, they will be doing it again.

THE END

THIRTEEN

H ER EYES FLICKER open to the sound of the doorbell. But she doesn't move. Just holds herself still and waits until it's gone.

She lay here all night staring at the clock. Now, after a thin and fleeting sleep, it's almost eleven and her muscles feel like wet cement.

She hasn't slept properly for a week. Not since—

The door again. That strident buzz.

Just make it stop.

She needs the bathroom. Kicks away the covers.

The blinds are down but there's enough light straining through to let her catch herself in the mirror. Nothing that she sees there pleases her. She tries at least to flatten down her hair. Ties her robe and falters out.

The doorbell sounds once more, and this time it won't stop.

From the bathroom, she makes it to the top of the stairs and there she slumps to the floor. Until the noise finally abates and as it does a voice she recognizes calls out from the street:

Nancy.

When she answers the door, she falls into her arms.

The blinds are down in the front room too. It feels unaired. They sit beside each other in silence. Eventually, Nancy speaks: Mame, she says, has been calling. Sounding worried. "She said you weren't answering your phone. That the two of you were supposed to visit your dad . . . ?"

But it doesn't even seem like Lizbeth hears. And then she says: "It was the funeral yesterday."

"Oh . . . Right."

"It was packed. People from town. His family. A lot of family. I sat near the back of the church and every time I looked up one of them would be staring at me . . . but when I caught their eye they'd look away. Like they knew . . ."

"Lizbeth, they were staring because of who you are . . . it's a big deal to them."

"Right. Like it was to George." She pulls the robe around herself.

"Seriously, Lizbeth . . . you told me no one knew you were there . . . right?"

"It doesn't look like it. I keep waiting for Lloyd Dreiz to say he heard a car horn outside . . . but maybe that won't happen. I think he was pretty fucked-up at the time. They played his nine-one-one on TV and he was sobbing . . . rambling . . ."

She clears her throat. "You know, now it's all come out, I just feel sorry for the guy. Wife dies. He spends three years drunk. Gets so bad they kick him off the bowling team the night before the biggest tournament of the year. That night of all nights. So he's at home with a bottle of Jim Beam, half passed out in his underwear, when he hears a noise downstairs . . ." She trails away.

"But he's not being . . ."

"Charged? No. It was a home invasion. He thought George had a gun. So there it ends . . ."

"And the police . . . they haven't wanted to talk to you again . . . ?"

"No . . . I mean, they knew I called him . . . right before Lloyd found him . . . but I told them I rang from here. Why should they think otherwise? Then they asked if George ever talked to me about the ill will between him and Lloyd. That it had been there years. I told them I didn't know anything about that. I haven't heard from them since. The reporters, though . . . once they knew I was here . . . that I knew George . . . I just stopped answering the door. The phone. But then, you know, even they drift off eventually. Different towns. New stories . . ."

Nancy heads into the kitchen. Makes tea. Surveys the empty cupboards, the scattered open cartons on the counter.

When she walks back in, Lizbeth sees the look on her face.

"I haven't made it to the store in a while," she says, ". . . with the snow the way it's been . . ." And she trails away again.

"Lizbeth, you know none of this is your fault? You know that, right?"

But Lizbeth doesn't answer that. Says nothing. Then: "These last few days . . . I've been thinking about the beach again. I mean, I wouldn't . . . I would never . . . but I just keep thinking about what it would be like . . ."

Nancy gets to her feet, and she says: "Are your bags upstairs?"

FOURTEEN

TWENTY PREGNANT WOMEN lie on rubber mats in the middle of a large white room, their knees bent and legs apart. They are huge, every one. Partners crouched at their shoulders, coaxing phantom deliveries.

Together, the women breathe. Suck in the air and hold it for a silent count of five. Release it. Twenty sighs billow through the room.

A second later, they do it again.

On a hardbacked chair off to the side of them, Lizbeth looks down at her own belly. Still the smallest here, for now, but not so totally dissimilar.

"Okay! That's *awesome*! Okay!"

A zippy young woman with cropped blond hair grins and applauds and then, as the pregnant women are hauled upright by their partners, she finds a word for each of them. When they start filing out, she heads over to Lizbeth. "So," she says, "how did you like the class?"

"It looked great. It looked . . . fun."

The woman smiles. "Listen, there's no pressure. Shop around. If you want to come, we'd be happy to have you. How far along did you say you were?"

"Twenty-three weeks."

"Okay. And he, she . . . they're kicking?"

"Like a Rockette."

"Well, listen, you need to go with whatever feels right for you. Although I should tell you I'm a massive fan . . . so I'd love to have you here."

On her way back to Quince Hill she plays Burning Spear: *Invasion*. At home she makes tea with the dogs fussing around her as steam fills the kitchen.

Upstairs in the study, there are no pictures tacked above her desk anymore. No card that demands A Page A Day.

She turns on her laptop and lets her mind hang open. Sits, and waits.

Sits, and waits.

Until at last her fingers start to twitch.

Enschell stared down at his desk. Then he gazed from the window. He thought of the cases that had filled his days for so long. So many murders. So much tragedy.

He stared at his desk once more.

Then he gazed back out of the window.

Delete.

She thought their time apart might have done them both good. She and Frederick. Revived whatever it was they shared. But it isn't working out like that.

Where, she asks herself, is her energy? What is it she wants out of herself?

Enschell braced himself against the chill. The body still face down on the cellar floor. A single bulb swinging over it.

He asks himself why he's even there. This is just the result of some sorrowful robbery. A desperate junkie meets a frightened homeowner. Nothing more than tomorrow's paperwork. Standard issue. Not his world.

But still they called him. Summoned him genie style and said something with this one didn't sit right. So he drove here with a sliver of a moon above him and a fat dub bassline filling the car, and now he's here.

A broken window, yellow tape, a pool of blood, the corpse. The same old same old. But when he crouches down and sees the face, he knows they weren't mistaken.

Full in the cheeks, soft skin, soft lips. This is no strung-out kid wanting cash and something pawnable to kill his jones. This is something different.

The local cops—trying to make like they're not giddy with excitement—say he owned a store in town. Sold books and souvenirs. Art crap, the cops say. Wouldn't hurt a fly. And then one leans in and mutters: "He was a fruit."

So Enschell says he wants to see the killer. The victim, if you choose to look at it that way. He's back at the station. Hollow cheeked and leathery. Recently drunk, shocked sober. Freaking out, like anybody would. Like any grieving lover would.

But no. That's not it either, is it?

Something, indeed, doesn't sit right with this one.

She stops typing. Reads back. It's the first thing she's done since returning here that she wouldn't cringe at seeing under her name.

She thinks of George's funeral and Lloyd Dreiz's 911 and it's all she can
do to keep her hand steady as she deletes it.

On the corner of her desk is her copy of *Settlers in a Misty Place*.

The guilt is never slow to come.

It waits for her in the spaces between thoughts. Because the truth, she
knows, is simple.

Had he never met her, George would at this moment be at the counter of
the gift shop. Maybe the Venus Restaurant Diner. Trying to read the *Expositor* without the pages trailing in his eggs.

But he did meet her.

She came into his life as much an agent of his death as the bullet that
tore through him. Left him sprawled face down in that cellar with his
blood all over the walls. She gave him her blessing and she let him go
there. And each time she thinks of it she feels more ashamed.

No apology will ever suffice.

She shuts her eyes and breathes, and opens them again.

The dressmaker's dummy stands in the corner. The trees sway outside.
Tork, Nes and Dolenz idle in the upstairs hallway, and the SUV waits in
the garage. The Volvo was sold the same day that the house in Essenville
was put back on the market. Now her old life reassembles. Like watching
breaking glass in rewind. Next week she's even having lunch with Inchy.
Going to Manhattan to discuss the future.

Next to the laptop is a small white handset with a soft gray pad in its
center. Her panic button. If pushed, it will activate a battery of alarms
while it sends an SOS to the police.

The panic button was their suggestion. In case of Leon Slocomb.

At night she keeps it by the bed while she lies there, unsleeping.

He called again within days of her return. The police don't know where
he is. He skipped out on the address he was paroled to.

The dogs won't be enough, they said. He could kill all three before she
even knew he was in the house.

But the panic button is not her only source of protection. In her bedside
drawer there's a handgun. A .38. Nancy went with her to the gun store
and helped pick it out. Lizbeth hasn't touched it since she got it home; but
once a day at least she opens the drawer and stares at it.

Now, she stretches out her legs beneath her desk and her foot brushes the cardboard box she keeps wedged under there. It holds everything that came out of her meetings with Wilson. The notes and recordings. She hasn't looked inside it since Essenville.

For a moment, she leans to the side, just enough to catch sight of it.

And when she straightens up her hands rise to the keys.

Enschell left the row of huts and tramped down the dirt path. The back of his neck was already burned. The sun here untameable. He took clipped, wary strides, uncertain of what he was being led to. The villagers jostling behind him, calling out in Spanish.

En los árboles, they said.

The boy led the way. The one who ran from here earlier, fled back to the village with blood on his cheek, screaming in fear.

The path began to fade out into unmarked dirt and a branch cracked under Enschell's foot. The boy, still scared, pointed to his right. A ring of lime trees, daubed with green. The villagers hung back now, but Enschell carried on. Pushed into the circle and there he saw.

The baby kicks. She lays her hand over her belly and when she tries to recapture her train of thought, it's gone.

And she rises from her desk and leaves before the guilt seeps through again.

Ossery wears pristine hiking boots and a tomato red ski jacket over his suit. His briefcase rests at his feet.

Lizbeth stares at him from the door of the house. The morning light thickening behind him.

"You're late," she says.

"Sorry. The traffic got chewed up outside Bridgeport."

She asks if he wants coffee but he holds up a still half-full Starbucks. So she leaves him where he is, and back inside she rounds up the dogs. Reappears with them straining at their leashes, and he almost falls backward in panic.

"Are they . . . I mean . . . in your condition . . . can you keep control of them?"

"Probably," she says.

She gestures for him to follow her around the side of the house and then into the woods. He keeps hold of his case and gulps at his coffee. Waxes over the scenery as they walk. Says he could picture himself here, one day.

They keep on as the woods get denser, the light more fractured, and Lizbeth gives in. Asks him why he wanted to meet her today. Told her on the phone that it couldn't wait. Why he's here in Quince Hill in brand-new hiking boots at a quarter past seven in the morning.

She lets the dogs off the leash, and they bound ahead, spring-loaded, rocketing into bushes, colliding with trees, each other.

"You left so abruptly," he says. "I guess we . . . Wilson and I . . . we wondered when you might be coming back. To carry on with the book."

"I don't know," she says, and then she hesitates. ". . . I think I need to step back from the material for a while."

"Right," he says. "I just thought it might have had something to do with . . ."

"With?"

"The guy that got shot. I heard you knew him."

"Oh, you did?"

She walks on. Away.

"I'm sorry," Ossery says as he catches up to her. "I didn't mean to . . . Miss Greene, he just wants to see you again. He's desperate to see you. That's the truth of it. That's why I'm here."

She holds her pace, says nothing. So he goes on.

"He's very down right now. Very low. Not having the interviews to look forward to . . . it really seems to have . . . *extinguished* him. He talks about you incessantly. He says meeting you was the most important event of his life. The way his face gets just saying your name . . . if you could even come back just once, I know it would lift his spirits so much . . ."

But she still doesn't respond.

". . . give him one thing to feel good about."

She feels herself tiring, her breath getting short. Finally, she turns to him. "I have to do what's right for the book," she says, ". . . but maybe . . . in a few days . . ."

The dogs lope on ahead.

"I didn't realize he was depressed."

"Oh, the atmosphere's getting bad up there. He's having problems with the guards. They keep screwing with him. Making him shower with the bugs. Messing with his food. They've fixed up brighter lights in the cells, so he keeps getting these headaches . . ."

He takes a swig of his coffee. "And the appeal review's so close now. Two weeks. Who knows which way it's going to swing? So he's terrified. He's terrified in two weeks he's going back to Ad-Seg."

They slow up and then stop as Lizbeth tries to catch her breath.

"He says he'll find a way to die if he has to. Rather than that . . ."

"Right. He said that to me as well."

"Let me show you something."

He puts his case down on the ground and squats to open it. Pulls out the *Times*. Turns to an inside page and hands it to her. And she reads of *a bipartisan campaign to all but end the right of convicts to appeal against their conditions in jail*. There is a photograph of Congressman Mitchell Rieber. He is, the story says, campaign spokesman. Pledged, as such, to end *"this obscene circus that clogs up our justice system and enriches lawyers while mocking victims."* Prison, he says, is not meant to be a place where the residents get comfortable.

And then he raises:

the case of the notorious ganglord Wilson Velez, convicted of issuing orders to kill while already serving a life sentence for racketeering. Held in solitary confinement and refused visitors as a result, Velez spent the next five years repeatedly appealing against those conditions, finally succeeding five months ago. Even then, however, the judges responsible were so unsure of their verdict that a formal review was immediately planned. It takes place early next month.

"And the taxpayer is once again left footing the bill," says Rieber [who points out that Velez's return to the general population of his prison has coincided with a rash of killings in his native Queens]. "Surely when the justice system is dealing with a man like this, it should be allowed to keep the public safe as it sees fit."

"As a nation, we need to stop criminals holding up the passage of justice—and our judges need to send out a message that their griping will get no reward in court."

"You can see what we're up against," Ossery says. "I don't tell Wilson about this kind of thing, but you know how he is . . . he reads your mood in a heartbeat."

Lizbeth hands him the paper and he slips it back into the case.

"Miss Greene, he just feels that with everything you shared, that—"

"What does that mean? 'Everything we shared'?"

"The experience of working on the book together. He just feels with that amount of energy each of you have put into this thing, for it to come to nothing now would be a great shame . . . because Miss Greene, frankly, God forbid, if the appeal review did go the wrong way and *then* you realized you needed more material, interviews, another chance to speak with him . . ."

But she makes no advance on her position. So they tramp back through the woods in silence.

It's not until they're outside the house that Ossery reaches into his case again. Hands Lizbeth a bundle of pages torn from a legal pad.

"He wants to know what you think."

In Wilson's handwriting it says: *THE MONSTERS OF GRAMERCY PARK AND THE STRANGE PALE SPELL.*

"It's the first chapter," Ossery says. "He said he wanted to know what you thought before he wrote any more of it . . ."

She stares down at the pages. There is a note attached to them. It reads:

Lizbeth, I know it will be difficult for you to judge this without knowing how it ends, but I hope it will be enough to let you know the nature of my ideas—and I also hope with every atom of my self that you will soon return to Essenville. I cannot say what I feel with any greater simplicity than this: Please Lizbeth—come back.

He signs it:

Yours with the utmost esteem and regard, Wilson Ulysses Velez.

"Plus it could be a while before we get anything else out of there . . . so I told him he might want to seize the day . . ."

Lizbeth peers at him, and he tells her Gang Intelligence is squeezing hard. That they've got Sosa censoring his mail from the Christian Ladies of Western Arizona so stringently half of it's blacked out. Next, they'll want it suspended. They'll call it a precaution. Just until the review. They've got to do something, he says. Three more shootings last week. One a boy of fourteen picking up his mother's glaucoma pills at Corona

Farmacia. No arrests. And when they've got to do something but they don't know what, they'll come after Wilson. "Put on a fireworks display," he says, "to convince *their* bosses they know what's really going on."

And Lizbeth says: "So do they?"

"You're kidding. Are you kidding? Oh, my God. I can't believe you even asked me that. All they want is a head on a pole. Something to justify their existence. You see that, right? I mean, you *know* Wilson. You know he's not that person anymore. He just couldn't do that. And you've been to Corona. You've seen the kids in the Royals now. These kids that got shot last week, they were nine years old when he went up to Moxanie. What are they to him? He doesn't even know who they are. You think he's going to get himself sent back to Ad-Seg for . . . what? I don't even know for what. It's nuts. Who do you think's helping him? Me? You think I'd put my family at risk like that? This is just bullshit. Dreamed up by incompetents. You know, the last time Gang Intelligence got anyone significant as far as a courtroom every last one of them was sitting in Burger King by lunchtime before they sued everyone in sight for false imprisonment. The Insane Stone Brotherhood in Sacramento. Look it up. That's all you need to know about these . . . *cretins.*"

He is as livid as she's seen him.

"You know, they've had the DOC transfer fifteen new Hispanics to ES-SUSP just so Sosa's guards can send them over to Wilson in the yard and try and have him incriminate himself. They just sidle up and start talking to him about how they've got a visitor next week. My five-year-old could see through it."

And Lizbeth hears herself say: "Do you know Alicia Mapp?"

"Oh," he says. "So they *did* come after you. I wondered about that."

"She asked if they could hear my tapes."

"And . . . ?"

"She said they didn't necessarily *want* to hear them. She just asked if they could."

"Miss Greene, they're just yanking your chain. If they want to listen to you and Wilson, they can listen to you and Wilson."

"Right. The camera in the lawyer's room. She told me they'd taped our last two meetings . . ."

"I'm sure they did."

"But I'm not sure that picks everything up . . . I mean, if you lower your voice or—"

"Right. But they don't just have the camera. You did know that?"

The dogs amble back inside as she feels her throat tighten and her skin start to prickle.

"There's bugs all over that room. Outside it too. You'll have been bugged since the first time you went to ESSUSP. It's the easiest thing in the world. They can slip one anywhere. You'll never know. Your phone. Your office. Bathroom. Car. It's a noble act these days, right? Any grunt can get the equipment. No, everything's getting recorded by someone—"

He opens up his car and throws his case inside. "—It's just a question of who." Then he spins back to face her. "So, listen, Miss Greene, I hope to speak with Wilson tomorrow . . . what do I tell him when he asks what your plans are?"

She mulls the question from the doorway.

"Tell him whatever you want to tell him. I can't come running out to Pennsylvania at a moment's notice. I'll think about it. I'll let you know."

"Okay, Miss Greene. So I guess that's what I'll tell him." He pauses before he gets into the car. "You know, Miss Greene, Wilson won't talk to me in any detail about what went on between you . . . what you talked about . . . but you've made a pretty deep impression on him . . . and God knows, he could use some comfort right now."

Before he can start the engine she turns and steps into the house. Watches from a downstairs window as he drives away.

THE MONSTERS OF GRAMERCY PARK AND THE STRANGE PALE SPELL. By Wilson Ulysses Velez.

Lizbeth stares at the title before sliding the pages into the box under her desk. Doesn't even read the first line. Just seeing his writing makes it all come back to her.

She gazes at the stacks of tapes. Thinks of his voice, and hers. Yet more strangers hearing every shaming disclosure. The visits to the beach, the night in Queensbridge Park. An iron ball chained to her ankle as she swims across bottomless water. The weight about to—

That evening she answers the door again but now in the place of Ossery is Ed. Holding orchids. His hair grown out a little, nudging his shoulders.

She smiles despite herself.

"Oh, my God," he says. "You look so . . ."

"Big?"

"Right. But good. You look good too. Big and good."

She finds a vase for the flowers and when she gets to the living room he's standing by the fire with his arms behind his back, tense as a first date.

"So, you're back now?" he says. "I mean, you're sticking around . . . ?"

"I don't know."

"Right."

"Ed, will you sit down? You're making me uncomfortable."

So they take facing couches and talk about his business and the nighthawks using the roof of his duplex as their nest. Twice she laughs at his jokes, and silently scolds herself both times.

Then briskly she tells him that whatever happens from here on, she wants him to be a father to this child. A real father. And that she always has.

"You didn't need to have your lawyer write to me," Lizbeth says. "You should know me better than that . . ."

He's sorry, he says. He just hadn't heard from her in so long. Started to get anxious.

"But everything's fine . . . ?" he says.

"With the baby? Sure."

"But you don't know what—"

"No. I don't. I guess we'll both find out in the summer."

His eyes drop to her belly before darting back up. "So," he says, "did you ever see the dentist again?"

She reaches into her mouth and pops out the false tooth. Holds it in her palm as they sit, facing.

And, later, when he's gone and it's just her and the dogs again, she moves through the house to check and recheck every lock; and when she goes to bed she peers at the gun in her bedside drawer and makes sure the panic button is beside her.

FIFTEEN

LIZBETH'S IN THE study when Alicia Mapp calls. Voice scratchy like she's fending off a cold.

She says certain recent events have persuaded the unit that Wilson may somehow be abusing the relaxation of his conditions. That a degree of coptering is under way as a result.

"The children's book," she says, "we understand was to be published pseudonymously . . . we've asked that it be pulled from the publisher's schedule . . . just on a temporary basis. There's a school of thought within the unit that it may be a vehicle for some kind of code. We realize it dates back a long way but we would still like the chance to take a closer look at it before it . . . goes any further. I also understand there's an issue over the exact destination of the monies paid by your publisher for the book . . . the nature of the charities that were nominated to receive them."

They've also asked Warden Sosa to suspend all mail to and from the Christian Ladies of Western Arizona at least until the appeal review (thirteen days now).

No conclusions are being drawn here, she says. These are, she stresses, simply precautions. Her voice gives way mid-syllable before righting itself. "Ms. Greene, I need to ask you if—in your opinion—anything Velez said to you suggested his involvement in something . . . untoward?"

"Untoward? I don't . . . think so."

"It wouldn't have to be explicit, Ms. Greene. It could just be something you . . . *interpreted* that way."

"I'm really not sure. Wait . . . is this conversation . . . official?"

"Would that be a problem, Ms. Greene?"

"No . . . of course not."

The dogs fuss outside the door, and Lizbeth takes the phone into the hallway.

"Ms. Greene, do you speak with anyone about the contents of your meetings with Velez? Anyone at all?"

"Only his lawyer. And you."

Alicia Mapp's voice catches again. "I take it you still have all the notes from your visits, Ms. Greene? The tapes?"

"Of course."

"You might want to get those in order now. So if . . . when . . . we need to check them over they'll be ready for us. Not missing anything."

She says okay, but knows she paused a beat too long.

"Also, we understand you may be in possession of another piece of his writing. If that is the case, a copy would be appreciated . . ."

"Okay. You want me to put it aside with the notes?"

"No, Ms. Greene. We'd actually like to see that now . . ."

She reads out a fax number, and then she asks when Lizbeth is planning to return to Essenville.

Lizbeth plays the question over. Tries to divine its intent. Glean whether she's just being toyed with now. But it's like reading tar.

"Is that relevant?"

"Why would it not be relevant, Ms. Greene?"

"Well . . . if I'm not going to be allowed to visit him, there's no point in me going back."

"Why would you not be allowed to visit him, Ms. Greene?" She falls into a coughing jag.

"I don't know . . . I just assumed . . ."

"No, Ms. Greene, the only reason we might take a step of that nature was if it was felt within the unit that you might have been enabling the passing of messages from Velez yourself. But that's clearly not the case." Her tone, once more, is unknowable.

Each of the dogs comes and lies beside her and she asks what this has all been inspired by? What latest tragedy has bloodied Corona?

"Nothing's happened in Corona, Ms. Greene. It's Ignacio Solis."

"Ojos?"

"Ojos. Right. He was found dead in his cell last night. Face down. He'd been stabbed in the throat and in the heart, Ms. Greene." She says nothing more. Coughs. Until Lizbeth gets it.

"*Wilson?* You think Wilson ordered this? That's . . . ridiculous."

"You might feel that way, Ms. Greene. We think it's a credible line of inquiry."

"But it makes no sense. Wilson idolize— . . . *idolized* Ojos. He'd never do that . . ."

"Even if he felt it might keep him out of Ad-Seg?"

"I don't . . . how . . ."

"What if Ojos was preparing to finally admit that Velez's letters did order the murders of Horace Gampas and Felix Cruz? *Or*, more pertinently, to disclose that he knew Velez had been in recent contact with certain of his followers and was directing events in Corona?"

"He was going to do that?"

"It seems possible."

"You don't know?"

"We think it's a credible line of inquiry." She pauses. "He had his Royal tattoos cut from his skin, Ms. Greene."

And the words hang there, brilliant, unfading.

"I imagine you know the significance of that. Only Velez can—"

"Order tattoos to be cut out."

Lizbeth slumps into the wall at her back.

"That's right. So we think we're looking at a scenario in which he may have somehow incited this and, by extension, if he is communicating these kind of messages, the likelihood of his being instrumental in the problems in Corona."

"But who . . . I mean . . . who's on the other end? In Corona? Hurricane? Almanza?"

"We simply don't know, Ms. Greene. Though to be candid, it would surprise me. We don't feel the Royals are quite the cherubs they like to portray themselves as, but the last few years have been notably free of these kind of . . . incidents. It's just not something we associate with Almanza. In fact, one scenario we're looking at now is that these episodes in Corona may be part of some kind of factional conflict . . . that Velez may even feel Almanza should be replaced by another Royal . . . however that has to be achieved. Have you ever had the impression he feels that way, Ms. Greene?"

"No . . . I really haven't. Not at all."

One by one, the dogs get up and pad downstairs.

"Oh, God."

"Is everything okay, Ms. Greene?"

"It's just . . . this is a lot to . . . process."

"Ms. Greene," Alicia Mapp says, "I realize that you've spent a lot of time with Velez in the last few months. But this is the Three Vee that *we* got to know. A man without conscience. A man who causes pain. If he feels threatened, he'll hurt somebody. If he feels angry, he'll hurt somebody. Other people's lives, they're disposable to him. Obviously, far be it from me to make suggestions to a writer as distinguished as yourself, but if you ever wanted to include a perspective from your subject's *victims*, I could certainly put you in contact with guys with some pretty rough stories to tell."

Lizbeth watches Tork return upstairs. Gaze at her quizzically.

"This is why the outcome of the appeal review is so vital. I mean, it's remarkable. The man's only been out of Ad-Seg a matter of weeks and look what he's done already." But her tone is suddenly breezy: "Anyway, we are hopeful of the picture becoming much clearer for the judges by the time it comes around . . ." Her cough rears up once more. "I'm sorry. Excuse me. Ms. Greene, I'll let you get on with your day. But if you could fax over that document . . . And perhaps get those tapes in order too."

Alicia Mapp pauses, and then she says: "By the way, I was sorry to hear about your friend in Essenville. It was a sad thing. Please do accept my sympathy."

And she coughs one more time before they say good-bye.

Lizbeth puzzles at the shock that rings through her. Why she's still, at her center, one percentage point unsure of his guilt.

But she is.

She sits cross-legged on the floor of the study with the open box in front of her. Stacks the tapes by the order of the dates written on the side of each case. Knows without even referring to them the one on which he says: *So . . . tell me what you took.*

Her head still reels with who knows what and where that knowledge will lead.

It's all unlocked now. Escaping.

But you keep on doing what you can because what else can you do?

She slips the tape into the machine, finds the sound of whispers and presses Record. Does the same with everything else the world was never meant to learn. Her notes too are scoured, and where his writing—*BREAK A LAW*—is followed by hers—*Air Freshener 7 UP, Mounds*—she rips out the page. Walks down to the kitchen and burns it over the sink. And as the last corner of the paper curls and turns to powder she thinks again of George. And then of Ojos. Face down on the cell floor.

She pictures Wilson's mouth set in rage as he learns of Ojos's treason.

His fury rising. And though it still butts against that flint of doubt, she pushes her imagination on. Until he decides his response—and that poisoned wish finds its way to Ojos's cell.

Face down. Both of them left face down.

All he needed, she supposes, was a channel. A—

Courier. She grabs a pen and, on the back of her left hand, she writes: COURIER.

The phone rings out from the desk above. Ossery. His voice battling against traffic noise, speeding cars en masse. He is, he says, on I-78.

He wants to know if she's thought any more about going back to Essenville. He doesn't want to pester her, he says, but he was down at the jail today. It's getting worse. The guards are abusing Wilson. They put him on the loaf, just like in Ad-Seg. He refused to eat it. So they force-fed him. Now he can barely talk from the tube they jammed down his throat. His tics are reemerging. His skin a bed of rashes.

"Also," he says over the roar of engines, "he's pretty distraught right now . . . He just got some bad news—"

"Ojos."

"Right. Ojos. How did you—"

"Alicia Mapp called."

Indignation fills Ossery's voice. "Oh, she did? So I guess you heard their little yarn. Ojos gets his ink cut out and Wilson's responsible. Isn't that something? Christ, what are they going to do the next time someone gets shot by a guy in a suit? Exhume John Gotti? But you know what? Fine. Fuck them. If they want to play this way, we can do that. We can file suit and make sure the whole world knows what a crowd of asses they are . . . we can bring down the kind of shitstorm that'll make the Insane Stone Brotherhood look like a flawless triumph of detective work . . ."

Just for a moment he stalls. Then: "This is just so entirely *fucked.* You know, I was supposed to be getting the first copies of *The Monsters of Gramercy Park* today? Now they're locked in a federal warehouse in Newark . . . and for those goons to be doing this now, right before the appeal review . . . I mean, of course, in any real sense, they've got nothing . . . but *symbolically* . . . the message it sends out—"

"I'd say the message was worse for Ojos."

"Of course. But Miss Greene, this has *destroyed* Wilson. I sat in the lawyer's room with that man for an hour today and I watched him weep the entire time. Weep like I haven't seen him weep in years . . . so for Alicia Mapp to be suggesting he was somehow *responsible* . . . in the name of her career . . . frankly, it makes me nauseous . . ."

And a memory bobs into Lizbeth's head. "Did he ever talk to you about Rinser?"

"Excuse me?"

"He's a bug. At the prison. Wilson . . . took exception to him."

"I'm not sure what you're getting at, Miss Greene. But no, I don't remember the name."

The traffic noise reaches a crescendo.

". . . Listen, Miss Greene, all I wanted was to check whether you were any closer to making a decision . . . but if you're not, then I'm sure we both have business to attend to . . ."

He pleads with her again before the end of the call.

That night, she reaches into the box under her desk, and from inside a notebook she pulls the photograph Hurricane gave her in Corona. *La realeza original.* Gazes at Ojos. Features alive with teenage bluster, a near-black mole on his cheek.

She sees his face as she lies in bed, and when she falls asleep it turns to George's. Until, an hour later, she wakes again. The baby kicking. Her mouth parched.

Lizbeth doesn't sleep again that night. Finally, she returns to the study. Sees the neat pile of tapes and the notes ready for copying. Then she sits on the floor beside her desk and pulls out the box once more. Takes off the lid and stares down at Wilson's story.

But she still doesn't read it.

When she looks back up, the sun is rising on the twelfth day before the appeal review, and the dogs are outside, demanding breakfast.

The days are getting longer now. They pass light and workless. Whenever Ossery calls she lets her machine answer. Every time the message a shade more desperate.

She still can't shake the uncertain haze that gathers every time she thinks of Wilson. Of what he might or might not have done.

Nine days before the appeal review she waits in the kitchen for Nancy to arrive with her groceries from Quince Hill. Sits at the table with the paper before her.

Front page, nothing of interest. Two, three, four, five. Nothing of use there either.

Then page six. The prison. ESSUSP. A photograph. The headline:

CORRUPTION SCANDAL ENGULFS PENNSYLVANIA SUPERMAX

And another picture. A Department of Corrections staff mugshot.
CO Sherwin Baines.
He was arrested yesterday. The climax of a long investigation. His crime

the trafficking of contraband and aiding of illicit communication for a number of the high-risk criminals that populate the facility.

A bank account has been discovered filled with the proceeds of what the paper calls

a wide range of services provided for a select group of inmates.

Drugs have been brought into the prison as routine, procured from the operations of dealers serving time in the facility. Inmates' semen has been smuggled out. The addresses of victims' families have been passed on to murderers, of victims themselves to rapists, of prosecuting attorneys to both. The names of informants within the facility have been distributed, and the locations of those who testified against inmates monitored. The whereabouts and potential transfers of gang members within the prison system have been tracked and made available.

She is ready at the start of every line for the mention of Wilson Velez. But it never comes. Instead, the story goes on to say that:

Lance Szletat, a former insurance investigator from Pittsburgh, has also been arrested amid reports he and Baines engaged in illegal surveillance at the request of inmates.

Visiting wives arriving by car have had those vehicles broken into and fitted with recording devices on behalf of suspicious husbands. The same has happened to the families of inmates that other inmates have a grudge against. Even other guards have been surveilled, on occasions in their homes, the information obtained then passed to inmates for use in at least one case of blackmail.

An unnamed DOC official admits that *the Department needs to look very closely at how this could have been allowed to happen.*

Warden Sosa has no comment.

She reads the entire story again, slowly moving from one word to the next, defining each in turn in the hope that will make this easier to process. Temper her astonishment.

The rest of the world suspended around her.

How many times did she walk with him through those endless corridors?

Then she shuts her eyes, and she is in the Venus Restaurant Diner. Watching as Sherwin Baines strolls in with his wife and daughter. Swaps cornball jokes with the waitresses and orders lunch. Receives every proud Essenvillian that comes by the table to wish him luck in the upcoming playoffs at the 'Drome. First strike's yours, Sherwin, they say. Then afterward he heads back to the prison. Punches in and fixes coffee in the mug he keeps in the staff kitchen, the one that says: *CAPTAIN.* Has a smoke as it brews. Shoots the breeze with another guard as he ambles up into the pods. And then, when it's just him, he raps on the door of a cell. Steps in. Takes a flattened paper bag from inside his shoe and lays it on the bed. Leaves again and heads down the pod, on to another cell; and here he slowly reads an address to a slick-haired, feral-eyed inmate, who scrawls it down and nods meaningfully.

At the third cell, he raps his baton on the door. And when he opens it, there inside is—

Wilson?

Ossery's line is busy when she calls. But Alicia Mapp picks up.

She apologizes for not giving Lizbeth prior warning of the arrest. Says she's sure, however, that Lizbeth appreciates the delicate nature of the operation, the number of agencies involved and, as such, the tortuous politics.

The surveillance these two pulled off was masterful, she says. Every bug gone as soon as the job was finished. This guy Szletat's a real talent, she says, admiringly.

Baines, she says, has not yet admitted to anything involving Wilson. But everyone at the unit is confident he will. Ojos. Corona. It'll all be in the open soon, she says.

An errand boy, she calls Baines. What he heard he passed on; what he passed on he would, if told to, act on.

"But then, an ordinary person with bills and responsibilities just like you and me, Ms. Greene, asked to perform certain favors while in a job which pays less than that person may feel his loyalty and experience deserve . . . it shouldn't take us aback that he might say yes."

Naturally, she says, she'll do everything she can to keep Lizbeth informed from now on. "Oh," she says, "incidentally . . . thank you for sending on those notes and tapes, Ms. Greene . . . and for Velez's story too. Obviously, for the moment our focus is on Baines . . . but what you've given us should prove more than useful."

When Nancy comes at eleven, Lizbeth says nothing of any of it. And then, alone again, she spends an hour by the pool at the back of the house with her feet in the water, letting it between her toes as her head fills with Ojos, and then—as ever—George.

Then Wilson.

Until the call she has resisted since Ossery's visit suddenly overwhelms her.

She dries her feet and makes for the study. Hurries across the room and to the box. Removes its lid and stares into it once more.

But this time she reaches in and from it she lifts out: *THE MONSTERS OF GRAMERCY PARK AND THE STRANGE PALE SPELL.*

And her eyes drop to the first few characters. The first few words. And then, without having even been aware of beginning, she's reading.

The night that everything went wrong again, Hector and Edmond sat on their perch above the front door of their building on Gramercy Park. A crowd of people were passing by, all dressed in their jewels and finery, on their way to supper at a high-class restaurant. With a ghastly creak of his vile old head, Hector turned to Edmond.

"Do you know what my favorite thing about people is, old friend?" he said.

"No, compadre," Edmond replied. "What is your favorite thing about people?"

"My favorite thing about people," Hector said, "is THIS!"

And with that he let out a bloodcurdling gargoyle cry and bulged his horrible gargoyle eyes and bared his foul pointy gargoyle teeth—and all of the fancy people shrieked with terror and ran from Gramercy Park!

Oh, how the gargoyles laughed—or at least they did until Hector saw the strange woman.

There she was again. Standing in front of the building, just as she had for the seven nights before this.

She had pale skin (so pale she was almost transparent) and black hair (as black as a raven down a coal mine at midnight). But this was not what made Hector notice her—no, he noticed her because while every other person that ever passed the building gasped with revulsion at the sight of the monsters, she did not so much as shiver. She just stood there, as small as a thimble, holding a huge leather-bound book with a loose scrap of paper inside of it.

But finally she turned and walked away. And just then the grandfather clock in the lobby struck ten, and with that the monsters flew from their residence and into the skies of New York. It felt such a wicked place to be that night! So full up with badness it could have burst! So the monsters made mischief and mayhem and malevolence and they fed and fed and fed!

They were all very tired by the time they flew back to Gramercy Park.

"Ah," Hector said, "another marvelous night in the most revolting city on earth."

"Indeed it was, old friend," Edmond replied. "Indeed it was."

At that very moment the sun began to rise over the East River. As it did, every gargoyle across the building—and there were, the last time anyone was able to count, 5,843 of them—drifted into a deep, contented sleep. And none was deeper and more contented than Hector's.

But then, from way down in his slumber, he heard a noise.

One scaly gargoyle eye peeled open.

The strange pale-skinned and black-haired woman was standing on a wooden crate on the steps of the building so that her head was next to Hector's. She held in her hands the huge leather-bound book and the loose scrap of paper—and it was that scrap of paper that she now started to read from.

Jeepers and more jeepers! Hector could not believe his horrible bat-like ears. What the woman was reading was a spell—a spell written in the ancient language of demons, one sometimes whispered about by gargoyles but one none of them had ever actually heard. But Hector knew what it was as soon as the strange woman started to speak.

A moment later, he opened his other scaly eye and she was gone. Then the sun went down over the Hudson and the rest of the monsters began to stir. Every one of them had been asleep as the woman read out the spell. Even Edmond.

"Good evening, old friend," he said now as he yawned and shook the dust from his wings and stretched out his grotesque claws.

"And good evening to you," Hector replied.

It must have been a dream. The strange pale woman and the spell. That was the only explanation. It had all just been a silly dream. Hector sighed with relief and a fat drop of rain fell to the sidewalk in front of him. Then another.

So, at the stroke of ten o'clock, the monsters flew once more from the face of their building toward a night of delightful chaos. By now it was raining like the clouds had whole oceans inside of them and with the rain came thunderclaps like cannons going off and bolts of lightning so bright they blinded your eyes. A perfect night for gargoyles, in fact— even if Hector did secretly feel quite strange as he and Edmond soared above Penn Station.

On the corner of West 57th and Broadway, they saw a very bad person indeed.

As the rain poured down, those unfortunate people without umbrellas were trying to take shelter in the covered doorway of a giant gleaming office building. But every time one of them even put their foot near the dry patch there, a sleazy security guard with terrible bad breath would run out yelling and chase them away with a baton in his hand.

Now, it should not have mattered to the security guard if people took shelter there. The doorway was as wide as a house and the people were doing no harm. So at first Hector and Edmond thought he was just being a busybody. But then they saw something else—that as he sat at his desk in the lobby of the building he was writing letters to famous celebrities. And oh, they were awful letters! Not awful like a gargoyle is awful but awful like only a person can be awful—nasty and mean and odious.

But just as Hector and Edmond were about to swoop down and cause a little havoc, Hector turned and saw the strangest thing he had ever seen—the pale woman with the black hair was right beside him, flapping her strange pale arms and flying through the air!

"Jeepers!" Hector and the woman said together. "It worked!"

Neither of them could quite believe it, but at the same time they both knew it was real. Because the spell the strange woman had read was a spell that broke all the laws of nature—a spell that gave a person the powers of a gargoyle!

"I was in the library," the woman said. "I have been writing a story about gargoyles and I found an old leather-bound book about them with the loose scrap of paper inside . . . and an old man even stranger than I am came up to me and told me that if I read it aloud to an actual monster, then this would happen. But I never thought it would come true!"

"Come on, old friend!" Edmond called out. "Let's pay a visit to this bad, bad person!"

And then Hector realized—only he, as the gargoyle to whom the strange pale woman had read out the spell, could see her in her current state! So he and Edmond swooped down, and the woman followed behind them, invisible to all but Hector.

Down on the street, the security guard saw an old couple trying to take refuge in the doorway of the office building and chased them away with his baton. Then he went back inside to keep on writing his mean and odious letters.

Suddenly, the door to the building flew open and a monstrous wind blew in. The security guard rushed to his feet and ran to close it but the wind was so high he had to struggle with all his might to do so. And then, as he sat back down, an even stronger gust tore through the building—and he followed the gust to the second story and found that every single window there had come open! He hurried from one to another closing them but every time he did another would open—and then the same thing happened on the next two stories as well!

Soon the security guard realized every window in the whole building was open and rain was pouring in and birds were now flying around the ceilings of the offices. Screaming with frustration, he ran back down to the lobby—and found to his horror that the door to the building was wide open and people from the street were now wandering into the lobby to take shelter. But when he tried to chase them out with his baton the strongest gust of wind yet picked up all of his mean, spiteful letters and blew them into the street!

Panicking, he ran out after them as they blew around the street. But he had barely gotten five steps from the building when there was a massive clap of thunder and a huge bolt of lightning forked down from the *sky—and it struck the security guard right on top of his head! He shook like he was dancing a crazy jig and his hair stood up on end with smoke billowing from it until finally he ran off screaming and gibbering, driven completely mad by everything that had just taken place!*

"Nice work, old friend!" Edmond shouted approvingly. "We haven't used lightning like that in years!"

But Hector knew he had not used the lightning at all. It had been the strange pale woman.

"Oh, my," she said as she flapped her arms. "That was really quite exciting!"

It was the same at every place they stopped throughout that night— every bad person that Hector and Edmond located, the strange woman found another way to torment them. Hector had not had so much fun in as long as he could remember!

At Penn Station, he turned to the woman to ask her what her name was. But suddenly, she was gone—as if she had never been there. And as the rest of the monsters gathered to return to Gramercy Park together, Edmond called out to them. "Hey, you guys! Old Hector here was like a new gargoyle tonight!"

Back at their beloved building, the vile and disgusting monsters fell into another deep sleep as the rain slowly stopped and the sun came up over the East River. Hector's own eyes got heavy, and started to close . . . but a moment later he found he was not asleep at all. He was on the platform of the 23rd Street subway station!

"You again!"

The strange pale woman was right there next to him. But although there were 100 other people crowding the platform, not one of them even looked at Hector—he was as invisible to them as the woman had been to the other monsters. He knew then that the other part of the woman's spell had come true as well. Not only could the strange woman now pass among gargoyles—Hector could pass among people! In fact, he had to—in accordance with the spell he would now have to spend the days in the world of people while his fellow monsters snoozed and snored back in Gramercy Park!

But do you know the strangest thing? As he folded up his wings and flattened down his ears and hopped like a toad onto the packed subway train, Hector was looking forward to the day ahead. Secretly, he had al-

ways been curious about what it would be like to behave like a person—and now, even though he knew the spell was very dangerous and that gargoyles and people should never *mix*, he was highly excited.

Soon they arrived at the place where the strange pale woman worked. Her name was Lenore Tamerlane. Hector knew this now because there was a sign that said it on her desk.

"So what do you want me to do?" Hector said.

"I don't know," the woman said. "I guess you could pass me that stapler."

And so he did. Quickly, he found out that he could not commit acts of gargoyle mischief here—but once again, in a strange kind of way, he did not mind. He just sat quietly under Lenore Tamerlane's desk and then he carried out some photocopying for her and made terrible faces behind her boss's back when he walked past. When the time came for lunch, he bounced along next to her as she picked up a sandwich from across the street—he even used his sharpest and most terrifying claw to open her can of soda.

He liked this, he decided. But as he followed her out of her office at the end of the day with the skies darkening over New York, Hector looked around him and suddenly she was not there—and then, in a flash, neither was he! Now he was back on his perch in Gramercy Park!

That night, once more, Lenore Tamerlane appeared beside him in the skies as he and Edmond searched for scenes of badness—and the next day he woke at the 23rd Street subway station, with her as his companion in the world of people.

He liked it more every time he saw her. And so it went on for a week—until on the eighth night, Hector waited on his perch as the rain began to fall, and with his usual dreadful creaking Edmond turned around.

"Good evening, old friend," he said. "Are you looking forward to an evening of badness?"

Indeed he was. But he did not tell Edmond why—that he was looking forward to this evening of badness more than usual because this evening he would see Lenore Tamerlane again. He almost felt nervous as his huge ugly wings carried him across the city. Then high above the Wollman ice rink, he and Edmond saw their first bad person of the night—a girl giving out skates who was secretly rubbing Vaseline over the blades of anyone that was prettier than her (which was a lot of peo-

ple). But as Hector got ready to swoop down, he looked around him and Lenore Tamerlane was not there.

She did not appear at the ice rink. And a few minutes later she did not appear when they saw the next bad person down on Roosevelt Island. She did not appear above Verdi Square or over the Apollo Theater.

Hector was sad, and worried too. Finally, at just after midnight, he flew off alone.

"Ay!" Edmond called after him. "Hector, where are you going, compadre?"

Hector wasn't even sure. He was using his seventh sense (the sense that only monsters have) to find Lenore Tamerlane. It worked. Soon, he had located her.

She lived in a tiny apartment high up in a proud old building not unlike the one in Gramercy Park. Hector could see that her light was on. So he flapped over and hovered at the window and there he saw her! She was sitting at her tiny kitchen table in a pretty dress with sequins all over it eating supper—with a man! An awkward-looking, balding man! Hector watched in horror, until finally the balding man got up to use the bathroom. Then the sad gargoyle approached the window and tapped on the glass with the same foul claw he had used to open Lenore Tamerlane's soda—but now when she saw him she screamed like she was going to explode! She was just as scared of gargoyles as every other person!

Although Hector did not know why she had done it, he knew what had happened. Lenore Tamerlane had decided to break her side of the spell—she could no longer make mischief with the gargoyles and she had now forgotten that she had even not been scared of them. So now when she saw Hector she just kept screaming!

He flew back alone and confused and miserable to Gramercy Park. But the worst was yet to come. Because, when all the gargoyles had returned and were drifting off to sleep, Hector's eyes drew closed—and he once more found himself on the 23rd Street subway station! Indeed, he saw Lenore Tamerlane—but now in the daytime he was as invisible to her as he was to every other person. (And of course at night he would just make her scream.)

So Hector spent the day wandering sadly through the world of people. Much to his own disgust, he even half wished he could be one of them. For him, at least, the spell was still in place. He stood in front of an electronics store and watched stupid TV shows. He smelled the greasy burgers that people ate as they walked and to him they smelled divine. When the cars in a traffic jam started blasting their horns, he even started wailing and moaning so he could try and be a part of it. But it was no good. Stuck between the world of people and the world of monsters, Hector had never felt so glum.

And so it went on for the next night, the next day, and the night after that. It was as if the strange pale woman had never flown with the monster. Yet even then he clung to a threadbare shred of hope. Returning from another night of melancholy troublemaking, he closed his eyes as he flew over the city in the last moments before dawn and felt sure that when he opened them he would know the purest joy—because she would be there. She would be standing in Gramercy Park just waiting for him to notice her.

Only she was not there. She did not come. So there was only one thing for it. The next evening, he told Edmond everything.

Edmond patted his old friend's hideous talons with his own.

"Don't worry, compadre. I know how to solve this problem."

The cure, he explained, was simple. Although Lenore Tamerlane had read the first spell with Hector there beside her, she must have undone it on her own. This meant that while she was free of it, he—obviously!—was not. So all he had to do was persuade Lenore Tamerlane to undo the spell again—but this time with both of them present. Then he would be free too!

The two frightful gargoyles split off from the rest above Penn Station as usual. But instead of flying off in search of havoc, they made for the apartment of Lenore Tamerlane.

"Okay," Edmond said, "now you just have to ask her to undo the spell again!"

So trying to make himself look as undisgusting as possible, Hector flapped up to the apartment window—but when he got there, the awkward, balding man was there again! Standing with his back to the glass so that Hector couldn't see past him!

But he could see one thing now—that Lenore Tamerlane had abandoned her monstrosity to spend her nights with this man instead.

Now just wanting to be rid of this idiotic spell, Hector flew around the building and found the back window of the apartment. But when he got there the balding man was in the middle of drawing the thick velvet curtains as if he owned the place! So the gargoyle beat his repulsive wings and returned to the front once more—and then he saw her. Sitting there in all her strange paleness. So Hector tapped the glass softly with his claw and when she did not look up, he called out her name in the least bloodcurdling voice he could muster—a noise that was somewhere a croak and a moan.

"Oh, Lenore," he called. "Lenore!"

But then the balding man put on some romantic music—and completely drowned him out!

"Ay!" Hector muttered to himself. "If I do not get this idiotic man out of the way then I will never find peace again."

Eventually, Lenore Tamerlane got up to use the bathroom. When she was gone, Hector saw the man reach into his coat pocket and pull out a pair of what looked like tickets—but as he did he spilled a bottle of red wine all over the table. Looking around the room in a panic, he grabbed a piece of paper from the mantel and used it to mop up the wine.

It was the spell!

Frozen in midair, Hector watched as the ink ran down the scrap of paper and the spell—far too complicated for anyone to ever be able to memorize—became unreadable. Then, when Lenore Tamerlane reappeared, the balding man balled up the soggy scrap of paper and stuffed it in his pocket where the tickets had been.

Edmond flapped up behind Hector.

"Oh, dear," he said. "There is only one way to remedy this predicament—you will have to put a spell on this awkward and balding man in order to get back the knowledge he has just destroyed!"

Then Edmond told Hector exactly what such a spell involved.

"Very well," Hector said. "If that is what I have to do, that is what I will do."

But at that very moment the romantic music suddenly ended—and as Hector put his cavernous ear up to the window he heard the most terrible and nightmarish news. His scaly old gargoyle skin turned white as the strange and pale Lenore Tamerlane herself.

"What is it, old friend?" Edmond said. "What did you hear?"

Hector turned around, aghast. "They're leaving New York! The balding man just gave her tickets for a tropical cruise! They're leaving first thing in the morning!"

And with that both gargoyles stared at each other in the purest ter-

ror. Hector would have to go with them—this monster of Gramercy Park would have to leave New York!

She doesn't move. Sits waxwork still. Cold filming the skin on her chest and face.

Can it be what it seems to be? Mean what it surely must mean?

What else can it be? What else could it mean?

It wasn't just Ojos. Wasn't just Corona.

Oh, God, Wilson. What did you do?

She looks back through the pages and it's clear enough to make her cry out.

Isn't it?

Be logical, she tells herself. Forensic. Think it through.

She summons her memories of the last few weeks. Months. Everything since she walked into the prison.

In the quiet of her study, she closes her eyes and lets it fill her mind. The central characters. Their motivations. Windows of opportunity. The intersections of why and how that she has sat here and mapped so many times times before in the service of Detective Enschell, the slow process that gradually scours away the mundane chronology of events to reveal the hidden order beneath. The real history.

And it fits. It all slots together. The awful intuition in her gut borne out, come true.

She looks down again at the page and sees what's there for what it is. His confession. Or his boast. Sitting on the floor of the study with her legs stretched out in front of her she picks out each detail like a pilot landing in fog.

He sits in the lawyer's room with the picture that he drew for her, and she's checking the machine as he talks. She looks up, and he glares across the table with such rage it puts a shiver in her.

"It's okay," he says, pouting like a spoiled child. "Really. I know why we're here."

Every time her attention left him, it was the same. That same toxic jealousy.

"It's just you seem very distracted today, Lizbeth." And so on.

"Still, I guess now you have your llllife in Essenville, your friends down there, it's going to keep you busy in the head."

But he could see one thing now—that Lenore Tamerlane had aban-
doned her monstrosity to spend her nights with this man instead.

As Alicia Mapp's voice echoes down the line: "If an inmate is smart enough, it's almost impossible to stop information getting out or coming in . . . Prison employees can be less than ideally scrupulous."

CO Sherwin Baines strolls through the gates of ESSUSP, as in the raw early morning Alan Ossery tells her: "It's the easiest thing in the world."

Everything, he says, gets recorded by someone.

And George turns to her in the kitchen of the house in Essenville—the house that would, with its patio doors and their chancy lock, its unsecured bathroom window, be so easy to discreetly break into—and says Lloyd Dreiz was always rotten. Mean spirited.

"Mean spirited. Whoa."

Before Wilson gazes across the table. And she watches as his features soften.

"You know, Lizbeth," he says, "I'm sorry if you feel I have been . . . hostile. Mean spirited. I did not mean to appear mean spirited—"

And something snags. But then the world spins on.

"Oh, mean spirited was the least of it," George says. Lloyd Dreiz was a bastard. A creep. A drunk.

And, in the wake of the missed interview, Wilson scowls once more: "So where were you? When you shoulddd have been here?"

In Essenville, she says. With a friend.

"What friend?"

"They can slip one anywhere," Ossery said. "You'll never know. Your phone. Your office. Bathroom. Car."

She sees the brown Volvo at ESSUSP. Baines slipping out into the empty parking lot. Maybe he chews the fat with the guard on duty there, talks about the game or gossips about the warden. Before he walks on to the car. Bug in his pocket. Picklock at the ready.

"What is it, old friend?" Edmond said. "What did you hear?"

And George stands on the lot of the gas station with the forest black behind him and stares into the backseat. And he tells her what he has to do.

"It's the state playoffs at the Bowldrome Monday night. Lloyd's bowling for the town. He'll be gone until eleven."

BAINES TO MURRYSVILLE—BRING IT ON, it says in the *Expositor*.

An errand boy, Alicia Mapp said. What is heard is passed on, and what's passed on is acted on.

As—like always—Lloyd Dreiz has a beer or maybe two before he heads up to the Bowlodrome and sure, fine, whatever, he's a little cheery by the time he gets there.

It helps his nerves. Everyone knows that.

Only this time his captain makes an executive decision.

"Lloyd, it's for the good of the team."

That night of all nights.

So the town gathers at the state playoffs, and Lloyd Dreiz climbs back into his Hummer.

"And he's at home with a bottle of Jim Beam, half passed out in his underwear, when he hears a noise downstairs . . ."

"*Oh, God.*"

A man without conscience, Alicia Mapp said. A man who causes pain. If he feels threatened, he'll hurt somebody. If he feels angry, he'll hurt somebody. Other people's lives, they're disposable to him.

The light came on upstairs. And Lloyd Dreiz rose and moved across the room.

"Very well," Hector said. "If that is what I have to do, that is what I will do."

She hears George's breath, and then he crosses the street. Disappears into the house.

"I'll be five minutes," he says.

And so he claimed George Finer. It was him. Jealous and malignant. He tore George from life as if his hands were wrapped around his throat.

She looks down at his note.

I hope it will be enough to let you know the nature of my ideas.

How could she tell herself she didn't know? She always knew. All this time she sat in the lawyer's room knowing just what he was, knowing it each time she started the tape or opened her notebook, but somehow never letting it inside. Not tasting it.

Now she tastes nothing but.

He wanted her attention. He has it. And she, with everything he took from her, that he knows of her, is bound to him. Helpless to act as he gloats. Her secrets his collateral.

She is, for a moment, certain.

Poor Rinser. Poor Ojos. Poor Corona.

Poor George.

She sobs for what became of him.

And for that single breath of time, she is secure in her belief. Distraught, but unequivocal.

Free of the random and unsolved.

It's only later her conviction starts to peel away. Doubt seeping in again, as doubt does.

Her version of events is, she realizes, just that. A notion. An interpretation. Built out of memory in all its frailty and deceit.

A story like any other.

All she feels now is the chill.

There is a parcel on her desk. Sent from Alicia Mapp. A sturdy brown cardboard crate in which are Lizbeth's tapes. Copies made now, and so returned to her.

She stands and unpacks them. Realizes she's holding the very first. Turns and reaches for the same machine that recorded it. Presses Play.

A dull hiss and then his voice: "I wasss born in Panama. My vvvillage was . . . —called Nolteros."

As the hours sink into one another, she listens to more of them. Long snatches of those early sessions when she walked into that room curious and eager. The ones that followed when she left destroyed.

Face down. Both of them face down. George, his cheek pressed to the dank cellar floor.

And her anger rises as she listens to Wilson rail at her. Her shame at how easily she folded.

She turns the volume up as high as it will go.

". . . your whole life is built on bullshit and lies and if anyone tells you thatttt, you start whining. That's unfair! That's unfair! *Wah! Wah!*"

Until, in the half second of silence that follows, she hears the phone from the desk. Pauses the tape as her machine clicks on.

It's Ossery. The same as usual. Lizbeth recoils as he talks.

The next time it rings, it's past two A.M.

She lies in bed with George Finer coursing through her thoughts and again she hears the machine.

Whoever's calling hangs up at the beep.

Then they call again. Hang up again.

The third time, Lizbeth speeds—cursing—from the bedroom. Picks up, breathless.

She listens to the caller. Then: "What?" she says. "What does that mean?"

She listens once more and then: "*I asked you once already—what does that mean?*"

SIXTEEN

THERE ARE SEVEN days until the appeal review.

Lizbeth brings the napkin to her mouth, and when she lowers it again it's smeared with lipstick.

"Anyway, they've told the bookstores Jim Rockford's sick with what might or might not be Lyme disease. So everything's on hold until the doctors know what they're dealing with."

Inchy Burden's voice floats above the lunchtime hum at Fifty Seven Fifty Seven. Lizbeth lays her napkin on the table.

"So, be honest with me, honey. Is this rigmarole going to be a problem for us? For the *real* book?"

"It'll be fine," Lizbeth says. "It's all going to be fine."

She stares down at what's left of her food. Can't eat without seeing herself at the Venus. Can't see herself at the Venus without George sitting opposite.

Everything is blurs and shadows now.

As the waiter removes their plates, Inchy says she has such a tingle. That every time Mitchell Rieber opens his mouth, she sees another copy of *God's Lonely Man* plucked from a stack of fifty in an airport bookstore.

Inchy, Lizbeth knows, votes for him.

They embrace on the street, and Inchy takes the first cab to appear.

In the backseat of the next, Lizbeth stares down at her hands as the driver butts through what's left of Manhattan. And then, as she lifts her head, she sees the Queensboro Bridge, its dense steel web of towers and trusses.

The East River seethes below her, and the face of Richard Cazet glares from the shoulders of every driver they pass. But she forces that from her mind and all she thinks of instead as they reach land and rattle down Queens Boulevard is the voice she didn't know on the phone last night, and the words it spoke:

To be near hurricanes is more dangerous than ever now.

And the same on through genteel Sunnyside and crowded-sky Woodside, until the cab pulls up on Martense Avenue and 103rd Street:

Corona.

From there she walks.

Down on Waldron Street, no Royals stand watch over the dilapidated house, and when she steps up to the door, no sound of work in progress clamors from inside.

On Van Cleef, Raymond Peres's church is locked up and deserted. As is, she finds, the annex.

No Royals anywhere. Just their graffiti.

But as she starts to walk away she sees a white-haired figure pause at the end of the block. Stare back at her.

Peres. And in a flash he crosses the street and hurries up 108th.

She calls out but he doesn't stop, and by the time she gets to the end of the block he's forty yards ahead and quickening.

He doesn't look back. Crosses the street once more and from there into the park.

She follows.

A pair of runners in hoods and beanies slog by the antique carousel. Lizbeth tries to keep up with him as he darts ahead, but she's getting wearier with every step.

He's still outpacing her as he reaches the New York Hall of Science. Takes a right turn and disappears. By the time she hits the same junction, almost exhausted now, she's certain he'll be out of sight. But no. There he is—just—at the other end of the pathway, only now about to spin around another corner and disappear from view.

Except, as he does, one foot stays just half a beat too long in the air and his arms fly up by his sides in the effort to keep his balance, but his leg crumples under him and then—one dilated moment later—he crashes face first to the ground.

When she catches up to him, she can see his face and hands are grazed.

"There was ice," he says, laboring to his feet. "A patch of ice."

She realizes two things. That his breath has enough gin on it to make her eyes water; and it was his voice on the phone. Him who called. Who spoke of hurricanes.

He must be the connection here. Reaching out before the net closes.

"Are you okay, Father?"

"I am fine. Thank you."

She takes his arm to steady him and leads him to a bench.

"I should have known you would come and find me," he says. "I should have known that as soon as I picked up the phone. I guess that is what I wanted. But the truth is I had drunk a little glass of something to warm me . . . and it made me rash. And now you're here, a part of me wishes I had never made that call. Because I am afraid to think what I have set in motion."

"You were right to call me. It was a brave thing to do. Father, I want to help. That's why I came. If Hurricane is in danger . . . from Wilson . . . then even if it feels like a betrayal . . . you need to protect him . . ."

The priest turns to Lizbeth, incredulous. "Protect *Hurricane*? From *Wilson*? Miss Greene, I thought you understood this situation."

He tries to rise from the bench, but doesn't quite make it. "Wilson is no danger to Hurricane. It is Hurricane that endangers Wilson. As he always has. Do you not see that?"

"Father," she says, "listen, I know these past few weeks must have been tough . . . but if you're drinking, it won't help . . . it'll just confuse things . . ."

"I wish I was confused. I wish I had that solace." He shakes his head, and his voice drops to a mutter. "I'm sorry, Miss Greene. I thought you knew the meaning of my call. So, okay . . . I will tell you more plainly. The blood spilled in this neighborhood has been spilled by the design of José Almanza and Mitchell Rieber—"

"Rieber? I don't—"

"Everyone cut down these last weeks has been cut down by their order." He sees Lizbeth's bemusement and sighs. "So that the world believes Three Vee is to blame. And he will be sent back to his isolation because of it."

A park worker in overalls cruises by them in a rusted buggy, and the priest waits until he's out of sight before he speaks again.

"Please understand that I have had no role in this situation, Miss Greene. To my disgrace I have known of it and done nothing . . . but I am not a participant. Just as I was not a participant to begin with. I ask you to remember that. Not until Hurricane came to me with this boy Slinky and asked me to speak with him . . ."

"Slinky? Slinky as in—"

"The *soplon* at Wilson's trial. That is when it started. At least when it started for me." He puts his head in his hands. Sits unmoving as seconds pass. Then: "Mitchell Rieber did not condemn Wilson alone. It was Hurricane also. It was the two of them. It was always the two of them. I don't know who had gone to who in the beginning. I just know that by the time

I learned of their understanding it had long been in place. Hurricane would deliver to Rieber the prize of Wilson Velez and in exchange, he would be left to conduct his business in peace when he took charge of the Royals. It was simple."

A pigeon struts along the back of the bench, then across the ground in front of them.

"They had found Slinky in Elmhurst. He belonged to the Royals there. He was a *tecato* and a thief. A dislikable kid. Anyway, word had got back to Hurricane that he was . . . *entertaining* men . . . to pay for his habit. So one night he found him . . . and he took him to a salvage yard up by the World's Fair Marina. I imagine that Slinky was ready for a beating . . . but it was just the two of them. And there Hurricane told Slinky he was to speak against Wilson. There was no way out of it. Otherwise he would let everyone know what kind of individual he was. But, if he spoke against Wilson, then he would be taken care of. Hurricane would make sure he was safe and well rewarded. So he told him to go to the police precinct on 43rd Avenue the following morning, and to ask to speak to Mitchell Rieber. They came to arrest Three Vee that same day. And I knew nothing of any of it until a week before the trial."

He stares ahead as if she isn't even there, his voice still little more than a mumble.

"I was asleep at home when my doorbell rang. It was after two A.M. When I answered it, Hurricane was there with this boy Slinky, with a refuse sack pulled over his head. I thought he was going to kill him right there in my house. I said to him, 'No, no, not here, what are you doing? This cannot happen here.' But Hurricane just dragged the boy into my kitchen, and took me into the living room. And there he told me what was taking place. What he and Mitchell Rieber had conceived of. But he said now Slinky was getting scared. Saying he wanted to back out. So he asked me to talk to him. Persuade him. He asked me to tell Slinky that the Lord wanted him to do this, and that as His emissary I would personally ensure Hurricane kept the promises he had made. So . . . I walked into the kitchen . . . and I did."

"But . . ." Lizbeth says, ". . . you were everything to Wilson. I mean . . . why?"

"Reasons that seduced me in that moment."

A Chinese boy dressed all in white paces by with outsize headphones clamped around his ears, the music so loud inside them that the *tsstsstsstss* is audible twenty seconds each side of his passing. Then, when it's faded: "Sometimes, an impossible choice still has to be made, Miss Greene." He shuts his eyes before he goes on.

"In those last months, Wilson seemed to have no sense of purpose. He was adrift. Who knows what the cause was? All I know is the older Wilson got, the more withdrawn he had became. Introverted. Melancholy. He watched movies all day. Walked around unshaven, barefoot. He didn't leave the apartment. He wouldn't even go to the grocery store . . . he had pee-wees run out to get him coffee and peanut butter. The only thing that seemed to bring him pleasure was thinking of the past. The salad days, you know? And he spent so long thinking of them, he couldn't see what was ahead of him . . ."

She stares up at a plane, outlined against the clouds, then disappearing into them.

"Toward the end, you know, I heard kids from here, from Corona itself, making jokes about him. About the way he looked, you know? Even a few weeks before that would have been . . . unimaginable. He had built this thing up so strong, but then it was as if he just . . . lost interest. And the kids coming up, you could see them look at this barefoot man in his dingy apartment and wonder why they were supposed to follow him. He and I spoke so many times of these plans for the Royals to become a positive force in the community, a source of change . . . but none of them ever came to be. And I knew they never would the night that Wilson turned to me and told me that he could never again be responsible for another act of violence. That the thought made him sick—"

"What? But surely you would have wanted that—"

"Oh, Miss Greene, to live in a world where that would have been possible, it would be wonderful. Delightful. But here in Corona, someone else would have come within hours and made this place theirs. Already there were grocery stores being robbed by *tecatos* right around the corner from my church . . . in Bushwick and Washington Heights, Royal chapters were threatening to break from the greater Nation . . . and he would not even rise from his chair. He would not put these elements down. This is what had changed in Wilson."

The priest makes sure to catch her eye. "And why even now I know that he could not be the author of any act of violence. Because that . . . *capacity* had gone from him. And when I realized that, I knew he was finished. You see, Miss Greene, what he had brought to Corona was order. Not a perfect order. But one that held. Except now, if he remained Sapa, sitting playing dominoes on 47th Avenue, all that was going to crumble. Someone from outside would come, and Wilson would have been left in a pool of blood on his couch . . . and all would be war."

He shakes his head. "But if somehow there was another way . . . a way in which the Royals would remain preeminent, and the work that Wilson always spoke of actually happen, and for him to live . . . not just to live, but to be cherished, as an icon . . . well, when Hurricane brought that boy Slinky to my house at two A.M. and told me what had been planned . . . everything just slotted together."

A moment goes by.

"So I know one day I will judged for what I did. And yes, I am not going to tell you that I and my church have not been rewarded for our cooperation. But I have also ensured that Hurricane carried out the work that Wilson and I spoke of so often. That was my price too . . ."

He lays his hands on his knees and then he gets to his feet. "So anyway, a week after Hurricane brought him to my house, Slinky gave his performance in court. Do you mind if we walk, Miss Greene? My joints are not so good, and I need to keep moving in this cold."

Lizbeth rises beside him, and slowly they move through the park.

"Of course, few plans are ever perfect in their execution. This one was no different. It seemed that for the younger Royals Wilson's memory was easier to respect than his actual presence. The gang was in chaos. Even though Hurricane was Wilson's deputy, many did not accept his ascent. Some laid claim to being the true successor to King Three Vee. There was much blood spilled. It was everything I hoped would not happen. And the whole time Slinky was a source of great consternation. The government had sent him up to Minneapolis with a new identity. He wasn't dealing with it so well. He would call Hurricane and complain that he was lonely. He said he was going to return to Queens and come clean. Beg forgiveness from the Royal masses. He would not mention us when explaining his betrayal, he said, but he just couldn't live this way. One time he even started hitching. Made it as far as Indiana before the federal agents caught him. The whole thing was becoming problematic . . . I tried to find some way of resolving it, but Hurricane said he and Rieber were running out of patience. And I guess he and Slinky must have been on the same wavelength, because when Hurricane showed up in Minneapolis to deal with him, Slinky was already gone."

They pass by the Queens Museum of Art and an elderly woman with a mutt on a leash.

"Hurricane came back to New York, but he sent another man to find Slinky. His name was Ramon Carvajal. He lived on 102nd Street. Not the kind of person you would want to get to know. Anyway, it took him two weeks, but eventually he found Slinky in a motel in—"

"Jerome, Idaho."

"Yes. Correct."

"And his head was—"

"Yes. But there was no big investigation. Even without evidence, the police assumed it was Wilson behind it . . . and with him already in jail for life, Slinky was just forgotten—"

For the first time Lizbeth interrupts: "Wait. I don't get that. Father, if the plan was to make people think it was Wilson, then why do that to Slinky's head? Why not just cut out his tattoos?"

"Oh, they would have, Miss Greene, had they been able. But from what I know Slinky only had one small sun and crown on his right arm. And after he turned *soplon,* the witness protection people, they told him to have it inked over. So apparently Ramon Carvajal broke in there and pulled up Slinky's sleeve with his pocket knife ready and found a picture of Snoopy instead . . ." He shrugs as he walks. "Of course, they didn't make the same mistake with Ojos."

Lizbeth realizes she's started lagging behind. But as the wind gathers behind them, the priest keeps tramping on, faster now, and he's still talking when she catches him.

". . . Anyway," he says, "it didn't seem to matter. Everyone still took it as the work of Three Vee. But, in one sense, that just made things more complicated. Because although now Hurricane was rid of Slinky and free of the blame for his death, Wilson was only becoming more celebrated among the younger Royals. It was as if by killing Slinky they had breathed life into Wilson's name. Now he was an all-powerful but unseen hand, you know? So the attempts to win his favor became more ferocious yet. No one took Hurricane seriously as the Sapa. People started to call him *la canguro.* The baby-sitter. You would hear them say to one another out loud, on the street, why not Ojos, or this person, or that person . . . and I guess that ate away at Hurricane . . . because then came the letters."

The priest walks quicker with each step, the ends of his words docked by breathlessness. "What he needed was some way of leaving the memory

309

of Wilson intact . . . as a symbol . . . but at the same time affirming himself as Sapa. And the one thing that made him look like *la canguro* more than any other was Wilson's letters from Moxanie. Because for many Royals, it was still him they turned to. His guidance they sought. And for Hurricane, that was an insult. So at first, all he wanted was to stop Wilson writing his letters. The idea of how . . . that came from Mitchell Rieber. He gave Hurricane the okay . . . and in the weeks to come, there was so much violence . . . every one who had badmouthed him or threatened him as Sapa . . . they were laid waste. Then the FBI raided Ojos and seized his letters from Wilson . . . and those killings were the ones they were accused of. And right before the trial it seemed once more like it was all going to collapse . . . the charges were coming apart, Hurricane and Rieber were squabbling, blaming each other . . . but two of them held up in court—"

"Hugo Gampas and Felix Cruz."

"Yes. In fact Ramon Carvajal killed them both. But Wilson was blamed. And even in their dreams I don't think Hurricane or Rieber expected that judge to deliver the sentence he did. It was like Christmas for them. I looked over at Hurricane when he heard . . . and saw him try not to laugh. Pretend to cry. Then in the weeks after Three Vee was taken into isolation, slowly the Royals began to accept Hurricane as Sapa. Wilson, of course, was venerated. But everyone knew he was gone now. And so at last there was an order . . ."

They are in front of the Unisphere. Lizbeth makes for a bench and sits. Peres follows.

"Did you miss him at all?" she says. "Or was that all a lie too?"

"No. Of course not. I would weep every time that I thought of what we had done . . . But as I told you, Miss Greene, the counsel God gives me is often less transparent than that with which He seems to favor others . . ."

He sighs again and now it seems unending.

"So that was how our neighborhood carried on . . . until the death of the judge. Rieber, he knew even before the reporters. And when he told Hurricane, the two of them . . . they panicked. They saw their work unraveling. The idea of Wilson in contact with the world again . . . that one day he might somehow connect the dots to them and seek retribution . . . with all they had to lose . . . it forced them to respond. So the same day Rieber had a cop kill Ramon Carvajal. To make sure he at least would never let it slip. And as soon as those judges allowed Three Vee out of isolation . . . that was when the full response was decided upon . . . the plan to create enough funerals so that even without proof of Wilson's guilt, no judge would look at him with any thought but sending him back . . ."

He takes an aged handkerchief from his pocket, blows his nose and replaces it. "Of course, all they have done is make sure the pee-wees of Corona think of Wilson with even greater reverence. He is a legend to them now. And Hurricane is *la canguro* once more. So a part of me . . . a part of me doesn't believe they will ever leave Wilson be now . . . because his very life serves to undermine Hurricane. So the best thing for him and Rieber would be the end of that life. And I know they would do it as easily as they would cross the street, because Hurricane is . . . *demente*. Out of control, yes? He has used this chance to put down anyone that has ever so much as ticked him off in the last five years. So many gone. There was never any call for so many. Their lives ripped away over the smallest grievance. And all I could think of when I called you . . . was that this had to be put right. I just wanted someone from outside of here to know . . . to take it from my hands and intervene . . . because, of course, were *I* ever asked to repeat what I am telling you now, I would deny it all." And he yells across the empty sprawl of the park. "Because I am a coward!" Then he slumps back. Turns to her. "But Miss Greene, when you came to Corona today . . . you really thought Wilson was guilty? Of what has taken place here . . . ?"

". . . I guess," she says, ". . . I was the one that was confused. It's been a strange time for me. For all of us. But now . . . hearing you . . ."

It's true. All she can think now is: How could I have been so wrong? It seemed so clear, for a while. Now, she's just dazed. Baffled.

The priest turns back. Gazes out at the park once more. "Miss Greene . . . as you have such knowledge of Wilson's case . . . may I ask what you think next week will hold? The review? I know the government will bring their entire weight down on him . . . but do you really believe the judges will return him to that place . . . ?"

She tries to home in on the question. Realizes, in her most honest assessment, that: "I don't know."

"I understand. It's just . . . I cannot bear to think of him there . . . suffering that way again."

They sit the width of a person apart, both facing front.

"Perhaps . . ." he says, and then he pauses. "Perhaps, in court . . . if a person as esteemed as you was to speak . . . on his behalf . . ."

She turns to him, but he's still fixed on the park.

311

"To have an advocate like yourself speak up for him with the judges . . . that would surely rebalance the scales. Then despite the injustice of the past, he might be treated with some degree of humanity . . . and you would have enabled that."

Her cheek smarts at a gust of wind, a slap of cold air.

"I . . . guess," she says. "That hadn't . . . occurred to me."

As the last word leaves her mouth, a swaggering crowd of boys in red, white and gold appear on the other side of the Unisphere.

Abruptly, the priest rises. Says nothing. Just bustles away. Turns back five steps later.

"Please, Miss Greene," he says, ". . . do not abandon him now."

Then he's gone.

She sits with her palms on her thighs for a moment before getting up. Walks out of the park toward the 111th Street subway and there she takes the 7 train.

A feline Latino man in a Mets cap stands to offers her his seat. It takes an age for her to even notice, to smile apologetically and lower herself into it as she tries to absorb what she's just been told.

With 111th in retreat behind her, she replays and replays the priest's story. Keeps it pinned down while its memory is still pristine.

She flips it over in her thoughts, and then again, running her finger down its spine, gazing at it, jabbing at it, scrutinizing. As the train shudders on, passengers blank or dozing, the flat Queens light dissolving through the window.

Poor Ojos. Poor George. Poor Wilson?

She thinks of him now and sees the scar down his forehead, his wrists bruised in their cuffs, his eyes flitting behind his glasses. But when she tries to step back and see the whole, the picture doesn't change. Only jams on these circling fragments.

How could she have been so wrong? How could she have been so wrong?

Or no. Perhaps, in fact, the question is—

Could she have been so wrong?

She rolls in her seat with the motion of the carriage, her head bowed in concentration.

When she next looks up, they're at Times Square, and the conductor is calling out that this is the end of the line.

SEVENTEEN

A MILK TRUCK HAS overturned in Quince Hill. The whole town's been left as one vast, sodden traffic jam. In Lizbeth's kitchen, Nancy shakes her head as she describes it. It is, she explains, the reason for her getting here forty minutes late.

But though Lizbeth nods and says, periodically, *Right, Uh-huh, Wow,* she is barely even present. She is, instead, with Wilson Velez. Trying to figure out why the priest's account still hasn't quite settled at her core.

All through the telling, she was rapt. But then, somewhere on that 7 train, her disbelief reared up.

God knows, she wishes that it hadn't. By now, she just wants something to be true.

After lunch, she and Nancy watch TV news in the living room, Lizbeth's hand resting on her belly. Gazing at the screen as it fills with footage of Sherwin Baines's arraignment, the same film of him in court in handcuffs and an orange jumpsuit that they show now every time there's an item on the case.

Three more guards from ESSUSP have been arrested, the voice-over says. Their photographs are shown in turn, but Lizbeth doesn't recognize them.

The arrests have come, the reporter says, as allegations emerge that Baines helped an inmate pass coded instructions to another man demanding the murder of a third party.

But when the inmate's face appears onscreen, she doesn't recognize him either.

Then the phone, across the room. Nancy mutes the TV.

"How are you, Ms. Greene?"

Alicia Mapp. Lizbeth wonders if she knows. If she's part of it. If there's an it to be part of.

"I was just watching the news . . . Baines."

"Oh, you were? Well, I have to say, Ms. Greene, even the guys leading the investigation have been pretty shocked by what he's been up to. But we think there's plenty more to come yet . . . and Velez's name is right around the corner. I'll tell you, it's an exciting time to be us right now."

She takes one of the soft gulps of breath which Lizbeth has come to know as a sign of an upcoming bend in the conversation; a tiny aural gear change. "Ms. Greene . . . were you recently in Corona?"

Lizbeth takes seconds to find her answer. Hears every one as an hour. Until: ". . . Did you people see . . . I mean . . . I did nothing wrong . . ."

"Please, Ms. Greene, relax. No one's implying otherwise. And you weren't followed. Nothing so . . . sinister. We just figured you might go out there. A few things that we overheard suggested it . . ."

"I'm not sure . . . what you mean . . ."

"I'll be frank with you, Ms. Greene. The unit recently became aware of extensive contact between Father Peres and Alan Ossery. They spoke eight times in the last week, actually. Every time on brand-new cell phones. It was quite a task to keep track of them . . ."

"I didn't know they were so . . . close."

"Peres and Ossery? Oh, sure. It was Peres that first introduced him to Velez. And the Father's always been quite the strategist . . ."

"I don't . . ."

"Ms. Greene, the two of them want the same thing. The right result for Velez at the appeal review. And, while it would be unprofessional of me to divulge exactly what we overheard, I can say that much of it involved you . . ."

She lowers her voice just slightly.

". . . Let's just say, after hearing those conversations, we assumed that you may have . . . received a strange phone call? That might have led you to visit Corona? Where you may have then heard a rather elaborate story . . . one that would be unlikely to ever have its veracity assessed in open court, but which would present Velez to you in a sympathetic light . . . And there might then have been an apparently spontaneous proposal that perhaps you might choose to speak up for him at the review. Am I warm here, Ms. Greene?"

But Lizbeth has no chance to speak before Alicia Mapp continues. "Ms. Greene, for those guys, having a celebrity with a profile like yours publicly support Velez would be invaluable. And how else to persuade you when all the evidence points to the need for Velez to be returned to isolation as swiftly as possible than to concoct some tall tale which presents him as the victim in all this? I guess if nothing else we should admire their ingenuity . . ."

Alicia Mapp pauses. Then she says: "Ms. Greene, don't be shocked. This is how Ossery makes his living. He's very good at it. Were I ever charged for racketeering, I'm sure I'd hire him too. And Peres? He's a virtuoso."

Lizbeth looks up and sees Nancy anxiously glance back at her from the couch.

"Anyway, Ms. Greene, if there'd been any confusion in your mind as to what to believe here, what you saw in Corona must have helped that . . ."

"What I saw?"

"The absence of people getting shot, Ms. Greene. A welcome consequence of Velez's lines of communication being severed."

Once Alicia Mapp's hung up, Lizbeth stands with the receiver still pressed to her ear.

Seasickness. That's what this is like. A ceaseless tilt and list of the ground beneath her.

She remembers every time in her life she has ever been cast as the dupe, the patsy, oblivious, misled. The sting, she realizes, is never forgotten.

"Is everything okay?"

Nancy half rises from the couch.

"It's fine. It was just . . . it's fine." Lizbeth belatedly hangs up, and the sound is returned to the TV.

An hour later, as Nancy gets ready to leave, she pulls a sheaf of mail from her bag. "I almost forgot," she says.

"Oh, right," Lizbeth says. "Thanks."

And so begins the once monthly handover of the fan mail sent on by Lizbeth's publisher that has, after being sifted through by Nancy, been found to need more than a form letter and an autograph in response. Nancy keeps one resealed envelope separate from the rest. "I thought you'd want to see this . . ."

Lizbeth pulls it open. Skims through for some clue as to what her assistant means.

Realizes and says: "Thanks."

"Do you want me to stick around . . . ?"

"No, I'm good," Lizbeth says.

"Was it okay for me to show you that . . . ? I didn't know if . . ."

"No, of course. I would have wanted to see this."

She waits until she hears the front door close before she reads it through again. Sent from San Diego. The writer—her name is Katherine Cash—begins like a typical fan: recalling when she first encountered Lizbeth's work, rhapsodizing about Enschell.

Then in the second paragraph she says the reason she's writing is that

I was an old (and I like to think good) friend of the late George Finer.

They met, the letter says, as substitute teachers in the spring of '86. Stayed close.

I saw you at the funeral in Essenville, but although I wanted to speak with you then, it somehow didn't seem appropriate.
So I'll say now what I wanted to say then—that while George's passing is a terrible waste of a much cherished life, you should know that what would prove to be the last weeks of his life were among the happiest he ever enjoyed.

And then, over the next three pages, Katherine Cash goes on to explain that George—a man possessed, she says, of a rare and unfailing kindness—had spoken frequently during their talks of his excitement at meeting Lizbeth. The thrill of their friendship developing. He did, he would often say, hope that he didn't bore or embarrass her.

He said that you were everything he always hoped you might be.
Please forgive me for rambling. I guess what I'm (clumsily) trying to say is that none of us are ever likely to know exactly what prompted George into such an unfathomable action on that dreadful night, but you can at least be certain of one thing—that he was proud to have become a friend of yours.

Lizbeth folds the letter back inside the envelope, and feels herself all but collapse as she does, engulfed by a vast wave of sorrow. It crashes down around her, touching with an uninvited intimacy everything she is, has ever been, would want to be, will ever be.

Then it passes. Just disappears. And in its aftermath she is left with the memory of George Finer and the incontrovertible faith that the cruel hand that wrested him from life had a name.

The name Wilson Velez.

But there's no anger. Just bemusement she could ever have doubted it. She could almost laugh.

Then she reaches for the phone and as calmly as if she was ordering Chinese food, she calls Alan Ossery.

When he answers, there's a furious tang to his voice. Wilson, he says, was returned to Ad-Seg yesterday. Just until this morning. A twenty-four-hour stay. They said he'd made an abusive comment to a guard.

"I only just found out from Sosa. He said Wilson was *subdued* when they brought him out. *Subdued*. Jesus, Miss Greene, can you imagine what he must have been going through . . . ? To be taken back there . . . ?"

There is silence at Lizbeth's end of the line.

"Miss Greene?"

"Right. I mean, God . . . that's terrible . . ."

"God only knows what kind of condition he's really in. I'm going to have to go down there and see him . . . but, you know, that whole place is in chaos now . . . after Baines, the rest of them are trying to prove what vicious hardasses they are . . . and Sosa's so desperate to keep his job he's firing them up . . . but, God . . . to take him back to that place . . ."

"It's awful," she says. She lays her free hand on the kitchen table. Will not be thrown, of course. "I'm calling about the appeal review."

Ossery lets a beat pass before he replies. "Okay?"

"I'd like . . . if it's something that you feel could be of value . . . I'd like to speak on Wilson's behalf. In court."

Another beat.

"No shit."

She tries unsuccessfully to glean the exact inference of those words and the tone in which they were said. Then she goes on. "I want to help. I don't know if you think my name will make a difference, but—"

"You're serious about this?"

"I am. And what's going on now . . . it's just confirmed it for me. The thought of him being sent back there permanently . . . I mean, if you think that my speaking to the judges might be beneficial . . . then I'd do it a thousand times over." She tries once more to read him as he gabbles delightedly.

This, he says, is just amazing. And with thick streaks of pleasure in his voice, he thanks her, and then he thanks her again. The power of her being there in court, her willingness to vouch for Wilson, the effect that will have on the judges, all are raised and eulogized.

He thanks her a third time and then he pauses. "And you'll come back to Essenville?" he says. "You'll see him again?"

She knew this was coming. "I will," she says.

She thinks of him now, the Sacred King Three Vee. Sees him reveling in what he has on her, over her. And she thinks of the appeal review, and how at a certain point in its progress she will walk into the courtroom and take the stand, and tell those assembled her name and business and the nature of her acquaintance with Wilson Velez.

If that's what Ossery and Peres want, then that they can have.

She will appear before them all and read from a prepared statement, and in that she will purge every noxious secret. Deprive him of his hold on her and admit it all. The thefts in Pittsburgh; nineteen years of dope; her nonabduction by Richard Cazet. And once the slate is clean and she has proved her desire to be nothing but honest with all that might entail, she will turn to Wilson Velez and—citing Ojos, George, the young males of Corona—declare with confidence and clarity that he is a thug, a liar, a bully, a killer. A man not fit to be among men.

She will watch as they lead him back to Ad-Seg, and that sight will make her glad.

For George.

That night she sleeps deeper than she has for weeks.

But with three days left before the review, it hits her the instant before she opens her eyes.

A crack has opened up along her conviction. The sudden loss of her cherished faith that she can do this. Can, and should.

She shuts her eyes again as a child would in the hope that when she reopens them, this misgiving will be gone, and the snug assurance of the last few days will still be wrapped in place around her.

But no. Some phantom in the night has spirited it away.

She heads downstairs with the dogs, and as she doles out their biscuits and fills up their water trough she tells herself this is ridiculous. The result of a life spent frothing up plot twists. She knows he's guilty. Knows his motive and his method.

Is that enough?

Ossery phones at nine. Calling from his condo in Essenville. Says after much berating of Sosa that he finally got to see Wilson.

"Of course, when I said *you* wanted to go down there, that was different," he says. "Then he's the gracious host. Anyway, listen . . . Wilson's not doing so good. He's pretty shaken up from Ad-Seg. His speech is screwed up again. He's flinching a lot. *But* he knows you're coming back . . . and that's really lifted him."

His tone rises into sunniness. "Also, he knows we've every reason to be confident . . . with the review. I mean, when Baines got taken in, sure, I felt a little rattled . . . but it's been a week now and what have they got? The typhoon that guy's facing, you'd think he'd have dropped Wilson's name by now if he could possibly make anything stick . . . And the judges will realize that. Plus, of course—"

He breaks off for what sounds like coffee. "—we have a certain guest speaker booked. Right?"

"How well do you know Raymond Peres?"

The words spill out, as much a surprise to Lizbeth as Ossery. They hang loudly in the pause that follows.

"The priest?"

"Right. The priest."

She hears him take another gulp of coffee. "Well, obviously, Miss Greene, we've spoken. We've conversed about Wilson a few times down the years. But I don't believe we've done so in quite some time."

The line hums, just once.

"We don't golf. We have no plans to catch a show together." And then again. "Do I get to find out why you're asking?"

"I was just . . . curious. It just . . . occurred to me I didn't know."

"Right. Okay. Well . . . there we are."

She lingers in the study after the call and gazes at *The Monsters of Gramercy Park and The Strange Pale Spell.*

Maps his guilt one more time. So many telltale details, too lucid and abundant to ever be coincidence.

But then—

She prints out the statement she's written for the appeal review. The damning of Wilson Velez. Honed to inescapability. She reads through its list of indictments; but it still doesn't make her sure. After rising and leaving the room, she paces the hallway. It's five minutes before she returns.

To the study, and her desk.

Here, she will find her resolution. If it all comes down to this, so be it.

Her eyes fix on the screen of her laptop as her fingers shape each word like a pianola hammering out its tune.

There it is. Hunts Point. The Bronx. What isn't burned out is rubble. What isn't rubble soon will be.

The date? January 3rd. 1983. The city stumbling back to its routines, still hungover and reeking.

Happy New Year NYC.

The boy waits behind the high steel gate at the exit of Spofford.

Spofford Juvenile Detention Center. A place of no forgiveness.

He takes a breath and the gate screeches into motion.

No one's on the other side. No one's come to meet him. His brother must be caught up with some hina *back in Queens. His mother? She's in Florida. Sipping rum on a poolside lounger.*

So it's just him.

He is twelve years old. His name is Nelson Valdez.

Nelson Valdez from Corona.

The sky is dirty laundry white. Sleet pelting down as the gate stands open.

Nelson Valdez doesn't move. A guard yells at him:

"You wanna come back in, Valdez? Go on, get your skinny spic ass out of here."

So the boy takes a step forward. Then another.

A second guard calls out:

"See you again soon, lambchop."

He takes the last few steps out of the gate with their laughter as his soundtrack.

Fourteen months. He's been here fourteen months.

But now it's January 3rd, 1983, and he's stepping out onto the ruined sidewalks of the South Bronx.

He turns right with his head down, hair already soaked. His clothes—the clothes he had on when he went in, returned to him an hour ago—don't fit him anymore. The sleeves of his parka end above his wrists, his jeans swing at his ankles.

His shabby red sports bag is slung across him.

They took his $10. Those puta *guards, they went into the pocket of his bag and they stole the $10 that he was keeping in there, the ten spot Father Pedroza gave him for emergencies. He's going to have to hop the subway. Or he could just keep walking, marching in the sleet; across* *the Triboro, over the Kill and Randall's Island, down into Astoria and then, after fourteen months—home.*

It doesn't matter. Either way it's OK. They stole his money but what he has in the bag is worth so much more. A tattered ring-bound notebook. Inside it what he's spent these last fourteen months getting ready. Preparing for this most glorious day:

The Manifesto.

She pauses to title the document:

GOD'S LONELY MAN 1:1

Then she cuts and pastes the text into another, and that becomes:

GOD'S LONELY MAN 2:1

And that night and for the days that follow, she sits with tea beside her and keeps both documents up on screen together. She adds a line to one, and then the other, a passage to the first and then the second, slipping between them, assembling them in tandem.

In one, she tells the story of a victim of circumstance. A gifted boy abandoned in a pitiless world. A kid who just does what he must to get by. Who builds himself an army. One that, in time, he wants to put to better ends. But before he can he's struck down, first by melancholy, then betrayal. Five years is spent alone in the lowest pit of the prison system, leaving him forever wrecked. It is, in a certain light, pure tragedy.

But the man she writes of in the second story deserves no sympathy. He is a murderer. Tyrant. Viral and without conscience. Just a thug with pretensions, buying Cokes and burritos for his goons with the crumpled dollars of black tar junkies. A leech whose only talent is goading others into violence, who even after five years of well-earned isolation still radiates malice. Able only to destroy. And so he does.

She writes with zest and fluency, the very act a joy, the screen effortlessly filling and refilling. Until finally she has two matching stacks of pages. Perfect negatives of one another.

A single copy of each is printed out, and she lays them side by side.

That night she takes them to bed, poring over them with just the baby's kicks for company. Trawls their contents for some eureka realization. Even with the light off their echoes ring through her. Her confusion in full bloom.

At just after one, she gives in. Gets up and makes tea. Sits in the kitchen and tries to clear her mind. Returns to bed. And now, at last, begins to drift.

Until:

What the—

Noise. From outside. A rattle at a downstairs window. Heavy. Persistent.

—fuck?

Her eyes are open. The dogs growling.

It stops. Then starts again. Then stops again. A second later there's a nonspecific clattering and—*are those footsteps?*—what sounds like someone trying to jimmy a door.

Yes, those are footsteps.

Moving to another door now.

Leon. And in a flash the dogs go from growling through snarling to barking, caught in a frantic stampede downstairs.

Lizbeth shrinks under the covers as her hand closes round the panic button, smooth in the hot damp of her palm. She presses two fingers into the spongy gray pad at its center and at once a battery of lights blaze on throughout the house, the howl of alarms their accompaniment. The dogs, of course, go into frenzy.

Then she pulls open the bedside drawer. Lifts out the gun with shaking hands.

Points it at the bedroom door and waits.

But nothing else happens. The dogs just keep barking, the alarms screaming, and after three and a half minutes, a blue light and a siren announce the arrival of the police.

Although they scour the house and the surrounding woodland, they find no one. No trace of anyone either.

Lizbeth apologizes. They tell her she was absolutely right to summon them. And they search the grounds of the house once more.

It's almost dawn by the time they leave.

She calls Nancy, and Nancy comes, and then she packs. She's at LaGuardia by lunchtime.

Pittsburgh as the sun sets.

It is the day before the appeal review.

Mame drives how she's driven all her life: index finger tapping at the wheel, foot leaving the gas pedal fleetingly and without enthusiasm.

The potholed highways of Pennsylvania jolt by, the snow just residual slush now. The safety belt rests beneath the swell of Lizbeth's belly like a shoestring under a grapefruit.

It is still early enough for breakfast to be fresh on their tongues. They left Altoona forty minutes ago, yawning and stretching out nighttime cricks. They couldn't agree on music, so the CD tray is empty and the radio off.

Lizbeth gazes out at the blur of old smokestacks, then turns to her sister. "So . . . about the stories . . ."

"You mean Nelson Valdez?"

"Right. I just wondered . . . which you thought was more convincing? Of the two?"

Mame glances at her sister, then turns back to the wheel. "As in which did I like more?"

"No . . . not that . . . I mean, which convinced you more? Which one seemed more believable? Truer?"

They speed on.

"God, Betty . . . it's hard to say . . . I mean, I only had last night to read them, you know? And I'm not a critic . . ."

"I know that."

"It's been a long time since you asked my opinion on your stuff . . ."

"I know. But this time I wanted it."

A sudden crater in the road jars them in their seats.

"So?"

"I don't know, honey. I guess one's as convincing as the other . . ."

"No, but . . . I mean . . . when you were reading . . . one of them must have felt more lifelike than the other . . . got you more absorbed . . ."

"But they're not the same thing, are they . . . lifelike and absorbing?"

"Mamie, just say. I'm not going to get mad. I don't mind either way . . . I just want to know what you think."

"*I don't know.* Maybe both. Couldn't they both be true?"

"I don't think so. I mean . . . no. They couldn't."

"Well, in that case, I don't know. I just don't. I mean . . . which one did *you* think was more convincing? When you were writing it?"

"They both convinced me when I was writing them."

"Well . . . exactly."

They accelerate past an umber pickup.

"Betty, I don't know why you're getting so hung up on this. Who cares which one's more convincing? They're just stories. I don't care if a book feels true. What is that anyway? I just enjoy it. Or I don't."

She glances across at her sister again. "God, the last thing I want from a story is something *lifelike*. I want it to make sense. Anyway, I don't get it . . . I thought you were writing the guy's biography . . . not another novel. And why did you change his name?"

"It's just . . . an exercise, you know? A writer's thing."

"Oh. A writer's thing. I see."

They pass another car, and as they do Mame checks that Lizbeth still wants to get to Essenville later today. The journey, after all, will be a chore. But Lizbeth says she'll just have to deal with it.

Tomorrow, she says, is the appeal review.

"Oh, God," Mame says. "I didn't realize. So this could be the last chance you get to—"

"Right."

"Okay, listen . . . we'll stop for lunch after we're done. Then I'll drive you down there . . ."

"Mame, that's ridiculous. It'll take hours. I'll just pick up a cab back in Altoona."

But Mame says: "I'm not going to argue with you, honey."

It's another ten minutes before they turn off the highway. The road narrowing as it winds downhill.

Although Lizbeth's only been here once before, the view is abruptly familiar. A sloping parade of gated bungalows. The trees at the roadside close enough for branches to jab the windows.

Mame drives on without speaking. Slower now.

Then there's another turnoff and after that, it's straight ahead. A two-story red brick complex with a black roof and lawns out front.

When they park, Mame sits with her hands fixed to the wheel before switching off the engine. Lizbeth hears herself swallow.

A plaque by the door reads: HERITAGE MANOR NURSING CENTER.

Inside there's a generic reception area. The carpet plush and royal blue and covered in a thick sheet of plastic. The walls made up of light wood panels on which are hung barely-there watercolors.

They walk on and the carpet gives way to lino, but there's no sign yet of what they call here *guests*. Then a moon-faced doctor spins around a corner. Greets Mame, then turns to Lizbeth. Doesn't wait to be introduced.

Just extends his hand and says he's a huge fan. Before he folds his arms and addresses each sister in turn.

"Anyway, he's doing okay. He got a little . . . *agitated* last night. There was something of a . . . tantrum. But I saw him up in his room an hour ago and he's doing fine. So go on up . . ."

Now for the first time Lizbeth sees a guest. A frail, chickenish woman in a flimsy nightshirt. Impossibly old. Wandering. She looks up and shrieks. Keeps shrieking.

The doctor excuses himself and calls for a nurse. Mame and Lizbeth continue.

There is, up a single flight of stairs, a set of double doors. Beyond those a corridor. More lino and wood paneling. Mame walks half a stride ahead as a low thump sounds from a room behind them. She goes on, then stops outside another. Asks if Lizbeth is okay, and when she says she is, she opens the door.

Their father sits at the window in a low vinyl chair.

Lizbeth can't help but gape. Such decline since she last saw him. Then he was dwindling. But this? This alien in pajamas, hairless and mumbling?

He seems wholly unaware of their presence. Sits hunched over in his chair, skin near translucent, toenails grown long and odd, deep in conversation with an unseen companion.

She and Mame take one step closer.

They have brought nothing for him. There's nothing he'd know what to do with.

"But I want to go to the Rivoli," he says. "I want to go to the Rivoli, Daddy."

Lizbeth peers at him.

"He's talking to Gramps," Mame says. "He does that a lot now."

"But it's just ten cents," he says.

Lizbeth stares around the room. A mattress, currently stripped of bedding, a built-in wardrobe, sink, another drab watercolor. The vinyl chair he sits in. Still talking.

She feels something brush against her hand and when she looks down she sees Mame twine their fingers together.

They stand that way for the next few minutes. Just watching.

"Bobby Tait's going to the Rivoli," he says. "Claude Lavery too."

When they leave, the shrieking woman is gone and in her place is a heavyset man, creaking open-jawed toward them. Staring in bafflement.

Neither Mame nor Lizbeth speaks as they drive away. But slowly, back on the highway, a giddy relief fills the car. There is laughter, boisterous conversation. Music is even played, if quickly squabbled over and then switched off.

It's only five miles outside Essenville that they fall silent once again.

EIGHTEEN

WILSON ULYSSES VELEZ steadies himself on the edge of the sink and raises his knee. Sets one bare foot on the bed. Then the other. Straightens his back.

His face draws level with the Plexiglas strip up by the ceiling. Half an inch thick.

Instantly, his breath mists the surface. He wipes it with his forearm and it's still filthy. But through it he can see, as always:

The observation post of a watchtower. A guard leaning up inside.

But then he lets his weight fall forward, splays his hands against the wall to support himself. Presses his face hard against the Plexiglas. And when he pulls back his head as far as he can and looks up, there is—above the flat roof of the tower—sky.

Washed out and magnificent.

Sometimes as he does this he thinks he sees a distant plane, a gleaming passenger jet en route to one or other coast and then beyond, away. Other times he knows it's just a midge, ambling its way up the other side of the Plexiglas.

He can only stand like this a minute at a time before his neck stiffens and protests.

But that's okay. The minute's only just begun.

And in the small, neat cemetery on the northwestern fringe of Essenville, Mame waits in the car as Lizbeth crouches at the grave of George Finer.

She's brought white chrysanthemums, but the headstone hasn't come yet. There's only a marker. A flat metal nameplate with his dates of birth and death.

She starts to speak but the words are drowned by self-consciousness. So she just lays the flowers on the ground. Her hand on the marker.

Back in the car, she gives her sister directions out onto the road that skirts the center of town. The one that leads, eventually, to the pylons and the brisk climb to ESSUSP.

"Jesus," Mame says when she sees it.

Lizbeth stares into the sullen face of the guard at the parking lot checkpoint, and does the same with the guard at the visitor's entrance. The one who picks up the phone and says: "It's her."

In the holding area, they pat her down, hands passing over her belly; and all the time she stares at them, their practiced deadpan.

As if Sherwin Baines had never been here.

She doesn't recognize her escort guard. Army manner, mustache and glasses.

Inside his office, Warden Sosa takes a mint from the packet in his drawer and says he thought they should catch up before she heads down to the lawyer's room. "So," he says, ". . . How have you been?"

"Oh, you know," she says. "Things have been a little crazy."

"I hear that," he says.

He lodges the mint in his cheek and sucks on it. Says nothing more. Then, eventually:

"How's Joan?" Lizbeth says.

"She's good. You know, as soon as I told her you were coming back, she asked me—ordered me, actually—to let you know you're always welcome in our home." He shifts in his chair, rubs his eyes. "So . . . I guess I've let you know." Then he rubs his eyes again. "I'm sorry, Miss Greene, I don't mean to sound curt. These last few days . . . I'm not going to tell you it's been easy . . . I'm all too aware that people from outside of the industry are talking very freely about the supposed shortcomings of this facility . . . of my supposed shortcomings . . . I don't know, maybe people inside the industry are talking about them too . . . at times like these, people aren't slow in reaching for the knife . . ."

She sees his face set in a mask of self-pity, before he bites down on the mint. Then he raises the subject of the book. Wonders how much of it is written now. When he might be able to see a sample.

"There's nothing worth seeing yet," she says. "It's just scribbled notes. I've been holding off anything else until after tomorrow . . . then I'll know what it is I'm actually writing."

"It's a sensible approach," he says. "I'd never fault a person for being sensible. Just as long as we're both still appreciative of the other's position." He gets to his feet and shows her out.

And Wilson stands on the gantry of his pod, head bowed as insisted on by the older of the two guards here (Dallow, his name tag reads). Then the younger (Lundersen) reaches out and tugs at his waist chain, his shackles yanking out his arms and bringing him up on tiptoes. A lifesize jiving puppet.

"Come on, Elvis," he says. "Let's get you to Priscilla."

They take up positions behind him.

As Lizbeth advances through the silent corridors of ESSUSP. Opens her bag as she walks to check she has the tape recorder. A fresh cassette still in its plastic.

She hears only her own steps.

The escort guard moves ahead of her to deal with the gate. Signs his name in the logbook that hangs on the wall beside it. Asks her to do the same.

Wilson maneuvers down endless stairways with Dallow and Lundersen at his back, each six inches taller than him.

He hums as he goes. They tell him to stop.

And as Lizbeth reaches the lawyer's room, she feels a pressing urge to stop, to turn away and head straight back out. But she stays where she is. She has come to settle this. To prise the truth from him. To give herself some peace. This will, after all, be her only chance to do to him what he did, so expertly, to her.

So when the escort guard opens up, she steps in. Takes up her position on the same side of the table as always. Looks up and into the camera.

As Wilson turns into the final corridor with his ankles, he knows, bleeding. Dallow grabs his shoulder to bring him to a halt and Lundersen steps forward to open the door.

Lizbeth spins and stares as they conduct him inside and push him down into the chair.

Then the guards leave.

He is, she sees, more ragged than last time. Weight lost. A raw circle of irritated scalp. He hunches slightly, his right hand trembling.

Their eyes meet, then skitter away. Bat around the room. Then meet once more.

The world outside receding.

"So . . . ddddo you have a name for ttttthe baby yettt?"

"Not yet. But I'm thinking."

"And yyyyyou still dddddon't know . . . if it is a boy orrrr a girl?"

She shakes her head, he lifts his chin.

Silence. Each listening to the other breathe. Then, finally:

"This is so ffucked up. I have thoughttt of so much thatttt I would say when—you were here agggain . . . but now you are . . ."

"I know what you mean."

She reaches into her bag and pulls out the tape recorder. Lays it on the table between them. "I didn't know if you'd be okay with this . . . I don't have to if you don't want me to . . ."

"No, of ccccourse . . . I hoped you would. Like the old dayssss, right?"

So she takes the cassette and unwraps its plastic.

"So, are you goinggggggg back to Quince Hill tonightttt, Lizbeth? Orrr—"

"I'm staying in Manhattan. So I can go straight down to the review . . ."

"Sure. I understandddd. And you will be stayingggg at . . . ?"

"I'll be at the Four Seasons."

"Oh, the Four Seasonsssss. Okay."

"So when are you—"

"Oh, they will come and tttttttake me from—my cell when ittttt is still dark . . . it's a long drive . . ." He shifts in his chair. Gets himself as comfortable as he can. "You know," he says, "I have thoughttt about you a lottttt while you hhave been away."

But she just slips the tape into the machine, and then she presses Record. Starts talking with her finger not yet even off the button. "How are you, Wilson? I was worried about you . . . being back in Ad-Seg . . ."

He shuts his eyes, lost in the roll of the tape. "It was the sssame cell. Did you know thatttt? They took me back to tttthe same cell as before. Like it—had jjjust been sitting . . . empty, waiting for me to rrreturn. And for the first few moments aftttter they locked me in there again, I tried to . . . make myself believe that it was a figment, *sabes*? That I was not actually there anddd, insttttteaad, a *thought* of myself there that I had conjured in my imagination had become caughttt in time. Like a piece of fabric snagged onnnnn a wire. And at any second it wouldddd snap and my imagination would lettttt me get back to wherever I *really* was. But that did nottt happen."

His eyes open. "But in one sense it is useful thattttttt I went back there. Because ittt reminded me of exactly—what tomorrow means. What will be waiting for me if I should lose. *Sabes*? So it has helped prepare me mentally for thatt eventuality. Whatttttttt my response must be."

Her gaze flickers over him as he stretches out his fingers.

"Wilson . . . I was so sorry to hear what happened to Ojos."

She stares into his face. Inspecting but not, she hopes, appearing to inspect.

He stares back. Then he nods.

"Me too," he says.

She tries again.

"It must have been so hard to find out how he died . . . when he was only in prison because of you."

"Yes," he says, almost under his breath. "Of ccourse, you are rrrrrright."

A moment passes.

"Can yyyyou believe these *cabronada* will not lettttt my book come out? After all that has stooddd between it and the world, it gets thissss far and *now* it is stifled . . ." He looks away. Begins, it seems, to lose focus. Zone out. Then he snaps back. "But did you like the bbbbbeginning of the new story? I have been sssso anxious wondering what you thought . . . Did you really think that itttt had promise?"

Her eyes sink into him, scanning once more for any hint, any tip-off. "Sure," she says. "I thought it was fascinating."

"That is so wonderful to hear. You know, while I was workinggggg on it, I worried that . . . that itttt could seem as if I was letting myself become too much of a part of it . . . and then the writingggg would lose its purity . . . and you would disapprove . . . But then I—looked again and thought, 'Wilsonnnn, it is fine. She will know itttt is only a story.' "

He sits back, expressionless.

She stays fixed on him. Her reason for being here.

"Wilson," she says, "you know . . . I'm sorry that I left so abruptly . . . I can understand if it made you angry . . ."

"It's nottttt important," he says. "You have come now."

"I was just very upset . . . things had got so out of whack between us . . . and a friend of mine . . . a friend of mine down in Essenville died." She measures out her pause, and then: "Did you know that, Wilson?"

"Yesss. Sure. Ossery tolddd me." He stares ahead at her. "I'm ssssorry for your loss, Lizbeth."

"Thank you. I mean, I say he died . . . but, in fact, he was killed. Shot. There was . . . I guess you'd call it a misunderstanding. A dreadful misunderstanding . . . and he was shot."

"That is ttttterrible."

331

"Oh, it is."

His right hand, she sees, is still trembling.

"I am ssssso glad that you came back, Lizbeth. I mean that ssssincerely."

"Sure, Wilson. I know."

"But I must tell you thatttttt although the news ggggave me such joy, I was surprised when Ossery said you would also speak at the review. Lizbeth, I honestly do notttt think that with a thousand dictionaries I could hope to . . . find words of sufficient gravity to tell you hhhow grateful I am. How much it means that you wouldddd do that—"

"It's fine, Wilson. It's . . . just something I felt was called for."

"But it's just so incredible," he says. "Because a person like you, of your status . . . your words could decide so much. You know thatttt, right?"

His head tilts as he gazes across the table. As she peers back, she realizes what it is she sees in his features—the exact same thing that's in her own. Fierce observation. Absolute watchfulness.

He leans forward with his eyes still on her. "So thank you, Lizbeth. I will always remember what you are about to do." He lets the silence build but doesn't look away. "Although, you know, nnnnow that you mention it . . . I did think for a long time that you mighttttt at least send a note . . . just a line or two . . . some kind of—explanation for leaving how you did . . . But you did notttt send a note. You sent nothing. Did nothing. And even when Ossery told you of my despair, all you said was thatttt you would think about it. *Oh, I will think about it. Tell Wilson I will think about it . . .*"

And suddenly his face is flushed. That old scowl returning. "I just felt so fuckinggg stupid . . . because a biggg part of me saidddd Wilson, this was always going to happen. Because this is the kind of person that she always was . . . a self-centered person . . . a self-servingggg person . . . And that parttt of me was very persuasive . . ."

The tape rolls on. Until, in a beat, his voice softens. All rancor vanished.

"But I know thatttt it was wrongg . . . it was just that . . . and now I feel like an idiot even sayinggggg this . . . but I got so scared that you had come to ttthink badly of me . . . that perhaps I had even been misusing my freedom from Ad-Seg somehow . . . and in my heartttt I knew you had reasons for leavinggg how you did . . . for instance, as you said, that your friend in Essenville met such a terrible end . . ."

She feels her jaw clench. Shoulders rise.

". . . but the longer that you stayed away the more I gggrew afraid.

Frightened that after all I had told you of myself you had decided I was worthless. Despicable. And thattt you would notttt care if I was sent back to that place . . . or if we never saw one another again . . ." He turns his head away from her. "You know, Lizbeth, I am sorry for how things got between us . . . I acted badly . . . speaking to you with sssssuch hostility . . . the things that I asked of you . . . it is nothinggg of which I am proud . . ."

And as he turns back, she sees her opportunity.

"Wilson," she says, "it wasn't your fault. I know that I was neglectful. I didn't show you the courtesy you deserved . . . I came here late . . . I didn't come at all . . ."

"No. It is kind of you to say these things, Lizbeth, but you were not at fault."

"But Wilson, I didn't realize how awful I was being . . . how disloyal . . . spending all my time with other people . . . making it so obvious I wanted to be with them . . . not you . . ."

His feet begin to tap. His lips purse. He breaks eye contact and stares down at the floor. Then he shrugs and shakes his head. "Two remarkable people like ourselves . . . I guess there was always goingggggggg to be creative differences. But that's okay. We are here now, talking like friends, right?" And he smiles, a slow upturn of the mouth.

"His name was George," she says. "My friend who died was named George Finer."

"Oh, okay."

"You know, I was up at his grave right before I came here."

"Oh. I . . . see."

"I couldn't help but think of the funeral. And that was such a sad day, Wilson. He was still young, this guy, you know? Younger than me, actually. And, sure, it wasn't like he was anyone noteworthy . . . there were no massed ranks of followers . . . but the people who were there, you could see it in their faces, how much he meant to them . . ."

"Righttt."

"It's just so unfair, Wilson . . . a person like George, his life snatched away like that . . ."

"Righttt."

"A person who never did any harm to anyone. Not one person."

"Righttt. Sure. I mmean—"

"And it's funny," she says, ". . . well, not really, but . . . I really think

the two of you would have gotten along well . . . if things had been different . . . if you'd got to meet each other . . ."

"Oh. Rrrright."

"I mean . . . you had so much in common. He was a writer too, you
know?"

He nods, barely perceptibly.

Lizbeth keeps her frustration in check. Keeps on working the angle.

"There was not one mean-spirited thing about him."

"No?"

"No. Not a mean-spirited bone in his body."

She thinks she sees him tensing up. "You know, all these times we came
here and talked, and I never asked you . . ."

His eyebrows raise.

". . . Did you like to bowl? When you were back in Queens?"

"Did I lllllike to bowl? No. Notttt especially, Lizbeth." He squints
from behind his glasses. "You know, I hhhave to tellll you . . . I'm a little
perplexedddd at this conversation . . ."

"I'm sorry, Wilson. It's just . . . especially with everything that's been
going on here recently . . . I guess I just found myself wondering what *you*
might have heard . . ."

"What I heard? Aboutttt what?"

"Oh, I don't know . . . just anything you might have picked up . . . on
the wire."

"Oh! Right! You mean Baines. *Claro.* Yeah, he'd cccome by my cell all
the ttttime . . . him and me, we used to chatttt every day . . . he would tell
me about his wife's sciatica, and I would ttttalk to him about fine art . . .
oh, and then we would each swapppppp places with the other for a while,
because we often enjoyed gettinggggg a little playful like thatttt, *sabes*?"

He sees her glowering. "Lizbeth, what do you wantttttt me to say? I can
ttttell you what Baines is to me . . . he is the reason why these fuckinggggg
jarabe have been pullinggg their sick shit on every *vato* in here. Why they
putttt me back into thatttttt fucking seven-by-ten casket. *That* is whatttt is
between me and CO Sherwin Baines." His feet are tapping fast and heavy
now. "You know, I'm not sure whattttt it is you're trying to achieve here,
Lizbeth—"

And she leans forward. Stops the tape. Pushes her notebook and pen
across to the other side of the table, close enough for him to reach.

"I'll still speak for you tomorrow."

"Excuse me?"

"It's okay. I'll still speak for you in court. Just tell me. Here. Face to face."

"Tell you whatttt here . . . face to face?"

"Just tell me. I just want to hear it from you. It's okay. Really."

"Lizbeth, I don'tttt know what ittt is you might be wanting to hear from me, but I will try and accommodate you as best I can—"

"Wilson, don't fuck with me again—"

He throws his hands up inside their cuffs. "But Lizbeth, I don'ttttt know what you—"

"George. I'm talking about George."

"Oh, *George*! *George*! Of cccccccourse! Okay. So—why are you are talkingggg about George? I am sorry aboutttt your dead friendddd George, Lizbeth, but—"

"Fine. Let's not talk about George. Let's talk about some other people. Let's talk about Rinser. How *is* Rinser, Wilson? Nasty fall he took on the stairway, right? Or why don't we talk about Ojos . . . *your* fucking dead friend Ojos . . . or, wait . . . let me find the names . . ."

She grabs her notebook back, and when she finds the relevant page she recites from it the names of every last murder victim in Corona.

When she's done she looks up and sees him calmly staring back at her.

And her own composure implodes right there. Her voice just one notch short of a scream. "Just tell me! Just tell me! Just tell me what you did! Don't put it in a fucking story! Just say it! *Say it! Here! Now! Tell me! Tell me!*"

There is silence. Not even the noise of the tape.

"*Dios mio,*" Wilson says, finally. "I'm goingggggg to court tomorrow to findddd out if my life is goinggggg to be taken from me again and you are the one who sits here yellingggggg. That is some irony."

He hauls himself forward to the edge of the table. "Okay, Lizbeth. I will tttttell you somethinggggggg now that you may finddd useful. You deserve to know thissss. Lizbeth, at one tttime I wrote a lot of stories, *sabes*? I mean . . . perhaps very fffffew had any true merit . . . but I wrote them nonetheless. Story after stttttory after story. And that taught me an unfailingggg lesson—that what makes a good story is notttt what it is in it, but what is absent from itttt."

Lizbeth sits with her head down.

"Now, somettttttimes it is very hardd, right? To recognize what is un-

335

necessary. A waste of ttttime. And then to actttt on it. Like a characttter, for instance. A minor character. Someone in the bbbbackground who *you* mightttt find interesting . . . but who really, whennn everything is looked at honestly, is just gettinggggg in the way of the *real* story. *Sabes?*"

He twists his head to one side, then back. "And Lizbeth, yyyyyou have to admit these thingggs to yourself. That tttthis little insignificant character that you have, for some reason, become attached to, this *speck,* is worth *nothingg* to the story. Right? Because the sssstory is the mostttt important thing. The story, and the *real* characters. Is that notttt the case, Lizbeth?"

She just keeps staring down.

"But the thinngg is, Lizbeth, the thinggg is that for a writer as *remarkable* as . . . you, I believe thatttt the real story *will* alwayssss triumph. *Sabes?* However it takes place, that unnecessary character who issss obscuring the story will fall away, eventualllllly. That is the natural . . . way of thingggs. And so what I am sayingggg with the utmostttt respect and admiration is that thisss process *just happens* . . . and you will benefit from not expending too much heartache on itttt. Do you understand me?"

"No," she says, without looking up. "I don't. Are you saying—"

"Lizbeth, it is like this . . . sometimes when I have been creatingggggg a story, I have realized thattttt I have to remove what is unimportantttt myself . . . and it has been a . . . terrible struggle for me ttttto accept that, and to rid my story of whatever it may be. It has been a painfullllll thinggg to do, and at the end of it, I have known that I and only I have taken this step. It has been my will, *sabes?* But at other ttttimes . . . at other times it is as if the story has taken charge of the problem itself. I have looked down at the page and there is not even a decision to make anyyyymore— because somehow it has been . . . made for me. It has already happened. I don't know whether itttt is the work of what you could call God, or fate, or if it is some other strange, unfettered spirit, but this other force has made tttthe decision, and taken the action. Do you see now? Sometimes, I have been responsible. At other ttttimes, it has haddd nothing to do with me. It has been this spirit. Fate, *sabes?* But either way, the resultttt is the same. And the story is the better for itttttt. You see?"

But she doesn't reply. Just feels her head drop a little lower.

"Okay, Lizbeth. Well, you shoulddddddd thinkk about that for a while, I gggguess. But also, you know, while you are here . . . there *is* something else that I need to tell you. Somethinggggg also of great importance to me."

At last, she looks back up. Numbly, instinctively, sets the tape rolling once more.

"Something came to me when I was back in Ad-Seg. A vision. It came when I wasss awake but it took me over like a dream. And at first it seemed absurd. Like nonsense. But the longer it has been since, the more real ittttt has felt . . ." He hesitates. "I think I finally found the meaning of the lime trees . . ." And he nods excitedly over the table. "That's right! I mean, I can hardly accept ittt myself . . . but since this dream, I have not thought of those trees again even one time . . . it issss like I finally have the answer, *sabes?*"

He takes a breath and then: "I dreamed, and I believe this dream may be tttrue, that I am not Wilson Ulysses Velez. I dreamed that I was, in fact, another boy who like Wilson Velez came ffffrom Nolteros village, a few miles from Penonomé, overlooking the Interamericana Highway . . . but that I am not him, and never was. Yet my own name and identity were lostttt so young that now I cannot remember them. You see, in the dream, I lived with my mother and my—father in a well-kept *bohio* that stood beside thatttt of the Velez family. But my parents did not lllike to have anythinggg to do with them, because the Velezes were not ggggood people. Not good at all. Julio the father wasssss a drunk. He had a foul temper. Always quick to use hissss fists. Just the mention of Nina the mother made my own mother scowl. She warneddd my father to stay away from her as often as she did me. They had an older sssson Eduardo. Although my parents did not approve of itttt, the two of us would often play together. Then there wasss a younger boy. Wilson. He was my age. In Nolteros, people called him *vacíe cabeza*. Empty head. He was . . . subnormal, *sabes?* He just stared around him all day, or he would laugh, but no one knew what at. Every day he ate the grass outside in the village and then he would be sick all over himself."

Lizbeth winces.

"The kids could be cruel to him, but the adults just ignoreddd him. His father, though, he was a *cabron*. He would come home from drivinggg his busted-ass truck around the province, so drunk he could barely see . . . but sober enough to chase Wilson through the village with a belt . . . and when he caughtttt him, he would drag him back to their *bohio,* and all of Nolteros would hear the screamsssss that followed . . ."

Fleetingly he shuts his eyes before he continues. "Anyway, in the dream, it was the nightttt after my fifth birthday. Everyone in the village was de-

337

lighted because the—next morning the Velezes were leavinggggg for America. It had all been arranged. Julio Velez had met a businessman from New York City who had given him some marvelous job andddd a plush apartment in a smart neighborhood. Their stuff was pppacked into their truck, and late that nightt you could hear Julio Velez outside his *bohio* drinking and singing lewd songgggggs. But I still woke early the next morning, before either of my parents . . . I pulled on a pair of old green ssshorts and when I went outside—it was already so hot that dogs were just laying on their sides, pantingggg. The only other people awake were the old women washing clothes . . . and I was always so full of energy at thatt age, even in that heat I started to run, just run, not going anywhere, just running . . . I ran through the middle of the village and then I turneddddd down the dirt path that led to the fields . . . and I jjjust kept running, my legs like pistons . . . until I got to the lime trees . . . and there I heard a strange noise from somewhere inside of them . . . I thought it mighttt be a macaw. But when I crept up close, what I saw was Wilson Velez . . . he looked like he wasss hiding . . . and then his father bursttt through the other side of the trees and grabbed him by the arm . . . He was cursinggg him, saying why did he have to ruin everything, that they were supposed to have left an hour ago buttttt Wilson had run—off and hidden and now thattt was ruined . . . and Wilson was giggling like it was all so funny . . . and then I felt a warm spray in my face . . . and I looked up and the sun had blinded me. I could see nothinggg. But a moment later it passed, and I saw Julio Velez standing with a—knife in his hand, and it was slick with— blood. And Wilson's body was limp on the ggground. Now I ran once more . . . back up the path, with mortal fear in my heart and my child's lungssss on fire . . . and I knew I could not run fasttt enough . . . I knew I would never make it home . . . and sure enough I felt myself being swepttt up and thrown into the long grass beside the path . . . and Julio Velez stood over me with that bloody knife, and I knew I was going to die. But then he lookeddddd at me and seemed to nod to himself, *sabes*? And instead of cutting my throat, he pulled off his T-shirt and ripped it in two and tied my hands and feet. Then he disappeared. I don't know how longggg I lay there. But then I hearddd an engine coming down the path and it was that truck . . . and Julio Velez got out and threw me into the back. And Nina andddd Eduardo Velez were there too, and I could hear Julio telling them Wilson had run away but they did notttt have time to find him, that they had to go now . . . and that they also had to take me because he had promised the businessman in America four pairs of handssss . . . that was the deal . . . otherwise it would all be off . . . and they shouldd be happy because now Wilson would be taken care of by ssssome kind old woman in the village while Eduardo could have a— brother he was not ashamed of, and Nina a son to cherish . . . But they were screaming, and I saw him about to hit them, and I screamed too . . . and he pulled over and gagged me . . . And I think then I must have passed out, because in the nextttt moment of my vision I was in Linneaus Place with a man's winter coat that stunk of paraffin around me . . . and Julio Velez was pushinggg me toward René the sweatshop owner and saying, 'This is Wilson.' "

He sits back now. "So that was my dream."

And Lizbeth tries to start a sentence four times over before she makes it as far as: "You . . . you think . . . that might be—"

"*No sé.* I have no idea. How am I ever goingggg to know? I never will. And I guess that is an importantttt lesson, *sabes?* To accept that some-times we will never know . . ."

"But Wilson . . . I mean . . ."

"I know. Maybe it is just garbage. It must be, right? It has to be. But then, like I told you, I haven't once dreamed of those lime trees sssince . . . so I guess some idiot part of me musttt believe it."

"But then—"

"Then what? It doesn't matter, Lizbeth. *It makes no difference now.* That is whatttt I am saying to you."

His anger seems to rise once more. Lodges in his voice without reaching his face. "After all, you are not the person the world thinks you are. And you have never chosen to correct that. So why shoulddddd I? Although then again, I guess you always measured yourself by different standards than the ones you used on me. *Anyway,* tomorrow before the jjjudges I am Wil-son Ulysses Velez . . . that is all that matters now." He shrugs like it's nothing so unusual.

She puts her fingers to her temples. Shakes her head as he leans forward as far as his shackles will allow. Looks her dead in the eyes. "So, tell me . . . what nice things are you goingggg to say about me in court tomorrow?"

She looks back and her voice is all but inaudible. "I don't know . . . if I . . ."

"No, Lizbeth. I wanttttt you to speak. As truthfully as I have ever saiddddd any word in my life, I wanttttt you to be there tomorrow to ttttell the court what you really think of Wilson Velez."

"But I don't . . . I mean . . ."

"I am serious, Lizbeth. Whatever you feel you have ttttto say about me, you should say aboutttt me. You know me welllll now. Your testimony will be all a judge coulddd wish for." His gaze has never been fiercer. He stares at her with such intensity, she buckles and looks away again. "So . . . I guess we will see hhhhow it turnsss out."

And then without warning the guards are suddenly marching in, claiming the room. Ordered to rise, Wilson rises; turns with deft coordination and begins to shuffle toward the door.

With a swell of urgency Lizbeth gets to her feet, tries to step toward him. But one of his guards extends an arm across the room as a barrier.

"Wilson," she says, "I'll see you tomorrow."

He nods as they steer him out. Already through the door when she hears him say: "It wasss nice to see you again, Lizbeth."

She presses the headphones over her ears and listens back to what has just passed. Breathes processed cabin air at 32,000 feet. Asks the stewardess for an extra pillow, and when it comes she wrestles it behind her head and turns toward the window.

Hears her voice, then his: "*No sé.* I have no idea. How am I ever goingggg to know? I never will. And I guess that is an importantttt lesson, *sabes*?"

She rewinds the tape. Listens back once more to the tale of another Wilson Velez. A fresh layer of confusion to set over the rest. She checks her watch. Eight forty-five. In a little over twelve hours, she will speak in court.

A stewardess gently pats her arm and points to the relit seatbelt sign, and as the plane makes the first calm slump of its descent, she takes off her headphones and sits in silence. Shuts her eyes and prepares for LaGuardia.

At the Four Seasons, she eats in her room. Balances the tray on the bed and absently squints at the TV.

The next time she checks her watch it's past eleven. Less than ten hours to make her decision.

She unpacks the stories. The competing summaries of *God's Lonely Man.*

With the TV still on she pores over the first. The torment of Nelson Valdez. Deceived at every turn. A life defined by other people's treachery. And now she lies here on fine cotton sheets ready to carry out hers; and a flush of shame washes over her.

Then she turns to the second. Its portrait of conscienceless spite. And she wonders how she could be so torn when she has so often been witness to his venom, his blackmail.

But she is.

Almost twelve now. Nine hours and counting.

In bed, in the dark, her eyes gaze up. And she sees herself in court. Sitting with her hands clasped primly in her lap as she readies herself to speak before the judges. Preparing her revenge.

She maneuvers out from under the covers and stands beside the bed. Pulls from her bag the statement she wrote with the iron intent of delivering tomorrow, and moves toward the dresser. Sits before its mirror.

"My name," she says to her reflection, "is Lizbeth Greene. In recent weeks, I have met with Wilson Velez at US Penitentiary Essenville on a number of occasions. During those meetings, I believe that I have come to know him better than perhaps anyone here. That I have come to know the real Wilson Velez. I have listened to his stories, and I have suffered his rages and intimidation. It is my staunch conviction that the man you are here to discuss today cannot and must not be allowed to maintain contact with the world outside his—"

Her voice falters as she pictures his face at each word. Lost in agony. Incomprehension. Injustice. She wonders how long she will spend waking up with that face as the first thing she sees every day, her first thought him, back there, the terrible gnaw that he didn't deserve it. And her own reputation will, of course, be rubble by then: Lizbeth Greene: junkie. Lizbeth Greene: thief. Lizbeth Greene: fraud.

Defeated yet again, she lays the statement on the bedside table and gets back into bed. For a moment, she sees nothing at all.

But then George lurches back into her thoughts. She pictures the cemetery when his headstone has arrived. How long will it take to get overgrown? An occasional cousin might pass through with a bunch of tiring carnations. Katherine Cash may bug the caretaker to clear the worst of the weeds. But that will be all.

Insignificant characters. Worth nothing. Removed by his will.

Suppose these things have been said in a story, she tells herself. Imagine writing them for a character. What could they be but a taunt? What else could they possibly mean?

But is it—she asks herself again, again, again—*enough?*

She rolls on to her side to check the clock.

Two-ten. Six hours and fifty minutes.

Rising, she steps to the window and pulls open the curtains. Looks down over the city. The narcotic lights. And her indecision rages on.

Again, she picks up the first story. Reads each densely typed passage over and again. Pauses at certain phrases, particular sentences. Until she reaches the last page and glances up.

It is two-fifty-five. Six hours, five minutes. And then she begins the second story, and when she's finished that it is three-twenty. Five hours forty.

She finds herself imagining the village of Nolteros. One son buried unmourned, another beloved and missing. And then the baby kicks and the carousel starts up once more.

Around. Around.

Four-oh-five. Four hours, fifty-five. Four-forty. Four-twenty.

She can't do this. Can't not. Must. Won't.

Five-ten. Three hours fifty. Five-forty-five. Three hours fifteen.

She stares at the pages but the words just dissolve. They mean nothing now. Just shapes on white paper.

Six. And the phone beside the bed rings out.

Her alarm call. Three hours now.

She starts to lay out her clothes. What she will wear as she stands up in court and—

But no. It doesn't work.

She takes a shower. Thinks of nothing but the water on her skin. Returns to the bedroom. Moves toward the stories. Ready now for one last attempt.

She looks down at them and—

Wait. Can that be . . . ? *Is that—*

It is.

Her decision is made.

Slipped up on her from nowhere. Simple. Obvious.

Why she only sees it now, she feels, doesn't matter. What matters is that she knows exactly what she's going to do. And this will hold.

At last.

She reaches for the statement and her fingers touch the corner of the paper.

Then the phone rings, again.

It is six-fifteen A.M.

"I already had my alarm call," she says.

"Miss Greene . . . it's Alan Ossery."

His voice is flat as he tells her Warden Sosa just called him.

That Wilson died this morning.

Her throat feels like it's closing up.

It happened in his cell.

Sosa said when the guards came to take Wilson to the truck, he refused. Then, when they entered his cell, he attacked them. Provoked a confrontation.

He went for them like a dervish. That's what the guards are saying.

His body's in the prison morgue. No decision has been made about the funeral.

She pushes the phone up against her ear even though he isn't talking anymore. And nothing that she feels is expressable.

Neither of them speaks again until they say good-bye.

After the call, she sits motionless on the edge of the bed.

Then she dresses and leaves the room. Takes the escalator down to the lobby and walks through the flawless opulence past the smiling concierge, the nodding doormen.

It's still dark. Just. Every step she takes is an act entirely unto itself, divorced from what precedes and follows. She heads down Park Avenue with the streetlights still lit, past the morning's first dog walkers, the pink-eyed janitors at the end of the night shift, stern-faced office workers making for the gym. She strides by the guidebook landmarks, the grand soar of greed and invention. Takes a left and hits Lexington at the base of the Chrysler. The grandest of them all.

She keeps walking, numb and inattentive, down block after block, unaware of how many she's covered or where that means she is. Just pacing by metal-grilled storefronts and the shabby awnings of all-night bodegas. Until in one unannounced instant her exhaustion consumes her—and she knows where it is she's going.

She flags down the next cab to pass and it takes her the rest of the way.

And with the sky slowly turning from blue-black to pearl they reach the very end of Lexington and come to Gramercy Park. The square of graceful town houses, and at its center the gardens and canopy locked behind iron gates.

She stands with her hands wrapped around the railings, and her legs feel like they're about to give way under her.

Turning, she stumbles back as far as a house of fine gray stone. Sinks onto its bottom step.

It was as if the strange pale woman had never flown with the monster. Yet even then he clung to a threadbare shred of hope. Returning from another night of melancholy troublemaking, he closed his eyes as he flew over the city in the last moments before dawn and felt sure that when he opened them he would know the purest joy—because she would be there. She would be standing in Gramercy Park just waiting for him to notice her.

And as the world stretches off around her and her sleepless eyes get bleary, she peers at the dawn. Her gaze lifting over the buildings to a cluster of shapes in the middle distance, high above the city, swooping down toward the park. And any second she will admit to herself that they are, of course, just birds. Local pigeons, hardy sparrows.

But for now, she doesn't have to.

A NOTE ON THE AUTHOR

Danny Leigh was born in 1972. He has previously worked as a musician and journalist. He lives in Brighton, England.

A NOTE ON THE TYPE

The text of this book is set in Linotype Sabon, named after the type founder Jacques Sabon. It was designed by Jan Tschichold and jointly developed by Linotype, Monotype, and Stempel, in response to a need for a typeface to be available in identical form for mechanical hot metal composition and hand composition using foundry type. Tschichold based his design for Sabon roman on a font engraved by Garamond, and Sabon italic on a font by Granjon. It was first used in 1966 and has proved an enduring modern classic.